TAKE ME
TO THE CAT

ALSO BY BRYANT A. LONEY

Exodus in Confluence

—

A NOVELLA

To Hear the Ocean Sigh

—

A NOVEL

BRYANT A. LONEY
TAKE ME TO THE CAT

VERONA BOOKSELLERS

TULSA

Published by VERONA BOOKSELLERS

Contact info@VeronaBooksellers.com for information about special discounts for bulk purchases.
The author does not in any way endorse, condone, or encourage engaging in any conduct
depicted in this story. The publisher does not assume responsibility over any website and
website content not owned by the publisher, as well as for changes that occur after publication.

Publisher's Cataloging-in-Publication Data

Names: Loney, Bryant A., author.
Title: Take me to the cat / Bryant A. Loney.
Description: Tulsa, OK: Verona Booksellers, 2017.
Identifiers: LCCN 2016920661
    ISBN 978-0-9971700-0-9 (pbk.)
    ISBN 978-0-9971700-1-6 (ebook)
    Summary: High school senior Michael Jackson reunites with former classmates
from elementary school but strange events from seven years prior put them in danger.

Subjects: LCSH Murder—Fiction. | Friendship—Fiction. | Oklahoma—Fiction. | Suspense fiction. |
Psychological fiction. | BISAC YOUNG ADULT FICTION / Thrillers & Suspense
Classification: LCC PZ7.L8336 Ta 2017 | DDC [Fic]

Published in Tulsa, Oklahoma, U.S.A. by Verona Booksellers
"Where Books Are Still Sold!" www.VeronaBooksellers.com

Cover design by Deranged Doctor Design
Book design by Inkstain Interior Book Designing
First Edition: June 2017
10 9 8 7 6 5 4 3 2 1

To my little sister Gracie.
You know you'll always be my favorite.

Happiness is an undeveloped neighborhood,

With high dirt mounds where houses should be,

And a little boy playing with toy soldiers,

Who get crushed in the uphill battle.

The father of the boy stands farther away

And watches the homes under construction.

The soldiers are buried and then dug out

Before it is time to leave this place.

The summer ends, and good men are lost.

Houses are transferred, and nothing stays the same.

But the neighborhood is still there,

In a permanent, haunting silence.

—MGKJ, "SOLDIERS ON DEATH MOUNTAIN"

When you are old and grey and full of sleep,

And nodding by the fire, take down this book,

And slowly read, and dream of the soft look

Your eyes had once, and of their shadows deep...

—W. B. YEATS, "WHEN YOU ARE OLD"

TAKE ME
TO THE CAT

PROLOGUE

Nostalgia. *It haunts us, it* destroys us, and sometimes, its sentimentality consumes us piece by piece so that we may realize our once-familiar circumstance may never again return. It is a state of mind best indulged infrequently.

It was this urge to reclaim the past that would remind me of Mr. Grantham, by no means a handsome man. My neighbor was pale from days spent under the shade of his awning while he read paperbacks and smoked cigarettes. His face was angular, and his thinning hair was combed over onto one side. His eyelids were pink around the edges, and they hung like a clothesline after a heavy shower in April. He also wore shirts and pants that were much too big for him. Mom used to say this was because Mrs. Grantham had bought her husband's outfits, and ever since she'd left him after their son Isaac drowned in the creek out by the elementary school, Mr. Grantham had grown frail.

Of course, my mother would finish any gossip about Mr. Grantham with the same phrase: "I don't like that man. He's a weirdo and I don't like him."

I don't think my mom had always referred to Mr. Grantham as a weirdo. When his family was still together, Mr. Grantham coached tee-ball. He had been happier then, but after the accident, he was a different man; he stopped speaking, stopped smiling, stopped waving to us kids as we passed his house. He read by day and smoked by night.

When I think about Mr. Grantham from before the accident, only a handful of memories come to mind. I can remember my parents throwing an open house party the month after we moved in next door to him. I was only six, and Isaac five. My parents briefly introduced me to Mr. Grantham and his wife Cyiarra, a Jamaican woman who was more into rural life than her husband. I recall eating cake while watching Isaac play with another boy named Christian, who was on Mr. Grantham's team that year. I still wonder if such a playdate ever existed.

Isaac drowned at recess near the end of his fourth-grade year. A recent downpour had flooded the nearby creek, permitting the water to rise exceptionally high. The teacher turned her head for a moment, and Isaac was gone. Mr. Grantham was never the same after that.

Cyiarra took the news the worst. She didn't even stay in town long enough for the funeral; her bags packed themselves, and she, like her son, vanished.

The weeds and the grass grew tall in front of their house, and Mr. Grantham began to develop his habit of eating two or more cans of tuna each day. I knew of this only because the neighborhood cats would show up on his lawn Sunday evenings, when he put the trash out for pick up the next morning. When a strong wind knocked over the bin one night, I woke up to find dozens of those aluminum cans—with jagged lids pried up, still partially attached—sprawled from his yard into ours.

This was the first time my mother cast Mr. Grantham in a bad light.

"What a crazy man. He's a weirdo and I don't like him."

Funny how memories change like that.

PART ONE: GHOSTS

"When I was younger I could remember anything, whether
it had happened or not; but my faculties are decaying, now,
and soon I shall be so I cannot remember
any but the things that happened."

—MARK TWAIN, 1907

t was in the lonely town of Dreary, Alabama, where I learned you can miss a lot of

a person's life when you don't keep in touch. It was in Madison, Oklahoma, where I

realized maybe that's the point.

"I need you to come and get me."

This was the second text I received that day—a Thursday during the first full week of

March. The first text, sent thirty minutes before at 9:02 p.m., was from Olivia, my girlfriend

at the time. She'd asked me to meet her at the Double Chin on King Street. So I went.

Olivia was in the booth where we first met, though her hair wasn't lavender then. I

walked over and sat across from her. We were both short but roughly the same height; I

was only a little taller with my own hair. We made eye contact. She was just as beautiful

as the day I fell in love with her, yet almost two years later, I was seventeen, she was

sixteen, I was a senior, and she was a junior. Love is not a theory but a construct, suggested a Romantic somewhere, probably. What's the difference? Only those with experience in the subject knew, and because I was not one of those select few, I could only admit that Olivia and I thought we were in love, when in reality, we were two strangers passing time, and much time had passed.

"I'm glad you're here," she said to me, then quickly added: "Not that you normally aren't! I mean, sure, some instances, yeah, but usually…"

I looked around at the customers of that Double Chin she and I held dear to our hearts. There was a mother standing beside her talkative little girl. There were two skater dudes: one had blond hair and wore a green leather jacket; the other wore an oversized hoodie and a beanie over his longer red hair; both had yo-yos and acne. I saw an older woman at the counter requesting her burger, and beside her was a balding man in a blue button-down shirt and jeans. In another booth were two older, bearded men: the one on the left was muscular, of Hispanic descent, and had a flashy gold wristwatch; the white guy on the right wore a ball cap. At a table was a large lady with pulled-back hair, and she ate alone. Last, there was a teenage couple dressed in formal attire, sharing both a meal and laughs at their table for two. I felt both envious of their current fortune and pity for their future loss. That was the pessimist in me talking, but I couldn't help it. Not on that night.

I imagined this cast of characters as my fellow survivors in a zombie apocalypse, as inappropriate an instance to do so as this may have been. The Double Chin's walls were made mostly of glass, so we would've needed to hold back the zombies that broke in from outside while eventually barricading ourselves in either a workroom or—and I have had this fear an unhealthy number of times—one of the restrooms. I predicted the balding man to be the first to die, and from a bite to the jugular at that. One of the skater dudes would sacrifice himself for the other, or make a cowardly and unsuccessful attempt to escape, and the young couple would be surrounded while trying to help the large lady to the safety of the stalls. The man with the beard and ball cap would get bit as well and end up eating the older woman, who never got her burger.

The remaining members of our makeshift group would consist of myself, Olivia, one of the skaters, the mother, her quiet and traumatized little girl, and the Hispanic man—not for racial diversity, but for his sheer strength. In a shocking twist, the skater who did not run from the zombies would use his yo-yo to somehow free us from the Double Chin and save the world in the process.

But this was real life, and my girlfriend was breaking up with me.

"… It's like you find everything but us interesting." Olivia was crying. As she took a moment to blow her nose into a napkin, I wondered what I had missed. "I don't know, Michael. I see how you avoid my texts to talk about your book online, then make up some excuse as to why you were too busy to respond. And I don't appreciate that. I deserve better, whether it be from you or someone else."

"Someone else," I repeated. "Look, I'm sorry if I've been ignoring you. That was never my intention. And this isn't an excuse, but with college coming up, I've had a lot on my mind. I want to spend more time with you and go on more dates, but I also have to focus on getting scholarships. Besides, didn't you say earlier I'm usually there for you?"

"That was me kidding myself," she said as she shook her head and fidgeted with the straw of her drink. "We have from now until Labor Day, if we're being generous. There's not a lot of time left for us, especially if you do go to California or North Carolina or *Oklahoma*, of all places. It's redder than here!"

"It has my major," I lied. I had been reminiscing as of late.

"Creative writing," she stated. "Your work will take you far."

"It's all I've got," I admitted. "My test scores are average, my grades are decent—"

My phone vibrated on the table. She sighed as I checked the text.

"It's Troy," I explained. "Says, 'I need you to come and get me.' He's at that concert. I think he and Clyde broke up."

"Won't be the only ones tonight," she muttered. "I get you were best friends before we all formed the group, but you spend more time with him than me, *your girlfriend!* Just the other week, you canceled our date plans because you had a fever, only to end up hanging out with him again the next day!"

"He was having relationship issues and needed my help," I reminded her. "And he got sick, too!"

"Were you both making out?"

"What the hell, Olivia?!"

"He worships you!" She said this as if it were the most obvious thing in the world. "You're always trying to make our evenings go from dates to double dates with him and Clyde, then Keegan and Leah, and before you know it, we're at a get-together without Eva!"

"You hang out with Rikki all the time—"

"We're just friends!"

"And that's what I'm saying about Troy and me!" I shouted, staring at her in complete disbelief. She took the lid off her drink. "But you're right—you defend her just as much as I defend Troy, the only difference being that Rikki has outright stated *she is in love with you.* 'Olivia is so amazing, but Michael is only getting in the way! I can't wait till he leaves for college! Oh, look, there they are together! I'll go tell them to have a gay Christmas because *I'm a lesbian and he's a hetero!*'"

Olivia hurled her drink at me. I stood up in shock. She still held the cup, though the front of my shirt was soaked.

"You are ridiculous!" she yelled at me. "You—!"

"No, let me finish!"

"THEN FUCKING FINISH!"

It was then I realized the whole restaurant had been watching our argument unfold. I took a deep breath.

"I love you," I told her. We had echoed it so many times before, it came naturally.

"And I know you always say the same. But you're just as guilty with Rikki as I am with Troy. We can work on this. We must. I mean… I love you, babe."

"Well, Michael dearest, you sure as shit don't act like it."

And just like that, Olivia moved out of the booth, stood up, and then walked away.

"Wait!" I called out to her. "Who's driving you home? Who's paying for your food?"

"I DIDN'T EAT ANYTHING!" she screamed at me without looking back, throwing her hands in the air.

One of the skater dudes shook his head in disgust. The mother scolded the little girl, who was giggling. The Hispanic man had been filming us with his phone, and I gave him the bird before running outside after her.

There was a light drizzle in the air, and with it being almost ten o'clock at night, I barely saw Olivia get into her father's gray sedan. But I did, as it reflected the light coming off the pink-and-yellow neon of the Double Chin. So I ran up to it, but she didn't roll down her window, and Mr. van Droogenbroeck—who had many times referred to me as "my son" and "my boy"—gave me a disappointed look before driving away.

I sighed and shivered in the cold. I had checked the temperatures before leaving the house and had known it would be in the lower thirties, yet I had still refused the hoodie my mother had offered. Hindsight's twenty-twenty, as the saying goes, and as with most situations I might later deem unpleasant, I had brought this upon myself.

Across from the Double Chin was a Taco Kick, and beside that was the single road leading to Dreary County High School, which I felt I was almost too familiar with. On that corner was a signpost listing the name of the intersection, Serling and King, and I wondered then if the town's planners were referring to a specific King or the lowercase title itself. It might not have mattered either way, but the thought was nonetheless a distraction from the weather, and the walk to the Big Nasty was a long one.

So named by Troy after an incident the previous June, the Big Nasty was an olive-green Alpinist SUV that had been gifted to me by my mother, who had owned it for fourteen years. The group and I had been on our way to the Gulf Coast, and among us was Clyde, the then-new guy who hardly spoke. He was so shy, in fact, he didn't know how to tell us he was getting carsick and needing to puke. So he did, right there, in the backseat. We then pulled up to the nearest gas station and hosed down both Clyde and the Alpinist. From then on, my ride was known as the Big Nasty, as the name—like the lingering smell—unfortunately stuck.

I got inside the Big Nasty and started the engine. Turning up the heater to full blast, I sat there, rubbing my hands until the hot air passed through the vents and onto my skin. Along with the warmth came the essence of Clyde's spew; it was as if the two could not be separated. I pulled out of the parking lot and drove in the direction of the Morrissey Ballroom.

Eva texted me then, my third text received that night. I checked it while driving, which was illegal and stupid, but so were a lot of the things we did. She wanted to know how the date had gone, if it could even be called that. Truth be told, I'd never imagined my breakup with Olivia happening like it had, so soon. My shirt was still damp from the water, and flakes were beginning to fall from the sky. I was too focused on the road ahead to pay them much attention other than mere recognition—as it had been with Olivia, no doubt.

There were three people smoking outside the building. They looked too old to be teenagers, yet young enough where no one would mistake them for parents. I felt as if I wouldn't look that way until I was thirty, the way puberty had hit me—slowly and inconsistently. This was unlike Troy Ricardo Valdez, who stood roughly six feet tall and could grow a full beard if he wanted. But he didn't, as that would have contrasted with his dyed blond hair, even though he usually wore beanies. If he had, I suspected people would've thought I was his little brother more than they already did, despite Troy being Costa Rican and only a month older than me.

He emerged from the entrance with an arm around Clyde, and both wandered out onto the curb. Troy surveyed the passing vehicles, pointed to the Big Nasty when he spotted it, and then pulled Clyde along with him.

"Hey, thanks, Mom," he said to me. "S'all right if Clyde rides with us?"

They were in before I could answer, and I found their behavior toward each other surprising; if they had broken up, they were handling this much better than Olivia and I had.

My phone vibrated with a notification from Coffeefolder. "Olivia van Droogenbroeck went from being 'in a relationship' to 'single,'" it read. My own relationship status stated something similar.

"God, that was a great concert," Troy announced to no one in particular. I put down my phone and started driving again. "Real, live bees! Just swarming everywhere!"

"Like that one in Raleigh," Clyde noted. He was smiling.

"And all my favorite songs." Troy rolled down the window and began howling and shouting lyrics into the chilly night. I continued in the direction of Clyde's neighborhood. "*One mile in the snow—*"

"*—is a mile that I'd gladly go,*" Clyde joined.

"*For you!*"

"*Always yooooouu!*"

"Yeow! *One mile in the snow!*"

"*Freezing temperatures!*"

"*Gonna miss my show!*"

"For you!"

"Yeah, baby."

"Oh, I'd miss it all for you-ou-ooooouu!"

They sang this last bit in unison, then fell onto each other, laughing. I looked in the rearview mirror and saw Clyde wipe tears from his eyes, both of which were closed as he continued to grin some more.

"Will you both *please* shut up?!" I yelled at them. "You have this sort of high from the concert and the weed you must've smoked, sure, I get that, but you broke up—*why are you still happy?!*" There was more to it than that, however; there was something I wasn't understanding, and Olivia had dumped me because of it. "So while I'm driving, please, oh please, keep your goddamn happiness to yourselves."

Troy snorted. "You said, 'penis.'"

"No, I did not."

He frowned, turned to Clyde, and then gestured past him.

"Get out of the car," Troy commanded.

"Wha—?"

"You heard me. We're done. I'm claiming friends, and I've got Mom. So get the fuck outta here!"

Clyde started to cry again, but this time, his tears were out of sadness. I glanced in the rearview mirror to see Troy roll his eyes, unbuckle both of their seat belts, and then lean over Clyde to hug him.

"Shhhh," he said, a finger to Clyde's blubbering lips. The storm whipped against the nearby trees. "Calm down. Calm down, all right? Just count to three with me. One."

"Two?" Clyde managed, looking into Troy's eyes.

"Three!"

Troy threw open the car door beside Clyde and pushed him out and onto the gravel road. I slammed my foot on the brake, bringing the SUV to a halt.

"Why did you do that?!" I demanded.

"No, no, keep going!" He reached over to grab the steering wheel, so I complied. "That butt-ass knew it was coming. This isn't the first time I've thrown him out of a moving vehicle."

"What did you mean back there?" I asked. "About claiming friends."

"I broke up with Clyde, and Droogen dumped your sorry ass," he noted. "There's bound to be some fallout within the group."

"Don't I get a say in who I choose?"

"You never have a say. Comes with the motherly instincts, I'm sure. They're going to hear from Droogen and think it was your fault. You're lucky to have me. Besides, you would've picked Troy Rico, anyway. You know that!"

I considered this as we passed Clyde's house.

"Keep your eyes forward," Troy told me, some shuffling going on in the back. "Don't look away, and slowly put your hand—your right hand—on the center console." He must have seen me hesitating, as he then added: "Just do it, OK?"

I did, then immediately regretted it as I grabbed a long, warm, slender, and questionably prized piece of male anatomy.

"You promised!" I reminded him. "You said you wouldn't do that again!"

"But I'm tired and hoooornyyy."

"You're drunk and disgusting."

"Fuck off, Mom. I'm the teen queen of this shitty town, *and I'm old!* You don't know how good you got it."

"So you tell me."

He withdrew his cock, and when I looked back, he was stroking it.

"Not in the car!"

"You just ran a stop sign."

"Huh? No, I didn't."

The scream of the siren proved otherwise, and soon after, a cop car, its lightbar flashing. I pulled over next to a two-story house, and the honest-to-God thought that popped into my head was not that I was probably going to get a ticket, and how was I going to pay it off—not that Troy might still have his pants down, and not of my recent breakup—but that I hoped the noise didn't wake the family inside the house— "motherly instincts" and all.

My head hurt. I felt like I'd done this before.

The police cruiser parked a couple of feet behind us. It was a ghostly white that stood out in the blackness surrounding Troy, the Big Nasty, and myself. An older man in uniform got out of the driver's seat, looked around briefly, spat into the grass, and then walked over to my window, red and blue reflecting in the side mirror. I lowered the window and shivered at the drop in temperature from the SUV's heater to the sudden snow.

"G'evening," the cop said to me. His identification read BLEAKMAN, and I prayed his name didn't match his personality.

"Hello, Officer," I managed as innocently as I could. I didn't have any drugs or alcohol in my possession—later that night would be anyone's guess, given the day's events—but Troy had certainly consumed the latter, not to mention tossing Clyde onto the road. I wondered if that was a chargeable crime, though I wasn't about to ask.

"You really wanted me to pull you over, didn't you?" Bleakman began with a slight laugh. "Young man, are you aware you ran a neighborhood stop sign at forty miles an hour back there?"

"Told ya," Troy said from the back. Bleakman craned his head to look inside—I heard his joints crack and pop as he did so—and stare at Troy, who was thankfully clothed.

Bleakman put a hand on his aging hips and looked at his watch. He wore an ugly yellow shirt with suit pants that matched the color of the Big Nasty. I looked in the rearview mirror at the cop car: DREARY est. 1824, it read on the hood. The fact people had been there for so long and hadn't all gotten up and left was astounding.

"So tell me what went through your mind just then," he asked of me. "Explain why you would drive your vehicle at such a speed at ten at night in the snow?"

I saw what he was getting at. The Big Nasty could've plowed into any car or person in my path when I'd run that stop sign, and my negligence would've been to blame. That and Troy's dick. *Troy's a dick*, I thought, but I couldn't share that with the cop. So I told him the truth.

"I was driving my friend home," I said. "He's a bit, erm, under the influence, and I was deemed the designated driver. As for the sign, well, I got a bit distracted." I gulped, and before I could stop myself, I added: "I like your shirt!"

Troy burst out laughing in the backseat. I struggled not to take off my shoe and beat him senseless with it.

"Uh-huh," Cop said. "Can I see your driver's license?" I had watched enough TV to know this was a command, not a request, so I slowly reached into my pocket and fished out my wallet. I pulled out the piece of plastic with my height, weight, eye color, hair color, and gender—whatever that meant, nowadays—and handed it to him while I waited for the inevitable.

It didn't come as fast as it should have. I assumed this was most likely because he was an older man, which factored in both physically and intellectually. Respectively: (1.) Bleakman held the license up to the streetlight to read it, and he squinted as he did so, which added to the waiting period, and (2.) while I was totally judging him by his looks and age, he probably didn't even recognize my namesake, which I then figured was practically impossible, given the awards and court cases.

"Michael Jackson!" he announced for the entire state of Alabama to hear, let alone the residents of the house beside us. "Your name is Michael Jackson!"

REALLY, OLD MAN? THANK YOU FOR TELLING ME THAT. NO, REALLY, THANK YOU SO MUCH FOR THE REMINDER. I HAD RECENTLY SUFFERED A FIT OF AMNESIA AND MOMENTARILY FORGOT WHAT MY PARENTS

NAMED ME. YOU ARE A TRUE AMERICAN HERO. GOD BLESS.

"Yeah, that's me," I said. "Sorry about running the stop sign."

"Oh, that's no problem," he assured me. "Probably just got your license, I bet." Untrue, but I wasn't going to argue with him. He smiled wide. "Michael Jackson, Michael Jackson. I remember when 'Thriller' came out, and my friend showed me a clip, and I went home to tell my folks, and Daddy said, 'That's of the devil.' I don't believe that, and I don't think anyone did but 'em extremists, but whatever he was, MJ became a sensation overnight, and I quickly learned all his songs, even though I weren't allowed to listen to rock while I was at the house." He closed his eyes and bobbed his head to a song only he heard. "Michael Jackson. Shame he passed the way he did."

I nodded. My mother and I had just pulled into the garage on a hot June afternoon when we'd heard over the radio that the King of Pop had died of a drug overdose at the age of fifty—and right before his big, final concert tour, too. I didn't have anything against the man, despite the countless accusations he'd had to endure, though I did wish my name was something a little more original and not associated with a music genre I tended to dislike.

"Y'know, you seem like a good kid, Michael Jackson," Bleakman said, his eyes gleaming with nostalgia. "I saw you run that sign and says to myself, 'Well, I gotta pull this guy over.' I'm going to let you off with a warning, so long as you pay more attention in the future. All good?"

I nodded, and he hesitated before giving me back my license. I pocketed it, then shook his outstretched hand.

"Drive safe now," Bleakman told me, as if I had a choice with him right there. "And get your friend home! This weather should pass within the hour."

I waved at the cop one last time before driving off into the quiet night. When Troy whined about wanting a theme song, I turned on my music to Miami Horror's "Real Slow" featuring Sarah Chernoff. Despite the mental pain Troy could cause me, I still liked him enough—though not in the way Olivia had suggested. Yet only once did I look back to check on my psycho of a best friend, who had fallen asleep with a hand down his pants.

Everyone has a group. At least, this had proven true thus far for my own high school experience. These societies could be the stereotypical preps, goths, nerds, whatever, and they could also be a combination of two or more, like the swimmers and the Speech & Debaters, both of which were cults. Mostly, though, you stuck to your core group of friends on the weekends; I knew of some people who would claim they were part of many factions, but they were the bullshitters.

My group consisted mainly of six individuals:

Olivia, a natural blonde who dyed her hair to match her mood.

Eva, a curvy black lesbian who had dyed her hair hot pink that week. She also didn't shave, consequently having more body hair than anyone I knew. Eva claimed it was a part of her feminist movement, so more power to her.

Keegan, who was half-black, half-Filipino, and couldn't cook to save his life, unlike his mother. He was also a bit of a loose cannon, which seemed to win him most arguments.

Leah was the ninth grader. She'd been dating Keegan for the past six months and hanging out with us more often than the rest of her cheer squad, which I found amusing.

Clyde was Keegan's ever-tired and sensitive drug dealer who should've graduated the year before, but he had gotten held back. Lucky for him, he was short like me, so he still fit in.

And then there was Troy, obviously.

Troy and I walked side by side that Friday morning to our group's corner within Dreary

County High School. There, Keegan, Clyde, Olivia, Leah, and Eva were sitting against the wall, all methodically picking off pieces of the baby-blue paint. Once they saw Troy and me, however, Keegan and Clyde stood up and positioned themselves in front of the girls for whatever reason. Clyde had a noticeable cut on his forehead. Keegan stepped forward.

"Got some balls showing up here after what you two did last night," he said to Troy and me. "Who do you sons of bitches think you are, throwing Clydesdale out of the Big Nasty and getting all mad at Droogen?"

"Buenos dias to you, too, Keegs," Troy said. "And it's funny you mention my balls—you being a homophobic asshole and everything."

"I'm not homophobic!" Keegan stated. "People have the right to fuck whoever they want, whether it be another girl or—"

"Makes sense, coming from the guy who's dating the freshman," Troy said, then laughed. "You know she's underage, right?"

"I'm sixteen!" Leah shouted.

"Honey, you're fifteen," Troy told her. "Stop kidding yourself. But that's all right—do what you like, fuck who you like. He likes his girls young, anyway. Got the consent forms and everything."

"Fuck you," Keegan said. "Mom went out with Droogen, and they're a grade apart."

"Sure, but they never fucked."

"What the hell, Troy?!" I exclaimed, hitting his side, then turned to Olivia. "I'm sorry about—"

"It's the truth!" he said to me. "You and I are more physical than you and Droogen ever were."

"I knew it," Olivia muttered. I shook my head. This wasn't how I wanted to start my day.

"Look," Eva said, standing up. "Troy, pushing Clyde out of the Big Nasty wasn't cool. And Keegan…" She sighed. "Mike and Livi's break up was more complicated than that."

"Whose side are you on?!" Olivia asked her.

"I'm not on any one person's side!" she explained. "Can't we all just talk about this? Like adults?"

"As I said," Troy continued, "Leah's underage."

"You motherfucker!" Keegan yelled, shoving Troy into me. He shoved Keegan back. "Go back to Cuba or Puerto Rico or wherever the hell you're from!" Keegan glared at me. "And you, chink-a-billy, can go back to Okla... *fucking-homo!*"

"Hey!" both Eva and Clyde exclaimed.

"Shove it up your ass, man," Troy told him, putting an arm around me and walking us away.

"'Cause that's how you fucking like it, you fucking fag!" Keegan shouted behind us, consequently getting a hard slap across the face from Eva. I grimaced at the sound, knowing Keegan would surely take his anger out on Leah afterward.

"We don't need them," Troy declared. "We're sixty-nine times better, all puns intended. And now we can start up that band we always wanted. What were we going to call it? Flamboyant Cuttlefish?"

"Look, man," I said to him, pushing his arm off. We stopped. "You're my best friend—my inappropriate, impulsive, and insensitive best friend. You know that, right?"

"You breaking up with me?" Troy joked with a grin.

"That's what I'm talking about! All these gay references to me and you—and I'm not talking 'gay' as an insult, 'cause you know me better than that, but 'gay' as in, well, gay! Just tone it down a bit, all right? I know that might be hard for the *illustrious* Troy Rico, but even so—"

"OK, OK, I feel you—get you. Really." We continued walking. "Besides, that breakup comment was probably too soon."

"Yeah, no kidding."

"And 'Flamboyant Cuttlefish,' like, what was I thinking? You can't play a recorder, let alone a dick!"

"I could in fifth grade," I told him, then cringed. "The recorder, I meant."

"You set yourself up for this kind of shit," Troy said, laughing. I joined him. It was probably true, anyway.

Our usual lunch spot on the lowered wall of the school's courtyard was empty by the time Troy and I arrived. Keegan and Leah were nowhere to be seen, though I did spy Olivia eating with a few junior girls—including Rikki—in the cafeteria, while Eva and Clyde ate at a table alone. He was crying, and it appeared she was comforting him. Troy rolled his eyes when I mentioned this, and we ate our food in silence.

I drove Troy home after school to his ritzy manor at the edge of town. His family's wealth was because Troy's maternal uncle was Julian Morrissey, a local college football player who'd gone on to make fancy and expensive wristwatches. For some reason, Mr. Morrissey had come back to Alabama, and with his fortune, he'd helped to improve the town and bring in new money. That was why, despite having a population of a little under five thousand, we could have a music venue with the ability to book rappers such as Narcissus and Thorax Wang, pop stars like Lita Candyce and Sabryn, and bands Pulsar Skies, the Orpheus, and Two-Thirds Denim, to name some of that month's performances. Thus, the Morrissey Ballroom was the only cool place to go to in Dreary aside from Troy Rico's notorious house parties, which featured not esteemed entertainers, but booze and marijuana.

Unlike Troy's house—which had been featured on the cover of October's *Southern Pride and Prestige*—mine had neither white columns, nor a heated pool, nor a concrete driveway, nor fourteen-foot ceilings, nor a formal dining room, nor a three-car garage, nor an attic, nor four bedrooms with a bath for each. Instead, the place I called home consisted of two bedrooms, a single living room, kitchen, den, and laundry space, and one working bathroom, all with wooden floors. It had been my grandmother's house before she'd passed away, and when she had, my mom and I had moved in. We didn't have a lot of money, so none of the antique furniture had been replaced. In short, my house was the literary foil to Troy's more modern abode.

He was having another one of his parties that Friday night, but I wasn't going, as I had yard work to do for my neighbor across the street. Mr. Bradford, who insisted I call him Aiden, was in his late fifties and had a bad back even after his fusion. So I'd offered to rake the leaves, trim the hedges, and mow the lawn for him whenever he needed the help. Each time, he paid me what he could, and in turn, we both were grateful.

Mr. Bradford was checking for mail when I got to the house after school. He was a wrinkled man with a sad smile and a crew-cut hairstyle. I pulled the Big Nasty into the garage, got out, and then met him by our conjoined mailboxes—which made it easier for the mail carrier, sure, but not Mr. Bradford, who always had to come over to my side of Miller Road to access the box.

"How you doing, Mikey?" he asked, holding out the hand that wasn't gripping notices from people he owed money. I shook it. "Kind of wish the snow had stuck around. Then we wouldn't have to see all these here leaves, huh?"

"Yes, sir," I said, "but less snow means easier driving."

"True, true." He ran the same hand through his little hair, which was gray with a hint of red. "Didn't snow like this in Oklahoma, that's for sure. Well, maybe." He kicked at the ground. "How's your old man over there? Didn't you say he got out of Red Springs Penitentiary? Because of good behavior or something?"

"Yes, sir. He has a house in Madison now."

"Beautiful little lake town. Not far from Arminster, too. You should see about visiting him this summer." Mr. Bradford smiled. "Sorry. It's just nice knowing someone who's also from Oklahoma. Most people hate hearing me ramble on and on… and on and on… and on…" He blinked. "But anyway, how's your mother?"

"She's fine. Tired. It's nice she'll be working from home now."

"Editing textbook-sized manuals for that oil company, right?"

"More or less," I answered, shrugging. "And your kids? How are they?"

"Oh, you know how it is." He looked down at his mail. "I sent my son birthday money a week or two ago, but he's at college, so I don't think he got it yet. Probably shouldn't've sent cash. Talked to my little girl on the phone Saturday. I worry she's not seeing me as her daddy anymore. Probably don't help she's had a stepdad, but still, Maisy doesn't call me anything. Just, 'I love you, too.' She's almost a teenager, though, so maybe that's normal for 'em. Probably shouldn't've signed those papers… I need to get her over here. Both, actually. Bought that house for its three rooms, thinking they'd visit more often, but that was years ago." He sighed. "I miss them, Mikey. I miss 'em real bad."

"I know you do," I told him, "and I'm sure they feel the same."

He laughed for some reason. "Anyway, it's getting too cold to talk out here. Go in your house and warm up and then get a jacket and gloves on. You know where I keep the rake, right?"

"In your workshop?"

"That's the place," he said with a smile, then put a hand on my shoulder. "And I know I always say this, but thanks again for helping me out. Means more than a lot." He put the hand in his pocket, glanced at his house, and then looked back. "I hope my boy's turned out like you."

With that, he left me by the mailboxes. I gathered what little was in mine, closed it, and then walked over the wet leaves to my dead grandmother's house. Soon after, I was outside again, marching across Mr. Bradford's lawn with his rake thrown over my shoulder, a job to do and time for my thoughts.

Mom was in the kitchen when I finished raking. She was preparing dinner—some tilapia and asparagus—and flipping through the mail as the fish fried in the skillet. I walked over, gave her a hug, and then kissed her freckled cheek, one of her many traits I had not inherited during DNA replication. In fact, I looked so much like my dad that an officer had pulled her over once to ask if that child in the backseat (*me*) belonged to her (*my mother*). Thanks, double helix. Fuck the cops.

"How was your day?" I asked her.

"The usual," she said. "Groceries to buy, packets to get, forms to fill. But I got that new work laptop! It's crazy how small computers are getting. I remember using my first one in a typing class in high school—absolutely massive. We had to type out the commands. And with all the privacy concerns on the news these days, the Internet freaks me out!"

"You're aging yourself," I said, smiling.

"I'm serious! You were proficient at the computer at fourteen months, sure, but that was when I got my first TSC email and signed up as PolkaNOK—Polka in Oklahoma. And then I joined the TSC group for runners because I was about to run my first marathon, and I thought I should try out the message board for tips, and I ended up talking to people from all over the world. But what I thought was crazy was that if someone put up my running time and information on the web—which is what they do for every race now—then they would be able to see everything under 'Heidi Jackson.' So I started signing up for races as 'Polka Jackson!' And it's all still there! Thank God I've changed my last name since." She caught herself ranting, laughed, and then handed me an envelope. "Speaking of which, that's a letter from your father. You must have missed it."

"Yeah, thanks." I turned it over and glanced at the return address. "Maybe I could go visit him sometime. Like, this summer or—"

"Maybe," she said, adjusting her ponytail and then pulling down at her sleeves, crossing her arms. "He didn't sound too right in the head the last time we talked. Of course, that was a while ago and before he tossed out his landline, but still, it might not be such a good idea. Besides, you'll be checking out Hartsett University in June, remember!"

She said this last bit with a wide smile on her face. I shook my head.

"You know I haven't gotten accepted yet. And Hartsett is all the way in California. We can't afford an extra flight there, let alone room and board."

"But you've got good scholarships. Plus, it helps they like that book you wrote, despite its, uh, questionable content."

"Mother!"

"I'm just saying!" she laughed. "Your Hartsett admissions counselor said their English department would be honored to have you, and they would work with us on your tuition. *You did it!* There's no way they won't accept you!"

"OK, OK," I said, wanting her to drop the whole college talk. "I'd rather wait to have this conversation until after I've been accepted or rejected. Can we do that? Please?"

"Fine," she agreed, still smiling, ever-so-hopeful. She returned her attention to the fish, and I took that as my opportunity to leave with my letter.

I went to my room and powered up my laptop. I checked the notifications from Chipper, Coffeefolder, Photofixer, Uprorrr, and my email, but there was nothing important—nothing about Hartsett and book sales. My colleges had until the first of April to send news of admittance, yet I was still concerned at having not received word from the places I'd applied to: Hartsett University in California; the University of North Carolina in Windhaven; even the University of Arminster in Oklahoma. The only news I had received was from Dreary Community College, which had accepted both Troy and me in February. It was the only Alabama school I'd queried, as I needed to get away from the state, and an institution of higher education seemed to be the only way out.

I tore open the letter from my dad and read his note. He wished me a happy early birthday and wanted to know how my senior year was going, and he had included two twenty-dollar bills and a ten. I put the money aside and thought of my childhood in Oklahoma and elementary school years spent in a town next to the city of Arminster called New Baines. It had been nearly seven years since I was last in Oklahoma, but like Mr. Bradford, I sure missed that place.

Feeling nostalgic for my youth, I went back to my laptop and looked up episodes of *Sea Breeze Academy*, a TV show from my adolescent years about a group of teens and their adventures at a fictional boarding school in Southern California. It was filmed at Hartsett during the summer months so the camera crew wouldn't interrupt classes, and if anybody said they hadn't ever wanted to go to school there, they were lying; *everyone* had wanted to attend SBA when they were a kid. And through Hartsett, this was my chance.

But for the time being, I was left experiencing what I could through the lives of transfer student Brooklyn "Rook" Rivers and Matthew Flynn, best friends who finally get romantically involved at the beginning of season four. *Sea Breeze Academy*, at the very least, gave me the opportunity to look at the stunning campus without having to use QuickSearch Maps. So I selected the episode "Double Trouble" and started it from the beginning. Chris—Matthew's best friend and roommate—wants to ask a girl out on a date, but he doesn't know how, so he comes to Matthew for advice.

"Just go for it, man," Matthew suggests. "If you like her, why not give it a shot?"

"Says the guy who still hasn't told Rook he loves her," Chris points out. Matthew frowns at this, but he doesn't say anything in return. He knows it's true, and so did I.

At noon on Saturday, Troy gallivanted into my room and fell on my bed while I was binge-watching *Sea Breeze Academy*. He then got up, peeked over my shoulder, and sighed his dissatisfaction over my taste in live-action television that had been off the air for nearly a decade.

"There are so many other shows you could be watching," he said, back on the bed while I was at my desk. He wore a white V-neck, dark skinny jeans, and a beanie over his hair. "Crap TV like *Rehab Runway* and *Penthouse Pursuit* are so much better than *Sea Breeze High* ever was."

"*Academy,*" I corrected him.

"What are they, thirteen? Look at their clothes!" He pointed to Matthew. "What is that? A long-sleeve button-down that's not even rolled up to his elbows? They're in SoCal! And look at her, with a tank top over a t-shirt! Jesus Christ. What year was this set in?"

"Their wardrobe gets better in the second season."

"They must not be rich like me. I'm rolling in it, baby!" He clapped his hands, then pulled out his phone. "Look at that case! *Solid motherfucking gold!* Can barely hold it in one hand! Tell me, author man: is that direct or indirect characterization, huh?" He gestured to the show. "You still writing fanfics for this stuff?"

"Those were my pre-BTM days."

"*Beneath the Makeup, Beneath the Makeup,*" he said to himself. "And somehow, I'm the homosexual. Isn't there a Michael Jackson song called 'Behind the Mask'?"

I thought about it for a moment, opened a new tab, QuickSearched it, sighed, and then returned to *SBA*. "Damn you, Troy Rico."

"And I'll be damned." He grinned. "How are your sales doing?"

I paused the show again, pulled up QuickSearch, and then typed in the name of my novella. The top result was its Coffeefolder page, and below that were links to the Marilyn Monroe quote I'd gotten the title from and included as the epigraph.

"Eight ebook copies sold this month," I told him after checking my reports. "Not amazing, but still good, for me. Better than February."

Troy shrugged, looked over my shoulder, and then started reading the description.

"'The Canopy Creek Sanatorium and Dr. Ian Gal—'"

"There's no reason for doing that!"

"'—both lost patient Madison Fitzgerald in less than a month,'" he continued, grinning some more. "'Admitted for punching a clown at her school's end-of-the-year festival, Madison fought against being placed with the real psychos, though it was her encounter with a creep of a clown at the town carnival that put her in the loony bin in the first place. Now Madison has run away, and it's that fair time of year again.'"

"Won the Dreary County Library's Writer's Spotlight," I beamed.

"Which I know because I'm one of your two hundred followers, as opposed to my two thousand."

"That's half the town!"

"Oh, please," he said. "Dreary's for the elderly. All the action's in Rochester, assuming you want to drive out for half an hour."

"Thirty minutes is nothing compared to Arminster County." I stopped to think. "Well, I suppose it is when everything here is five minutes away—and that's not saying much—but still."

"But still," he echoed, mocking me. "For a guy who's lived in Alabama the past seven years now—four of them being here in Dreary—you sure talk about Oklahoma a lot."

"I know, I know."

I got up from my desk and looked out the window to the gravel driveway and the Big Nasty parked along the side of our property. Dreary was, simply put, too quiet for me—too simplistic and old-fashioned, despite the slight LGBT+ movement going through its youth. Troy was right: the malls and movie theaters and Brick & Mortar were all in Rochester, the teen scene there coming to Dreary solely for the Morrissey Ballroom. In fact, the local gas stations all had a monopoly on Dreary—raising their prices because we were so isolated by forests. As Troy had once said, it's tough being young in a sleepy town; there isn't a whole lot left to explore.

"I'm just not… I'm not happy here anymore," I told him. Myself, really. "I don't think I ever have been."

"Hey, now!" Troy said, putting one hand on my left shoulder and using his right to sweep across his imaginary sky and my field of vision. "We've had *plenty* of fun times together! Sooooo many parties."

"Not even you like your parties," I pointed out.

"This is true," he admitted. "In any event, when *were* you last happy, huh? Your birthday party in my pool last year? Some date with Droogen? Me taking you to your first concert? Man, that was the shit—"

"Hayes Elementary."

"Hayes Elementary?"

"Where I went from first to fifth grade, yeah."

I moved over to my bed and crouched beside it, shuffling through the various items underneath. Eventually, I pulled out my Rutherford B. Hayes Elementary School yearbook, which featured pictures of safari animals on the cover and stated, "WILD ABOUT LEARNING." As if.

I tossed the worn paperback to Troy, who skimmed through its black-and-white pages and, within seconds, found what he was looking for: Ms. Albertine's Fifth-Grade Class. I was in the second row and right in the middle, wearing a plain t-shirt and smiling wide for the camera. I was even missing a tooth.

"Aww, look at you," Troy said, pointing at the picture, looking from past-me to present-me, then back again. "You were a cutie! Should've kept that haircut."

"That's vaguely pedophilic of you," I noted.

"All the more reason to keep this away from Keegs," he declared, then laughed at his joke. "Oh, God, I hate that fuck. Hey, your teacher is wearing two different earrings. What's up with that? Worse than those *Sea Breeze* kids!"

"Yeah, she was an interesting lady. Would always switch her scarves throughout the day, too. I forget why, though. Some sort of visual test, maybe?"

"Isn't 'Harper Albertine' the name of a porn star?"

"Since when you do you watch straight porn?"

"For the giggles." He took out his phone and went to the Internet. "What town did you say you were from?"

"New Baines," I answered. "Very picturesque. The school was by the neighborhood, so my friends and I would all meet at the—"

"Says here that Harper Albertine, not affiliated with the porn industry, was killed after a head-on collision with a semi on the New Baines Expressway," he read from his phone. "This is the year after you left, too. She's buried at Shaughnessy Grove Cemetery."

"Let me see that," I said, and he gave me his phone. "Damn."

"Was she a cool teacher or one of the boring kinds?"

"We liked her. She was wacky and enjoyed teaching outside more than in, so that was fun. This was before the Board of Education put in standardized testing and whatnot, so maybe it's a good thing she wasn't around for that. Probably would've drove her even crazier."

Troy snorted. "Bad choice of words, Mom. But anyway, that sucks for Ms. Albertine."

I handed his phone back to him, and he gave me the yearbook in return. I sat down at my desk with it, exited out of *Sea Breeze Academy*, and then went to my Coffeefolder account. *"Your business is our business!"* the site's slogan read.

"Yep, I know, nobody uses Coffeefolder anymore," I told him. "I get it. Still, it leaves an electronic trail for mice like me to follow." I flipped open the yearbook and turned to the appropriate page. "First guy on the left. Christian Battenfield."

I typed in his name, and he immediately appeared under the search bar: Christian Battenfield; New Baines High School; New Baines, Oklahoma. His profile picture was of him and a girl on a couch in some home. It was three years old, but even so, I could still see the Christian I remembered—the one who read his Bible for fun and was good at every sport he played.

"What a tool," Troy commented as we continued. "A mirror selfie? Really? And what's with that fauxhawk haircut? Oh, look—there's that girl again. Bet you they went to junior prom together."

"Look at the timestamp," I said, pointing. "A lot can change in three years."

"Even more can change in seven," he countered, then pointed. "Ha! The shaggy-hair-over-the-eyes phase of his life!"

"Which you're still going through?"

"Yeah, OK, Mom. I'll cut my bangs when Hell freezes over. No graphic tee, though—and now he's back to the fauxhawk. Look at that girl's comment: 'I MISS YOUR HAIR!' Sad emoji! See, that's what everyone would say to me. Let's look at his posts—except nobody posts anything to Coffeefolder but parents, so let's look at his *mom's* posts. What does that even mean, 'Coffeefolder'? Isn't that just two random words thrown together? We *celebrate* that kind of ingenuity? I can't believe in this country that… well, all right, I guess I can—"

"So Christian chose baseball over soccer," I observed, remembering his fondness for both.

"With a name like Battenfield, wouldn't you?" Troy joked. "Though, by that logic, it's like asking if you, Michael Jackson, want to sing some high notes, thrust your pelvis, bleach your skin, and burn your hair off—and not necessarily in that order." We continued. "Way too many posts. Um, college tours… birthday car… older brother's cute… wow, look at that TSC flip phone on the counter…" He clapped his hands. "OK, next person—wait, wait, click on that one!"

He pointed to a tab labeled "Recent Pictures" beneath Christian's headshot. These were much more current: there was an image of Christian as he posed with his New Baines baseball team, one of him flexing in a tank top with a friend inside a department store, and another of him wearing low jeans and an open shirt, revealing his six-pack abs.

"Not only is he a tool, but a twink, too," Troy commented. "Skinny with, like, no body hair." He turned to me. "Kind of like you, Mom. You'd make a perfect twink!"

"Yeah, maybe, but *I'm not gay.*"

"I'm so confused," he went on. "Christian went from a wannabe to I-wannabe-in-his-pants. And who's posting these?! Click on her name!"

"Belle Bottomley," I said, laughing, then pointed from her name on the screen to her picture in the yearbook. Back then, she'd had straight blonde hair, big teeth, and round glasses. Troy grimaced, but that soon changed once we saw her profile.

"Oh, shit!" Troy said. "Shit, shit, shit! Belle got hot! And she's got a hot car to match! I mean, she has to if she wants to make up for 'Bottomley,' right? Holy fuck, that's unfortunate."

Belle was surprisingly pretty. She had been sweet in fifth grade—maybe even cute, to be generous—but now she had curved legs, shoulders you couldn't help wanting to kiss, and a smile that would turn any nonbeliever into a saint; she was simple, yet almighty. There was something odd about her gaze, though, in the more recent pictures.

"That girl knows fashion," he continued. "Oh, well, duh, since she works at Ivy's Innuendo. Shit, I wonder if she gets free lingerie from there. That ass…"

"Are you still gay?" I asked, laughing some more as he caught himself trailing off. "No wonder Eva's always preaching about fluidity—look at you! What happened to the Troy Rico-slash-Christian Battenfield story in the works from a minute ago? Did that ship already sail?"

"They don't call me 'Troy Rico, Queen of Dreary Dicks' for nothing, straightboy." He considered this. "Actually, no one calls me that. Besides, I can acknowledge when someone's got sex appeal. But seriously, do you think we can get Belle to hook up the Christian from three years ago with some proper clothes? I mean, it says they go to the same school, for Christ's sake. LOOK AT THOSE JEANS! SHE WEARS THEM

LIKE A MOTHER HOLDS HER CHILD: SNUG AND WITH PURPOSE!"

"Gaah. Gross. You're creeping me out."

"You know you're thinking it!" Troy exclaimed. He was right; she was hot, but she reminded me too much of Olivia before the hair-dying. "Go back to Christian's profile pic for a second... uh-huh... yep, I knew it. Belle's the girl. They totally hooked up three years ago. No wonder he got a fitting pair of pants then. Went back to the shaggy hair, too."

Belle had been a bookworm in elementary school, so it made sense she volunteered with the library's summer reading program for kids and would post all about her favorite novels coming out soon. It was her sister—equally attractive—who wrote the post on Belle meeting the author of *Rudderless at Sea* and getting a picture with him; Belle was generous, yet modest. She was the girl every heterosexual boy wanted to bring home to his mother.

Next to Belle in the yearbook was Gabriel Cabello, who was arguably one of my better friends at Hayes. I remembered he would come over to my house on the weekends to play computer games and drink lemonade. In fact, Gabe was the one to help me come up with my first short story about a dog named Obie that would attack the bullies of the third-grade protagonist. "*Obie* was *obedient*," I told Troy, who just rolled his eyes. "What? We were eight. I thought it was clever."

Gabe, however, was not on Coffeefolder, or if he was, Troy and I could find neither Gabriel, nor Gabe, nor Briel Cabello. The search found an older man in California and another in Argentina, but they weren't my guy. So we expanded our hunt to include QuickSearch, which didn't bring up any relevant results. Christian and Belle weren't faking their virtual smiles in 120 characters or less on Chipper, either, as its slogan went, but Belle was on Photofixer—and her profile was set to private. Figured.

So we moved on to Franklin "Blank Frank" Chambers, lovingly named so because he had always drawn a blank when taking our multiplication tests. To be fair, it was

Frank who had told me to email him so we could keep in touch during middle school, though we never did. He had signed my yearbook, "I miss you so much," which had thrown me off in the moment, since we weren't best friends or anything, and we hadn't left the school yet. Like Belle, I remembered Frank as being nice and caring, which made the New Baines *Ledger* article Troy and I discovered all the sadder.

"He shot himself," Troy summarized after we'd finished our silent reading, "during a freshman biology test. *Damn*. Just took a gun out, put it to his head, and… All he wrote on his answer sheet was 'Too big to keep.' God, that's messed up."

Willow Dusett, a red-haired girl who had struggled with schoolwork, was now in Madison, Oklahoma, as stated by Coffeefolder. She was a scene kid at one point, with neon colors and zebra prints, and she'd worn a lot of eyeliner and mascara. Willow also wasn't afraid of showing off a little—or a lot—of her cleavage, at least according to the doctored pictures she'd posted over the years. Troy laughed at a comment from a girl that read, "No homo but ur really pretty," then pointed to a post further down the page.

"Not only does she work as a hairstylist for her mom's salon," he said, "but she's had a baby, too. Kid turned three last month." He laughed. "Real country-type shit. And I'm from Alabama!"

Beginning the next row was Peter Fortescue, who had invited me to my first sleepover party in second grade. It was mostly us guys running around and shooting each other with fake pistols, but it was still fun, even if Pete was a smelly kid with caterpillar eyebrows and hair so short he was almost bald. He only ever wore green clothes, too. And while I was at his house, I had opened one of the drawers in the kitchen to find a random mound of ground beef and shredded cheese within. His little brother had then grinned at me before running off down the hall. My mother picked me up soon after.

"Can't see his posts," I said to Troy. "Just that he goes to New Baines South Intermediate High School." I clicked around. "No cover photo, either. His profile picture is him with two medals for... Brazilian jiu-jitsu? Three years ago, anyway. Is that when people stopped updating these things?"

"Longer than that," Troy said. "Damn, this guy is private. I QuickSearched him, and all that came up was the Hayes Elementary Honor Roll for your class seven years ago." He scrolled. "Pete got A's and B's, as did Belle, Christian... you, too! Frank got all A's. The rest of the names, I don't recognize." He smiled. "Not yet, that is!"

◆———◆·◆———◆

"James 'Jimmy' Hickman," I said as I typed. "Nothing. Oh, here he is as Jim Hickman. Moved to Red Springs, Oklahoma. Bought a pickup... there's him with a bloody buck head and a rifle... bass fishing... a bulldozer... Hickman Construction is his dad's company, and... oh, perfect. Waving the Confederate flag. He has a Photofixer, too."

Troy made a noise of disgust. "Get off his page—I don't need that negativity in my life." He pointed to the picture of fifth-grade me. "There's you again! Type in yourself, hotshot!"

My Coffeefolder page was pathetic: advertisements for my book on sale, excerpts, and links to my website on Uprorrr, which featured reblogged quotes on writing and photos of the beach. My profile picture was of Olivia and myself tangled in Christmas lights; I'd been meaning to change it, and now I had an excuse. My Chipper consisted of musings I thought were funny enough to share, and my Photofixer contained pics of my dumb friends and me. My SextMe was private, and only Olivia knew the username. We hadn't used it in a couple of months.

"Who's after me?" I asked.

"Samuel Kidd and Samantha Lykke," Troy answered, then smiled wide. "Hey! Two Sams, side by side! Did they totally crush on each other? No, no, I bet Sammy over here had a thing for Pete. Am I right?"

"Nah, but it was rumored Frank and Pete were gay for each other. Apparently caught kissing during recess one day. Ms. Albertine was *furious* about all the gossiping. She was chill about them, though."

"Uh-huh. So Sam Kidd and Sam Lykke?"

"Right. Um, they were a couple, sort of. I think Sam—girl Sam—wanted to wait to make it official or whatever until they were older, but they always hung out together, and we kids catch on quick to stuff like that."

"Yeah, yeah, yeah, that's great and all, but are they still together?" he begged me.

They weren't. Samuel had moved to Red Springs, while Samantha went to a high school in Arminster. The former had only one picture on his page—him with his guitar—whereas the latter's was packed with tagged posts by various boyfriends, as her relationship status seemed to change every other month. Sam and Sam had the same brown hair and skin tone; they could have been siblings, really.

Zach and Morgan Millburn, on the other hand, were brother and sister. They were the coolest of the fifth graders at Hayes, and their summer pool parties were always the talk of each May. They'd even gotten me a paid *Everblade Online* account for my ninth birthday, as *Everblade* was a fantasy online role-playing game that was popular back then, and everyone seemed to have one.

Per Coffeefolder, after the Millburns had moved to Texas, Zach cut off most of his golden hair and became an offensive lineman for his high school football team, while Morgan became somewhat of a part-time hipster, part-time volleyball player.

"I know you're not supposed to 'ship real-life people," Troy began, "but I 'ship those two. I 'ship 'em hard. Look at the chemistry in that picture of them at the homecoming dance! Are they stepsiblings, at least?"

"Blood," I answered, laughing. "Don't worry—our whole Hayes class thought they should be together, since we didn't know any better. I think they were just as confused, to be honest."

"Like how?"

"I dunno. Is it weird for siblings to hold hands and talk about each other like they're lovers? I mean, that's what Zach did at Christian's house one time. They both had a crush on Morgan."

"Wait, wait, you—Mom, *Michael Jackson*—were hanging out at sleepovers with Christian the Twink Battenfield and Zach the Popular Ten-Year-Old Millburn? *Were you popular?!*"

Troy put his hands to his cheeks and opened his mouth, feigning surprise. I rolled my eyes.

"It was easier then," I explained. "We were just… children. Popularity didn't matter as much. No one cared who looked better or whose parents made more money. If you were nice, you got to hang out with everybody. It was that simple."

"Even for li'l ol' Emily Pitts?" He pointed to the girl who was after the Millburns, then looked up as I typed in her name. "And her profile is… anime. And short, emo haircuts. A fedora, too? And her posts are all poetry. Can we go back to Belle and Christian now?"

"And miss out on Bobby Royals?" I asked him. He shrugged, then looked back at the yearbook.

"YES! FINALLY, MY RACIAL DIVERSITY! THE TOKEN BLACK GUY IN THE MIDDLE OF OKLAHOMA, A.K.A. WHITE PEOPLE LAND!"

"I wonder what my mother thinks of what she overhears from you," I told him, laughing. "Two things: first, New Baines is in the northeastern part of the state, not the center. Second, Bobby is French Polynesian. Gabe is Mexican, both Sams are Native American, and the Millburns are part Japanese on their mom's side. Besides, I'm half-Chinese, half-Polish!"

"Polish?"

"Like… You know. Poland? That country in the middle of Europe?"

"Oh, how *convenient*," Troy teased. "Well, it's a good thing you said something, or I might've assumed everyone was white." He laughed with me. "So no black people, huh?"

"B-Love is half-black, yes."

"B-Love? What?" Troy looked at Bobby's yearbook picture again. "WHAT?! YOU WENT TO ELEMENTARY SCHOOL WITH B-LOVE ROYALS?! WHY DIDN'T YOU TELL ME EARLIER, YOU SELFISH FUCK! Forget Belle and Christian and Millburn incest—*this is news!* Was this before or after he was discovered by Narcissus?!"

"Bobby left Hayes during winter break in fifth grade to check out Los Angeles with Nar," I said, then shrugged. "Signed a record deal and never came back."

"Well, shit, I know I wouldn't." Troy shook his head in disbelief. "B-Love never went to middle school. Who would've thunk it? OK, OK, everyone, really. Still! I own all his albums! *'If you wanna get love, you gotta B-Love, nigga!'*"

I grimaced, and we continued.

"I can already tell 'Rachel Schoenhals-Zajac' is less interesting than Black Bobby B-Love," Troy observed. "Ugh. She's the same big girl with flat blonde hair who likes to wear sweatshirts, right? Yep, she confirms it. Goes to New Baines South Intermediate and everything."

"She was sweet," I told him. "And there, she's decorating for a pep rally. That's something!"

"You said Belle was sweet, too, but at least she turned out pretty. And the people who decorate for pep rallies are the ones too pathetic to play sports." He yawned. "I'm bored. Give me a harder one."

"Nathanial Oakley," I said, pointing at the screen. "He went by Nate."

"Isn't Oakley out of alphabetical order from Schoen… whoever? Anyway, let's see this punk. Short kid, glasses, too much product in his hair. Thin, dark mustache. His phone doesn't have a case on it—see the mirror selfie?—and his watch is too nice. Why do people pay a lot of money for a watch that can't even get Internet? Oh well. Total drug dealer."

"Because of his watch?!"

"No high school senior can afford a twenty-seven-thousand-dollar Julian Morrissey Nautilus Oyster eighteen-karat solid gold wristwatch unless they've got a sugar daddy *or* they just so happen to sell a shitload of molly after school on Wednesdays. I went out with Clyde, remember? Got frat boy dealers in Rochester with coke, Mexicans behind the Double Chin off Serling with pills and weed... They're easy to spot once you've seen 'em. Your friend Nathan here's a seller. Maybe even a user, too. I'd put my money on him and the Kush."

"He wasn't my friend, though," I said a bit too defensively. "He was kind of a perv, now that I think about it. The girls didn't like him at all."

"How big was your class size?"

"There were nineteen of us."

"And how many are left?"

"Three," I answered, then pointed to the last guy on the list. "Richard Skinner. His middle name's Bryce, which he went by."

"He looks like the leader," Troy noted. "Five-foot-eleven and one-eighty, according to his baseball info for New Baines High. Eighteen years old. Clean-shaven, handsome blond guy. Wears button-down shirts and pleated pants. Oh! There's a pic with Belle on his back, and they're both smiling. Wait... they're dating! They're currently in a relationship! Oh, there's a picture with him and a different girl, too. Two years ago. Then there's Bryce, Christian, Belle, other girl, and Nate hanging out in middle school—is Nathan *their* dealer?"

"Richard Bryce Skinner? Not that kind of guy."

"Wait, S-K-I-N-N-E-R? Richard Skinner? *Dick Skinner?!*" Troy fell over in hysterics. He laughed so hard, he cried. "IF MY NAME WAS 'DICK SKINNER,' I'D GO BY BRYCE, TOO!" He wiped the tears from his eyes. "Oh, God, I can't breathe. I am dead. I am deceased. Lord Jesus, save me."

"Get up, you atheist," I said, helping him back onto the bed as he continued to be annoying. "Anyway, you know how I said that as long as you were friendly, you were basically accepted by everyone in the class?" Troy nodded. "Well, that wasn't exactly the case with Bryce—at least, he was damn passive-aggressive about it for a long time. He had this set of rules, and they weren't even religious ones—and I say that because his dad was a preacher before he died of a heart attack—but they were just… Bryce was picky. Conservative. He was the only one who got legitimately angry at Frank and Pete when the rumors of them kissing started cropping up. Like, we only teased them a little, I think, but Bryce? He was ruthless, kind of like Keegan yesterday. He flipped out when Christian put a lollipop stick in his mouth and pretended it was a cigarette, got mad when Sam and Sam were sitting close to each other while playing video games in their swimsuits, hated people cussing…"

"Sounds like a fun guy to be around," Troy said with a frown.

"Well, he wasn't all that bad. I remember him being funny and smart. You're right in that he sort of was our leader, though that might've been because he was the tallest of us. Weird how that works. But I never disliked him, even when he liked the same girl I did."

"Who?" Troy asked. He seemed genuinely curious, so I tapped the face of the girl beside Bryce—the same one in his profile picture from two years before. Troy smiled. "Catherine Thomas. A brunette with glasses. Cute. She your Billie Jean?" He laughed. I didn't. "Kidding. You should look her up, too."

I already had many times in the past—so much so that whenever I would type "Coffeefolder" into the address bar, Coffeefolder.com/catherine.thomas.918 would autofill. Cath was the reason I missed New Baines and my days spent at Hayes Elementary so much. She was, without a doubt, my best friend during childhood. We would make up stories together, then act them out in my backyard. We would explore the nearby creeks and construction sites like the dumb little kids we were, always searching for the next adventure. We played computer games together, watched TV together, and ate just about every lunch together, whether it be during the school year or summer break.

But I had gotten the stupid notion from Nate, Christian, and Jimmy that guys can never be just friends with a girl. It's impossible, they said. One always has a crush on the other. So I manufactured an infatuation with her, even though it was real and I'd always secretly felt it. But Bryce had liked her as well, which put Catherine in the awkward position of having to choose between two of her best friends.

Then fifth grade ended, my dad was arrested, my mom and I moved away, and Bryce and Catherine started dating in middle school.

"Catherine Anne Thomas... does not update her Coffeefolder or Chipper accounts," Troy noted. "Two years without a single post or picture on either. But boy, she looks like a party animal. Would've fit right in with us, huh?"

He nudged me. I pushed him off.

"Not even close," I stated. "She would never—"

"Hey, hey, hey! Look at that sideboob, loverboy! And that bikini... God, she's a woman. A cute little woman with a psycho for a boyfriend."

"Two years ago."

"When we were all sixteen, save Clyde and Leah. Little Miss Catherine likes to wear oversized tees, aviators, short shorts, high-tops, and crop tops. Switched over to contacts, too. Belle was a pear, but your girl here is an hourglass, Mom!"

"Cut it out!" I demanded. "Not funny at all."

"Mae, chill. You haven't seen these people in, like, seven years. They've changed. And for a lot of them, we don't even know what they've been up to the past forty-eight months. She's cool—she *looks* cool—but she doesn't know you anymore. None of these people do. So stop being so emotional."

The most frustrating phrases are, in order: "Stop being so emotional," "Everything happens for a reason," and "You can't eat that whole thing by yourself." So I ignored Troy, instead browsing through all the pictures on Catherine's Chipper profile since she'd joined three years before: pictures taken with a group of friends drinking slushies in a parking lot, pictures taken in backseats, pictures of Catherine in full-out New Baines High spirit attire. Posts about Bryce being her #ManCrushMonday and Belle being her #WomanCrushWednesday. Christian serving Catherine and another girl lattes at a coffeehouse. Catherine in a sports bra and sweatpants, covered in painted paw prints, smiling wide at the New Baines High homecoming game.

Those were supposed to have been my pictures—*my experiences.* I was meant to grow up in that town with those people. Not in Dreary. Not with Troy.

"You don't understand," I said simply. "And I don't expect you to, either."

"The fuck is that supposed to mean?"

"Do you really think I planned on—?!" I started, then lowered my voice. "Do you really think I saw myself in high school smoking weed with you and Eva and Keegan?"

"No, you thought you'd be having hot sex with Catherine Thomas, asshole." He was angry; I could tell when Troy wasn't masquerading as Troy Rico any longer. So he grabbed my yearbook, squinted at it, and then dropped it back on the desk. "Who's the last bitch?"

"Mekenzie Willis," I answered as I typed. "Looks like she relocated to North Carolina in seventh grade."

He took the mouse and scrolled down. "Of course she's cute. Oklahoma breeds pretty girls. And she lives in Windhaven. Didn't you apply to UNC Windhaven? For their creative writing program?" Before I could respond: "Awww, her dad died six years ago. I bet you that's why they moved. I mean, that's how come you and Ms. K ended up in the Heart of Dixie—because of your father. Man, what is it with our generation and daddy issues?"

"Doesn't your stepdad still believe you're going through a phase?"

"Step-dork? Yeah. Let's see… profile pics by the pier, Ferris wheel, a huge-ass war boat… a bikini shot! But she's thirteen. Kids these days. Or rather, four years ago. So confusing. She talks about nightmares a lot. Oh, look, and she even played softball with Catherine at New Baines."

"Really?!"

"No, I made that one up. Sorry." He yawned again and pulled away from the laptop. "So who or what do we have to blame for this gross nostalgia trip?"

I leaned over and picked up an old photograph taken with an instant camera. It had been propped up on my desk against the wall since Olivia and I had discovered it in January while we had cleaned out some of my drawers of various short stories. It was included in my copy of the Hayes yearbook and featured the twenty of us. The front row: Belle, Morgan, Samantha, Mekenzie, and Catherine. The second row: Rachel, Emily, Gabe, Samuel, Willow, Nate, and myself. The third row: Bryce, Christian, Bobby, Frank, Jimmy, Zach, Pete, and Ms. Albertine, who had her hands on my shoulders. In the background was a review of fractions on the chalkboard, and above that, pictographs of various constellations.

"That's actually kind of neat," Troy said after I'd finished explaining it to him. "What did Droogen say when you found it?"

"She just asked who they were, and I said they're my friends."

"But we're your friends."

"Not after yesterday," I reminded him.

"Ah, well. At least you've still got Troy Rico!"

He put one of his lanky arms around me. I shrugged him off.

Troy left soon after to make lunch at his house for his little sisters. I stayed with my yearbook, flipping through its pages and reading over the various signatures.

"Michael—you are a terrific student, and I have been so lucky to be your teacher," Ms. Albertine wrote. "Have a fun sixth-grade year, and celebrate your creativity! I know you will have a bright and successful future."

"You are funny," Christian had added. "You are cool. We'll hang out!"

"Me and Zach will miss you so very much!" Morgan wrote. "Have fun at your new school and stay on *Everblade!* morgan566126283."

"I signed your crack," Gabe had written where the two pages met in the middle. "It needs some cleaning now!"

"You always make me laugh," Belle wrote. "You are an amazing friend!"

"I will see you this summer," said Catherine, "so I won't miss you too much! I love your crazy, awesome, smart self. Like Matthew in *SBA*. See you at Clarkson!"

"You're a good friend, Cookie," Bryce finished. "Come swimming with me, okay?"

I never did go to the pool with Bryce, nor did I attend Clarkson Middle School with Catherine. Christian and I only saw each other once that summer—at a convenience store with our mothers by accident. I had my father and his alcohol dependency to blame for this. The day after fifth grade ended, he took the SUV to Arminster International, got real drunk, hijacked an airport rental shuttle, and then drove off into traffic. *He literally took a bus.*

My old man ended up killing one and wounding two that day: a preschooler and her parents, respectively. He got charged with vehicular homicide and driving while intoxicated; thus, he was sentenced to five years in Red Springs Penitentiary with good behavior. My dad had begged for the forgiveness of the court and the family of the deceased, but it was no good for my mother, who'd had enough. So she packed up our belongings and moved the two of us into an apartment in Rochester, Alabama. My maternal grandmother lived thirty minutes away, and when she died three years later, we took her house in Dreary. And that was that.

I searched my cluttered desk for the card from my father, found the envelope, opened it, and then reread his brief message, written in all caps: "HAPPY EARLY

BIRTHDAY. SON I AM SO PROUD OF YOU. HOW IS YOUR SENIOR YEAR? SEND ME A COPY OF YOUR BOOK, KAY? I LOVE YOU. DAD."

Troy came back then with mail for me: a bank statement and a Happy Birthday! card from my uncle in Arminster, despite my birthday not being for another two weeks.

"Check it for money!" Troy commanded. "All Uncle Julian sends are—"

"Watches?" I guessed.

Troy grinned. "And not even his nice ones for me to resell!"

Inside the card—Happy Birthday to a Happy Boy!—were cash and an inscription: "Michael! You have accomplished so much already. You teens impress me constantly with both your wits and stupidity (for you, the former, and for my classes, the latter). Congrats, fine sir! Oh, and sorry for the lame-ass card. Enjoy the $25, 'kay? Give Heidi my love. Uncle Herbert."

"Well, that was nice of him," Troy said.

"Yeah," I agreed, flipping the card over and back again.

"Is that one from your dad?" he asked, pointing. I nodded and gestured for him to take it. He did, looked at it, squinted, checked the envelope, and then reached for the one from my uncle. I let him. "Where does Uncle Herb live?"

"Arminster. He has a teaching job there. He's got a lake house in Madison, too. He bought it for cheap after there was some kind of structural collapse or—"

"Is the lake house at 902 Honey Deer Drive?"

"Huh? I don't know. Maybe."

Troy moved over to my laptop and opened QuickSearch Maps. There, he typed in the return address in question and clicked for the street view, and just like that, we were outside my uncle's cabin in the woods.

"Yep, that's it," I told Troy. "Well, I've only seen the pictures my uncle sent to my mom and me, but he's always invited us over—"

"Mae," he said. "That's the address your dad wrote you from."

"Huh?"

"I'm sorry, man."

I was confused. I got up and checked both envelopes.

"What are you talking about?" I asked.

"The handwriting's too similar, even in caps," he explained. "They also both write, 'kay,' followed by a question mark. And look—the capital K in your dad's letter is the same as the one in your uncle's last name on his envelope. Don't get me wrong, I'm just as weirded out as you, but I think it's safe to say *at the very least*... your uncle wrote both messages on those cards you got."

My vision blurred. I got on the floor and reached under my bed for a shoebox two sizes too small for me. Inside were not sandals, but various mementos from my childhood, including several letters my dad had written while locked up. I'd thrown away the cards from Uncle Herbert, but I had his current one to go by. Sure enough, the handwriting was the same except for one written four months into my dad's sentence— before the phone calls had stopped.

"Hey," Troy began, his phone in his hands. "You've never QuickSearched your dad, have you?"

"No," I answered, "and I don't want to hear it, whatever it is."

"Well, I just did, and I think you ought to read this article from—"

I took his phone and skimmed the report.

"A prison riot," Troy told me. "An officer was seriously hurt, but the four 'fatalities' were all inmates. One of them was your dad. I'm so sorry, Mom."

I was enraged, embarrassed, hurt. I gathered up the evidence, ran from the room, and pushed open the door to the den. My mother was typing something on her new laptop. She sat comfortably.

"What's the matter?" she asked, her look of concern obscured by reading glasses. "What's wrong?"

I dropped everything on the table beside her. She stared at it all, her mouth half-open, as if she were going to say something. I *wanted* her to say something, to say anything, to *deny* my suspicions. I wanted something to happen to prove to me it was all a dream—for zombies to attack, for Troy to kiss a girl, for Olivia to say she still loved me.

"Yo, Ms. K," Troy said to her from the doorway. "I'm gonna be going now, but thanks for dinner the other night—"

"No, stay," I told him, then turned to my mom: "He can stay the night, right?"

"But..." she started. "I... Yes, he can, Michael, but..."

"But what? Are you going to explain all of this?!"

"I'm sorry—"

"For moving me around? For my lack of a father figure?" I snatched the letters and held them in front of her. "For having Uncle Herbert read about my sucky life and for him having to pretend he gives a crap about my dates or grades or wherever the hell I'm going to college?!"

She was blubbering. My mother was honest-to-God blubbering. She wasn't going to say anything. I didn't know what I was expecting.

I left her there in her tears and pushed past Troy to lock myself in my room. He showed up again an hour later with food from Taco Kick. So together, we marathoned season two of *Sea Breeze Academy*, and not once did he complain.

That night, in my waking nightmare, the rain fell without pattern. From the water formed a lake, and what floated to the top was a box of lies, all our names etched across the top in a bloody, childlike scrawl.

＊━━━━━＊━＊━━━━━＊

"The fuck are you doing up this early on a Sunday?" Troy asked the next morning from the blowup mattress in the corner. "You set your clock forward an hour or something?

I know you aren't going to church."

"Isn't that where your family's at?" I said from my desk, laptop open.

"Yeah, but you know how I feel about organized religion," he said. "Always trying to make you feel bad just for living and shit."

"I'm not sure it's that simple."

Troy got up and stretched, naked save for his lucky neon green Kleidüng boxer briefs. A snail trail of brunet hair ran from his belly button down, and the hair on his head—no longer covered by a beanie—was a long blond mess. He then put it into a bun, scratched his ass, and strolled over.

"What are you doing?" he asked again.

"Writing my own version of the Bible," I lied.

"What's different about it?"

"Someone else dies on the cross."

"Who?"

"Haven't gotten that far."

But I was planning something, and Troy knew this. So he read over my shoulder the message I had drafted.

MICHAEL G. JACKSON

Hey there. I doubt you remember me, but I went to Hayes Elementary with you. Michael Jackson? Ring any bells? Maybe not, but that's OK. I moved to Alabama after leaving New Baines seven years ago. Now we're all seniors. Crazy, right?

It's raining. It's been raining. I'm not sure exactly why I'm writing this to you or if you'll even get it. I mean, who truly uses Coffeefolder anymore? Even so, I hope you managed to keep in touch with our fifth-grade class better than myself. That's why I'm planning a reunion for all of us, so to speak. It'll be at my uncle's cabin at 902 Honey Deer Drive in Madison, Oklahoma, on Lake Nasagarreset, from six to eleven this Saturday. RSVP if you can make it, and if so, consider bringing snacks or something to drink.

I miss you. I miss us. I hope life treated you well.

Michael

"A reunion," Troy said with a tone of disgust. "Seems a bit quick after having just learned your dad's dead. Is this your way of coping? Did you even ask your uncle if you could use his lake house?" He laughed. "I mean, Mom, seriously. Why do you even think they'd want to see each other again? Wouldn't they have already? Wouldn't they have contacted you if they wanted to find out where li'l ol' Mikey boy disappeared to? Have you lost your mind?"

"That's why I'm doing this!" I exclaimed. "I can't be the only nostalgic high school senior, right? No, don't answer that. Point is, my classmates all have relatively easy names to QuickSearch—'Christian Battenfield,' 'Rachel Schoenhals-Zajac,' 'Emily Pitts,' 'Willow Dusett,' 'Pete Fortescue,' to name a few. Me? I'm stuck with *Michael Jackson*. Go ahead! Try searching anywhere for Michael Jackson, you know who you get? Of course you do. Everybody does! I'm unsearchable; I'm under the radar. In fact, I'm tempted to write a story about a kid named Stephen King who just wants to writes children's books, but everyone thinks he's into vampires, horrors, and the supernatural!"

"Whores and the supernatural?!"

"What? No, *horrors*. Like… Look, if all those kids from Hayes have tried to look me up only to find the King of Pop, think about colleges! What if it's the same for them?! 'Michael' is the fourth most common name in the United States, while 'Jackson' is eighteenth in the number of most frequent last names. If there are 4,264,636 people in the United States with the first name Michael and 797,477 people in the United States with the last name Jackson, that is—*I shit you not*—10,531 people in the US of A named Michael Jackson, meaning—"

"Mom, Mom, enough with the numbers already." He rubbed at his temples. "Just go by your middle name, why don't you?"

"GUY!" I shouted at Troy. "I WAS NAMED AFTER MY FATHER! MY NAME IS *MICHAEL GUY JACKSON!*"

"OK, OK!" he said, laughing. "Sixth through eighth grade in Rochester must've sucked if all you care about are your elementary school pals."

"A fifth grader couldn't have asked for a better group of friends," I told him, then shook my head. "Middle school had nothing on them."

"So what's your plan, then? How're you getting to Oklahoma by Saturday?"

"Plane tickets are way too expensive, but a nine-hour drive with stops isn't too bad, assuming I leave early to get there by night. Since the party would be this Saturday— the first day of spring break—I'd need to leave on Friday to have time to get food and drinks and make sure the lake house is ready."

Troy started pacing the room. Then he picked up his watch, scrolled a bit, and paced again.

"Well, this sounds like a two-person heist," he said, "and you'll need a benefactor, anyway—for gas and beer and party supplies and whatnot. Basically, my queeniness will do half the work for you. And it's not like I have plans, with Clyde and me no longer a thing and my mom staying home next week with my sisters."

"Won't it be awkward—you not knowing anyone?" I asked. "Are you... are you one hundred percent sure you'd want to do this?"

"But of course!" He hugged me from behind. I felt his bulge against my back. "We stick together, remember? Besides, you're broke, and I have my own bank account. I'm rich as balls in this town. Well, crystal balls, maybe. *We're set!* Oh, and I also feel personally invested in this enterprise, given that I spent a good half hour or so with you yesterday scrolling through the virtual lives of your former classmates." He paused and turned me around to face him. "We good?"

"Yeah," I said. "Definitely. Just, um ..." I looked away. "Put some pants on, all right?"

Troy grinned. I smiled. Together, we sent out the invitations individually from my account to each member we could find of my fifth-grade class at Rutherford B. Hayes Elementary School of 8800 South Horne Place, New Baines, Arminster County, Oklahoma, USA.

RACHEL SCHOENHALS-ZAJAC

Omg. Ya i remember u! How could i not? U were hilarious! i'll bring chips for us to eat. i can't believe your doing this, haha! Are you inviting Bryce & Cath?

PETE FORTESCUE

Wow. It's been way too long man. Good to hear from you!!! And all the way out in Bama? Yeah I'll be there at your party.

MORGAN MILLBURN

That's great! We are doing well ourselves. Zach and I arrive in Arminster that day for spring break, so we'll see, but we want to come! :-)

CHRISTIAN BATTENFIELD

Hey! I'm doing good! What about you? Haven't heard from you in a while. I'll be there, bro! Who all else did you invite?

JIM HICKMAN

Hey Mike. I just got your message because I just got home after bass fishing this weekend. Thanks for notifying me about your party on Lake Nasagarresett (awful for fishing). I will be there with drinks. P.S. I did type this. I know its a shock with me saying a big word like: notifying. I'll talk to you later.

WILLOW DUSETT

Michael – Thank you so much for the invite to your party, but I will have to pass on this one unfortunately!! With my son and work, it's pretty hard to do anything like that on weekend nights. (Does Bryce know? What about 5/29?) Anyway... if you ever need a haircut, don't hesitate to stop by! You've always had nice hair lol.

SAM KIDD

Hey Michael how's it been? I'll certainly try to drive on over to hang out with you all for a few hours. Jim mentioned bringing stuff. I can probably give rides. Did you invite Sam? Is she still around?

EMILY PITTS

hey inhaven't talked to u in a long time i'm sorry i will try to be there i kiss everyone even Nate ts really sad sorry not kiss mjiss miss you cookie you ok?

B-LOVE ROYALS (OFFICIAL)

yoooo! wus qood doqq. it cool u tryna chill wit everybody. i real busy wit the latest and bestest sounds u ever hear **god status** i holla at cha if i make it from LA.

SAMANTHA KAYLA LYKKESBOYS

COOKIE! What are you up to!!! so this is your Coffeefolder wow thats cool and strange! Hey do you know Cath's number or email i kinda need it. If you do know it, please tell me so i can email her. Thanks hahahahaha. Oh and i will be at your party so thank you!!!

NATHANIAL OAKLEY

Yo M-dog. Been some time! Almost seven years to be exact. I'll make your party. You invite Cath and Cabello? I will make sure Bryce knows. Also: Blank Frank is dead. (Last one wasn't a blank lmao.) Remember when we used to call you Cookie?

BELLE BOTTOMLEY

Oh my goodness thank you so much!! Sorry I'm a totally awful person for not replying earlier and just now getting back to you. I've been so busy these past few days, but I'm so glad you messaged me! I miss you and all our friends from Hayes! I will definitely come to see you and everyone so we can catch up! Thanks again I appreciate it!!

MEKENZIE WILLIS

Hi there! It's so funny to hear from you our senior year of high school haha. I live in Windhaven, NC, now and that's not close at all to Oklahoma, so I don't think I can come! :-(But tell everyone I said hello!! I miss you and Catherine and Belle and Sam and Christian and Gabe! Bryce, well...

BRYCE SKINNER

Hello from New Baines, Mr. Famous Author. Didn't think I'd hear from you again after fifth grade ended. To answer your question, yes, I've been keeping tabs on our elementary school friends. Most of us have remained in the state, so that should make it easier for your party. Mekenzie is in North Carolina, the Millburns are in Texas, and Bobby is a "rapper" in California. Franklin Chambers is no longer with us, as you might already know. Gabe changed names, though I believe Christian has already extended the invitation on your behalf.

Let me know if there's anything I can do to help. I'm glad you reached out.

The week before spring break was tedious, but Troy and I got through it well enough. In our free time, we talked about provisions we would need to pack, which roads we would plan to take, and various expenses we would need to cover with or without a generous loan from the National Bank of Troy Rico Valdez.

Eva was there with us as well, though she would move from our lunch spot to sit with Keegan and Leah, then to Clyde, to Olivia, and back our way again; she was trying to keep the peace. Troy argued she needed to find new friends, but I could see how it would be tough for Eva to merge into a previously established group during the last semester of high school, especially with us already being the misfits.

By Thursday night, I had two backpacks ready, along with some blankets and pillows in the back of the SUV in case we had to spend the night on the road for whatever reason. One backpack was filled with toiletries such as my toothbrush, toothpaste, facial moisturizer, hair shampoo, and conditioner. The other carried necessities such as my laptop, balloons for the party, extra copies of *Beneath the Makeup*, and *Krijg de Tering*, our assigned reading book written by Dutch poet Ard van der Kolk.

Troy, on the other hand, left his four suitcases with me to take home after school so I could simply drive over to his house at seven the next morning, wake him up, and then drag him out to the Big Nasty without him having to put in too much effort. He and I would switch driving every three hours until we made it to Madison, Oklahoma. We had a plan, and I was ready to stick with it to see my friends again.

My mother was gone when my alarm sounded on Friday. I remembered the previous night while making friendly conversation—as I was still furious with her—that she had gone to get some software package or another from Rochester. So I left a note on my bed explaining the spring break situation; I was desperate, not heartless, and I wasn't about to leave her in the dark.

Mr. Bradford was getting ready to walk his dog as I pulled the Big Nasty out of the garage twenty minutes later. He waved and started limping over. I rolled down my window.

"I have your money for last week's work," he told me, reaching behind him and pulling out his wallet.

"Keep it," I said, glancing at the dashboard. "I have to get on the road, anyway."

"To school?" he asked, confused. "Saw your mom leave earlier. She's getting too thin—"

"Oklahoma," I explained. "It's complicated. My dad's been dead for seven years. I'll say hi to your daughter if I see her."

"Maisy," he said quickly. "Twelve. Lives in Arminster with her mom and stepdad. Red hair like mine." He felt the top of his head and smiled softly. "Was like mine, anyway."

"Will do, Mr. Brad—"

"And tell her momma…" He stopped, then pulled at his sweatshirt momentarily. The dog sniffed around him. "Tell Charlene I'm sorry. And let her know I still have the trampoline."

"Trampoline, got it," I said as Mr. Bradford laughed to himself. I wasn't sure exactly what he kept in his backyard, but we both nodded our mutual understanding before parting ways once more.

I found Troy sitting in his driveway. Despite knowing he would be spending much of the day in a heated SUV, whether driving or sleeping, Troy was impractically dressed to impress with his diamond-patterned shirt, fur coat, skinny jeans, and maroon shoes. I, meanwhile, wore jeans and a purple plaid button-up under my hoodie. I'd thought it was too cold to think about fashion, but clearly, I was mistaken.

"We ready to blow this joint?" he asked as he got into the passenger seat. "Buh-bye, Dreary, and hello, Madison!"

"I think so," I told him, squinting at the rearview mirror. "Wait, is that—?"

"Fucking Eva," Troy said.

She parked behind us, blocking most of our exit. I got out of the Big Nasty and walked over to the driver's side of her red and rusty sedan. She got up then, pulling her backpack over her shoulder as she stepped into the yellowed grass beside me.

"Hey," Eva said, "I want to come with you guys."

"Huh?" I asked. "Why would—?"

"Because I have no other friends!" she blurted out, then stepped back. "Sorry. It's just… well, when you and Olivia broke up—and Troy and Clyde did, too—it split us all up. Livi's got her junior friends, Keegan and Leah have each other, and you two have been talking about this road trip all week!" She sighed with discontent. "I… want to belong somewhere. I want us—"

The Big Nasty lurched onto Troy's front porch, reversed into the grass, and then sped past Eva's car, nearly taking off her side mirror as it came to a harsh stop.

"Get in, get in!" Troy commanded at me through the open window, then to Eva: "You can't come!"

"And why the hell not?!" she yelled at him.

"Because this is a bonding experience between Mom and me. So go and be a traitor with your traitor friends, why don't you!"

"It's not like that, you dick!"

Troy reversed the SUV to where the passenger door was in front of me.

"Eva, this is an adventure duo," he explained to her, "not a trio. Mom and I are going to have a shitload of fun together to convince him to stay in town for college, so really, this is best for everyone involved, yourself included. But wait! Guess what! Your complaining is costing us time we're running out of! We should already be in Tennessee by now! So get back in your little I-don't-even-know-the-brand-of-that-clunker-it's-so-generic, find someone else to bother, and let us go on our way." He looked at me. "Big Nasty. Now."

I turned to Eva. She was staring at her shoes, and she had let her bag slump on the ground next to her.

I opened the door and sat beside Troy. He then drove away from his mansion and Eva, and a minute later, we had made it onto King Street.

"That was messed up," I told him after a while. "What the hell was that?!"

"That, Mom, was how you stop an uninvited guest from ruining your party and running off with all your beer and toilet paper. Besides, I already know you're going to college with me, and it's not like we wanted to hear her feminist rants the whole ride to Oklahoma."

"I'm a feminist," I reminded Troy.

"And so am I!" he said. "But she's too into it. She needs to get fucking laid, like, bad. I keep telling her to try online hookups—it's what everyone's doing nowadays. You can even find friends online, through video games and fandom sites and forums… It's crazy, really. *Technology*. Look at this."

He grabbed onto the wheel with one hand, stood up as much as he could, and then somehow managed to pull his oversized phone/tablet hybrid out of his jeans. As he did so, we passed the "You are now leaving Dreary" sign. *Hallelujah.*

"Engineers are the true magicians," he continued. "This screen you're looking at? The work of an engineer. Try to tell me you're not amazed by this sorcery!" He put it in the cup holder before I could answer. "Everything's different. Everything's changing so much all the time. I, Troy Rico Valdez, am eighteen years old. And do you know who I party with? *Fucking sophomores!* The fifteen-to-sixteen-year-old crowd of jailbait is more active than us seventeen-to-eighteen jerkoffs, all of who besides me are looking for a serious goddamn relationship—they all want to settle down for whatever reason before shitting all over it when college starts and they all move away. That guy with the hair in physics? He proposed to his girlfriend with a keychain! A fucking keychain! *And she said yes!* There are more *freshmen and sophomores* at my parties than upperclassmen. I'm a has-been! I'm too old for this game! Me and the Morrissey Ballroom are all this stupid-ass town has left—and for how long? When did this happen?!"

"I don't know exactly what you want me to say—"

"SOCIAL MEDIA!" he screamed. "Social fuckyoufuckyoufuckyou media." He hit the horn for emphasis. There was no one around to hear us. "They're all too concerned about getting so wasted that someone manages to take a picture of it, crop everyone else out, add a stupid-ass filter, and then post it on Chipper or Photofixer or someplace with the victim's name clearly available for QuickSearch to pick up and for colleges to brood over. *Social media killed partying.* And now a third of the people I know are dating from their phones and apps instead of going to my stupid-ass parties. 'He's twenty-four! He has credit cards! *He's been in the Navy!*' Fucking hell. I mean, can you even be truly friends with someone—let alone 'in a relationship'—if you've never met them face-to-face?"

"I'm sure there's a Young Adult novel on the subject."

"And I'll bet you the main character is white," he finished, looking at the road as if he wanted to rip it off and choke someone with it. "OK. OK. I'm done ranting. I just need to calm down to some music. Unlock my phone—six-five-eight-seven—and go to the playlist I made for you. It's the one called 'Fetish for Fifth Graders.'"

I rolled my eyes and did as he instructed. His mix included bands with names such as "Panama," "XYLØ," "XY&O," and even "Kaleo."

"Are these for real?" I asked him, laughing.

"What kind of question is that?" he countered. "Of course they're actual songs.

Symbolic, too. So give them a listen! Look 'em up, if you don't believe me!"

I shrugged, selected the first song, and then looked out at the forest of leafless trees as Troy bobbed his head to "Always" by Panama. And as the music played, the woods gave way to valleys of green on all sides. We were the only car on a two-lane road with the rising sun behind us, and God, did it feel good to finally be heading home again.

"Don't slow down," I whispered. "Please. Keep going."

He sped up. The view stretched on forever, and what I could see was beautiful.

"Hola, Mami, cómo está?" Troy said as he answered his phone. I was driving, he was chilling. We'd been making headway for a little over three hours, leaving Alabama and Mississippi behind to enter the state of Tennessee. "No... No, I'm with Michael. We're going to Oklahoma to see his friends... No, we're—no, that's not fair, Mami... *Mami!* ... But I didn't even—what? No, I told you... Yeah, yeah. Sí, lo haré... Uh-huh... OK, you, too. Cuídese."

He ended the call and dropped his phone in the cup holder again.

"No music?" I asked as I saw the highway sign for Memphis. I glanced at the QuickSearch Maps app on my own phone, verified where we were, and then put on my turn signal.

"I get why you want to see these people," he told me, "and are, like, wondering if they've tried looking you up. I used to play a lot of *Everblade Online* in middle school—when being gay in Alabama was even less of a cool thing than it is now—and I didn't have a lot of friends, so I spent my weeknights and weekends on the computer fighting monsters and forging alliances with other so-called losers like me. Anyway, I was part of this settlement in a village called Harmony, despite it being everything except harmonious thanks to butt-ass Ghoul being put in charge and having a wall built around the town to keep the slashers out—the irony being I was killed by a slasher—and that's when—"

"Whoa, hold on," I said. "Don't mean to interrupt—"

"Hasn't stopped you before."

"—but we're close to empty, so I'm gonna pull into this gas station up ahead."

"Make sure to use my card," he offered, waving the piece of silver plastic. I took it. "Least I can do for *boring you* with my MMORPG history."

"No, no, I want to hear it. I actually had an account—" His face lit up. "—but I only played for a weekend in fifth grade." His smile faded. "Morgan Millburn used to play, though. She was the one who bought me the membership."

"Huh? Girls don't play video games," Troy joked, then in Eva's voice: "Don't be sexist, Troy! Women make up half of the gaming market! We're underrepresented as protagonists! We're harassed in multiplayer! *No warrior would ever wear an armor-plated bikini to battle!*" He laughed. I shrugged. "Do I look like a game developer to her? And you know I'm kidding. It's just all I see on her Uprorrr, is all. What was Morgan's username?"

"Um… her name with a bunch of numbers after it."

"Then I don't think I knew her." He sighed. "Oh well. No me importa. Let's go fill up the Big Nasty with some hot, hot—"

"Are we *still* making Big Nasty jokes like that?"

He smiled. I did, too.

We left the Come N' Pull Out close to eleven with a full tank of gas and a couple of Southern chicken wraps for the road. The scenery got greener by the hour as we drove away from Dreary, and I wondered if there'd be any yellow left by the time we got to Madison.

"I can't believe you won't let us stop in Memphis," Troy continued to lament.

"Memphis is gay, baby. I'm gay. It's a match made in heaven!" He rubbed his cheeks. "Think I'm gonna grow out my beard on this trip. See what it looks like now."

"So *Everblade*," I reminded him. "I never got into it. What do you even do besides kill those slasher-things?"

"The slashers are only one type of enemy," he explained. "More of a nuisance than anything. But anyway, the game is about survival and commerce between players. You explore and meet other people and make your house next to them so you can protect each other. Or you rob them. That's always fun. But if you die—"

"You have to make a new account, right?"

"Pretty much. It takes a lot to kill your character, but still, it happens, and it sucks when it does. But like I said earlier, I was part of this community called Harmony, which was made up of about twenty or so people, which was cool, since that meant there were twenty-odd players in a world of killers who weren't, well, killing each other. And we were, like, thirteen, too, and you know how teenage angst fucks things up. Like Ghoul! Long story short, he was voted to be the mayor of our town, he had two homes destroyed to make way for his mansion, he put a huge-ass wall around the town to keep raiders and slashers away, and then finally, when we needed more room for people who were outside the wall and seeking sanctuary, he said, 'Screw them!' Nobody was allowed in or out without clearing it by him. It's like we were back in 1984. *Ridiculous.*"

"Not to keep interrupting—"

"Unlikely, knowing you."

"—but you missed the Arkansas sign to share with your Chipper followers. 'The Natural State! Buckle Up for Safety!'"

"Goddammit." He considered this. "Actually, it's fine. I hire people to do analytics and stuff like that—*graphs*, if you will. I know what the people want, and I deliver. Arkansas? Not a trending topic in the world of Troy Rico."

"Is that why you leaked your own nudes last month?"

"That never happened!"

"So what did you do? About Mayor Ghoul?"

"See, there were talks of a revolt in the works, and there was also this guy named Maestro who was tired of Mayor Ghoul bossing us all around. And at this point, Ghoul had basically told us that if we had a problem with his style of governing, we could leave, but then we wouldn't have the wall's protection. So Maestro, a skilled carpenter, built his house outside the wall and put a larger house—Maestro's Home for the Weary—right next to it for others to stay in while they transitioned out of Harmony. Mayor Ghoul, of course, didn't like that at all, so he had his loyal subjects attack the Home for the Weary in the middle of the night. I was hurt from the fight, but I ended up dying to a slasher attack. I could've made another account, but I was too angry. So I didn't, though I wish I had."

"For Maestro?"

"No, not Maestro," Troy said, as if I'd missed an important detail in his story. "For Swear, or Swearyouloveme. She was, like, my best friend for two years."

"Oh, a girl?" I teased.

"Yeah, yeah, métete el dedo," he said. "But I forgot to keep in touch. All I know is she has an older sister named Maddie. QuickSearching her username brings up nothing 'cept for some rearranged Lita Candyce song lyrics—*that's* how you become anonymous. A fake name you only use once, or a name so common, you're unsearchable." He stopped to think. "She mentioned she was in the CST time zone... I dunno. But anyway, I can relate to you wanting to get everyone together. Fighting with those guys was the shit—Griffinity, Lotzataters, Bunnicaro, Hockeygirl01, Racingwheeler, Mountaines, Swear... and me, Troixe. Swear was my favorite, though. Troixe was a bit of an asshole."

"Well, maybe Morgan knows one of them," I offered.

"Nah, it's all right. It's not like they tried contacting me."

Troy rolled down his window and looked out at the expanse of fields and scattered trees with clouds above them. It was scheduled to rain all week in Dreary—maybe even snow—but the weather was supposed to be clear and sunny in Madison, just as I'd envisioned it. We were getting closer by the mile, and soon, I'd be home.

◆━━◆◆◆━━◆

"Shit," Troy said as he woke up from his nap. "I lost the game."

"You lost the what?" I asked.

"The game," he said, as if repeating it made it any clearer. "The object of the game is not to think about the game. If you do, you lose."

"Oh." I thought about this. "Well, crap. I lost, too."

A delivery truck passed ahead of us then, proudly displaying the Big-Box logo on its sides and back, along with the Big-Box slogan: "American proud."

"I gave my first blowjob at the Big-Box we have in Dreary," Troy said as he struggled to recline the passenger seat. He then put his bare feet up on the dash, revealing the UFO stick-and-poke tattoo on his ankle. "Oh, and this was during one of your shifts, by the way, between two vending machines. I miss that, sort of. You'll have to introduce me to Pete and Christian!"

"No way," I told him. His toes left prints on the windshield. "At least, not like that. This party isn't about hooking up with people; it's fifteen or so former classmates getting together to reminisce over the good ol' days, when—"

Troy yawned. "That's not gonna happen. Belle and Bryce are dating now, and she went out with Christian before. Both Sams liked each other, the Millburns might still, I'll bet you Emily is horny as fuck… and weren't you finally going to ask out Catherine? And didn't she date Bryce in middle school?"

"And part of high school. But that doesn't matter because *that's not gonna happen.* She didn't even reply to my message, anyway."

"Maybe someone texted her the info," Troy suggested. "Like Christian with Incognito Gabe."

"Maybe," I allowed. "How are you remembering all this, anyway? I mean, I know it's a lot, but to be fair, it wouldn't be an elementary school reunion with only, like, five people there."

"I get that," he said, pulling out his phone. "Critics won't, though, in the movie they make of this. They'll be all, 'There's too many characters to keep track of! Combine them!' Whatever. That's why I made a list in my notes app. This way, I can refer to it for reference. I even crossed out the people who can't come and bookmarked the page so I don't lose it. I'm *that good* of a friend. Here, take a look."

"I'm driving."

Michael's Fifth-Grade Class at Hayes Elementary School:

Teacher: Ms. Harper Albertine (dead)

Christian Battenfield (plays baseball) [New Baines, OK]

Belle Bottomley (is dating Bryce) [New Baines, OK]

Gabe Cabello (MIA) [New Baines, OK]

~~Franklin "Blank Frank" Chambers (gay with Pete, dead) [New Baines, OK]~~

~~Willow Dusett (hairstylist, mother) [Madison, OK]~~

Pete Fortescue (gay with Frank, jiu-jitsu) [New Baines, SI, OK]

Jim Hickman (total redneck) [Red Springs, OK]

Michael Jackson (not the pop singer) [Dreary, AL]

Sammy Kidd (boy Sam, likes girl Sam) [Red Springs, OK]

Samantha Kayla Lykke (girl Sam, liked boy Sam) [Arminster, OK]

Morgan Millburn (possible incest) [TX]

Zach Millburn (probable incest) [TX]

Emily Pitts (uninteresting) [Arminster, OK]

Bobby "B-Love" Royals (the famous rapper!) [Los Angeles, CA]

Rachel Schoenhals-Zajac (uninteresting) [New Baines, SI, OK]

Nate Oakley (most likely a drug dealer) [New Baines, OK]

Richard "Bryce" Skinner (dude creeps me out) [New Baines, OK]

Catherine Thomas (Michael's elusive love interest) [Arminster, OK]

~~Mekenzie Willis (girl has nightmares) (Windhaven, NC)~~

"Wow," I said. "Insensitive, but impressive—"

"YOU ARE FOUR HOURS AND FORTY-SEVEN MINUTES AWAY FROM YOUR DESTINATION," QuickSearch Maps announced. "IN SEVENTY-TWO POINT SEVEN MILES, MERGE ONTO—"

Troy quickly turned down my phone's volume. "Oww. Why? Gaah. I'll just read you the directions. Fuck." He picked up his own phone and spoke into it: "Cyiarra, put my playlist 'Fetish for Fifth Graders' on shuffle." He paused, and I sat up straight. "Please."

"Wha… what did you name your phone?" I asked him.

"Cyiarra," Troy answered. "Madison's Jamaican stepmom in *Beneath the Makeup*. You know, that book you wrote and won't shut up about? Or are you still as high as when you wrote it?"

I eased up a bit. "Nevermind. I… don't know what I was—"

"Though if I give my personal assistant a predominantly female name," he went on, "is that being sexist and reinforcing gender stereotypes? But if I named it, like, Troy, wouldn't that be sexist against men, or just egotistical? Names don't have genders, do they? Like, that's just a social construct? I should probably stop specifying the gender binary, too. Right? Fuck, I confuse myself. Things were so much easier a decade ago."

We stopped at a Come N' Pull Out for another refill of gas at 1:20. Troy and I switched seats, and then he was driving again. I took the opportunity to enjoy the momentary peace around us: tall pines, far-off towns, power lines, concrete dividers, a water tower in the distance, a river to the left, and so many roadblocks attempting to slow us down.

The temperature was a pleasant fifty-two degrees Fahrenheit. The box trucks ahead of us carried supplies to various Taco Kicks out west. A woman behind us was taking her teenage son and daughter to a place with no name. It rained for thirty minutes, and then the sun was out once more. The local radio stations talked about spring break sales in the area, the murder of an Arkansas legislator's granddaughter, a drug bust gone wrong, a girl's body found in the woods, Mexican tapeworm dieting, and former reality TV star Jake Palaver's new talk show featuring washed-up celebrities and their crazy sex stories.

I closed my eyes, but only to tease the notion of sleep. I didn't open them again for another three hours. Even when a blue prison bus caught up to us—nineteen men and women in chains staring down at me—my mind was elsewhere, my head against the window, dreaming.

Troy pulled into a rest stop at 4:31, waking me up as he turned into the parking lot, which was fine, as it was my turn to drive, anyway. *The final stretch. Not far, as the woodpecker flies.*

"Just gotta take a piss," he informed me, turning off the car and dropping the keys in my lap. "You coming?"

"No, I'm fine," I assured him. "Haven't had much water. Didn't want us to have to stop more times than—"

"OK," he said, slamming the door as he left. I decided to get out to stretch.

The rest area was shaped like a triangle with a roof that jutted out to provide shelter from rain and wind. On the sides were doors for men, and the two in the middle were designated for women. Between each door were water fountains and signs that stated video surveillance was a service provided by the Parks Department; yes, George, Big Brother was still out there. A machine taking quarters provided road maps of the state, which seemed obsolete, given QuickSearch Maps. Free pamphlets talked about how travelers could keep Arkansas beautiful by reporting any littering to the number provided. A bulletin board behind glass hosted posters of children, faces blurred, all missing seven years ago.

There was only one other vehicle in the parking lot, though it appeared the Chinese family getting into the station wagon was just about ready to leave. I walked over to the vending machines—secured by a metal gate—and bought some chips through the slits. Then, realizing I did have to pee, I unlocked the Big Nasty, tossed the bag inside, locked it again, and went into the men's restroom on the right.

Troy must've gone in the other one, as he wasn't inside the restroom I'd chosen. All the mirrors had been shattered, and the toilets were caked with red. I did my business quickly, the result as yellow as the stained urinals and graffiti-covered walls. I read the inscriptions after washing my hands: "Sure is hot but it's gunna be OK #roadtrap2k15; N+K, HAPPY 23 YEARS; LUSSO COSTO WILL NOT SAVE YOUR SOUL; Thine hands have made me, yet thou dost destroy me; Kyrie Eleison lost virginity here 5/2/18; Jennas really pritty; KISS ME LORI I LOVE YOU." I knew neither Lori nor the last writer, though I hoped they both got what they wanted.

A tall man with unkempt long black hair, beard, and mustache was talking with Troy when I walked outside. The stranger wore a denim button-up, dark jeans, and cowboy boots, and what little of his arms I could see were covered with indecipherable tattoos. He looked like he belonged to a biker gang, the way he was dressed and leaning against the building, which made me curious as to where the rest of his friends were waiting.

"Mom," Troy started when he noticed me, "this guy's been mugged! He's going to Madison, too."

"Some punk-ass kid jumped me in the bathroom," the man explained, wincing as he touched his left leg. Blood had soaked through his pants beneath the kneecap. "Stole my wallet and the keys to my Privateer and left me here 'bout fifteen minutes ago." He took a quick breath. "I know I need to go the hospital—that's clear to me—but my sister's in labor. She lives in Madison, Oklahoma, you see. I'll go right after, I swear."

I studied the man. He didn't look too dirty, aside from his clothes and hair—which might've been covered in lice—but other than that, he looked almost gentlemanly in a supernatural sort of way.

"You're not an axe murderer?" I asked him.

"I'm not an axe murderer," he told me, grinning as he winced.

"Mom, this isn't the time for jokes!" Troy exclaimed, despite him always being the jester between us. "Can he come or not?!"

"Uh, I don't know… Fine!" I told them both. Troy was already helping the man limp toward the Big Nasty. "Just… keep your leg up, and try not to get blood anywhere, all right?"

In the grass near the Big Nasty were two duffel bags. The man pointed to them as I unlocked the SUV.

"At least the kid had the decency to leave my things," he said. Troy picked up the bags and put them behind the driver's seat. The man sat behind Troy. "Name's Charlie, by the way. I appreciate you doing this for me."

"Not a problem," I told him as I started up the Big Nasty and began pulling out of the parking lot. I didn't like the idea of having Charlie ride along with us, but the man needed our help, and it was a relatively easy request to fulfill.

As we left the rest area, Troy pointed to a sign with a red "No" symbol around man's purported best friend.

"No dogs equals no happiness," he declared.

"I don't like dogs," Charlie said. "I blame my neighbors from when I was little. They had mean dogs. Mean, vicious mutts that would bark as soon as you went outside and would bite if you got too close. My mom taught 'em right, though, before she died. Wrapped some zolpidem in ham and fed it to those tail-waggers. Never bothered me again."

"That sounds… illegal," I noted.

"It's Occam's razor," Charlie went on. "Not *my* razor—haven't used that in a while. Basically, if you have two or more options to choose from, the simpler one is probably the best. No need to complicate things. No need to get passive-aggressive and not return my calls. Women are the worst at that. I wouldn't hurt an animal, 'cause they're only out to try and survive… but I might just want to choke a woman for teasing me. If they wanna *feel* something, I'll sure as hell give it to 'em."

"Dude, that's awful!"

"No, no, think about it," Troy said, shocking me. "Don't get me wrong, I'd never do it, but haven't you ever gotten so mad at Olivia that you just wanted to slap the shit out of her? Or Eva for being so goddamn indecisive? Not just the girls, either, but Clyde, too? Even me! But you're bound by social conventions. You've *never* wanted to knock some sense into any of us?"

"Um, no?! You sound like Keegan and his excuses for Leah's bruises!"

"My mom left bruises on my dad," Charlie told us, "so he took his rifle and shot her. Then he pointed it up and shot himself. She had worked at a cash register, see, the only reason she got the job being her manager liked the way she looked in a skirt. And he married her. And he shot her. What a cycle. Too complicated. Messy. Should've saved the near-forty years and killed her in the beginning."

"Jesus Christ," Troy said.

"Not really," Charlie deadpanned. I imagined him slicing my throat as I drove. "But anyway, it's been a long day for me, and I'm real tired. You guys got any songs up there?

Maybe… country?"

Troy groaned, and to reach a stalemate, I went through my phone and selected "Daylight" by Mandolin Orange. The rich, story-driven lyrics by the Americana/folk duo reminded me a bit of Olivia, but mostly Catherine. I wondered why she hadn't replied to my message, and why a couple of others had asked about her as well. I wondered what she looked like and what she was up to. I wondered if she'd even recognize me, assuming she was coming to the reunion after all.

Even so, we continued. We passed semitrailer trucks and off-road accidents. We drove through patches of clouds and one instance of sudden rain. We followed the same white van for thirty-five miles on I-49 to Missouri. From there, we went west. Charlie didn't talk again, and neither did Troy. So I played the rest of the *Such Jubilee* album on shuffle, and time passed as we set our sights on the slowly setting sun.

Troy and I dropped Charlie off at his insistence beside Madison's welcoming sign, "Your Home Away from Home!" He grabbed his duffel bag, thanked us for our generosity, and then started his walk away from the SUV and down the forested road.

"Huh," Troy said, looking back as I continued driving. "His leg seems fine to me."

"That guy was nuts," I added. "I can't believe you offered to let him come along with us!"

"You could've said no."

"Not with you going on about his injury and mugged-ness."

"I've only helped one other hitchhiker before," Troy told me, "and that was a girl on the Gulf Coast—maybe fifteen years old. I mean, it was clear she was running away from home, but I didn't want some weirdo being creepy with her. So I drove her to the Rochester homeless shelter, and now we follow each other on Photofixer. She ended up in California. Go figure."

I thought then of *Sea Breeze Academy* and Hartsett University. I thought about how my colleges had yet to find me, but how I had found my fifth-grade friends. And how, in twenty-four hours, I'd be seeing them again for the first time in seven long years.

·— ··———— ◆·◆·◆ ————·· —◆

This was small-town Oklahoma.

American flags and gravel roads. Pickup trucks and compact cars. Country stores, bars, and a laundromat. Cops taking down homemade signs promoting a guy named "Harry Ballitch" for District Attorney. Arrows pointing to the town's only tourist attraction: a lake without fish but plenty of speedboats. That's where all the wealthy city folk lived. The people who put up the notices? They were the locals; they were the dedicated few whose lives were at the mercy of both the weather and vacationers. It was little more than a sad sight from a different time.

Past the Mr. Swanky's market and gas station was the turnoff for Lake Nasagarresett. Once Troy and I found it, we were driving with a perfect view of the lake and its many occupants—all of them ready to start off their spring break with barbeque meat and drunken fireworks. The sky was pink on the horizon and purple up top, with the water an indigo blue and calming from the last of the sailors. Little orange lights from cabins were additional signs of life, and from the ones we could see, there must've been hundreds of people along the shoreline and into the woods.

"This is a white person's wet dream," Troy observed as he gawked at the view. "Massive income inequality. Put *that* on Uprorrr, why don't you? 'Get excited about the things you care about!' says Uprorrr. Good God. Get a *life*, why don't you? I mean, why make these houses so big if you're only gonna stay in them three weeks a year?"

"I'm guessing a lot of these are family-owned," I said, then looked over at Troy, who was admiring the view, despite his complaints. "Either that, or by people who can afford the extra mortgage. So where do I need to go?"

"Honey Deer Drive is on the other side," he told me, following the blue blip on his watch, "so take the left road for about ten or fifteen more minutes."

We continued to snake around the many cabins and the sports cars, convertibles, and luxury SUVs parked in front, as opposed to the good ol' Big Nasty and its V4LD3Z vanity plate. Men with beer bellies and wrinkled women with visors sat on their porches and sneered at us as we drove by. Troy just flipped them off. It'd been a long day, and we were too tired to deal with retirees fifty years older than us.

At last, we reached Honey Deer Drive, and soon after, house 902. It was a one-story structure less ambitious in design than the surrounding cabins, as it featured only raw wood shakes and a wraparound porch on the front and sides as its architectural decoration. The patchy driveway led to the property at an angle, and from where Troy and I were idling, we could see the back of the house was built on stilts hanging off the edge of a small cliff. It appeared that a wooden walkway led down to the shore, where I presumed was the dock we had seen from QuickSearch Maps during our research. A black coupe and a green motorcycle were parked in the nearby grass.

"Is Herbert home?" Troy asked me. I shrugged, but then I felt a sudden anger rising in my chest at the mention of my uncle. He was the reason we were there, after all— because he'd been impersonating my father for the past six or seven years.

"Let's get this over with."

"Wait, did you ever end up asking him if he was cool with this?"

"Nope. I told my mom, though, in the note I left her." I checked my phone. "Still hasn't called, of course. Why would she?"

I killed the ignition and got out of the SUV. Troy did the same, and together, we walked up the steps to the front door. A hand-carved sign above it read: HOME OF THE CUCKOOS.

I knocked on the door, waited a few seconds, and then opened it.

An older blonde-haired woman in a dark green bathrobe pushed past Troy and me and ran straight for the coupe. She was clutching the robe shut with her right hand, and in her left, she struggled to pull her keys out of a plastic Big-Box bag and unlock the car door.

"TULIP!" a voice called out from within the house. I recognized it as the voice of my uncle, and this was confirmed when I saw him: a heavy-built man with a large midsection and tufts of graying brown hair on the sides of his head. He had a full beard and mustache, however, which seemed trimmed for the first time since I'd known him. He was wearing only his red boxers—his baby dick sticking out like a sore thumb— and he waved a pair of pink fuzzy handcuffs in the air as he chased after the woman to her car. "COME BACK! I WASN'T EXPECTING ANYONE!"

But it was no use to her, as she then put her car in gear and sped off, away from the Home of the Cuckoos.

Uncle Herbert turned to me, furious, a hand down his boxers as he readjusted himself, contents having shifted during flight.

"What the hell are you doing here?!" he demanded, and then to Troy: "And who's this?!"

"What the hell are *you* doing pretending to be my dad?!" I countered.

His anger dropped, and an honest look of regret replaced it. "Oh, Mikey... I—"

"This is a nice bike you got, Uncle Herbert," Troy observed while circling it. "Trying to be one of the cool teachers, right?"

"Puh-lease," my uncle said. "And call me Kukowski—all my students do. 'Uncle Herbert' makes me feel my age." He turned to me. "You, too, kiddo."

He held on to his back as he eased his way down to the front steps leading to the door. Kukowski seemed to admire the swirling stars in the cobalt sky for a moment before sighing and scratching at his chest.

"Seems my hair flew south for the winter and decided to retire there," he said in my direction. I had noticed in the commotion he had a new tattoo across the top of his right arm, though I didn't ask about it. "So when'd you find out? Did Heidi finally tell you?"

"The handwriting on my birthday cards." I tried to make eye contact with him, but he wouldn't look my way. "I noticed they were the same."

"Well, *actually,* I was the one who noticed," Troy amended, then stuck out his hand. "Troyton Ricardo Campos Valdez-Souse. And call me Troy Rico—all the gays do."

Kukowski glanced down at the fuzzy cuffs, then clasped one around Troy's outstretched hand and the other onto the railing.

"What the fuck, Uncle K?!" Troy exclaimed, tugging at it.

"Don't call me that," Kukowski said as he pulled down at his tired eyes. "Come on, Mikey. Let's get inside. The mosquitos are still hibernating, but it's getting chilly, and I'm half-naked. If I were thirty years younger, that'd be OK around these parts, but—"

"HELLO?!" Troy shouted. "Mom, get me out of here!"

I laughed as Troy continued to struggle while we went inside, closing the wooden door behind us.

The lake house opened to a small hallway, a door on each side. Past that was the living room, which was the main area of the cabin. Dirty rugs lined the floor and overlapped in an odd pattern, and the only furniture was a couple of couches and a single leather armchair around a coffee table. The walls—darkened by woodsmoke—contained three of the same painting in different sizes, all crooked, as well as raccoon skins, a decorative elk head, and a mallard statue on a shelf. In the corner was a massive taxidermy bear, while fish on plaques were placed against empty shelves and beside unopened boxes. It looked pretty ridiculous.

Some of the interior design was nice, however, such as the stone fireplace, a grandfather clock with no hands, and a bookcase full of dusty paperbacks and board games. Surprisingly, the kitchen seemed to be from this decade, with a new toaster, microwave, blender, refrigerator, and oven. It didn't look like Kukowski spent a lot of time here; it was as if he were still trying to figure out what to do with the place.

"Sorry 'bout the mess," he said as he reached into the fridge. "Want some passion fruit juice? Gave up drinking a few years back."

"Sure, thanks," I said. He took out the carton, poured the juice into an old glass, and got another for himself, and then we clinked them together. "To what are we toasting?"

"The end of an era." Kukowski sat in a chair at the kitchen table and took a big gulp. "I quit my job, you're graduating high school…" He squinted his eyes at me and cocked his head. "Why are you here, anyway? And where's your mom at?"

There was the sound of breaking wood outside, and then the door burst open— nearly falling off its rusted hinges as Troy stumbled inside.

"Michael and Michael's uncle!" he started, catching his breath. "There's *someone* or *something* outside!"

Kukowski laughed. "We're in the middle of a forest, kid. Could be a fox or even a stray dog…" He shook his head. "God, I hate dogs."

"Someone was *watching* me!" Troy went on, holding the broken piece of railing in his hands, the handcuffs keeping them together. "Some guy was out there!"

"Well, where's he now?" I asked.

"I don't know! I think I heard a truck engine and some whispering—"

"Welcome to Lake Nasagarresett," Kukowski said, raising his glass to Troy and smiling. "Waterskiing behind a bass boat, overweight girls in Confederate flag *buh*-kinis who think they should be wearing that, and rednecks with three teeth and a cigar in their mouth. But that's lake life for you boys." He kicked back and put his feet on the table. "Welcome to paradise!"

Troy looked to me. I shrugged. Kukowski left the room, went somewhere else, and soon returned with a key. He then slid it across the table to Troy, who eagerly freed himself from the clutches of the fuzzy handcuffs.

"We're here for my fifth-grade reunion party," I finally answered. "Mom wasn't invited to tag along, given the whole my-dad's-been-dead-for-years situation."

"I see," Kukowski said. "So you're here for a get-together in New Baines?"

"No, here," Troy told him, grinning.

"What's Valdez-Souse yammering on about?" Kukowski asked me.

"Your sweet and innocent nephew invited eighteen or so high school seniors to a party at your lake house here in Madison," Troy summed up. "Why? Because he's disgusting, that's why. He's too sentimental! I mean, Christ, he's probably wearing a *Sea Breeze Academy* t-shirt underneath that button-up. He's a hipster! He can't let go!"

"Enough," Kukowski commanded. He turned to me. "Look, I'm sorry for... for pretending to be your dad. That wasn't cool of me, and Heidi didn't like it, either. But we knew moving and changing schools and friends was going to be hard on you, and she didn't want to add to your stress. After what he'd do to Heidi..." Kukowski shook his head, fists clenched. "Don't be hard on her, all right? It's my fault this got out of hand and lasted as long as it did. So if you and this Troy fella need to stay here for a night or a couple of days or a week, that's fine. Just..." He glanced down, then back up to me. "I'm sorry. 'Kay? This wasn't my intention."

I hugged him. I hugged my near-naked uncle in the middle of his cabin in the woods. I missed my dad, but I wasn't going to hold that against the only family I had left.

Timed perfectly, my phone then began to vibrate in my pocket, and I checked it to see an incoming call from my mother. I excused myself, tears in my eyes, and Kukowski pointed me to the bathroom, which was directly across from the kitchen. I went inside, locked the door, and then slid a finger across the screen.

"Mom?" I answered.

"You were right," she told me. I could tell she'd been crying, too. "You do have a sucky life."

"Wait, what?"

"Look at Mrs. Souse!" she exclaimed, referring to Troy's mom. "She has the perfect American Dream story: a little girl who comes into this country not knowing a word of English, and by the time she's in her twenties, she's a telephone operator. And her brother—a quarterback who realized he had a thing for nice watches—changes his name from 'Julio Valdez' to 'Julian Morrissey' to get a job when no one's hiring Hispanics, and voilà, he's a multimillionaire. And now Troy's mom and her husband are living off his money! And what do we have? Your grandmother's house and all her furniture." I could picture my mom's hand on her face as she slowly sank into her armchair in the den. "I... I expected there to be more for you—*for us*. Your father and I never saw eye to eye when it came to money. He was never satisfied. I didn't *plan* on him going off and getting drunk and plowing into that family and their four-door. I didn't *plan* on divorcing him, either. Not exactly. I didn't *want* to move! It just happened. It all *just happened*. So I'm sorry you got caught in the middle of it. I'm sorry it wasn't everything I had hoped for you. And I'm sorry it took me this long to apologize."

By this point, I was crying with her. But it was necessary, and I was thankful to hear her say all those things—and I told her this. Then she apologized some more, and I did as well, and then she said something funny, and I laughed, and she did, too. We talked about my spring break plans and the reunion, and ultimately, she was OK with Troy and me staying the week in Madison with Kukowski.

"Be safe, all right?" she said as our conversation was ending. "Those kids might not all be as nice as they were seven years ago. People change, for better or worse."

"I'll be fine," I assured her. "I love you."

"I love you, too," she told me. "Good night, my little ootsie-wootsie!"

I laughed again. "Bye, Mom."

I hung up and caught my reflection in the mirror. I felt older. Confident. Ready to take on the world and see my friends again.

I opened the door and bumped into Troy.

"Oh, sorry," I told him.

"No problem, ootsie-wootsie," he said with a smirk. "Kukowski and I already brought the bags inside. That guy's actually pretty cool."

"Well, I'm glad," I said, smiling. "Where are we staying?"

"When you walk in from the front, the door on the left is your uncle's room, but the room on the right has a leftover bunk bed from the previous owners, so he said we can stay in there."

"And speaking of the former proprietors of this fine piece of land," Kukowski added, leading us to the door to the back deck and opening it, "this is why we never go out the rear entrance, 'kay?"

There was about a child's step of room on the deck before it stopped, jagged and splintered, the rest having snapped off and fallen below onto the shore. Troy took out his phone and turned on the flashlight feature, allowing us to see broken planks and rotted bits of railing sticking out of the black water beneath us.

"That's how you got this place so cheap, huh?" I asked.

"A lake house party gone wrong," Kukowski answered with a shake of his head. "The last family thought it'd be a good idea to get everyone and their cousin out on the back deck for a selfie. The phone was on a timer, and it was recovered in the wreckage. Three people died, including twins who couldn't swim yet. The guy who sold it to me wanted nothing more to do with this cabin. I paid in cash, too." Kukowski corralled us back inside and locked the door. "This lake has a weird history of unexplained deaths and disappearances. So be careful tomorrow during your party. 'Kay? Last thing I need is a frickin' lawsuit."

"Of course," I said.

"I won't even make you pay rent, unlike my son at our house in Arminster. He pays half now, but I'm goin' to increase it even more than that 'cause of what a frickin' slob that kid is." Kukowski rubbed at his temples. "Oh my God. Troy: when you go out and start dating and make that fateful, humongous mistake by going, 'Yes, yes, let's get married!' Please. Take note of how big of a mess your guy is, 'kay? Just spot-check every now and again. I walk in, there's crap all over my son's room. I look in his car, it's a disaster area! He's twenty-seven!"

I laughed and thanked Kukowski again for letting us stay there. He said it was no problem, and then Troy led me away to our room. It featured the bunk bed against the wall, along with a desk by the window, a wastebasket with a used condom on the rim, a side table with empty pill bottles in the drawer, a braided rug over the wood floor, and our bags in the corner.

I took my laptop out of my backpack and put it on the desk. I then took out my phone charger and plugged it into the wall outlet, as did Troy with his. I grabbed my toiletries and went back to the bathroom, which was like the kitchen in that it had a much more modern appearance than the living room, at least regarding its amenities.

Kukowski was on the phone in his room when I was done washing up, so I didn't disturb him. Troy had fallen asleep while masturbating in his button-up and skinny jeans on the top bunk, but his shoes were beside the desk. I didn't blame him; it'd been a long day for us, and I was plenty beat. So I powered down my phone, turned off the lights, and then shut the blinds so the moonlight wouldn't keep us up. But the moon was only half-full, and it wasn't bright, either. In fact, it barely gave off any light at all; it just sort of sat there in the sky, bobbing along in empty space.

Some creature was clawing in the walls, trying to escape. My mind wouldn't sleep, so I thought of Catherine again in that bottom bunk. I thought of Bryce, too. And at the same time, I wondered what it was in those missing years that had brought them together—and ultimately, what had driven them apart.

An owl hooted in the forest. In the distance, sirens.

I woke up the next morning with a headache, which I attributed to dehydration. Troy lay asleep, so I went to the kitchen, rinsed out my glass from the night before, filled it up from the sink, and then took a much-needed sip of water. It tasted coppery.

"DON'T DRINK THAT!" my uncle yelled at me, causing me to spit the water out all over the countertop. "Sorry. You just can't drink the tap here in Madison. The rain mixes with the soil, and there's a bunch of flooding in the spring—and if all those fish died out in that lake, why the hell would you be drinking what they were swimming in?"

"I don't know!" I said while wiping up the mess with the sleeve of my shirt. "But I guess that makes sense, with you being a biology teacher."

"Chemistry," he corrected me. "Formerly, too. Anyway, go take a shower or watch an entire season of *Rehab Runway* on your laptop or something while I make the three of us some omelets, 'kay?"

I did as he instructed, making sure not to get any of the shower water in my mouth while I struggled to scrub away my fears. When I had finished, with steam clouding the small and poorly lit room, I went over to the mirror and turned on the metallic shrill of the faucet. I splashed some water onto my face then, staring deep at the reflection. I wiped a hand across the glass, clearing it up a bit, and watched as memories bubbled up from the sink and resurfaced. There was much I still didn't know, but I'd kept my head above water for this long; I didn't mind treading some more to get the answers I so desperately wanted. My actions were crazy—traveling states on a whim to reunite everyone. I needed them, but I was also sure, somewhere in the years of grave distance, they needed me back. There was no other option.

———◆————◆—◆————◆

"I can't believe Madison doesn't have a Big-Box," Troy commented as we drove away from the rustic cabin and into town. The sky was cloudy, though it didn't look like it was going to rain, so the boating continued on Lake Nasagarresett. "Big-Box is everywhere! Even Dreary's got one!"

"One," I repeated. "And I can believe it. Look at this place."

"No Big-Box, no Taco Kick, no Double Chin… not even a Happy Cow! Where's the capitalism? Everything's local!"

"That's probably what they want."

"I guess," he said, then pointed. "That the place? Mr. Swanky's? Your uncle says it's the last gas station in America where a sandwich won't kill your system."

We parked nearby. Outside were notices on a bulletin board: an almost-new pet carrier for forty dollars; a cancer benefit for a schoolteacher in two weeks; fresh goat milk at a nearby farm; a computer technician offering services at a reduced rate; and "Whoever stole my orange tabby from my yard, please bring her back, as she has sentimental value. There will be NO PENALTY and NO QUESTIONS ASKED. $200.00 reward." Inside Mr. Swanky's were typical convenience store items and goods, with racks full of March's edition of *Hollywood's Highest*, boxes of candy and flavored gum, and entire aisles dedicated to soda and potato chips.

"So it's all generic, huh?" Troy whispered.

I elbowed him. "Just find some snacks for the party tonight, OK?"

"Fine, fine!" he said, then grabbed some tortilla chips and salsa on sale.

After five or so minutes of scouring the store, we brought the tortilla chips, salsa, some sugar cookies, chocolate-covered pretzels, soda, and baby carrots and ranch for the athletes up to the front.

The girl at the cash register had been ringing up the items as we set them down in front of her. She had soft blonde hair, black eyeliner, and perfect lips. Troy inserted his card into the reader before she told him the total price.

"Oh, a well-to-do guy, are you?" she asked, laughing and smacking the gum she was chewing. Her name tag read "Kelli." She wore a red visor, tight black pants, and an equally tight red polo, which was unbuttoned enough to expose just a little of her black bra. "You guys here on vacation?"

"Came all this way just to see your pretty face," Troy said with a crooked smile. "And where might you say we're from?"

"Hmm…" Kelli put a finger on her chin, then pointed to me. "You're from China, and you're from, uh… Mexico?"

He cringed. "No, Alabama. I'll take the receipt."

"Should've known, since only white guys buy the salsa here." She finished bagging up the goods. "Still a long drive to see a dumb ol' lake. I been here all my life, and I ain't seen nothing yet impressive 'bout it."

"What happened to the fish?" I asked.

She handed us the bags. "It was that school bus they pulled out of the water nearly a decade ago—I know that for fact. Damn thing must've had some radiation. That's what Daddy said."

"Is he the owner? Mr. Swanky?"

"Who?" she asked, then giggled. "Nah. My dad ran out when I was ten." She noticed Troy leaving. "Enjoy the weather!"

"Thanks!" he called out, rolling his eyes as he walked in the direction of the Big Nasty. I quickly followed.

"Hey, look," I said as he started putting our groceries in the back. "She wrote her number on the receipt. Do you think it's for me or you?"

"Doesn't matter," he stated after a quick glance. "It's a 5-5-5, anyway, and Kelli here's a 5-5-5 kind of girl."

"That could be a six right there," I noted. I wouldn't have minded getting to know her, no matter her racial ignorance. She was cute, I was lonely. "And you're the one who started flirting with her."

"Yeah, but I'm naturally charismatic. You're just pitiful. That's why I'm glad your party's tonight." He clapped my back. "Gotta get you out of this funk!"

He grinned at me. I merely shook my head at him and started up the SUV. I could only hope it would be that simple.

❖ ⸻ ❖ ⸻ ❖

The green motorcycle was gone when we got back, and on the porch, I found a note:

Gone back to Arminster for the weekend.
My number is on the fridge.
The door to my room is locked.
Text me how the party goes.
Kukowski

Troy offered to unload all the bags onto the kitchen table, so I decided to take another look at 902 Honey Deer Drive, as my uncle wasn't there to give me the daylight tour. The cabin had only the one level, but the ceiling in the main room was tall, and a couple of canoes were stored underneath the house between the many stilts that kept it standing. An empty toolshed sat to the right of the property, and in the middle of the cabin and the shed was a faint path that led to the set of stairs to the actual lake, which was dark green and choppy that afternoon. It was a simpler paradise.

Down the walkway was the 902 dock, and moored beside it was an old speedboat with "Caldecota" written on the side. It was partially covered with a tarp that matched the water's color, but from what I could tell, it had plenty of room for passengers. I thought about asking Kukowski to take Troy and me out on the lake at some point, but it was then I noticed our neighbors had forgotten to turn off their dock beacon, as it still flashed Gatsby's green light. I wondered if that made me Daisy from Fitzgerald's novel, but I couldn't picture anyone thinking of me as an enchanted object, dehumanizing or not. I figured it wasn't likely, and that whoever lived in the lake house several miles directly across from ours was more annoyed by the light than enamored with it.

Troy was unpacking the groceries when I went back inside, and as I approached, he looked at me with a glimmer of excitement in his eyes.

"Mae!" he exclaimed. "Charlie left one of his duffel bags in the car when we dropped him off, and inside—"

"—are the axe and the chopped-off bits of his victims?"

"What? You're so morbid. No, Mom, he left us a case of Gletscher!" Troy stepped aside so I could see the twenty-four beer cans lined up along the counter. "It's watered-down bliss! An act of God!"

"I've always wondered about that. Why do you, a proud atheist, say things like 'Goddamn' and 'Go to hell' when you actively state on Uprorrr and the like that you believe in neither God nor Heaven nor Hell?"

Troy thought about this. "Force of habit? I guess it helps I have nothing to fear for saying those things. And did you know those apostles in the Bible weren't, like, old men with beards? I read somewhere that only Jesus paid the temple tax, aside from Peter. That places most of the disciples at under twenty. *Teenagers.*" He tossed me a Gletscher Light, warm in my hands. "But enough of that nonsense. With these, you'll have a real party tonight! You're set!"

"I don't know... I'm not sure a lot of those kids are the drinking type."

"You're not sure of anything, Mom. You haven't seen them in years. They could all be party animals and sex addicts and cocaine drug lords for all you know—or those axe murderers you keep going on about."

He put his hands on my shoulders to face me directly. I tried to shrug him off, but Troy didn't let up.

"With beer at your party, you're set," he told me. "Sure, we all pretend to like it because of social norms and whatnot, since all alcohol pretty much tastes the same without something fruity in it, but now all you need is Kush, and really, that's optional. You did it, Mom! You're officially a young adult!"

That made me laugh. "Well, it's about time."

He grinned with me. "And right before your next birthday, too. How old will you be turning? Fourteen?"

"Thirteen," I joked. "Still holding out on that growth spurt, too."

"You'll catch up," he said, and I could tell he was being momentarily heartfelt. "But first! You have a party in five hours, and I haven't eaten lunch yet. Gotta brush up on your former classmates with that list I made, too. What did Kukowski leave us?"

I peered in the fridge. "Uhh... cottage cheese, ketchup, raspberry yogurt, more ranch, passion fruit juice, milk, a whole lot of bottled water, some green herbs, health drinks, and..." I opened the freezer. "Frozen pizza, chicken nuggets, mixed vegetables, taquitos, and a tray of ice."

"You want the pizza or the nuggets?"

"I'm trying to relive my time as a child in elementary school," I pointed out. "Dinosaur chicken nuggets all the way, man." We smiled. "Some things never change, do they?"

"Let's hope not," he said.

<hr>

"We've got utensils in that drawer, some garlic powder in that cabinet, no TV, no sound system..." Troy paused. "I guess we could use your laptop for music. You texted

Kukowski about the WiFi password, right?"

"Most people are going to be talking, anyway," I said. "At least, that's what I imagine them doing. You know. Like, catching up and stuff."

"So innocent." He strolled by and patted my head three times. I instinctively fixed my hair. "So naïve and youthful. Mom, they get drunk first, and only then do they talk. They may also get high."

"I've many times attended the parties of the magnificent and vain Troy Rico Valdez, I'll have you know," I reminded him. "But this won't be like that. We all haven't seen each other for the past—"

"We all haven't seen each other for the past—"

"What?"

"We all haven't seen each other for the past—"

"What are you—?"

"WE ALL HAVEN'T SEEN EACH OTHER FOR THE PAST—!" He took a deep breath. "Sorry, the song got stuck on loop there. But seriously! I get it! *Seven years!* I know this is a big deal for you. Catherine might be here tonight. You've got this. Just, please, chill out, all right?"

"OK," I promised. "I also brought a pack of balloons from when we had Eva's party. They're in my backpack."

Troy looked at me as if he were a devoted father and I had just taken a large and greasy crap on his only child; it was a raw combination of shock, anger, and utter disgust at the very mention of my idea.

"Balloons!" he cried out. "You brought balloons!" He closed his eyes quickly, opened them again, and when he was certain he wasn't dreaming, he grabbed me by the shirt and then slammed me against the wall. "YOU BROUGHT FUCKING BALLOONS TO DECORATE A PARTY THAT TROY RICO IS SPONSORING?! WHAT THE FUCK!"

"They're maroon!"

"CARAJILLO, YOU'LL BE MAROON IF YOU EVEN THINK YOU'RE GONNA HANG UP BALLOONS IN THIS HOUSE!"

"And a spirit board!" I said, struggling to breathe. "I found… a spirit board in the bookcase! It's on the coffee table!"

"Oh, hell no!" he declared, quickly letting me go so he could get it. I took a moment to catch my breath and watched him grab the spirit board, examine it, shake it, and then head off with it in the direction of the back deck. "I'm not superstitious, but I'm also not stupid. Nothing good comes from these things! *I've seen teen slasher films!* A bunch of drunk kids at an isolated cabin on a lake with a dark secret and ghosts in the water—" He stopped, then looked at the box. "No. No, no, no way, and not today. I refuse to end up in a horror movie!"

"Really, Troy?" I asked, half-annoyed with his antics. "What are you even doing?"

He threw open the door and hurled the spirit board below. I walked over to him and peered down to see it land in the water between some rocks.

"VESSEL OF DARKNESS, LEAVE US IN PEACE!" he shouted to nothing. "BEGONE, SPIRITS! BEGONE, I SAY!"

"I'm sure you only provoked them further," I suggested. "So nice going, hero. Now we're really in a horror novel!"

"BEGONE!" Troy continued, on his knees with hands outstretched. "BEGONE!"

My phone buzzed repeatedly in my pocket. I excused myself from him.

"Hello?" I asked.

"Hey, this is your uncle," Kukowski said on the other line. "To answer the question from your text, the WiFi password is 'Caldecota' with a capital C. It's written on the side of the boat at the dock—the previous owner sold me it, too. But anyway, are you in the living room?"

"Yes?"

"Another thing. Pushed against the wall on top of the mantel above the fireplace is a

Leiden 21. That's a semiautomatic pistol designed and produced by Leiden Ges.m.b.H. You shoot?"

"Whiskey?"

"No. In case there's a home invasion. Look, just either make sure it's still up against the wall or hide it somewhere during your party, 'kay? You can't see it from the ground unless you're tall and looking for it, so it should be safe where it is. Just thought I'd let you know."

"Yeah... Thank you."

"Another thing: if you or your friends are smoking real cigarettes and not 'vaping' or whatever, please put your butt in the proper place—not your *butt*-butt, but your butt-butt, 'cause I am sick and tired of seeing them all over the lakefront. I think it's littering. 'Kay? Be considerate. Light it on fire, attach it to a stick of dynamite, and put it down a barking dog's mouth." A car horn sounded. "All right, talk to you later. Traffic is bad, and my bike is—*oh, you son of a mother!*"

He hung up. I looked down at phone. It was 5:30.

"What was that about?" Troy asked.

"The WiFi password is 'Caldecota,' C-A-L-D-E-C-O-T-A, capital C." My stomach felt like it was tightening. "OK, uh, do me a favor and heat up some taquitos for us, then put the chips, paper plates, cups, salsa, snacks, soda, and napkins out. I'm gonna go change into my purple plaid, move the Big Nasty up, go to the bathroom, clip my fingernails, brush my teeth—"

"You should probably brush your teeth after you eat the taquitos," Troy suggested, grinning at my nervousness.

"Right. OK." I started fast-walking to our room. "We got thirty minutes!"

"Go put on some new boxers!" He laughed. "I think you pissed yourself, Mom."

"TWENTY-NINE MINUTES!"

"Yeah, yeah, go fuck yourself."

At six o'clock sharp, a small, blue three-door hatchback drove up the gravel road to 902 Honey Deer Drive. I moved from room to room to watch the car through the blinds and attempt to identify its driver, who parked the hatchback beside my SUV, waited, and then killed the engine.

A girl with chin-length, side-swept dark hair got out of the car, looked around, checked her phone, and then looked around again. She wore long sleeves and pants, even in the heat. The sun was still an hour from setting, and from it, I noticed she was wearing pink lip gloss and eyeliner as she approached the door, grimacing with each step.

I opened it.

We stared at each other. Then she smiled.

"I thought I'd see you again one of these days," the girl said softly. She was short, my height, and her voice was pleasant, if not a little deep.

She hugged me. I stood stiff, thinking it all wasn't real, but it was. So I hugged her back and felt the tears welling up inside me.

"Michael, if you cry, I swear to God," Troy started from behind me, then extended a hand to the girl. "Troy Rico Valdez. I'm his best friend."

"Emily Pitts," she told him, looking up at Troy, still smiling. She turned to me. "Am I the first one here?"

"What?" I asked. "Oh. Oh, yeah, you're the first. That's my SUV out there." I pointed in the general direction. "Um, there are chocolate pretzels and chips and salsa and baby carrots and ranch on the table in the kitchen—if you want."

"Awesome," she said. "I brought some chips, too. They're in the car. I'll be right back."

"Yeah, OK, cool."

Emily left, closing the door behind her.

"Shit, shit, shit," I said, pacing. Troy laughed. "This isn't funny! This is, like, a disaster!"

"It's three minutes after six," he reminded me. "She's not as goth as her profile led me to believe. Maybe she changed up her aesthetic? Anyway, just remember the important details: she likes poetry, anime, she lives in Arminster—"

The door opened, and I almost screamed. Troy lightly hit me on the back of the head and pointed forward. I groaned, then walked ahead.

"Rachel!" I said to the blonde girl who looked the same as her profile picture: big smile, square face, red sweatshirt, and jeans. When I took a closer look, however, her hair appeared broken—of varying lengths and with blunt ends—and her eyebrows had been poorly drawn. She'd brought chips as well. "Good… to see you!"

"You, too, Cookie," she said, and she hugged me like Emily had. I hugged her back, trying not to pop the bag between us.

"Isn't that, like, sort of racist?" Troy asked, then to Rachel specifically: "I'm Troy. Michael's friend in Alabama."

"Oh, my goodness, I'm so sorry!" Rachel exclaimed, covering her mouth with her hands. "That is racist, isn't it? That's just what we called you—your nickname—when we were kids." She shook her head. "I guess I didn't realize… I'm so—"

"Hey, no, it's totally fine," I assured her. "Really. I mean, yeah, in hindsight, that probably wasn't cool, but we didn't know any better. Hell, I know I didn't mind. I like fortune cookies as much as the next guy."

"OK," Rachel agreed as Emily rejoined us. "OK. Gosh, that was stupid. Bryce came up with it, anyway." She scanned the cabin. "Is he, um… is he here? Bryce?"

"Uh, no," I told her. "He should be here soon, though. He said he was coming."

"And he's cool with…" Emily began, then gestured at the living room. "This?"

"Why wouldn't he be?" Troy asked, raising an eyebrow.

Someone else was at the door. I opened it to see a slender guy wearing cargo shorts and a red t-shirt. He had gelled blond hair, and I could tell by the low growl behind me that Troy was already disliking Jimmy Hickman, Confederate flag-waver and bass fisherman extraordinaire. Next to him, I recognized Samuel Kidd, who wore a red shirt with the sleeves rolled up and jeans that hardly fit his slim structure. His hair was just as short as I remembered it, though his baby face had turned into something skeletal. Sam had gotten taller since the fifth grade, though; I'd give him that.

"Hey, Mike," Jimmy said. We fist-bumped, then I did the same with Sam. "How're ya doing? You remember Sam."

"Of course he does!" Sam exclaimed, grinning wide. Whereas I was lean, he looked underweight. "We missed you, man! Should've moved with us to Red Springs—less drama than in New Baines, I hear."

We then walked into the living room, where Emily and Rachel were sitting on one of the couches. They stood up when they saw us, and the guys walked over to hug them both.

"It's been so long," Emily stated. It looked like she was about to cry, though she was still smiling. She had always smiled; I remembered that from elementary school. Even when her dad had once yelled out the window that she was a useless child while dropping her off by the flagpole, she'd smiled as she walked past us, as if nothing had happened. It wasn't necessarily a good trait to have, always smiling past the pain, but it was courageous. *Emily* was courageous.

"Tell me about it," Sam said as he sat down with Jimmy on the opposite couch. "It's been… Oh, how long has it been now?"

"Seven years," Troy told them, then smiled. "Hi, I'm Troy."

"Hello, Troy," Jimmy said from the couch. He looked at Troy's rainbow bracelet, rolled his eyes, and then looked to Rachel. "You're still in New Baines, right? How're things?"

"Well, I go to New Baines South Intermediate," she told us, "not the main high school. So I don't know everything that's gone on."

"Bryce goin' to be here?" Jimmy asked me.

"What about Sam?" Sam asked. "Do you know if she's coming?"

"Yes and yes," I said. "That's not a problem, is it, Jimmy?"

"I go by 'Jim' now," he informed me, then stretched his feet out underneath the coffee table. "And it better not be. You remember how Bryce was."

"And Sam goes by her middle name," Emily told Sam. "We both go to Hennigan High School in Arminster." She lowered her smile. "We don't hang out, though. Different crowds."

"Wait, she goes by 'Kayla' now?" Sam asked, bemused. "But that's… that's not what we promised each other. That's just—"

The door opened, and in walked Pete Fortescue, wearing a ball cap, jeans, and a blue track jacket. Beside him was Samantha "Kayla" Lykke, with long, dark hair, perfect teeth, a turquoise tank top, and tight jeans around her wide hips.

"Hey, Rachel," Pete said, waving to her. He then blushed and explained to me: "We have English together. It's good to see you, man. Thanks for having us."

"No problem at all," I said, smiling. We shook hands, but then Kayla moved her way in to hug me. I wasn't used to all this physical contact with different women, but of course I still hugged her back.

"Oh, it's so good to see you!" she said as she looked me over, then hugged me again. "All of you—really!"

Sam stood up. "It's nice to see you, too," he told her, his hands together in front of him.

"Sam!" Kayla exclaimed, then ran over to hug him as well. "How've you been?! What are you up to?!"

"Not exactly the easiest place to find," Pete whispered to me. There were different conversations happening, and I'd known Pete to be the kind of guy not to interrupt. "Kinda spooky, all the way out here, secluded… Little cliché, actually. Did you plan it this way? How genre-savvy are you?" He laughed. "I'm kidding. It's a nice cabin you got. Or is it your uncle's?"

"My uncle's," I told him. "Herbert Kukowski."

"Herbert *Eugene* Kukowski?" Kayla clarified, turning back to us. "He was my chemistry teacher at Hennigan during sophomore year."

"Mine, too," Emily noted. "Small world."

"You go to Hennigan, Amy?" Kayla asked her.

"It's Emily," she said flatly. "And yeah." She looked to me. "Your uncle's a... pretty weird dude."

"Total jackass, more like," Kayla went on. "I was always late to his class 'cause it was right after lunch, so one day, he called my house and said to my mom, 'You know, she always comes in smelling like marijuana. I don't know for sure—it's been so long since I've smoked it. Is doing drugs OK in your house? I didn't know you were so progressive!' or some crap like that." She shook her head. "Got a seventy-eight in that class, and he refused to round it up. Ugh, that man."

I laughed at her anecdote. Emily's smile returned to normal levels.

"By the way," I told them, raising my voice to get their attention. "There are snacks, bottled water, off-brand soda, and, um, Gletscher in the kitchen, if you want any." Troy gave me a thumbs-up. "But seriously, feel free to keep talking, since there isn't, like, an itinerary for the night." I looked again at Troy, who shook his head in his hands. "But I do want to thank each of you for coming. I mean, we're all seniors. I thought it'd be nice—"

"Guess who!" a girl said behind me, her arms around my waist. I turned around to see Morgan Millburn, as gorgeous as ever, with her long and wavy dark hair and sideless Ivy's Innuendo t-shirt, which revealed a blue lace bra underneath.

"Morgan!" Kayla shouted, and they both ran to hug each other.

"What's up, MJ?" Zach said from the door. I walked over to shake his hand, but he embraced me instead. "It's been too long, brother!"

"Y-you're squee... squeezing me," I stammered.

Zach let go. "Oh, sorry, man." He looked around. "Why're all you guys so skinny?" He began to laugh, then quickly stopped. "Not that there's anything wrong with that—

don't get me wrong, I—"

"Hey, Zach," Emily said sheepishly. He smiled wide, picked her up, and then started spinning her in the air.

"How have you been?" he asked when he put her down, the both of them laughing. Then he hugged her, too, and I smiled at everyone interacting with one another.

"Peter was nice enough to give me a ride," Kayla told Morgan from the couches.

Sam frowned beside them, to which Pete pulled him aside and said, "I forgot you had a crush on her. I meant nothing by it. Honest!"

Kayla looked around before whispering to Morgan, *"He's big!"* They then both burst out laughing, and I saw Sam leave the room, with Pete fast-walking after him. "Oh. Oh, wait. We're failing that Bechdel test, aren't we?"

"Yeah, you're right," Morgan said. "My boyfriend taught me that. We should talk about something other than guys, I guess." She looked down. "Like your Lusso Costo handbag! Oh my God!"

"Thanks." Kayla laughed. "It's an imitation. I bought it in Progreso, Mexico, for, like, twenty bucks. Then I wanted the real thing, so I paid two thousand dollars for one in an online auction. But I like this better. And no one can tell the difference!"

"So, like, compulsive shopping?" Morgan asked.

"No, not… that," Kayla said defensively. "I don't… have a problem." She looked at her bag and held it closer. "It makes me happy. It's a distraction."

"How are you liking Texas?" Jim asked Zach in the kitchen. "You've got hotter weather down there, right?"

"Sometimes," he admitted, "but we still get freak hail and such. Besides, I'm an Okie cowboy at heart, man. All the way."

"Nice," Jim said, raising his can of beer in approval to Zach, who raised his own before they drank their allegiance to the state.

"Arminster's about as big as I could go," Rachel told Emily by the windows. "Well, maybe. I mean, I've been a country girl my whole life. The tallest building in New Baines is four stories! Downtown Arminster is just so…" She shook her head. "Whew."

Emily laughed. "Didn't they completely revamp Main Street in New Baines?"

"Yeah, and I helped with the flower potting and painting." Rachel smiled. "You should come visit sometime."

"I think I will," Emily agreed. "You can give me the grand tour!"

They both laughed. I turned my attention to Pete and Sam near the front door.

"I didn't know you and Kayla were dating!" Pete tried to explain. "I wouldn't have—"

"We're not!" Sam admitted. "And don't call her that! Besides, I thought you were gay. What happened to you and Blank Frank making out at recess in fifth grade?!"

"Don't talk about Franklin," Pete said, taller than Sam by a few inches. "Besides, it doesn't matter. I'm bi."

"Bisexual?!" Sam exclaimed, throwing his hands in the air. "What the hell does that mean! You either like boys or girls—why can't you people make up your damn minds?!" He shook his head. "If Jim hadn't driven me here, I'd sure as hell be gone from you and this bullcrap."

Troy was also listening in on their conversation. We made eye contact. He nodded and momentarily disappeared into the kitchen.

"Think about what you're going to say next before it rolls off your tongue," Pete commanded, his fists clenched, "or I'll see you leave here in an ambulance instead."

"Fellas, fellas, please," Troy said with a beer in each hand as he walked up to them. "Let's all just take a drink, mingle around, and relax, all right?"

Sam took a Gletscher from Troy and went outside. Pete rolled his eyes and went to join the others in the living room.

"The trials of party management," Troy told me. "Feelings are hurt, coffee mugs go missing, and no one ever leaves the first time you ask."

"You do this every weekend?" I asked.

"And somehow, I enjoy myself," he laughed. "But for the most part, everyone seems to be having a good time. You did good, Mom! Be proud! Sure, not all your friends showed up, but at least there weren't any uninvited guests or—"

The door opened, pushing Troy against the wall. I expected it to be Sam again, but instead, I was eye to eye with a girl with dark braided hair. She wore a faded denim jacket with the sleeves rolled up, tight jeans, boots, a light scarf, and a dark blue beanie on her head. Her mouth opened wide in surprise, but I didn't recognize her at all.

"Michael!" She hugged me harder than the other girls. I patted her back a couple of times. "Oh my God, it's been so long since we last—"

She looked at me again, and a deep sadness suddenly overtook her expression. She then stared down at her boots.

"I, uh…" she tried, voice light but thoughts heavy. "I…"

A guy had accompanied her, and he—Christian—was familiar to me. He'd also kept the shaggy hair, much to Troy's noticeable delight.

"Michael, good to see you again," Christian said slowly, then gestured with his head to the girl. "This is Gabriella." After a moment of hesitation, he gestured again. "Gabriella Cabello."

"Gabby," she said, smiling again and tucking some loose hair behind her ears. "It's, um, certainly been a long time."

I hugged her. She held me tighter that time.

"And you look great," I told her. She started to cry on my shoulder, so I continued to comfort her, wondering where the years had gone and why I hadn't gotten in touch with these people sooner. Why *I* had waited for *them*.

As she pulled away, Gabby mouthed a *thank you* to me before both Morgan and Kayla came over to hug her at the same time. I smiled, imagining the journey she must have gone through, and so did Troy. He then gave me another thumbs-up.

"Christian, this is my best friend Troy," I explained. They fist-bumped. "He came with me from Alabama to help set this up."

"You must really be a friend, then," Christian affirmed. "And a friend of Mikey's a friend of mine."

"Thanks, man," Troy said with a sly smile, though I knew he was fangirling on the inside. "Michael says you're into baseball."

"Yeah, you play?"

"No, but I like to watch."

"Oh," Christian said, then laughed. "I played for the New Baines Cougars all of high school, but I tore my ACL in October, so I've been out since then."

"Wow, that sucks," I told him. Troy gave me a quick look that suggested I had stated the obvious. "But, um, how is your leg now?"

"It's better," he explained, pulling up the right side of his pink shorts so we could see the surgery scar around his kneecap. I could hear Troy just about squealing with joy at the sight of Christian's exposed skin. "Coach made me a trainer, so I still got to help with practices. It's all good, and I even got a full baseball scholarship to Northeastern Oklahoma State College, so it worked out in the end." He sighed. "Well, I'm not as fast as I used to be, but that's no biggie. Where are you both going in the fall?"

"Dreary Community College," Troy answered. "That's the town we live in."

"Well, I might go to Hartsett in California," I pointed out, more to Troy than to Christian. "Maybe even the University of Arminster or the University of North Carolina in Windhaven. It all depends on money, really, and I'm still waiting to hear back on whether I've been accepted."

"Well, I wish you both only the best," Christian told us, and I could tell he meant it. He glanced back toward the front door. "Anyway, my mom made some desserts, and I promised I'd bring them in." He smiled at me. "You remember my mom, right?"

"Of course!" I said. "She baked those chocolate chip cookies every year for the Valentine's Day parties at school, and she made the welcoming cake when my family and I moved into the neighborhood." I smiled at the memory. "And you were playing with Mr. Grantham's kid, right? Wasn't Mr. Grantham your tee-ball coach?"

"Mr. Grantham?" Christian asked. "Oh, you mean—" He stopped himself. Sirens blared in the distance, as if an afterthought. "I better go get those cookies."

"Do you need any help?"

"Nah, I got this," he said, then excused himself out the door.

Troy then grabbed me and hugged me, as I supposed he was feeling left out, so I hugged him back.

"Like I said, great job," he praised, then released me. "Everyone's talking to each other and having fun. Aside from Sam, that is, and Jim keeps messing with his goddamn phone…"

"Should I go talk to Sam?" I asked.

"Not yet. Besides, good-guy Christian will probably do it for you. So enjoy yourself. Don't stress."

"I've stressed all week," I reminded him. "This is me enjoying myself!"

"Whatever, Mom," he said, grinning some more.

I was going to follow him back to the couches to socialize until I saw a short guy in the corner, all by himself. He was pale and skinny, and only when I approached him did I realize he was indeed a member of my fifth-grade class at Hayes Elementary: Franklin Chambers, the boy who committed suicide.

"Franklin?" I said as I got closer. He turned to face me. "Oh my God, Frankie, it is you! I thought you were dead! I thought… I thought you killed—"

"Maybe you were thinking of a different Franklin," he suggested. He sounded and looked the same as his fifth-grade self, yet he was a little taller than he'd been back then—though still shorter than me, surprisingly. "How have you been?"

"I have… been good," I told him. "Sorry I never emailed you—"

"Did you know all the lakes in Oklahoma are man-made?" he asked me, then looked out the window. We couldn't see Lake Nasagarresett from where we were standing, but past the tall trees, it was out there, somewhere. "Put a dam wherever you want, and overnight, you'll have one. At least, that's what they tell me. You want to know what else I hear?" He grabbed my arm as I tried to back away, and I shivered as I felt his wet skin against mine. "The dam is leaking, Michael. And when it breaks, the lake will flood, and it'll take you with it. You know that, right?"

I pulled my arm out of his grasp and turned around—hoping Troy had witnessed the incident and was on his way to help. But Troy was with my friends, and when I looked back, Franklin Chambers was nowhere to be seen.

When Christian didn't come back inside for a while, I wondered what was taking him so long. So I looked out to see by the porch light that he and Sam were talking, and Pete had slipped out with them. By nightfall, the three of them returned to the living room to join the rest of us on the couches.

The hours passed on by while we shared stories of our lives.

"Oh, I was completely obsessed with *Sea Breeze Academy,*" Morgan admitted in response to Kayla. "I decorated my room to look just like Rookie's dorm—same wallpaper and everything. I even had SBA bedsheets!"

"It was ridiculous," Zach affirmed, causing us to laugh. "She had the biggest crush on Matthew, too."

"Did not!" Morgan threw a pillow at her twin brother. Then she thought about it. "OK, maybe a little."

"And you were also into *Everblade Online,*" Kayla noted. "Well, we all were, somewhat, except for Peter, who liked that *Annihilation!* video game."

"So did other people!" he professed. "Like this kid named Jake. My mom worked with his mom, and he would come over to my house and..."

Troy leaned over to Morgan and said, "You didn't happen to run across anyone in *Everblade* named 'Swearyouloveme,' did you? In a town called Harmony?"

"I remember Harmony," she told him, "and vaguely who you're talking about. Was her dad a rabbi? Did she hate the demon wraiths?"

"I'm... not sure," he said, shaking his head. "Doesn't matter. Nevermind."

"So, Sam, where're you going to college?" Christian asked him.

"You can't just say it like that," Gabby told Christian. "Not everyone goes to college anymore, with how expensive it is and how shitty student loans are." She cringed. "Sorry—didn't mean to curse!"

"It's fine," Kayla said. "Bryce isn't here to scold us about it."

"How is he?" Morgan asked, appearing genuinely concerned. "How is Bryce?"

"He's good," Christian said. "Better. Keeps to himself."

"And his stepfather is the mayor," Rachel told us, frowning. "New Baines is corrupt, and it's all Mayor Hill's fault. The NBPD, the *Ledger*..." She shook her head. "Sorry, I—"

"But yeah," Kayla went on. "Come fall, it's no longer about smarts and studying, but how much money you've got in your bank account." She turned to Sam. "Anyway, where are you going, if you're going?"

"Well, I was actually enlisted in the Israeli Defense Force for three or four years," he said. "I've been taking classes on the weekends to help with my Hebrew, but it's not mandatory to learn. Everyone in my family volunteers. It's like a tradition. I start in August."

"Wait, you're being serious right now?" Troy asked, legitimately surprised.

"I thought you were Native American," I said.

"A Jewish Native American, yeah," Jim explained. "He's telling the truth."

"Wow," Kayla said. "You're so brave! I could never fight in the army, especially one that wasn't, like, the United States or anything. No offense."

"I got a deferral," Sam continued, "but like I said, I want to go. It's kind of a cool situation for me." He looked down at the wooden floor. "I should beef up, though."

"Well, we'll be thinking of you," Kayla said. He smiled at this.

"Hey, that's right," Rachel said. "Didn't you write a book, Michael? I saw you posted something about it on your Chipper after you sent us the invites."

"Oooooh, a book!" Morgan exclaimed, then turned to face me. "What's it about? Love? Death? Adventure?!"

"People doing people-things?" Pete guessed. I laughed.

"It's a psychological thriller," I said. "A Young Adult novella about this girl named Madison whose stepmom takes her to see a therapist after she punches a clown at her school's end-of-the-year carnival."

"Why did the stepmom sock the clown?" Zach asked.

"No, babe, Madison hit the clown," Morgan corrected him. To me: "Continue."

"Well, throughout the story, we learn she had a really messed-up encounter with a different clown during the town fair—"

"Say no more," Christian said, taking out his wallet. "How much for a copy?"

"Yeah, I'll buy one," Emily joined in. "I don't read enough as it is."

"Same," Pete agreed. "Can I buy it on my tablet?"

"And aren't you in a band, Pete?" Rachel asked.

"The latest member of Seymour and the Cancer Survivors!" he told us.

"Oh, God," I said. "I'm so sorry—"

"No, no, they just needed a new bass player," he explained. "Turns out the last guy relapsed. But anyway, your book?"

"There aren't any fish in the lake," Pete explained, "because of the nitrates from all those Fourth of July fireworks. That stuff's toxic on—"

"Man, that doesn't make any sense," Jim said. "And it's not 'global warming,' neither. Everybody sane knows that climate change is a hoax."

"It's probably the fishermen depleting the population," Zach said. "That's what's happening in the oceans right now. Either that or sewage waste. Phosphorus content is hell on the environment."

"But that's no fun!" Kayla joked. "You have to think outside the box, like… like a tornado came by ten years ago and swept them all away!"

"A tornado *did* sweep my house away," Pete reminded her. "That's why my family moved to Shaughnessy Estates in the first place."

"Oh, right. Um, sorry about that."

"Ten years ago is when that missing school bus was found here," Christian stated, "but without the nineteen kids inside."

"That's what the cashier mentioned at Mr. Swanky's," I said. "She told me and Troy it must've been something in the bus they pulled out of the water."

"Huh? No, that's not what happened." Christian shook his head. "The locals like to blow it out of proportion, but they're the ones who stopped calling this place 'Catfish Crater' after the bus went missing and the fish went with it. The whole thing was weird because the bus was found on a deserted shore here on Lake Nasagarresett. There were no roads between the trees, so it was like a UFO or something beamed up the bus, took the children out, and then dropped it back down in the middle of nowhere."

"And they never found the missing nineteen?" Troy asked.

"Never," Christian told us. "And that's when the fish died."

Troy pulled me aside while the conversations continued.

"How are you?" he asked.

"Asian," I answered.

"Good, I almost forgot."

There was a beat coming from outside, and soon after, the door opened, and B-Love himself walked through the entrance in a white fur coat, gold chains, and with a burly bodyguard behind him.

"WHAT'S UP, MY NIGGAS?!" Bobby shouted as he walked inside. "Morgasm! Christiano! Pete Forte-screw-yo-momma-in-her-vagina, motherfucker!" He stopped in front of Rachel, his finger pointed toward her. "I don't know you. Sorry." Then to me: "Cookie! Thanks for the invite!"

"Yeah, no problem, Bobby."

"Please," he said. "I'm only 'Bobby' under the 'Born as' section on my QuickSearch page." He looked around. "Where's the music? No music?"

"B-Love," Troy started, a permanent marker in one hand and his phone in the other. "My name is Troy, and I'm a huge fan of yours—"

"Course you are, nigga," he suggested, taking the marker and signing the back of the phone. "Gold, huh? I like you, Trey. And your bracelet! Half my fan base is gay. Faggots make the best entertainers for parties!"

"I know, right?" Troy agreed, then winked at me.

"It's cool, it's cool," B-Love told the bodyguard. "Don't come back till you hear from me, all right?" Then, as the man hesitated: "Go!"

Mr. Clipboard and Earpiece left the cabin, and B-Love immediately relaxed.

"Sorry about all that," he said, his B-Love persona gone and replaced with the kid I once knew. "I have to keep up the act around him. Everybody, really. And sorry I'm late, too. Bad weather stalled the jet." He looked at the grandfather clock. "What time is it?"

"You're lookin' at the time," Jim pointed out.

"I can't read those things."

"Traditional clocks?"

Bobby sighed. "Troy—or was it Trey?" He shook his head. "What time is it?"

"It's ten oh two, B-Love."

"Please, just call me Bobby," he insisted. "I'm B-Love way too often nowadays. And my bad for calling you a faggot. Not cool of me. It's like a flashback to—"

"Seven years ago," everyone said at the same time. We all then looked at each other and laughed.

"How did it get so late?" Emily asked, yawning.

"Time flies when you're having fun," Morgan answered, smiling at her.

"Where's Catherine?" Bobby asked, looking around. "Her, Willow, Mekenzie…"

There was a knock at the door.

"Ooooh, shit, I did that, didn't I?" B-Love asked me, nudging my shoulder. "That's the magic of *God Status*, nigga!" He then shook his head. "Sorry, sorry. This is all still new to me. I didn't even like the name of that album."

I ignored him and moved in the direction of the door. My feet were devoid of sensory input; I floated there, my heart pounding. So I took a deep breath and turned the knob.

Belle stood on the porch. She wore a white V-neck and bright red running shorts, and her highlighted blonde hair fell neatly down to her shoulders. Behind her was Nate, who was cleaning his glasses and had on a light pink button-down and corduroy pants.

"Michael!" Belle exclaimed as she hugged me. "How are you?! This is crazy! It's so good to see you again!"

"I'm glad to see you, too," I told her honestly. She kept on smiling.

"Hey, guys!" Belle said as she walked into the living room. "So sorry we're late—"

Gabby, Morgan, and Kayla all got up and ran over to tackle-hug her. They laughed as she squeezed each of them back.

"Cookie, my bro," Nate said to me, clasping my back with his hand. "Thanks for the invite." He then scanned the room. *"And hello, Morgan!"*

"Hey, Nate," she said, shaking her head, though I could see she was still smiling.

Jim offered me a cup of Gletscher, which I gladly accepted; it was time to celebrate, so celebrate I did.

The chattering went on throughout the night, and things were going well. *Really well.* I continued walking around and participating as per the social demands of party management, as Troy had called it. The topic of college was a popular one, and I learned from my rounds that most of my former classmates were staying in-state at either Eastern Oklahoma University or Oklahoma State College, including the Millburn twins. Rachel was going to Saint Christopher's University in Arminster, Sam planned on attending a school for music after his time in the IDF, Emily was going to Arminster Community College to save money, Pete was going to the University of Arminster, and Bobby was continuing his career on the West Coast. But the other nine were either EOU- or OSC-bound, and by their loud discussions, they sure were proud of it.

At some point, the door opened. At another, it slammed shut, and Bryce Skinner walked inside.

Everyone got quiet.

Bryce turned to me, examined the situation, and then held out his hand for me to shake.

"Good to see you, Michael," he said.

I took it. "And good to see you, Bryce."

Sirens blared in the distance.

"Yo yo yo, if it isn't Dicky Skinner!" Bobby exclaimed with a mix of B-Love in his greeting. He walked up to Bryce and started fake-punching his chest. "You still as much of a tight-ass as you were back in elementary school, bro?"

Bryce chuckled. I'd never heard anyone chuckle in real life before, but Bryce did right then, and it unsettled me in a place in my core I didn't know existed.

"I'm fine, thanks," Bryce said coolly. He then patted down the top of his perfectly combed blond hair. "And how are you, Bobby? How's the rapping coming along?"

"I'm at the fucking top, motherfucker!" B-Love told him, crouching and jumping and then crouching again for some reason. He grinned. "My boy Narcissus and I got the whole industry as our bitch. We got the motherfucking *God Status*, nigga!" Bobby then relaxed again, extending a hand and laughing. "I'm just playing with you, man. I'm not like that."

"*God Status*, huh?" Bryce asked Bobby, leaving him hanging. No one was talking except for those two. "That what you call it?" He looked to me. "Breaking the rules?"

"What rules?" I asked him.

"Five Twenty-Nine," Rachel whispered to herself. Bryce looked over at her, then to Troy.

"Who are you?" Bryce asked.

"The name is Troy Rico," he told him. They were about the same height, and from where I was standing, it looked like they were having a stare-off with each other.

"Your bracelet." Bryce pointed. "The rainbow one. What does it signify?"

"That I support LGBTQIA rights," Troy answered. "But I see what you're getting at, so let's skip to the chase. I'm gay."

"You're gay," Bryce said. "Morgan, what do you think about gay people?"

"I think they deserve the same respect as anyone else," she answered sternly.

"Uh-huh. What about you, Rachel? What do you think about gay marriage?"

"Oh, I, um…" I could tell Rachel didn't like being put on the spot. "I, well, I think that gay people should be allowed to marry whomever they want." She gulped. "But I don't think being gay is a… natural concept."

"That so?" he asked, though it wasn't a question. "And you, Jim?"

"Marriage should be between a man and a woman," he stated. "That much is clear, and that's what our Founding Fathers intended in the Constitution. I think gay people can be allowed to date and whatever they need to do to get off, but if they want to marry each other, they shouldn't call it marriage. Call it 'commitment.'"

Troy groaned.

"What about you, Emily?" Bryce continued. "Your thoughts on the topic of LGBT rights?"

"I… have a lot of gay friends," she said. "And I like hanging out with them. I believe they should have equal opportunities. But what bothers me—the only thing that bothers me—is how… I don't know… *excited* they get about the whole thing. Like the gay pride parades where everyone's dressed in tie-dye. I used to love wearing rainbow stuff until people started believing I'm a lesbian. And I think it's great if you've come out as one, but that's just not who I am. I have a boyfriend. I don't understand why they have to flaunt it around as much as they do." She took a deep breath. "If gay people acted like normal people, there wouldn't be such a stigma around them as a group." She looked over to me apologetically. "Sorry, Michael."

"Wait, why?" I asked.

"Well…" She glanced at Troy, then back to me. "Aren't you gay? Isn't he your…

partner?" A couple of others nodded, agreeing with Emily and her assumptions of me.

"No!" I shouted a little too loud. "No, I'm not gay! God, no!"

"You act like it's a fucking disease," Troy said, rolling his eyes.

"And it's not," Gabby added. "It's biological, *not a choice*. You don't choose your sexual orientation."

"Says the crossdresser," Jim muttered, but we all heard him.

"Hey!" Christian exclaimed. "Gabe went through a difficult—!"

"GABE?!" she repeated.

"Gabriella! I'm sorry! I sometimes forget—"

"I think we all get a little confused every now and again," Bryce stated, pacing the room. "I think that sometimes we forget the rules we agreed to seven years ago… and the consequences we established for breaking them."

"Man, to hell with your rules," Zach told him. "Nobody's told, and everything's fine. If Pete is bisexual, let him be bi. If Gabby sees herself as a girl, let her be a girl. And Emily, just be thankful you don't need a symbol to celebrate your own pride. But, Bryce, man, none of that has anything to do with—"

"The fuck are you all talking about?" Bobby asked. Or maybe it was B-Love. I was just as confused, regardless. "Y'all crazy motherfuckers. I'm about out of here—"

"To continue to be as crude as you are in your influential music?" Bryce went on. "If you can even call it that. And for you, Kayla, to continue to sleep around with any guy who offers you a ride? And for you both, Zach and Morgan, to carry on with your… *incestuous* relationship?"

"What the fuck?!" they shouted at him.

"You're behind the times, Bryce," Kayla told him, "and you're acting like a parent. I know your dad was a preacher—"

"Don't you talk about my father."

"—but whether this is about religion or *whatever*, you need to grow up and get out of our business. God, do you actually believe that people who are living on this planet *right now* should have less of a say in how they lead their lives than Someone or Something you've never… oh, what's the expression? Broken bread with? So long as people aren't harming one another—or *discriminating* against each other—then there isn't a problem with their behavior, got it? So quit making such a big deal out of this!"

"Gay people are the ones making a mess of everything," Jim told her. "Like Emily said, if they would just act normal and stop getting bothered about every headline or law passed—"

"Well, no, they have a right to be upset," Emily clarified. "What I meant was—"

"They support the freedom of speech if it's not against themselves," Jim went on. "Seems hypocritical to me."

"Rednecks act the same way," Kayla countered with a sneer.

"Oh, cry me a river, you weak-minded slut."

"NO SLUT SHAMING!" most of the girls and Troy shouted at once.

"Can't believe you said that in front of a bunch of feminazis," Nate told Jim, shaking his head and laughing. "It's like watching those angry Chihuahuas on Uprorrr. 'You can't be racist against white people!' The literal definition of racism is—"

"What the actual fuck are you going on about?" Troy asked him.

"That unless you're a white, cis, upper-middle-class male, it's totally cool to talk about societal issues and the exclusion of others, according to Social Justice Warriors or whatever. Uprorrr is so hostile, no one will take you seriously unless you put in your bio you're either queer or a Person of Color or have this certain medical diagnosis no one's ever heard of—why? Because they're made up so people will listen to you! All you people do is scream out 'Racist!' and 'Transphobia!' whenever someone tries to give an opinion that's different from yours. 'Check your privilege! Check your privilege!'"

"*As you should!*" Morgan yelled at him. "Because it's sooo much harder being a white, heterosexual, whatever-the-crap-you-just-went-on-about than it is being a minority *in real life!"*

"And it's extremists like you, Nate, who make us religious people look stupid!" Gabby shouted.

That did it, as all but two people immediately began talking over one another—yelling, screaming, cursing, and all on the verge of violence. As party manager, I only watched the chaos ensue without participating, wondering how things had gotten out of hand so quickly. It was while doing this that I noticed the other silent person was Bryce, who had fanned these flames and was happily watching my lake house burn because of it.

"Everyone, please, cut it out with the theatrics!" Christian demanded above the noise. They quieted, and Christian looked to Bryce. "Man, you know I'm your best friend, and I usually have your back. But this? *This is crazy!* Save the sermon for Sunday! Yeah, not everyone is how you pictured them being after seven years—but people change! I mean, take Catherine, for example: she honestly thinks she's a… a cat!"

"A cat?!" Kayla, Zach, Morgan, Jim, Sam, and I all asked at once.

"Yeah, I'm out," Bobby said, standing up to leave.

Bryce reached above the mantel, took the handgun, and then pointed it at Bobby.

And just like that, everyone started talking again.

"Oh my God!"

"Jesus Christ, he's got a gun!"

"Fuck! Fuck!"

"Richard, please!" Belle begged him. She had been softly crying since he had started his rant, but only then did she speak up to him. "Stop this. It's not worth it!"

"Up against the wall," Bryce commanded to us, waving the gun. "Do it! Maybe now you'll all start *paying attention."*

We started to move slowly—all of us, including his girlfriend.

"Not you, Belle," Bryce told her. "In fact, not you, Nate, Jim, Sam, Rachel, Emily…

and Christian. You all step away from them. This is about identity, after all. What we're proud of. Who we believe we are and could be." He paused, looked me in the eye. "And what we did."

They shuffled over to the couches. It was then the Millburns, Bobby, Pete, Kayla, Gabby, Troy, and myself against the wall.

Bryce strolled over and put the gun to Zach's forehead. Zach stood still with his fists clenched and eyes closed, but Morgan's were wide in fear.

"No," she pleaded softly, her knees bent forward, her head shaking left and right. "Bryce, Bryce, no, God, please, I don't know what you think or want to happen, but *fuck*, please don't—"

"Hell calls hell," Bryce said simply, then shot Zach dead in the head.

"NO!" Belle screamed, but Nate held her back.

"BRYCE, YOU MOTHERFUCKER!" Morgan cried out as she fell beside her twin brother. Her wails filled the room; the lake was nothing compared to her tears. She looked up, heartbroken. "HOW COULD YOU?!"

"*Hell calls hell!*" he repeated—hands shaking—and with the twitch of a finger, he shot Morgan in the eye, then Bobby.

Sam and Rachel puked to the side. Pete grabbed Bryce's arm and twisted his fingers backward, causing Bryce to drop the gun in alarm. Troy then ran into Bryce and knocked him hard onto the floor; something cracked, and I didn't think it was the wood beneath him. As he fell, Bryce slid down the hall toward the kitchen, so I ran around and positioned myself behind him so he couldn't run away. But Bryce was a man of action, not words, and when he managed to get up, all I could see was hellfire in his raging eyes.

He lunged forward, knocking him and me against the back wall. Then he rolled over, and with our combined weight against the door, it snapped off its hinges, and we fell onto the back porch.

"MOM!" Troy yelled as he ran over to the open doorframe. *"MICHAEL!"*

Bryce kept fighting, and so we toppled over the edge together for what felt like an eternity spent in total darkness. The light from the cabin grew fainter until it was only a speck in the night as we crashed into water. It was sudden and cold as it collapsed into my mouth, and while I struggled, I only took in more of it. I was a vessel, and I was sinking, and no matter my efforts to save myself from taking on water, we continued still to plummet deeper into the abyss.

As I drowned, I thought not of the corpses in my uncle's cabin, nor of Catherine and Troy. I thought of the missing fish, the missing bus, and how scared and confused the missing children must have felt when everything had suddenly gone wrong, and there was nothing they could do about how it was going to hurt their families, how it was affecting so much more than the lives around them, how it was 7:40 in the morning as the second bus drove off from Clarkson Middle School one humid day in late May.

PART TWO:
REMEMBER THE TIME

*"When I was younger I could remember anything, whether
it had happened or not; but I am getting old, and soon
I shall remember only the latter."*

—MARK TWAIN, 1912

I t was 7:40 in the morning as the second bus drove off from Clarkson Middle School one humid day in late May. The students on board hoped the damp weather would be a sign of heavy rain—preferably enough to cancel the end-of-the-year field trip to an outdoor American Civil War historical museum; they were originally going to Coaster King City, but it turned out not being in the school's budget last-minute. Most of the kids on Bus #2 were either playing handheld games or listening to their music, which greatly annoyed the teachers who were trying to read magazines such as *Hollywood's Highest* while planning the upcoming week's curriculum.

Ian Gallagher looked from his spot in the eighth row back to the third bus, still parked and waiting for teens to hop on. Bus #3 was referred to as "the bisexual bus" by most of the students, as it was co-ed. The teachers had tried to separate the boys and girls by putting them on different buses, but with 115 kids in the eighth grade, an extra bus was needed for the remaining students.

Ian knew his best friend Karina Tamerlane was on the bisexual bus, probably waiting for him to text her, "I see you, babe." Ian and Karina were an interesting pair. They weren't technically dating—despite the flirting—as Karina's parents wouldn't let her even look at boys until high school, though you could tell by the way they acted they had something special going on. This confused the girls who had crushes on Ian and the guys who had a thing for Karina, but they both didn't mind. It kept things "drama-free," as Karina put it. Yet Ian promised himself that he would ask Karina out the first day of ninth grade, no matter what.

It was a two-hour drive from Oklahoma to Missouri to reach the museum, and Ian was bummed he couldn't spend the four-hour roundtrip with Karina. He was stuck on the all-boys "gay bus" instead, and what was even worse was that Robert was probably sitting right behind her.

Robert Schlimme was the perverted class clown of Clarkson Middle School. None of the girls respected him, nor did the boys, but he thought highly of himself regardless. He would often push others out of their seats or describe his twisted fantasies aloud in the hopes this would somehow impress Karina, who he obnoxiously made clear was his "bride to be," despite her numerous denials. Ian wondered if Robert had paid off one of the teachers to let him sit on the bisexual bus, for there was no way fate would've allowed Robert the chance to hit on Karina without Ian being there to stop it. "Boys will be boys," the teachers had told her. For a group of educators, Ian thought they were a bunch of idiots.

"Don't worry about it, man," Aiden—Ian's best friend since the first grade—told him. "I'm sure that stupid Woodpecker got himself stuck in the bathroom again and can't get out."

Ian laughed, remembering the time the cheerleaders had put a chair in front of the door and prevented Robert from leaving the restroom for a whole lunch period.

"I certainly hope so," Ian said, smiling.

It was almost ten o'clock when Ian's cell phone buzzed with a new text message. He had spent the last couple of hours texting Karina, who wished he was there with her. Ian was about to text her that he was going to catch some z's when the cell phone vibrated repeatedly in his hands, indicating Karina was calling him. He answered, happy to hear her voice.

"E? It's *so* boring here!" she told him. "All I see out the windows are trees and yellow-green grass, and the roads are *terrible!*"

"I know, right?" he said, laughing. "I can't believe we both paid twenty bucks to do this for a day."

"At least you have air conditioning! Ours broke down a while ago. It's so hot—"

"Hey, hey, hey!" a voice cut in. "How are ya, Mr. E?"

"Give it back, Schlimme!" Ian commanded into the phone. A couple of students stared, but he didn't notice.

"Sorry, Ian," Robert said, "but me and your *girlfriend* are gonna have some fun now, so I'm goin' to hafta let you go." There was some shuffling on the other end. "Ooh, you like that, huh? Yeah, girl."

Ian heard the phone drop onto the seat of the bus. He imagined the Woodpecker wrapping his greasy fingers around Karina's soft hair and holding her too close to his rank body. Ian felt claustrophobic just thinking about it.

When I get off this lousy bus, I'm gonna break his goddamn nose.

Karina or somebody hung up then. Ian tried calling her back, but she didn't pick up. He tried again to no answer. Furious with Robert, he turned off his phone to save the last of the battery life, assuring himself that Karina could take care of herself, and Ian wasn't missing anything by not being there. But in his gut, he knew he *was* missing something.

Ian didn't realize he had fallen asleep until after he awoke to the sound of panic coming from the students. His bus had stopped at a gas station with Bus #1. The police were outside talking to the teachers. He was confused, and it took Aiden a while to explain everything to him: the bisexual bus had disappeared, and neither the teachers nor the other bus drivers could get a hold of it.

A surge of emotions ran through him. He was worried for Karina, but he was also angry at Robert for taunting him and groping her with his sweaty palms.

Where were they? How could they have just vanished? Maybe the bisexual bus ran out of gas midway, and the bus driver was busy calling a tow truck, or…

Yeah, that seemed more likely. He decided to check his phone for any text messages from Karina. As soon as it was done booting up, it chimed, indicating someone had left him a voicemail. He pressed play.

"The water's cold, E." He could tell it was Karina's voice, but it sounded different. "We're waiting for you."

It came off as emotionless—dull and monotonous, as if computer-generated. She sounded as if she were in a trance. She sounded as if she were *possessed*.

"I'm bleeding, Ian," she continued. "I need you. E, where are you?"

The voicemail ended. He replayed it, listening for anything he might've missed. Then he played the message a third time, just to be sure he wasn't hallucinating. Later, after he made Aiden swear not to tell a soul, he tried to find the voicemail again for him.

It was gone.

"Are you blind or something?" Aiden asked, then looked at Ian as if he were making it all up. "Nothing's there."

"Nevermind," Ian muttered, shaking his head. He felt dejected and sat in silence for the rest of the bus ride back to Clarkson, as did the other students.

It was two days before school let out in June when Clarkson Middle School was informed of the whereabouts of the missing bus. Police officers had found it at Catfish Crater, also known as Lake Nasagarresett, a large, secluded body of water about twenty miles southwest of the gas station where the buses had stopped. The bisexual bus was empty—no backpacks, no sign of human life, nothing. The doors and windows were reported to be wide open, and there was no damage to the exterior of the bus. Law enforcement was still looking for the nineteen missing children.

An odd note on the police report: "All the fish were dead … *more or less.*"

The sky outside was white, and the memories were fading. The entire cabin was engulfed in a thick fog, and when it cleared momentarily, it was apparent there was steam rising from the lake as if to taunt early-morning swimmers into its warm, murky depths. But there was no one out on the water, and not a ripple stirred its surface. So there it sat, silent and foreboding.

I awoke on the couch with a blanket covering me. I was heated and relaxed, though that only led to a sudden panic. I quickly got up—slipping on the rug and tripping in the process—and ran over to the back of the house to examine the wall.

The door was there. It hadn't always been.

"What the fuck," I said, my fingers on the wood. "What the fuck."

There was a knock on the door at the other end of the cabin. I noticed I was still wearing my clothes from the night before, and they were dry, which was a good sign, but I didn't know what that meant.

I opened the front door. The fog only permitted me to view about five yards in all directions, but what I could see was a middle-aged white guy with slightly thinning hair he probably colored every few weeks. He wore a dark-gray trenchcoat and an emerald-green tie around the collar of his off-white shirt. From where I stood, he seemed to lean against solid air; as I shut the door and walked down the steps, however, I could see his black sedan, which was new and shiny, save for a bit of dirt around the right-rear tire.

"That's the type of car police officers use," I said to the stranger, pointing. He looked behind him, then back. "Is it unmarked?"

"No," he told me, smiling faintly. "I retired three years ago, but you know what they say about old habits." The man reached inside his coat, startling me. As I grabbed for the door handle, he put up a hand, then fished out his wallet and produced a business card for me. I took it. "My name is Michael Northcott. I'm a private investigator."

"Uh-huh." I flipped the card over in my hands, reading it carefully. It listed a phone number, a website, and an email, as well as his name and his occupation of private detective. "And what exactly are you investigating?"

"Not much these days," Northcott said, stretching his arms out and popping his wrists. His voice was raspy, like that of a smoker. "But Mr. and Mrs. Dusett are friends of mine, so I suppose I have a more personal interest in finding their daughter."

"Dusett?" I asked, remembering my fifth-grade friend who couldn't make it: the hairstylist, the mother, the girl most concerned about Bryce being at the party. "As in Willow Dusett?"

"That's her," he affirmed. "Willow went missing last night after her shift. She was the last one, so she locked up, got in her car, turned it on..." He stopped, whether for dramatic effect or to catch his breath. "She never got home. So her mother and Willow's boyfriend went out to the shop to check. They called me late last night. This happened right in town, and those are all the facts I have as of now." He smiled. "But you know what else I know? I know you and she went to elementary school together, and you invited her to a party that just so happened to be on the same night as her disappearance. Kind of strange, don't you think?"

"I don't know where Willow is," I told him. I could feel the sweat dripping down the inside of my shirt, but I knew I told the truth, so I attributed my nervousness to the fact he used to be a cop. Northcott unsettled me, and maybe it was the way he looked like the kind of guy a kid would want as their uncle—the ones who were people-persons and knew how to use their charisma and demeanor to their advantage.

"And I believe you, Michael," he said. "I just have a couple of questions. Is that all right?"

I nodded, so he pulled out his phone. I recognized it as an old TSC Serenade, the same model my mom had bought as her first smartphone.

WILLOW DUSETT

Michael – Thank you so much for the invite to your party, but I will have to pass on this one unfortunately!! With my son and work, it's pretty hard to do anything like that on weekend nights. (Does Bryce know? What about 5/29?) Anyway... if you ever need a haircut, don't hesitate to stop by! You've always had nice hair lol.

"What's Five Twenty-Nine?" Northcott asked, referring to Willow's message to me on the screen. "Is it a date?"

"I'm not sure," I told him. He held out his phone, and when I reached for it, he hesitated.

"What's that written on your arm?" he continued. I looked down and saw, written in handwriting other than my own, a phone number with the 918 Arminster County area code. I only recognized the name above it. "Who's Gabby?"

"I guess it's her number. She must've written it last night."

"During your party." Northcott started typing something into his phone. "This your family's lake house?"

"My uncle owns it. He's a teacher for Arminster Public Schools. Or, he used to be."

"And who is Bryce?"

I thought of the previous night's events: Bryce's entrance, the arguments, the gun, the screams, Zach, Morgan, Bobby, and the lake.

"His full name is Richard Bryce Skinner," I said. "He went to Hayes Elementary with us. He still lives in New Baines."

Northcott continued typing, then looked up. "Can I have a look around outside?"

"Sure," I answered. So he did.

There were a lot of tire tracks around the Big Nasty, and Northcott inspected these. He then continued toward the back of the house. If he were a home inspector, he most certainly would have condemned the cabin on the spot for the structural collapse that was the back porch. Instead, he pointed to the ground, at two thin lines running parallel to each other about two feet apart. With our eyes, we followed the lines from the front steps to the side of the house and ending at the drop-off to the shore below, where a crushed wheelchair had joined the spirit board.

"What's that?" he asked.

"Not sure," I answered, and as I noticed the hint of frustration in his furrowed brow, added: "Sorry."

"No, it's all right." He craned his head around. "Did anyone *not* come to your party? Maybe they were out… doing other things?"

"Mekenzie Willis, who lives in North Carolina, and Catherine Thomas. She never responded."

He wrote this down.

"Did Bryce arrive to your party by land or sea?" Northcott asked. I shrugged. "OK. Do you know what time he got here?"

"Late," I answered. "After ten."

Northcott wrote this down as well. "Did Bryce come with someone else or by himself?"

"He came alone."

"And do you think he would harm Willow for Five Twenty-Nine?"

I thought of Morgan begging Bryce for her brother's life. The rules. *Hell calls hell.*

"I'm sorry," Northcott said, correcting himself. "I don't know why I asked that." He put his phone back into his suit pants, put a mint in his mouth, and then popped his wrists again. "You have my card. Call me if you remember anything that might help us find Willow. OK, Michael?"

"I will," I told him.

Northcott nodded and walked to his car. From there, he nodded at me, and then he drove off and away from 902 Honey Deer Drive.

I shook my head, perturbed and disoriented, and went inside.

Troy was in the living room pacing, an act the two of us often associated with myself rather than him, as I was the nervous one, whereas he was calm and confident. Unlike me, Troy was in his boxer briefs again, though this time a neon blue rather than green.

"Mae," he said, grabbing my shoulders and looking me in the eye. "Last night…" He shuddered. "So crazy."

"Dude, it was fucked up!" I shouted. "I've never been so scared in my life, I—"

"*You* were scared?" he exclaimed, legitimately shocked. "I'm the one who had sex with a *girl!*"

"What are you talking about?!"

"What are *you* talking about?!"

"Last night!"

"After you passed out," Troy explained, "from the Gletscher. The Millburn twins totally made out in our room, by the way. And you threw up outside near the end of the party. I put you on the couch, remember?"

"Um, no?!"

"Well, I did. But Gabby…" He sighed, more out of rapture than sorrow. "I don't know, man. Something about her." He shook his head. "No. No! That's what I'm saying,

Mom! *I'm gay.* You know that, my mother knows that, my sisters know that, our friends know that, and I've known that since preschool, when all the little boys were chasing after Betsy-Rae Pighauler, but I wanted Hank Dirtsower, so we started holding hands during nap time. I don't *like* girls. I find a lot of them annoying. I find a lot of *people* annoying. But Gabby, I'm not sure. We just started talking and … one thing led to another."

"That's what happened?"

"That's what happened."

"What about *Bryce,* though? What about him and Zach and Morgan and Bobby, and then I fell out the back and drowned—"

"Mom, chill out," Troy said. "*Everything is always about you!* I get it. My problems don't matter, but the ones about you and your fifth-grade friends do. Diay, Mamita, do you even listen to yourself?" He rolled his eyes. "No, of course you don't. That's why I'm here, right?"

"*Do you not understand what went down last night?!*" I shouted. "With Bryce walking in and talking about gay marriage and lining us all up and murdering Zach, Morgan, and Bobby—"

"What I understand is that *you* got *really drunk.* So did I, Mom. We *all* got wasted last night. That's how I ended up with Gabriella. Did I like it—being with her? Yeah, I did, *which is why I'm so fucking confused!*"

"GAAH!" I screamed at him, then held up my hands and went to the kitchen. I opened the fridge, took out the passion fruit juice carton, poured myself a glass, sat down, and then drank it all, both hands around the cup, eyes wide with anger. Troy was clueless; that much I got. He thought I was a boy crying wolf. Without proof, there was no point in discussing it further with him.

From my phone, I went to B-Love's Chipper account. I scrolled and refreshed, yet I soon concluded there hadn't been a new status from the rapper since the day before. So I checked Zach's Chipper and then Morgan's Photofixer, but each was updated about once or twice every week. This meant nothing to me, which made it even more frustrating.

"Are you gonna call her?" Troy asked from the entryway.

"What?" I asked. "Who?"

"Gabby," he told me, holding up his arm. I checked mine. "You asked about seeing Catherine, and she said she could hook you up in the morning. It's ten oh two."

I ran my hands through my hair, pulled on a tuft, and then typed in her number. She answered on the third ring.

"Who—?"

"It's Michael," I explained. "You said… Troy said to call you in the morning."

"Oh. Oh, yeah." There was some shuffling on her end. "Sorry. A bit, uh, hungover, you know? Anyway, you said you wanted to see Catherine, right?"

"I mean, I do, yeah."

"And you're going to be cool?"

"Why wouldn't I be?"

"OK," she said. "Cat lives in a gated community in South Arminster called Mountain Vista, passcode zero-seven-zero-four. It's on a big hill. Her house is 1123 Palmer Drive. And please, Michael… Don't fuck this up, OK?"

"I won't!" I told her, then glanced up at Troy, who'd been watching me with a look of pity in his eyes. I took a deep breath. "Sorry. It's just, with last night and Bryce—"

"I know," she assured me. "But we can't talk about that, remember?"

"Huh?"

"They say the fog'll clear up in an hour or so," she continued, either cryptically or literally, "and I told Troy I'd show him downtown today. Drop him off by Ricchezza's at around noon on your way to Cat's, all right? You remember it. The Italian place?"

"Yeah, I got it," I said, then ended the call.

"What's the plan?" Troy asked as I stood up and headed for our room.

"Take a shower, eat, and get dressed," I told him. "We're going to Arminster."

The drive was a bit troublesome, given the weather. QuickSearch Maps knew where to go, but that didn't mean we could see the road in front of us. I jumped a little in my seat each time a car appeared out of nowhere, so much so that I had to turn down the end of XYLØ's "Between the Devil and the Deep Blue Sea" to concentrate ahead.

"Are you wearing the same outfit three days in a row?" Troy asked. "Good thing you didn't barf on it."

"Yeah, but I don't sweat," I noted, "and you're the only one who's seen me in it. You saw it Friday, my friends saw it Saturday night, and now Catherine will see it today."

"And what about when Gabby sees you when I get dropped off?"

"Oh well," I told him.

Troy laughed. "No es importante para ti? At least it's not a red leather jacket with a bunch of zippers. Or the one from *Thriller*. Anyway, what about the party? Are you happy you got your answers?"

"I haven't got anything yet," I stated. "Just directions."

"You have me."

"I've had you."

"You had them, too. Once seven years ago, and again last night. What more do you want?"

"I want to see Catherine."

"Fair enough."

We continued south down the highway once we passed through Red Springs. I vaguely remembered the road from drives with my dad, but that was when I was in the passenger seat. This was different.

"So," I started. "You mentioned you and Gabby...?"

"Gabby and I?"

"… had sex?"

"Yes, sir."

"I see," I said. "And did she have, uh… you know. I don't mean to pry… I'm just curious, is all. She has the boobs, so maybe—"

He laughed again. "Are you asking if she's had an operation?"

"I'm asking if you noticed," I clarified, looking over to wink at him.

"It was definitely different," he told me. "And… I think it's something I'd do again. I just can't explain it, though. I know I'm not bi." He shook his head, then sneezed. "It's the damn lake air trying to kill me, messing with my head. You heard what Sammy went on about. How you can't be liking both boys and girls—how it's always one or the other."

"Man, you don't seriously believe that shit, do you?"

"No! I don't know! Christ, it's complicated. Maybe even biphobic…"

"It *is* complicated," I reminded him.

"*But I've been gay all my life!*" he exclaimed. "Then this girl comes along and… and fucks it all up! What am I going to tell people? What do I tell all the little gays who look up to me, huh? 'Oh, my bad! I was just kidding!' Dreary's gonna get a kick out of that. Step-douche, too." Troy put his head in his hands. "How far until we reach Arminster?"

Immediately, the veil was lifted; the fog began to clear, and we could see the three skyscrapers in the distance that represented Downtown Arminster. It was a sight picture-perfect for Photofixer, and the sun seemed to agree. The weather app had stated it was going to be a warm day, and with the view ahead, I could believe it.

"Oh," Troy said, his head raised slightly to look at the buildings as we crossed the river. I'd remembered it being brown from all the earth washed in during rainstorms, but now it was blue and welcoming. "Oh, wow. That… is a city."

"And the rest of Arminster is spread out around it," I told him as he steadied his hands to take a picture for his followers. "Same average temperature as Santa Barbara, too. It's an easy city to navigate because it was built on a grid. Memorize the street names, and there's no way you can get lost—'specially with QuickSearch Maps. I mean, look at those skyscrapers!"

"I... don't have a fear of heights," he assured me, "but I do have a fear of falling."

"Hey, tell that to Gabby, not me," I reminded him with a gentle nudge.

"Yeah," Troy said. He gulped. "Yeah."

The Mountain Vista neighborhood was small but private. As Gabby had mentioned and reaffirmed when I'd dropped off Troy, the community had been built on a big hill in stark contrast to the rest of flat Oklahoma. The surrounding wall was at least ten feet tall, denying anybody a peek inside without the passcode—and not even the ivy was climbable.

I pulled up the Big Nasty to the front gate with the big MV in gold lettering, stopping about a foot away from it. Sharp rods protruded from the gate at a level with the SUV's grille guard, and a large sign stated there was a $250 minimum fine for any damages. That gate was just too high to get over and too low to get under. No wonder QuickSearch Maps didn't have a street-level view of Catherine's house; the QuickSearch driver hadn't been able to get in to take the pictures. Perhaps that was the appeal.

I typed the code into the available keypad, and slowly but surely, the gate came to life and retreated out of my way, revealing the winding road onward. I took notice of the NO SOLICITING and WARNING: THIS IS A CRIME WATCH COMMUNITY signs, then drove up at a little over five miles an hour, making sure not to bump into any cars or mailboxes as I approached the top of the hill and the homes above. Her house was two stories, made of brick, and at the very peak, facing inward. The backyard, I imagined, had a swell view of the city and neighbors below—probably to their annoyance, at that.

The address was 1123 Palmer Drive, as Gabby had said. I was going to text her to be sure when I saw I'd received a message from Troy wishing me good luck, followed by a smiling emoji wearing sunglasses. So I cleared my head, parked uphill, checked my hair in the rearview mirror, and then got out of the SUV. The sun warmed my head as I knocked on the front door.

After two minutes of waiting, I knocked again.

A small, slender woman with thick, straight, dark hair opened the door. I recognized her as Catherine's mother, and from her instant smile, I could tell she recognized me as well.

"Michael!" she announced, stepping closer and hugging me. "I remember you as a little boy on his bike. You're all grown up!"

"Thank you," I said, smiling. "How are you, Ms. Varsha? I see that you moved."

"Oh, we're good, we're good." She let go and looked from my right eye to the left and back again, still smiling. "I work from home with Adveston now."

"My mom's starting to work from home, too."

"I keep waiting on Mr. Thomas," she told me. "He's why we have this house. He goes missing for months, puts a check for a lot of money in the mail, and so we move from the apartment and into Mountain Vista." She sighed. "That stupid man. He writes twice a year, but that's it! I'll bet you he's started up another family."

"Sorry to hear that."

"That's all right." Ms. Varsha glanced around. "Are you in town? Your mother said you had moved, too, on Coffeefolder. How did you get into the neighborhood?"

I started sweating. "I, uh… Did Gabby not say I was visiting?"

"Gabby hasn't been here in a while."

"Oh, well, um, she said—I said I wanted to see Catherine, and so she gave me your address and passcode."

"Cat gave you the passcode?"

"No, Gabby."

Ms. Varsha looked at me skeptically, as if I were some kid up to no good. But then she shrugged, peered up inside the house, and studied me.

"OK," she said finally. "We don't get too many visitors anymore since Lizzy went off to college at Eastern Oklahoma, so it's only been us two for some time."

Ms. Varsha led me inside her home, and immediately, I saw stacks upon stacks of boxes, books, and odds and ends lining the left-side wall. Between ten and eleven o'clock from the entrance was a staircase leading up and around. Past the foyer was the living room with tall windows and a large TV above the fireplace. To the right was an open kitchen with granite countertops, followed by a bathroom, a dining room, and a home office, from what I could see. On the walls were various tapestries of circular design, and on the shelves were statues of elephants of all sizes. There were also vases of different shapes and colors, and within each, a green plant flourishing with life and taking over much of the surrounding area. The rugs were crimson, and the furniture a dark brown to match. It looked to be an organized mess, but I wasn't there to judge their preference in décor. I was there for a girl named Catherine.

Behind the staircase was a door, which Ms. Varsha opened and then held up a finger for me to wait.

"Caaaaat!" she called out in a singsong voice. She waited. "Cat, you have a visitor!" She waited some more, then looked at me. "I'm sure it's fine. Just be sure to knock first."

"Yes, ma'am," I said, then descended into the dark.

I could see a white light up ahead. It was faint but there, and it grew with each step, slowly illuminating the hall. I could vaguely see the bottom of the stairs, and soon, my feet.

There was a voice, too, singing soft and sweetly from someplace else. It was lovely, and it belonged to Catherine.

Now won't you listen honey while I say:
How could you tell me that you're going away?
Don't say that we must part.
Don't break your baby's heart.

I passed by what looked to be a room with a treadmill, washing machine, and dryer, followed by a bathroom on the opposite side of the hall. And then, through the open door directly ahead, I saw Catherine's room.

You know I loved you for these many years—
Loved you night and day.
Oh, honey, baby, can't you see my tears?
Listen while I say.

The walls were painted a dark red without decoration of any kind, and the carpet featured alternating red and salmon-colored zigzag stripes. The room was a rectangle, and on the shorter side opposite to where I stood were curtains as red as blood, presumably covering a window. There was little furniture in the room besides two floor lamps, a desk with a laptop, a gray mannequin, and a large mound of brown blankets on a mattress.

Catherine stood in the middle of the room, sauntering barefoot away from me. She had her mother's dark brown hair, cut an inch or two below the shoulders, as well as her mother's dark brown skin. She was as wondrous as I remembered her to be.

She continued singing, flowingly beautiful.

After you've gone and left me crying;
After you've gone, there's no denying

You'll feel blue, you'll feel sad,
You'll miss the bestest pal you've ever had.

There'll come a time, now don't forget it;
There'll come a time when you'll regret it.
Oh, babe! Think what you're doing.
You know my love for you will drive me to ruin

After you've gone,
After you've gone away.

She turned around, saw me, and stopped her singing. So we stared at each other.

Catherine was roughly my height—maybe taller by an inch. She met all the modern standards of beauty, though her eyebrows were unkempt, and her lips were noticeably chapped. She wore a teal tank top and gray athletic shorts. Her eyes were a bright brown and showed no signs of age, stress-related or otherwise. She looked well rested, as opposed to myself.

"Michael," she said, sounding surprised. "I had a dream about you the other night."

"Really?" I asked, trying to conceal my wonder.

"Not about you specifically," she elaborated, stepping closer, "but you were in it. Everyone from Hayes was there. Gabby had mentioned you were having a reunion party, but I didn't think you'd come to my house."

"Oh, sorry."

"No, you're fine," she clarified. "It's just shocking, is all." She looked around. "Well, this is my room."

"It's…"

"Empty?" She laughed to herself. Her smile was all sorts of lovely. "Yeah, with the clutter upstairs, I thought I'd keep my own space neat and tidy."

Catherine slowly strolled over to the many blankets and pillows and curled herself up in them. Then, extending her free hand, she patted the spot beside her.

"Aren't you already hot enough?" I joked, even though I could feel the sweat under my arms.

"That's how I like it! Nice and warm like a summer day. I *love* natural light. Normally, I have the curtains open, but I was testing the lighting for a video."

"A video?"

She pointed to an expensive-looking camera on a tripod in the corner.

"I sing these old songs people request and then upload the video. If people like it enough, they usually buy the audio. Not all of it's great, but I like the process."

"A singer," I observed. "But when I typed in your name, QuickSearch didn't bring up any results other than your Chipper and Coffeefolder."

"When you...?"

"To send out the reunion invitations."

"Gotcha." She smiled. "I don't use my real name for my music, so that's probably why you couldn't find me, which is good. There are some people I don't want seeing my stuff, you know?" Catherine then got up, walked to the desk, and pulled out a familiar book from one of the drawers. "Speaking of our work and online selves, you should totally sign my copy of *Beneath the Makeup*."

She handed me my novella, so I flipped through it. Corners of some of the pages were folded, and Catherine had highlighted a few passages. She'd also drawn a mustache on the minimalist clown on the front cover.

"How'd you find out about this?" I asked as I looked through it some more.

"Your mom posted the link on her Coffeefolder, and my mom saw it, so she told me about it. It's a good read, even if the hospital scenes aren't at all accurate. I would've posted about it on my Uprorrr, but your cover contains a pretty big trigger, so, you know, I decided against it."

I thought of Zach with the gun on his forehead.

"A trigger?"

"Yeah, the clown. Mountebank might not scare everyone, but he's still a clown, and clowns are always creepy, and that affects some people when they see it—brings up repressed memories. Like, some people don't like the mentioning of abuse or war or self-inflicting pain because it reminds them of awful things, and then they might have a panic attack. A trigger can be anything from a word or phrase or sight, or even a sound and smell. Taste, too. I suppose I could tag it, but even so, not everybody—"

There was a knock on the wall beside the door. We turned around to see Ms. Varsha with a plate of what appeared to be raw meat. As she got closer, though, I could see it was thick cut, peppered jerky.

"Sorry to interrupt," she interrupted, "but it's time for your snack, Cat."

"Awesome, thank you!" Catherine exclaimed as she eagerly took the plate. Ms. Varsha then left, allowing me to be the sole witness of this eighteen-year-old girl ripping and drooling over big, tough pieces of meat with her teeth. She held a slab in her hands like one would hold a corn on the cob, and I could've sworn she growled momentarily while tearing at her meal.

"Um," I started, not knowing how. "Catherine?"

"Call me Cat," she stated between bites. "I'm a domestic cat therian."

My heart pierced deeper into my chest as I watched her in disbelief.

"You're a… what?"

She sighed, put the plate down, and then started licking her fingers. I gripped tighter onto my book.

"I'm part of the felinekin community," she tried to explain. "The word 'Otherkin' is sort of an umbrella term for Otherkin and therians. Simply put, someone who is Otherkin believes that—on some level—they are not entirely human. For example,

I believe that in another life, I was a cat, and I was meant to be a cat, but for whatever reason, I ended up with the body of a human." She looked at me. I stared back. She sighed again. "I know. You think I'm making this up."

"Well…" I faltered. "Catherine—Cat—I mean… how could you not?"

"It's a struggle, OK?" She pushed one of the pillows aside with her foot. "I thought Gabby would have told you. Very few outsiders take us Otherkin seriously, and even when they do, there's still a lot of hate and ignorance. So I'm going to try to walk you through it how I did with Gabby and Christian: I know, right now, I am not physically a cat. I have the anatomy of a human. What I do have is a spiritual connection to domestic cats. I believe—and not all Otherkin are like this—but I believe I was reincarnated as a human and that I still retain some of the memories I had as a cat. Does that make any sense?"

"Uh…" I scratched my head. "On paper… sure. And maybe science fiction. Is this, like, clinical lycanthropy? Psychosomatic? I learned about that in psychology junior year."

"No, it's not that simple," she told me. "I do have a therapist I talk to, and I do take medication for my mood disorder, but this isn't some mental illness or connected to serotonin levels or my upbringing or…" She trailed off. "It's different for each Otherkin member, and the community itself is extremely diverse, which makes it harder to say anything concrete. You won't find a single, correct definition of what we are. My beliefs are my own. They're spiritual and not physical, which is why I like to say that I act like a cat who has been raised by humans for eighteen years, rather than outright stating, 'Oh, I'm a cat.' Species identity is the key here, and not necessarily species dysphoria à la gender dysphoria."

"But the pillows and blankets," I pointed out, "and the… the jerky…"

"Like I said, I'm not physically a cat. That kind of operation doesn't exist as of now, which makes me sad, but doing things that remind me of what it felt like to be a cat makes it easier for me to—"

"I'm sorry," I said, "but by 'operation,' you don't mean—if it was possible, which it isn't—you would change your body to be more… catlike?"

"I would do that in a heartbeat, yes."

I laughed. I didn't mean to, but it was sudden, and when she glared at me, I only laughed some more.

"Catherine," I began, wiping a tear from my eye, then corrected myself. "Cat. You can't be serious right now. You couldn't possibly be—"

"Well, I am," she told me, standing up. "I get enough ridicule elsewhere, so I would appreciate it if you didn't make my own home—my last safe place—a harmful and counterproductive environment."

"But what you're claiming is impossible!" I told her, standing up as well and leaving my book on her bed of sorts. "You're not… you're not *trapped* in a human's body. *That's ridiculous!* I mean, I like cats just as much as the next person, but you're—"

"Michael," Ms. Varsha said from the doorway, "I think it's time for you to go."

I looked to Catherine for relief, but her face was stern and a bit repulsed—I assumed at my behavior. I merely shook my head and went to Ms. Varsha to follow.

"I must be dreaming," I whispered to myself.

"No, you're just a dick," Catherine stated from her room. I considered this, took a deep breath, and then walked behind Ms. Varsha up the stairs and out the front door.

The singing picked up where Catherine had left off.

Don't you remember how you used to say,
You'd always love me in the same old way?
And now it's very strange
That you should ever change…

"Gabby didn't tell you?" Ms. Varsha asked once we were outside on the porch. The pale-blue sky had gotten cloudy, and the trees leaned slightly with the wind. She held a white-and-gold Lusso Costo handbag close to her side, as if someone were out to steal it.

"Tell me what?!" I countered. "That Catherine—?!"

"Good-bye, Michael," she said simply, then shut the door in my face, followed by a *click* of the lock.

"Fucking hell," I muttered, imagining what Troy would say, then kicked at the ground with the toe of my shoe. This wasn't how I'd expected my reunion with Catherine to be. This wasn't how I'd expected *her* to be. She was insane, and this was crazy. *Catherine* was crazy. Either that, or a good actor to go along with her singing.

I got in the Big Nasty and called Troy from my phone. I was beyond furious.

"Yo, Mom, what's up?" he asked after the third ring.

"She thinks she's a cat," I said.

"What?"

"Look, where are you? I'm ready to go back to the cabin."

"Oh, well, we're still downtown. This place has a *huge* arts district! It's awesome! I'll have to talk to Uncle Julian about Arminster. But if you're heading back to the lake—" Someone said something on the other end. "Uh, Gabby says she can take me back later today, if that's easier, so she can keep showing me around."

"Fine, whatever," I said, then hung up.

I started up the Big Nasty and headed down the twisting slope to the gate below. While it opened, I wondered how much force it would take to knock it down. "Take It Back" by Liza Anne played on the radio as I drove away from Mountain Vista, and that was the end of that.

◆━━━━◆━◆━━━◆

"Hold on," Troy said as I finished recounting my twenty minutes with Catherine and her mother to him. We were outside, and Gabby was there with us, next to her hybrid electric, four-door liftback. "Did Catherine say she was a cat or a cat-person? Like, my sisters both love swimming and collecting dolphin plushies or whatever, but that doesn't mean—"

"Cat is a cat in a human's body," Gabby stated, annoyed with us. "How is that so hard to understand?"

"Uh, it's very hard to understand," Troy answered for us. "The whole concept is—"

"Look, are you both cisgender?" she asked. We nodded. "Well, as a trans girl, it's sort of like that feeling of discomfort—knowing you were born as something you aren't."

"Whoa, whoa, whoa, whoa," Troy said. "What Catherine—or Cat?—means is completely different from the experiences of a trans person, and you should know that! If someone's transgender, they're at the very least talking about keeping most of their body parts and replacing or removing the ones that make them feel uncomfortable because of their identity. *But another species entirely?* That's… delusional! Gender is a social concept we made up, and gender dysphoria is medically recognized. You can get *oppressed* for that. But pretending you're an animal, you'll just be bullied. Maybe even get a reality show."

"I don't think you have a right to talk about trans experiences," Gabby countered. I could see she was suppressing her anger. "You're not exactly in a position to know."

"You're right, but I do have a trans friend in Rochester, Alabama, and extremists burned their house down last summer. My house would be a target, too, if step-shit didn't spread his lies about how he's getting me therapy and psychoanalysts and a bunch of other crap to 'correct' my—"

"Don't insurance companies have to cover transitioning costs for trans people?" I asked her. "Like, the medicine and treatment?"

"Some jobs have it in their plan," Gabby said, "which is wonderful, but it's not an every-healthcare kind of deal, and it still doesn't remove the stigma. Just because gay people can marry in all fifty states doesn't mean everyone's willing to accept it, even years after the decision was made. With Cat and the Otherkin, outsiders see it as some form of mental insanity or a role-playing game gone a little too far. How is believing that non-humans can manifest as humans any different than concluding that humans have been to the afterlife and back, that a deity once walked the earth in mortal form, or that the spirits of our ancestors exist around us? Forty percent of Americans believe houses can be haunted. How is it that only humans can reincarnate, huh? They're all just different claims. Why is this one so hard to wrap your head around?"

"It's impossible," Troy told her. "All of that is. The LGBTQIA community can be backed by biology, physiology, and psychology. You can't explain thinking you're a cat."

"Unless it's a coping mechanism," I added.

"And it's not," Gabby declared. "Cat is a felinekin. She's a domestic cat in spirit and soul. It's not something she chose because she was bored and homeschooled; it's who she is, and that's all there is to it."

"Does she wear fake tails?" Troy asked me. "Does she paint whiskers on her face and wear cat-ear headbands?"

"So what if she does?!" Gabby told him. "If it makes her feel more comfortable in her skin, why the fuck shouldn't she be allowed to eat food or wear accessories that are closer to the diet and lifestyle she prefers?"

"Yeah, OK," he allowed. "But does she shit in a litter box?"

"CAT KNOWS SHE IS NOT A DOMESTIC CAT!" Gabby screamed at Troy. His eyes widened. "SHE HAS AN IDENTITY-BASED BELIEF WHICH JUST SO HAPPENS TO INCLUDE NON-HUMAN ENTITIES." She was fuming. "Cat knows she is a human with a human life. While she would prefer to be a cat as she once was, she acknowledges there are many, many benefits to being human—but there is no such thing as human privilege. Only people mocking the community will say dumb shit like that. Some Otherkin wish they could transition into their original species, and some do not. It's a complex group of individuals, and this has been going on publicly since at least the nineties. They don't feel like they need to be represented in the LGBTQIAP spectrum, and they assert this repeatedly. If they identify as LGBTQIAP, it's because they're bi or trans or asexual and the like *in addition to* their kinship, *not* because of it. This isn't escapism-gone-wrong, either. It's a reality for Cat and a lot of other people."

"That sounds like it came straight from Uprorrr," Troy noted.

"A lot of Otherkin are on Uprorrr because that site is supposed to be a safe place for progressive thinkers."

"Meaning not cis, heterosexual, middle-class, white male Republicans who believe angels exist," I said.

She frowned. "That kind of mindset is what gives Uprorrr a bad name."

"That and the extremists," Troy stated. "Fanaticism goes both ways. There are a lot of crazy Social Justice Warriors and alt-right conservatives on the Internet." He laughed. "The perks of being a Democrat born in Alabama—you get to hear and appreciate the opinions of all parties."

"Well, I believe an opinion is valid so long as it doesn't discriminate or spread hate," Gabby told us, feeling for the cross she wore around her neck. "Cat's identity and spiritual belief system are true to her. That said, they don't define her. She does schoolwork, she has friends, she sells her music online, and she drives to Big-Box to get groceries. *She isn't a freak.* She's a cat therian."

"Do a lot of Otherkin take antidepressants?" I asked her. "Catherine mentioned a mood disorder."

"I can't really speak for them, but many of the Otherkin I've talked to online have said that they do take medicine."

"Figures," Troy muttered.

"Well, it makes sense," she went on, scowling at him. "There's something wrong with them—they're humans who should be animals. I don't blame them. I'd need drugs and a doctor, too, if I were going through that sort of realization."

"What other types of therians are there?" I continued.

"Oh, I don't know. Deer, cats, dogs, swans… a shark, I heard."

"Do the dogs and cats dislike each other?"

"Instinctually, maybe, but like I said, they're cognizant that they're human, and they can rationalize what's acceptable in our society. And before you suggest it, this isn't a group of twelve-year-olds who've read a book series or watched a show about wolves or their favorite animal and are just pretending to be those things. That's role-playing. These aren't the grownups at comic conventions dressed in fur suits. That's cosplaying. Do Otherkin dress up on occasion? Absolutely, especially if it makes them feel more comfortable and closer to their former selves, like I said. But for the Otherkin community, this is real and serious." Gabby turned to me. "So if you're going to make fun of Cat and secretly think she belongs at St. Luke's, forget it. Stay here at your cabin. She's been through enough."

"What does her mom think of all this?" I asked.

"I think she's just glad to have her daughter alive and happy."

"And Bryce?"

Gabby's eyes widened, and she quickly looked around.

"He, um," she started. "He didn't like it. They were dating when she was awakened. They had a big fight, and when people found out, things got dramatic. They nailed rats to wooden boards and would leave them on her doorstep in the mornings. She got depressed then, and her mom pulled her out of New Baines. It was…" Gabby looked away. "Really sad. I was very disappointed at my school then. Of course, I wasn't treated any better, but I transitioned in middle school, so they had time to get used to me. I kept the root of my name because I didn't feel a need to dissociate myself with the gender binary at that age. Still, it's hard."

"I don't think I like Oklahoma anymore," Troy said, shuddering. "I mean… God, that's awful. To both of you. I still don't get the whole cat-thing, but even so—"

"In Oklahoma's defense, Arminster is much more liberal," I explained. "When you look at the results from elections, Oklahoma is red, but that tiny blue dot in the northeast part of the state is always Arminster. But New Baines, I can see as being… traditional and old-fashioned."

"Conformist," Gabby added. "Orthodox. But anyway, I should be heading back—"

"Wait," I said, glancing first at Troy, then back to Gabby. I was tempted to bring up Bryce again—to get answers about Zach and Morgan and the night before—but I was thinking more for myself. "Our fifth-grade class. Did you all ever… talk about me, over the years? Or miss me? Do you remember 'Obie' from third grade?"

"Huh?" Gabby asked.

"That short story you helped me write? The family got the kid a dog named Obie, and the dad accidentally ran it over, so they got a doppelgänger of the dog, but that dog was, like, evil and would kill the bullies and—" I stopped myself. "It died in the fire at the end?"

She smiled out of pity. "Sorry, I don't. But, um, you were mentioned, sure, in, like, stories from when we were in elementary school. And yeah, sometimes we wondered what you were up to, but…" She sighed. "Well, you know. It was difficult with—"

Her phone vibrated from her pocket. She took it out, shook her head, and then backed away slowly, swiping her finger across the screen and putting the phone up to her head without breaking eye contact.

"Hello?" she asked. Her eyes widened. "Bryce! Oh, um, what's up?" Silence. "No, I don't know what *Michael and his friend are up to.*" Troy and I looked at each other. "Who saw us downtown? No, I was… yes, alone."

Gabby turned away from us—still listening to Bryce—and walked to her car. She then went inside, started up the engine, and drove off.

"What the dick was that about?" Troy asked me.

"I'm… not sure," I told him, which was the truth. "I'm not sure what's been going on recently."

"Recently?" Troy echoed, laughing. "More like since you first left this place. Did Cat act catlike then?"

"I don't think so," I said. "I mean, I—" I felt close to crying. "God, I am so… *emotionally wrecked*. I don't—"

"Wait, did you say, 'wrecked' or 'erect' just then? 'Cause I kinda like both." He laughed, I didn't. "Well, anyway, I'll see what I can learn from Gabby. She's taking me to this famous museum and gardens in Arminster tomorrow at one o'clock… which I need a ride to, by the way."

"Yeah, OK," I said. "But, um, with Cat…"

"I dunno, Mom. I've never heard any of that stuff before. I'd just play along—respectfully, of course. That's the courteous thing to do, I guess, even though it all sounds bat-shit crazy." He paused. "Or should I say, *cat-shit crazy!*"

He was proud of his joke, but I was confused and worried. I didn't know what was going on. I didn't know anything.

Troy and I spent the rest of the evening alone at the lake house eating leftover chips and salsa with our taquitos. Troy showed me how he liked to mix ketchup and ranch together—which he called "kranch"—and dip his taquitos in it, which I thought was disgusting. He then talked about exploring downtown with Gabby, including visits to a clay sculpture painting studio and the Crossed Flintlocks coffeehouse, which had people playing music out front and selling homemade soap and pottery. I, in turn, talked about the Mountain Vista neighborhood and what Catherine's house and bedroom looked like.

Sometime after, Troy did his own thing in the kitchen while I updated my website on my laptop in our shared room. I was mulling over whether I should delete a pretty bad piece of prose I'd come up with on traveling when my phone buzzed beside me. I checked the text, and it was from Gabby's number.

"KittyCath228," it read.

I didn't know what she meant, so I typed it into QuickSearch, and lo and behold, I found kittycath228.uprorrr.com, Catherine's blog from seventh to tenth grade. After reading a couple of posts, I realized this was more along the lines of Catherine's diary, preserved via the wonders of the Internet.

The posts started out simple enough, with drama about two of her best friends and then Catherine missing her father. Her blog was updated rarely back then—maybe once a month. There were posts about her mom's male coworkers bringing Catherine home from school and then having long talks with her mom upstairs, and on one occasion, eating dinner with the family. In an entry from eighth grade, she talked about how her friend Nate smoked an e-cig while she and her friends ate chicken sandwiches at Happy Cow, and another where she helped her friend Willow buy condoms, even though neither girl knew what they were doing.

Near the end of eighth grade, Willow got pregnant and moved to Madison to be closer to family. Catherine soon started seeing a counselor for a mood disorder. One day, she saw her dad in an online advertisement for a superhero movie called *Live to Rise*. She looked him up, emailed him, and then found out he was living in Hollywood. He had a new wife and a toddler. He wanted to help and send her money, but Catherine said she wanted nothing to do with him. He sent a check for $300,000 the next week. She didn't tell her mom why.

In ninth grade, her mom walked in on her watching lesbian porn, hugged Catherine, and then said she loved her no matter what. Catherine was searching for a reason why she wasn't yet sexually attracted to boys, and as it turned out, she wasn't too interested in girls, either.

Catherine started going to this place at night in Arminster where LGBT+ kids could hang out and drink free coffee. She went with a friend named Gabby, but the scene wasn't for Catherine. ("They have different problems than I do, and I feel like I'm intruding by being there.") At one point, a fight broke out, and the cops came. Catherine could barely be seen running in the corner of a picture the newspaper had printed, and when her boyfriend found out, he was furious. He asked if she was gay. She said she wasn't anything. That only made him angrier. This was all in a construction yard.

Catherine was a cat for Halloween. She wrote that even if she dressed as a cat every year, she still liked it, and it made her feel just a little better about herself.

In February of her ninth-grade year, Catherine wrote that she felt she wasn't attracted to humans. "Not bestiality," she explained, "but I'm just not straight or gay or bi. I don't know what I am. It's killing me, not knowing."

Her doctor gave her new medication, and for the most part, the spring went by smoothly. At the same time, Catherine was discovering the Otherkin, a group of people with whom she could identify. She was skeptical of people claiming they were once animals in a former life, however, so she largely ignored it.

During the summer, she went to parties with her boyfriend and volunteered at the local animal shelter. She liked helping cats the most. "They get me," she wrote.

She put that all behind her during sophomore year, as she wanted to try to fit in with the other kids in her grade. It worked, for the most part: she danced and drank and had a good time, but the alcohol messed with her medication, so she started lashing out and stopped doing her homework. She didn't tell her boyfriend the personal bits of her life anymore. Her writing stopped.

When she returned to blogging the next year, she revealed she had planned to kill herself with pills she'd gotten from a friend; Catherine felt she wasn't doing anyone any good, let alone herself. Her mom had found the drugs and took her to stay at St. Luke's to recuperate. A nurse brought her a copy of Ernest Hemingway's *The Old Man and the Sea* one day, and as Catherine read about the main character Santiago dreaming about lions on the beach in Africa, she had a revelation—her Awakening.

In the hospital, Catherine felt her connection with her past self as a domestic cat in India. It was gradual, but it overtook her completely. She remembered being a little kid and staring up at her parents and thinking they were strange, foreign, and hideous. She hated the way she looked growing up, even if all the boys loved her. She didn't feel right as a human. For the longest time, she thought it was related to her sexuality or her identity as a girl. It wasn't.

"How does one come out as trans-species?" she asked to no response.

She concluded she was a cat in a girl's body. Later, with the Otherkin community's help on Uprorrr, she confirmed this.

"I want to be an advocate for teens who are just as confused," she wrote. "I now have a purpose in life, and I know what I want to do with it. The fact is that people who identify as Otherkin all share a common need to allow our desires the expression we deserve while at the same time finding the balance that permits us to function as healthy humans. We should not attempt to repress our spirituality, but rather, we must embrace the memories, patterns, feelings, and sensations that make us who we are. My name was Catherine, but as of today, I am Cat."

She came back to school in late April, finished up the year with better grades, and then waited as her mother finally found a new house for them in South Arminster. Her mother was helpful, but Cat still had to tell her friends.

"My mother, sister, and I had a long talk," she stated. "They are both supportive of me and will love me as I rediscover myself. We move next week on June second.

Mom took me to see the place, and it's truly a palace. I haven't told anyone yet, about anything. Not even my boyfriend. It will come as a shock, but I'm hoping it will go well with him and my friends. I'm scared, though, and I've only been this scared once before. But that's okay. This is only the beginning."

That was the last entry.

I felt awful. This felinekin concept was real to her, and all I'd done was make fun of her for it. It wasn't a tangible belief, but then again, such was faith—acceptance without needed proof.

I thanked Gabby through text, closed my laptop, and then told Troy I was going to bed early that night. I had a lot to think about, and an apology was due; I needed to take it all back. So I went to the bathroom, brushed my teeth, washed my face, put on some pajama pants and a t-shirt, and then lay there on the bottom bunk, waiting. But sleep came much later than I had anticipated, leaving me to my thoughts and deepest regrets.

Ian awoke in a sweat. The left side of his head throbbed with needle pushes of pain, and he struggled to think clearly. He would be celebrating his twenty-third birthday in a week—he remembered that. It was a Monday, which he had read on the Internet is the most popular day to commit suicide, call in sick, and surf the web in the Netherlands, but that wasn't relevant.

Another frigid morning in upstate New York, and Ian's small apartment was freezing. He quickly slipped on a shirt and turned up the heat. He was living with Makenna Williams, a part-time hairstylist and part-time girlfriend with serene sky-blue eyes. She was the first woman in years to find interest in him despite his quirky behavior, and he greatly appreciated her company. That's why he had moved to New York in the first place—to start a new life.

He rubbed his hands across the stubble covering his cheeks as he checked the time. Starving, he made himself a bowl of cereal, sat down on the couch with it, turned on the TV, and then clicked through the channels, though he found nothing remotely interesting. Anything but the news. Too depressing. Too real.

Ten years had passed since the bisexual bus had gone missing.

Ian didn't know what to make of it. He got so desperate, he started seeing therapists, wondering if even they could unravel what was becoming of him. He used to tell himself that his favorite part of life was that not even he knew what was to come next.

How ironic… my own words taunting me.

One of the problems was that Ian couldn't distinguish between the real and the unreal; judging reality from nightmares grew difficult for him. He knew the third bus had gone missing—that much was fact. He also knew the police had found it a couple of weeks later, but with no one inside. *Karina* wasn't inside. She was missing. She had also left him a voicemail, which had vanished like disappearing ink. At least, he *thought* she had.

These were the things Ian told his therapists, but so many gave up on him that he started referring to them as "stupid shrinks." They would tell him the mind will latch onto anything to explain itself, even a story completely unrelated. One therapist got so frustrated with Ian that the man had yelled at him, "You're wasting your life by hanging on to fragmented memories of an *eighth-grade field trip*, for crying out loud! So many years of denial, and you aren't even responsible! Yet you still think she's out there— somewhere! But that's where you're wrong, Ian, and you just can't accept the simplest truth hidden behind your guilt-ridden hallucinations. KARINA IS DEAD! WAKE UP AND SMELL THE DAMN COFFEE!"

A more forgiving, sympathetic psychiatrist had concluded he was in a state of what she referred to as "paranoid delusion."

"We all have normal schedules we rely on, Mr. Gallagher," the psychiatrist said while Ian stared out the window. "When something abnormal occurs that we weren't expecting, several aspects of life may change without warning. Suddenly, with little room for flexibility, the anxiety builds up, and your mind doesn't know what to do or think. This is the irregularity, and what often follows is a living nightmare."

Ian had to agree with this; his whole life had taken a turn for the worse after he'd lost Karina. He started suffering from chronic headaches, paranoia, and depression. *Lamentations.* That Old Testament book was like a comedy when compared to his miserable life. He had even developed a phobia of telephones, fearing if he answered one, he would hear the robotic voice of Karina whispering to him, "I'm bleeding, Ian." That voice, *her* voice, was the one keeping him up at night—the whispers of an angel followed by Satan's wicked laughter.

Even years later, when people trying to help him move on brought up dating, Ian frowned. Having more than a friendship with another girl didn't seem possible.

"There's no one out there for me," he would repeat to himself as if it were a chant. "There's no one out there for me. I'm not the touchy-feely type. I'm not the kind of person to keep a relationship."

Libby, a smart and pretty girl he often ran across in the community college coffee shop, reached out and touched his hand one afternoon.

"Someone got hurt, and you feel bad about it," she'd said. "You're blaming yourself, but you shouldn't. Your eyes are kind. Whatever it is, it couldn't be that bad."

That bad. That bad. If only she knew.

He couldn't remember exactly what had happened next. Only that he'd dropped his coffee and woken up hours later in his apartment, Libby's caring words replaced by the Woodpecker's constant beating away at his mind, his memory, and his loosening grip on his sanity.

Ian was almost finished with his bowl when he heard the droning ring of the only phone in the apartment. Ian had desperately tried to convince Makenna not to buy it, but she'd persisted.

"You don't even have to answer it if you don't want to," she had assured him, vaguely understanding his telephobia. "Just listen for the voicemail in case I need to reach you from the salon, OK, baby?" When she said it like that, Ian couldn't argue with Makenna, so he caved in—so long as the phone was out of sight.

Assuming it was her, Ian let it go to voicemail. The answering machine picked up on the eighth ring, and Ian hit the MUTE button on the remote so he could hear the message.

"Staying late again?" he asked in the phone's direction. "Why do so many people get haircuts in March?" Now that he thought about it, he was also in need of a good trim and shave.

His trail of thought was interrupted by the voice the answering machine projected into the living room: "E?! Are you there?!"

It wasn't Makenna's voice, but another woman's. She sounded eerily familiar.

"Ian, answer the phone! I'm so scared! E, where are you?!"

Karina Tamerlane.

Ian knocked over the coffee table, causing a glass of water to shatter as he rushed to the phone. The voice from the answering machine was undeniably Karina's, yet it was strangely distorted.

"—but we were different! And I didn't—"

"Karina!" he panted. "Karina, I'm here!"

"Oh my God, it's been *ten years!*" She sounded panicked. "Why didn't you try to save me?!"

"What? *Where are you?!*" This was the question he had wanted to ask her for as long as he could remember. Now, a decade later, he would finally get his answer.

"*I don't know!*" she sobbed, and Ian almost felt bad for asking. "It's kind of… um…" He could sense she was trying to hold back tears.

For a few moments, there was silence. Ian worried he had lost the connection. "Karina? You still there?!"

"I'm sorry, E—Ian," she quickly corrected herself. "This isn't going to work. I'm so sorry, I just… I just know it won't. Don't bother looking for me."

"No! Karina, wait—"

"You're making this harder than it should be!" she sobbed. "There's nothing out here, dammit! Nothing but fish, and they were luckier than us… they… oh, God!"

The sound Ian heard next was so loud, he dropped the phone and fell back, grasping his ear in pain. It lasted only a second, but the scream a butterfly would make if someone held both of its wings and ripped them off simultaneously was enough to make anyone cry out in anguish.

At least now he knew she was alive. *Karina Tamerlane was alive!* He wasn't crazy. The voicemail was real, the phone call was real, but she wanted him to stay away. Yet he had just spoken to the dead woman he had loved for so many years; he wasn't about to stop loving her now. Ian *had* to find her—and he had a hunch where to start.

Troy and I were out the door by 11:30 the next morning. I felt like I needed to buy Cat a gift to present along with my apology, so we swung by Mr. Swanky's on the way out of town, just in case the convenience store was that. Curiously, we found police cars had blocked the entrance in front of the establishment, denying access within. So we left for Arminster instead.

There was a Big-Box four miles from the Protzig Art and Gardens where Troy was meeting Gabby, so we decided to stop there to search for my offering to Cat and some pajama pants for Troy, as he'd forgotten to pack a pair.

As we parked, I shuddered at the ridiculously large building in front of us, a sea of cars between. The inside of the supermarket was as unsettling as the one in Dreary, with tall aisles, metal walls, scuffed tile, and an awful air surrounding us. The intercom beeped three times, followed by a typical Big-Box prerecorded message: "Tires, groceries, credit card data—we've got it all. Big-Box: American proud."

"Oh, the joys of consumerism," Troy said. "Every product looks the same. The people, too. They're all exhausted and smelly. But anyway, I'll go look for the pajamas, you find a gift, and we'll meet up at the Big Nasty in ten, all right?"

I nodded, and so we split up.

Buying Cat a card, funny or not, seemed cheap and impersonal, so I decided against it. Instead, I went to the candy section, but the entire stock was Easter-related. So I picked out a chocolate bunny, figuring that since some cats kill rabbits, maybe Cat would appreciate the gesture.

As I turned the corner, I noticed a little girl with red curls talking to an older woman with the same color hair. The kid was energetic and couldn't have been older than thirteen, whereas the mom looked exhausted and in her late forties. They were arguing about something the girl wanted to buy.

"I don't care what all your friends have!" the woman told the girl with a slight country accent. She wore a pair of pink monogrammed sweatpants and a black kind of sweater-top. "Their mommas have the money to spend! George has a nice job and all, but I'm out of work—"

"But you said you wooooouuld," the girl whined.

"Maisy Diana Bradford, you cut that horseshit attitude right this second!" the mom commanded, then shook her head. "I mean, Maisy Diana… ah, forget it."

"Excuse me," I said, walking over to where they were standing. I looked at the girl. "Sorry to interrupt, but does your father live in Alabama?"

"My dad lives here," Maisy answered matter-of-factly. I frowned.

"Her biological father is in Dreary," the mom answered. "Why?"

"Aiden Bradford lives across the street from me," I explained. "Are you Charlene?"

She hesitated. "I am."

"Well, he misses his kids," I told her. "And he said to tell you he's sorry. Oh, and, uh, he says he kept the trampoline, whatever that means."

Charlene instantly blushed and covered her mouth with the hand that wasn't holding on to the shopping cart. It looked like she was smiling.

"He did, did he?" she said, then laughed a little. She turned to Maisy. "In that case, maybe we ought to go out and visit your daddy this summer."

"I guess," Maisy said with a shrug.

"Thank you," Charlene told me, and I hoped she was being sincere. Mr. Bradford needed that interaction with his daughter. Why hadn't they sensed that? It was a miracle I'd found them—for his sake, anyway. That dog of his could only do so much.

Troy wasn't at the front of the store when I got there, so I went ahead to checkout lane number three without him. There was only one other guy before me, and when he turned his head to flirt with the cashier, he looked familiar to me—almost gentlemanly in a supernatural sort of way. I didn't recognize his face, though, which was clean-shaven with neatly cut black hair on top. But I ignored it, and after he left with a case of Gletscher in each hand, I pushed the chocolate Easter bunny closer to the cashier.

"Thanks for shopping at Big-Box," she said with emotionless eyes and an artificial smile. I knew the script. "We're American big—"

"—and American proud. Did you find everything you're looking for?" I finished with her. She laughed. "I worked at a Big-Box in Alabama for a while."

"So you must know how much fun I'm having," she joked, ringing up the bunny.

The girl was dark-skinned and young—maybe a little older than me—but when she bent down to spit her gum into the trash can, I noticed she had a faint, diagonal scar across her left cheek. She caught me staring. "Bake sale accident."

"Oh," I said, averting my eyes to her name tag. "Sorry, Meg."

"You and everyone else who chooses number three," she countered. "That'll be five twenty-nine."

I gave her six dollars. "You can keep the change."

"Thanks," she said, covering her scar with her dark hair. "Enjoy your chocolate."

With my gift and Troy's pajamas, we drove to the museum, and after that, I went back to Mountain Vista and typed in the code. Ms. Varsha was collecting the mail as I pulled up to her house in the hills.

"Another Michael," she said as I got out of the SUV. She crossed her arms against her chest. "You came back. Why did you?"

"To apologize," I told her. "I was wrong, and I'm really sorry." I showed her the chocolate bunny. "I brought this for Cat as a way of saying—"

Ms. Varsha snatched it away from me.

"Cat is allergic," she informed me, then looked at it and raised an eyebrow. "What made you change your mind?"

I gulped.

"Um, research," I answered, "about therians and the Otherkin community."

Ms. Varsha sighed. "I understand why you don't understand. It seems weird, at first. But Cat discovered what she believes she is, and if she's happy, I will support her. If you truly are sorry, then you can go speak with her." She pointed a stern finger at me. "But if you mock her again, Michael, I won't allow you back into my home. We clear?"

"Crystal."

She stepped aside, and as I passed through the papier-mâché elephant wall hangings and walked into the foyer, I realized how much of a sanctuary this gated community must have felt to Cat after coming out as a felinekin to her classmates and receiving such backlash. With her sister in college, and her mother as the only person she saw every day, it was no wonder her online group was so important to her; they were all she had. Her home was a place of vulnerability, and more so than most.

I opened the door to the basement slowly. I could hear Cat singing the same song as before while I descended the staircase.

Perhaps some other sweetie's won your heart—
Tempted you away.
But let me warn you, though we're miles apart,
You'll regret someday.

She was sitting on a stool in the middle of her room, sheet music with red marks scattered beneath her. Once again, she was facing away from me.

After you've gone and left me crying;
After you've gone, there's no denying
You'll feel blue, you'll feel sad,
You'll miss the bestest pal you've ever had—

I knocked twice.

She turned around, saw me, and stopped her singing. So we stared at each other.

"Michael," she said, a bit surprised. "I had a dream about you the other night."

"Really?" I asked, trying to conceal my wonder.

"Not about you, specifically," she elaborated, getting up and stepping closer, "but you were in it. Everyone from Hayes was there. We were in a well-lit room, and you were all wearing these hooded robes, and you guys were chanting something in Hebrew, and I don't even speak Hebrew. I just sort of… knew. Anyway, the room gets dark, and one of you in the middle presents me a birthday cake. Then that same person sticks out their hand, and with a bony finger, they extinguish one of the five candles." She paused. "And then I woke up."

"That's, uh… morbid," I noted.

She shrugged. "Gabby mentioned she spoke with you. Is that why you're here?"

"I'm sorry for the way I reacted," I explained. "That wasn't cool of me."

"No, but it was the standard response." She got up from the stool. "Sometimes I think I'm insane, but I have to remind myself I'm not, you know? It's personal to me, which is why I got so mad at you yesterday. Sure, I'd expect that type of reaction from other people, but… I don't know. Not from you. Not from my best friend those seven years ago."

"Well." I plopped myself on her mattress and pulled my knees to my chest. "I feel awful about it."

"Good," she said, smiling some. "It's an important part of me, but it's not everything. I sing, I exercise, I like to watch old shows from when we were kids… I'm proud of once being a cat, don't get me wrong—I wouldn't try to hide it—but it doesn't define who I am. It might come up now and again, but yeah. At the same time, people shouldn't discourage others from promoting those parts that make them who they are, whether it's being a Buddhist, or black, or a schoolteacher, or gay. Or a gay, black Buddhist who teaches at New Baines. For me, it's my animal spirit. *Not* my spirit animal. That's cultural appropriation."

"OK," I said. "That makes sense."

Cat laughed. "Now sign my book!"

She reached over to her desk and tossed me her copy of *Beneath the Makeup*. I then pretended to sign my name with my finger, so she threw a pen at my head. I took it, smiling, and then personalized it for her: *Cat — Thanks for being a friend after all these years. Michael G. Jackson.*

She sauntered over and took the space next to me. She wore a tank top and athletic shorts once again. She picked at her nails, and as she did so, I noticed she had a circular scar the size of a pinto bean in the middle of both her hands. Then I realized, from the way she'd positioned herself, it might seem as if I were staring down her top. So I did, involuntarily, then looked away.

Cat fell back against the mattress. "Tell me a story."

"This one?" I asked, holding up the book.

"Sure," she said. "There are some things in there I'd like to talk about."

"The clown raped her," Cat noted with a frown as I finished reading. "Another trigger. That's messed up."

"It is."

"But you wrote it so abruptly," she told me. "Like it's a fact of life or something."

"Did you want me to go into detail?" I asked, laughing.

She shook her head. "Tell me this: have you ever been raped?"

"God, no!"

"So why would you write about something so sensitive like that and then just gloss over it? You set it up nicely enough: an email from Dr. Ivan Galloway to the investigator of Madison's AMBER Alert, saying he's attaching Madison's case notes in hopes it'll help in some way—even though, if this were real, Dr. Galloway would have his license revoked for the distribution of confidential information. Anyway, flashback a month before: Madison is complaining about her stepmom to Dr. Galloway, then they talk about her punching the clown at school, then Madison's strange dream, then the carnival, and it all leads up to Madison meeting that creep of a clown Mountebank and following him into the storage room for her prize." Cat sighed. "And another thing! The mental hospital. You portrayed it as an insane asylum, so I'm assuming you've never been in one of those, either. Let me tell you from experience: *they do good in there.* No chains and psycho nurses out to get you. I get that it's fiction, but the only true paragraphs are the final three."

Confused at her unforeseen criticism, I flipped to the ending. Madison was talking to Dr. Galloway after stating Mountebank had raped her during the tenth annual Canopy Creek Carnival.

No, I didn't tell my parents. They were concerned when I got home late, but that was it. I mean, what would they think? Would they be mad at me? I was fifteen, for Christ's sake! So when I saw that other clown at the school fair a few weeks ago, I just... I could've sworn I saw Mountebank. But it was some random guy instead. And that's what frightens me the most.

What if Mountebank is out there, waiting for me, somewhere? I'm... I'm so terrified of crowds and baseball games—I don't even go to the mall! He could be anyone. Anywhere. I don't know what the hell was beneath the makeup, like going to a costume party the night of Halloween. That scares me, Dr. Galloway. And I'm not sure what to do at this point. What if he's my principal? Or my band teacher, or my bus driver?

What if he's you?

I looked over to Cat, but she was looking away. Then she got up, stretched, and went over to the door.

"You wrote that part well," she said. "True to life. Now come on. Let's watch some TV."

"But—"

"Please," Cat asked of me. So I followed her out of the room and up the stairs.

Cat mentioned her mom spent most weekday afternoons managing client requests in her home office, so we had the living room and kitchen to ourselves. Like Cat's room, the couches all had too many pillows of different designs and textures, as well as a blanket or two. The TV was massive—a bit excessive, though, given the rest of the house, not out of place.

She gestured to the couches for me to sit. I picked the one in the middle so I would have a nice view of whatever we were going to watch, making sure there was enough room for Cat to sit on either side of me. Meanwhile, she worked in the kitchen, pouring what looked like milk into a saucepan, followed by syrup and other ingredients.

After a few minutes, Cat brought two yellow mugs to the couches and set them both on a couple of coasters on the coffee table in front of me.

"Behold! A felinekin delectable," she announced, smiling widely. "Well, not really. The recipe is easy enough, and I can't have store-bought milk." She picked up a cup. "It's pretty much soy milk, real maple syrup, vanilla, a dash of nutmeg, and a little cinnamon for the senses. It's good! Try it!"

I did, and it was indeed good, if not uncomfortably warm going down. Still, I drank it with her sitting beside me. I liked it, overall.

"I'm not a fan of the way it settles in my stomach," I admitted, "but you're right—it is good!" I peered inside the empty mug. "Does this help? Making you feel more catlike, I mean."

"It does," she told me, then took another sip. "I like to base my afternoon meals around a feline diet. Sometimes evenings, too, but eating only what cats eat would be unhealthy; I'm *human*, after all." She smiled. "Do you always take the drinks people offer you?"

"What do you mean?" I asked, then looked down and gulped. "Did you—?"

"I'm just saying," she said. "You haven't seen me in, what, seven years? Studies have found that the victims of assaults frequently know their offenders in some way. Makes you think twice about who you let close to you." Cat picked up the remote. "What're you in the mood for? Anything but *Rehab Runway*. That show just never seems to go away." She clicked around. "I've got… *Weeks Without WiFi, Animal Nannies, Supermodel Plastic Surgeons, Finding Former Child Stars… 2 Many Kids 2 Count, My Stepsister is a Hoarder, Sex-Related Injuries with Jake Palaver…* recorded episodes of *Sea Breeze Academy, Growing Up Sucks—*"

"You have *Sea Breeze Academy*?!" I asked, sitting upright so fast I nearly slipped off the couch.

"Yeah," Cat said, as if it weren't a big deal. "I set the TV to record all episodes sans repeats, and now we have all sixty-one!" She considered this. "Well, sixty. 'Checkmate' rarely airs in North America."

"Wow." I stared at her in sheer amazement. "I thought I was the only one left who stilled cared about *SBA*. That's incredible."

"If you say so," Cat said with small laugh. "I'm surprised there hasn't been a spinoff show yet. Seems like everything gets a rerun, reboot, or revival nowadays. Whatever. Help me find the 'Heatwave' episode. Either that or 'Blackmail' with Chris's crazy ex. Maybe even 'Double Date,' which introduces her. All of them are good."

"Or we could start with season three and see how far we get," I suggested. "That includes the episodes you mentioned."

"Yeah, season three's probably the best of the four."

"Agreed," I noted, still smiling. "The last one's all about dating—and everyone's with the wrong person, at that. How are Rook and Matthew supposed to get it on while he's away in Alaska?"

"Gaah." She shuddered. "Please, no innuendos, sexual or otherwise. There's too much of that in the world as it is."

Cat found and selected the 3x01 episode "Campus, Sweet Campus," in which Rook, Matthew, and the gang return to Sea Breeze Academy to start their junior year after being separated during summer vacation. It was nostalgic and beautiful—like the girl sitting next to me—and watching the characters hug, fist-bump, and talk to each other then made me really, really happy for some reason. Cat could tell, too, and with each episode we watched, she positioned herself closer to me as we kept our eyes on the screen.

At one point, I tried to put my arm around her, but she shrugged her right shoulder so that my hand was in her hair, above the neck. When I absentmindedly started to scratch her skin, she put her head up against me, and I could've sworn I heard her purr a little. So I scratched some more, and she nuzzled closer by my chest as her response, an intimate warmth radiating from her soft skin.

"I wish you'd stayed in Oklahoma," she whispered after some time had passed.

"Me, too," I told her, sighing deeply. It was the most honest statement I'd made in recent years.

The rain fell at a steady pace against the roof, and with the air conditioning, it made the house seem colder despite us being so physically close to one another.

The lights flickered briefly. Cat switched the channel to the weather station.

"—with torrential rain leading to tree damage," the meteorologist said. "A trail of intense winds, hail, and lightning continues to push east into Arminster County. On our radar, we can see more heavy rain that has the potential for some serious flash flooding—"

"I hate the rain," I muttered.

Cat looked up from my chest. "You, too?"

"It's such an inconvenience," I went on. "It's not even that pretty. And the smell…"

"Oh." She sat up and put her back against the couch. "I thought you meant—"

Thunder sounded from nearby outside. Cat jumped, then recomposed herself.

"I should've brought more blankets," she told me. "My CD player, too, and *The Essential Billy Joel* album. I saw him in concert, Billy Joel, three years ago—"

The thunder boomed once more, shaking the house. She stood up this time.

I laughed. "Are you scared of storms? Like, because of the whole cat-thing?"

She glared at me. "Not funny. You of all people—" More thunder. "*Fuck!* It's close to us. Why in the world do we live on top of a hill?!"

Cat left and disappeared down the stairs. When she returned, she was carrying a lot more blankets and pillows. She dropped them on the couch to the left, then walked over to where I sat.

"Build a pillow fort with me."

"What?"

"Come on!" she pleaded. "Like we used to do in your old house! Pleeeease?"

"I wouldn't know how to start," I admitted.

"With the walls and supports," she said, then proceeded to show me with two couch cushions. "But first, help me clear some space."

Within twenty minutes, our fortress was complete, and we were laughing inside. The thunderstorm raged on, but for the moment, we were safe and protected from the world beyond our sheets and pillows; nothing else mattered then but us and our makeshift haven.

"Things were so much better ten years ago," I said, leaning back for a second before realizing my leg was pulling on one of the blankets.

"How so?" she asked, smiling some more.

"It just was!" I continued, smiling with her. "You, me, Christian, Gabby, Pete, Belle, the Sams, and the Millburns all living in that neighborhood—"

"Well, me in the apartment complex."

"—and goofing off and just being kids. We played and swam and all went to Hayes. It was the best."

"No, Hayes was the *worst*," she countered, laughing. "Remember first grade? Hayes Elementary was a disgusting… chaotic mess. Kids running around everywhere, the boys hitting each other—total *Lord of the Flies*. Didn't your mom have to pick you up one time because someone in another grade had peed all over you in the bathroom?"

"Oh, yeah." I pushed my hair back with one hand. "I forgot about that."

"Yeah, don't go romanticizing elementary school. Crappy lunches, fire drills, and learning long division weren't anything to get sentimental over." She sighed. "Wishing to be in a different moment, remembering what it was like to be a little kid, reminiscing over time spent with friends and loved ones—all are methods of escape."

"But the people," I argued. "The friends we made."

"And look where we are now," she countered, gesturing, getting up close to my left ear and whispering: *"The lone survivors!"*

"You know what I mean."

"Not really," she said with a shrug. "Just a bunch of children running around at recess, pretending they were Matthew or Brooklyn from *Sea Breeze Academy* and acting like boyfriend and girlfriend—whatever that meant when we were nine. We were kids playing with fire." She looked at me, frowning. "They don't care about us. I bet they're still assholes."

"Who?"

"Belle, Christian, Nate, and Bryce. People you don't know. You saw them. Are they still acting as if the friendships we make in elementary, middle, and high school will matter after graduation? Hell, they're just buying time."

"Is that what we're doing now?" I asked solemnly.

"Huh?" She smiled again. "No. No, Michael, not at all. No, we're different. You have your book, I have my singing, and I'm also assisting kids like me. We're starting our careers years before everyone else—you as a novelist, me as a social justice worker. We *know* what we want to do with our lives. The people at school—they'll join national volunteer organizations so they can put it on their college applications, right? But they don't give a crap about helping people outside their own realm of self-absorbed problems. 'Who's going to be Homecoming Queen?' and 'I don't have enough to put on my résumé!' Are you kidding me? That's their concern? You and I are doing something real, whereas everyone else is worrying about some physics project that won't even—"

"You don't miss it, though? Because you're homeschooled?"

"What I miss is people believing I'm getting a proper education, even though I've finished a year early and have almost completed a semester of college. I don't have busy work or annoying teachers, and I get to go at my own pace. I mean, I was more disciplined in the beginning—up by eight, eating meals at specific times, keeping to a schedule—but I'm more prepared for college because I've been teaching myself."

"Well…" I sighed. "Fine. I suppose the public education system isn't all it's cracked up to be."

"Except for Ms. Albertine," she said with a wink. "I liked her a lot. She was probably my favorite teacher. They buried her in the same cemetery as your dad." Cat's eyes then widened in the dark. "Oh, I'm—I'm sorry, I wasn't thinking. Um. Well, a lot of people are buried at Shaughnessy Grove."

"How did you know my dad died?" I asked. "I found out last week."

"How come you—?"

"It's complicated," I answered. "Basically, my mom didn't want me to know, so she had my uncle write me letters, pretending to be my dad."

"Wow." Cat cleared her throat. "Sorry you… that happened to you. Uh, my mom told me a few days after it happened, I think. It was on the news? Oh, but you were in Alabama then. How is your town?"

"It's fine. Dreary's the kind of place where just about everybody knows everyone, and with each telling of a story, they add their own slander. The worst are the barbers and dentists. The town is small enough where the woman on the real estate billboard is also the keyboard player at church on Sundays. Most of the kids at Troy's parties are from the neighboring, wealthier town."

"Troy?" She tilted her head with a puzzled expression. "Who's Troy?"

"Oh, God, he's, like, my best friend in Dreary. He came with me here to help with the party at the lake. He's a bit over the top."

"So... where is he now?"

"With Gabby at the Protzig."

Cat laughed. "Remember when Ms. Albertine took us there for something, and the guards couldn't get Blank Frank off the statue in that big fountain? Because he couldn't swim?"

I laughed with her. "He was always a strange one."

"Yeah..." She sighed. "I can't believe he killed himself. It must've been tough for him, living with the pain he had, but even so—"

"What?" I asked. "No, Frankie's alive."

Cat looked at me with pity. "Frank committed suicide during a biology test freshman year. I heard the gunshot from the hallway. The school got a licensed psychologist, the yearbook was dedicated in his memory..."

"No, no, that's..." I shook my head. "He was there, at my party. He was there, but he didn't look so good. He talked about the water flooding, how I would drown... I saw him. He was standing in the corner."

"Michael," she said. "*That's impossible.* Franklin Chambers was struck by a white van in the seventh grade. His aunt's sedan broke down on I-40, and when he got out of her car to see what was wrong... Collision. Wheelchair-bound. We never played kickball again." She looked down. "Not like we did, anyway, with Bryce."

"But when I QuickSearched Franklin, that didn't show up."

"The papers didn't print his name," she explained. "When a child is involved, they usually don't. To... you know... protect their identity."

"I..." My head was spinning. "I don't feel so good..."

"Do you want something to drink?" she asked me. "Some aspirin?"

"I think..." I shifted downward, briefly supporting my weight on my right hand as I eased myself to the floor. "I think I'm gonna lie here for a second."

"Yeah," Cat said. "Yeah, sure." She got down on the ground and positioned herself beside me. "Anything you need. I'm here for you."

"This is nice," I told her. "Being with you is what I've needed."

"And I'm happy to help," she added, nestling up against me, then purring softly as I stroked her hair again.

We rested there in a peaceful quiet, the only sounds coming from the ticking of the wall clock, the low hum of the air conditioning, and the rain outside. Cat was gorgeous—there was no doubt about it. Yet something still felt off about us.

"Remember how I had said I liked you?" I asked her. "Like, like-liked you. In fifth grade? And Bryce did the same?"

"Let's not do this now."

"If I'd stayed in New Baines..." I watched her face, and as she opened her eyes, she considered mine. "Who would you have picked? I know you ended up with Bryce in middle and high school, but—"

"I don't want to talk about it," she said. "Not in front of *them*."

"In front of who?" I asked. She looked past me. I turned around, saw nothing.

"I would have picked you," she stated. "Is that what you wanted to hear?"

"Well, yeah," I said, grinning wide. She rolled her eyes, though she was smiling all the same. "I thought of you the whole time I've been away."

"Even when you were dating Olivia van Droogenbroeck?" she pointed out, taking me by surprise.

Time spent alone with Olivia immediately came to mind: making out in the fantasy section of a used bookstore, watching *Polar Opposites* on my couch, going to Rochester to see the Christmas lights display, going on late-night drives to Taco Kick, taking her shirt off in her bedroom, listening to Mandolin Orange on loop, reading *The Master and Margarita* to each other, talking about the future, wondering if God exists, and imagining how our lives might've been different had we not met at that one Double Chin by accident those many months ago.

"Yes," I told her.

"No," Cat said, and I could tell she was being serious. "Don't admit to that, even if you mean it." She pulled a smaller blanket over her. "I saw that relationship status on Coffeefolder about you both breaking up. I used my mom's account. Olivia's pretty."

"She broke up with me," I explained, "because of this. Well, not *this*, specifically, but because of how I'm so... *obsessive* over the past. Our past. Of Oklahoma and childhood and my writing and..." I rubbed at my temples. "It needed to happen, but that doesn't mean I wanted it to."

"Hey," she said, taking my hands. I noticed again the scars on her own. "You are not alone. You made it back. *You're a time traveler.* And you've got me."

"Yeah?" I asked, raising an eyebrow and watching her face in the dim light.

"Well," Cat backtracked as she let go, "maybe not like *that.*"

"Then how?" I pressed.

She smiled again, just as teasing.

"Let's play a game," she said, causing me to wonder if she was changing the subject or exciting me further. Whichever it was, Cat stood up, and the roof of our fortress rose above us, making her the center pole of the circus tent. She grabbed my hands again, pulling me along with her. "Come on! It'll be fun!"

I followed her, briefly lamenting the destruction of our little home of quilts and couch cushions as we plowed through toward the TV. There, Cat got on her knees and ruffled through a container appropriately labeled STUFF. After five or so seconds, she produced the Big-Box special edition of *Michael Jackson: Dance Party*.

"No way," I stated, standing my ground. "Not in a million—"

"Pleeeeaase?" she begged. I shook my head. "Hey, that's not fair! Do you know what you've done to my brain? I can't hear the King of Pop's name without thinking about that little boy I had a crush on in fifth grade. Do you know how problematic that made eighth-grade formal when they played 'Thriller,' or 'Heal the World' during the Black History Month presentation at New Baines each year? *The least you can do* is trip the light fantastic with me to the voice of one of the greatest musical artists, like, ever. Can you do that for me? Can you swallow your pride enough for a song or several?"

"You had a crush on me?"

Cat rolled her eyes—still smiling with those white teeth of hers—and handed me a controller. She then connected the wrist strap of her own to her hand, booted up the console, selected the game, and assigned me the role of Player 2.

"Which one am I?" I asked, referring to the avatars onscreen.

"For this song, you're the backup dancer," she explained. "I'm Michael."

"But I'm Michael," I pointed out.

"Sure, but you're not ready to moonwalk just yet."

Cat was right, as evidenced by my score at the end of "Will You Be There," "Leave Me Alone," "Black or White," "Behind the Mask," and "The Girl is Mine," for the latter of which she remained Michael Jackson while I played as Paul McCartney. She was obviously the more experienced dancer, but I wasn't so bad myself as I mirrored the Michael lookalikes onscreen while they grooved to the music—no blood on the dance floor or anything.

Of the many moves we performed, I did recognize his signature pelvic thrust, which I happily attempted at the beginning of "Who Is It."

"Oh, gross," Cat commented, unamused for some reason.

"What's the matter?" I asked, laughing as I sloppily tried to move my feet to imitate famous-Michael Jackson. The game was only tracking right-arm motions, but still—go big or go home to Dreary.

"Nothing," she said simply. "It's just… MJ's the reason why the pop industry is so hypersexualized. Like, he basically started it all. Him, Elvis, and Marilyn Monroe. They're why we see Lita Candyce twerking her ass off during award shows and Thorax Wang running around with a pool noodle between his legs and getting all over Averyl, Sabryn, and Piri in his music video with the dolphins. I dunno. It's fine if people do that kind of stuff, really. I only wish it wasn't thrown in our faces all the damn time."

"What do you mean?"

"What do I mean?" she asked, pausing the game. "Sex is everywhere! Even the LGBT community is hypersexualized to the point where asexuals don't feel comfortable identifying as part of the community because they're so excluded. They're 'not gay enough' or whatever bullshit—" She sighed, then started up the music again. "Forget it."

Cat didn't allow me enough time to consider what she'd said, as I was too busy trying to keep up with Michael's moves as he sang about a lover who had left him for someone else. She ended the song with a score of 9,274. Mine didn't come close at all. Even so, we were having fun, and I could see Cat enjoyed having me around—someone to play and laugh with, just like the good ol' days, despite her being so opposed to them.

"OK," Cat said, panting slightly. "You choose the next song."

"Gaah, my arm."

"The next song?" She started scrolling through the selection screen.

"I don't listen to Michael Jackson," I admitted. "I wouldn't know."

"What?! But—" Cat looked at me in shock. "You don't listen to your own namesake?! You need to inform yourself! When people make fun of you for MJ, do you even catch the references?!"

"Most of them!" I told her. "I think."

"Here," she said, grabbing my hand with the controller in it. She moved through the albums for me. "Pick something you like—or think you'd like. Life's too short to pretend to hate pop music."

"Uh…" They were all a blur. "How about… there. *Dangerous*, 1991. 'Remember the Time.' Is that one good?"

Her sudden laugh was genuine and hopeful. I did the same, as I'd made her happy once again.

"Yes," Cat told me. "That song's perfect for—"

She stopped herself. I waited for the rest of her sentence, but she clicked "Play" instead, and so we danced. It was our toast to a youthful love affair, as the lyrics described, and I enjoyed every moment of it.

A little after six o'clock, Ms. Varsha came into the living room to see Cat and me shaking away to "Love Never Felt So Good." She was smiling, which was a good sign for me, and then asked if I wanted to stay for dinner. I told them I should probably get going, as I still needed to pick up my friend, a.k.a. Troy. I then wrote my number down on a napkin and left it with Ms. Varsha.

Cat walked with me to the front door, and outside, we laughed over a video her mom had secretly taken of us dancing, if my flailing motions could even be called that. The rain had passed without our knowing, and though it was cloudy, nothing could block her light from my eyes.

"Thanks for coming back," Cat said to me after. "And thank you for apologizing."

"I'm diagnosing myself with an underdeveloped prefrontal cortex," I told her. She didn't reply. "I've, uh, taken psychology classes. The prefrontal cortex affects behavior and decision making."

"Ah," she said, smiling again. "Well, anyway, it means a lot. So thanks." She grabbed her left wrist and stretched her arms forward to pop it. The action looked familiar. "Same time tomorrow?"

"What do you mean?"

"Do you want to come over again?"

"Oh!" I exclaimed. "Yeah, of course! And where do you post your music? I want to listen."

"Black Missy dot Uprorrr dot com," she told me. "Like the Black Dahlia. 'Uprorrr' with no A and three R's at the end." She then added with a light punch to my shoulder: "I've even covered a Michael Jackson song."

I pretended to stagger backward. She laughed.

"And I'll do my research on him," I promised.

"But not from trashy websites! That's what 'Leave Me Alone,' 'Tabloid Junkie,' and 'Scream' were all about: mass media and how horrible they were to Michael. He was a good guy with a strange childhood and a lot of awful accusations thrown at him. So try to have an open mind, and stay away from *Hollywood's Highest* and their gossip articles."

"Will do," I said. "I'd do anything for you."

"Don't say that," she told me, "or I'll ask for too much."

"Try me," I answered playfully. "You do have my number."

Cat hugged me. It was a full embrace—one from a girl who didn't receive a lot of company. Whereas I felt lonely, Cat truly was alone.

I hugged her back, and after a couple of seconds, she released me.

"See you soon," she stated.

"See you soon," I agreed.

We waved our good-byes then, and I got in the Big Nasty. As Cat went inside her home, I started up the SUV and headed down the hill, careful not to hit any of the lawn decorations that littered the sides of the narrow streets. I couldn't see myself living in a neighborhood like Mountain Vista, but I could appreciate Ms. Varsha's decision to relocate her youngest daughter there; whether or not her mother knew it at the time, Cat was safer there—physically and emotionally—hiding behind the gates, windows, and screens. It was a place of healing, and I was already starting to feel better myself, even if it wasn't reality.

At the bottom of the hill was a familiar black sedan, and within, a familiar private eye. Once my side of the gate automatically opened and let me out, I drove up beside the car and rolled down my window.

"Detective Northcott," I said to him. He looked up, then ran a hand through his receding brown hair. As I watched the investigator, I could tell he must've been a better-looking man at one point who just hadn't aged so handsomely. "What are you doing here?"

"You mentioned yesterday that Catherine Thomas wasn't at your party," he reminded me. "I'm only here to ask her a few questions."

"Don't bother," I told him. "You'd be wasting your time. She's pretty reclusive."

"Or is she a pretty recluse?" he added. "Doesn't matter, I suppose, since I don't have the code."

"Guess not," I said as he put a mint in his mouth. "Anyway, bye."

"Wait," he called out. "Did you say Franklin Chambers was at your lake house on Saturday?"

"No," I lied.

"Huh." He scratched his head, consulting his notes. "All right. Thanks again."

I drove away quickly, perturbed by his presence there. I didn't like Northcott investigating into our private affairs, especially since Willow disappearing had nothing to do with the party or whatever had happened Saturday night. I might've been losing my mind, or I might've lost it long before, but that didn't matter anymore; what was important was my relationship with Cat, a prisoner with no parole. She was the purpose of my journey, after all, and seeing her again and being normal together was significant—nothing else.

At a red light on Seventy-First Street, I texted Troy, asking where I should pick him up. He replied simply that he was already at the cabin. Pleased with myself and my playdate with Cat, I found the aux cord, plugged my phone into it, scrolled through Troy's playlist, and then selected "Lights On" by XY&O.

The road had been long, but soon, it would be mine.

◆━━━◆◆━━━◆

Troy sat on the front porch steps while vaping as I pulled up to the lake house. I got out and walked over to him, and I could see his eyes were a faint red, as if he'd been crying.

"What's wrong?" I asked him.

He took a long drag of his e-cig, then hurled his personalized vaporizer somewhere in the tall grass.

"She denied it," Troy told me, sniffling. "Gabby. She says we never had sex, and then she got all mad at me for even suggesting that we had." He spat to the side. "Fucking hell. That's what I get, isn't it? Now I'm the one going crazy. I don't understand…"

I let Troy babble, which I'd recognized before as one of his coping mechanisms for dealing with stress when things weren't going his way; I'd sit back, close my eyes, and let him talk as long as he needed. Did that make me an ass? Maybe. I didn't think he required an audience, as there were many times when I would walk into his room to find him chatting with the air around him. He liked hearing his own voice. I liked reading my own words. Nothing to it, and few people outside my friends and family had bought my book, anyway.

He stood up, studying me. "You look happy. I take it she accepted your apology?"

"Yeah, but her mom threw away the Easter bunny."

"Qué horror!" Troy said, sniffling and smirking. "Of course she did. Cats can't have chocolate. Everybody knows that."

I thought about this, then shrugged and walked past Troy into the cabin. He followed.

The door opened behind us, and in came a large monitor on a pair of hairy legs. As it got closer and turned to the side, however, it became Kukowski in flip-flops, cargo shorts, and an orange button-up. He was out of breath. The years had been hard on him, too.

"Help me," he breathed heavily, "put above the mantel."

"Good to see you, too, Havana Shirt Herbert," Troy commented.

"Whereas I'm just… glad to see… y'all didn't burn the house down," he countered.

Troy and I each took two corners of the TV, and together, the three of us lifted it above the fireplace. But it faced the wrong way, so we took our same sides and turned the TV around toward the couches as the handgun fell to the floor.

"There we go." Kukowski picked up his gun, sat down, and then admired his forty-inch TV in relaxed comfort. "I saw this kid selling used computers in a parking lot, and I'm like, 'Hey, I need a TV.' So I paid him a hundred bucks. Got a friend coming by later to help set it up. It's all still new to me." He looked at us both. "So how'd the party go? You have fun?"

Troy caught Kukowski up to speed for the most part—again with the talking—yet he did leave out a few crucial details of the Bryce variety. I decided it wasn't worth arguing with him again, so I kept to myself. Troy, nonetheless, did mention most us getting drunk off our asses.

"Kids these days," Kukowski said, setting the gun back on the mantel. I shivered. "But I'm glad you had your fun. It's Heisenberg's uncertainty principle: you can't measure something without altering it—in this case, your pleasure levels and state of mind." He took out his phone, then glanced out the window. "There's still daylight left. You both wanna go on the lake? I can get my captain's hat!"

We laughed, and sure enough, he went into his room and came back with a white yacht cap on his head. I imagined him wearing solely this while he was with the woman and the fuzzy handcuffs from Friday night, causing me to gag momentarily before Troy and I followed Kukowski outside and down to the dock.

"Behold! The *Caldecota*." Kukowski held out his hands toward a cruiser speedboat with a blue paintjob, spoiler, and retractable canvas roof. "I know what you're thinking: it's a heavy boat—big whoop. But in calm waters, this li'l sucker can go up to eighty without a sweat. So *fuck you*, Hennigan High and your dumbass principal! Who's got the boat? I got the boat."

"What do you mean?" I asked while Kukowski stuck his middle fingers high in the air for all of Lake Nasagarresett to see.

"Nevermind that. Hop on in, and I'll show you how to work this beauty. It's not that hard. There's always a couple different ways to skin the cat, but if I can teach a bunch of kiddos the ideal gas law, I think I can get you two to drive a boat proper."

And he did, showing Troy and me how to move the throttle and trim the bow, as well as the correct way to turn at high speeds. When the sun was close to setting, I was getting a good hang of it, and for once, I felt in control—not just of the boat, but of my life and future.

I made a sharp turn to the left, and Kukowski immediately grabbed my shoulder as we rolled across the choppy water.

"Mikey, what'd I tell ya?!" He pointed behind us. "Always look back in the direction you want to go before you turn! Safety's the most important part of sailing."

"Is that why we aren't wearing life jackets?" Troy said as I slowed down and he took over. "Watch me hit a Republican with this thing."

Kukowski merely shook his head. He was sweating, so he unbuttoned his Havana shirt and stowed it under his seat. Now that he wore only a muscle shirt, I could see the tattoo across his upper-right arm more clearly. "PV=nRT," it read.

"What's that?" I asked, pointing.

"Good Lord." He took a quick peek at it. "That's the ideal gas law I was talking about. Huge pain in the rear for my tenth graders. Reason I quit, too."

"Oh, do tell!" Troy said sarcastically.

"Long story short—I have a rambling problem, Valdez—I made a deal with one of my classes that if they did well on their semester final and raised sixty dollars, I'd get a tattoo of 'PV equals nRT,' their favorite mathematical equation. Eventually, they got to their sixty bucks, took the final, and they did better than usual, I'll admit. So after winter break, I go out and get it, *bzzzzt*, and there it is." He flexed his arm. "I like it 'cause when I run in a sleeveless shirt, women think it says, 'pervert,' and they come up and talk to me."

"But how did it cost you your job?" Troy asked, laughing with him.

"Well, a few weeks go by, and I get called to the principal. It's not my first. And usually, when the principal starts his bitching and that kind of crap, I go, 'Listen, does this affect my paycheck?' I've always done that, and he goes, 'No, but—' and I get up and leave. I say, 'When it affects my paycheck, I'll care about it. If not, I'm gone.'

"So I sit down this time, and he goes, 'So, I hear your class paid for a tattoo,' and I'm kind of like, 'Yeah, yeah, does this affect my paycheck?' And he says, 'This time, it might,' and you could just see that smartass look on his face. But anyway, he has this whole letter written up that says, 'It's a violation of Arminster Public Schools Board Policy Fifty/Fifty to receive money from blah blah blah,' and I say, 'OK, good, but what'll happen?' 'Well, you're goin' to get a letter put in your file.' *Oh my God! Really? Take me out and beat me with a stick instead of putting a letter in my file, please, my God, I can't have that!*"

Troy was in hysterics—so much, he had to slow down the boat to keep us from capsizing against the homes of families, tearing fathers from children or vice versa.

"Now, remind me," Kukowski said. "Where'd the money come from?"

"The students," we answered.

"And what did it look like? *A frickin' jar of pennies, nickels, and dimes.* You gonna go up to a tattoo artist and say, 'Hey, dude,' with your mayonnaise jar—have you seen a tattoo artist? If you throw that sucker down and say, 'Can you start countin' it?' then you're goin' to get a tattoo, all right. But it's not goin' to be in the right place, it'll be misspelled, and you're gonna have Hepatitis C when you walk outta there. And so *clearly* I did not use their money—I still had the jar in my room—but Principal was too stupid to figure it out."

I should have laughed, but I couldn't stop thinking about what Cat had told me about Franklin Chambers. In my mind's eye, I saw him standing there, alone in the corner. Troy said I'd passed out; Cat said Franklin was dead. My recollection began to fugue into uncertainty. Had Franklin issued me a warning? Had he given me a threat?

"Who's gonna read this file?" Kukowski went on. "No one. New employer can't read the file, 'cause there could be a slander suit. So I told him something to the point of, 'You're an idiot who wouldn't understand true brilliance if it punched you in the face, and I know because I used to teach next to you, and you sucked then! Put *that* in my file!' Valdez, why're you shaking your head no?"

"You did not say that," Troy said, grinning wide.

"Did, too! I figured I could quit two ways: resign the second week of school in August, get ten more sick days—which they'd have to pay me for—*and* I'd get the stipend, *and* I'd leave their ass hanging without a chemistry teacher. Or I could get it over with. So I quit, after eleven years there, and boy, was it fun. I have a real bad temper. Sorry. So you boys remember that when you make me mad. I might go, 'Hmm. Thirty-five years in the pen, but hey! Three full meals, free TV, *and* a roommate, *and* a boyfriend, *and* the satisfaction of knowing I slaughtered some teenager after years of fantasizing about it…' I don't know." He shrugged. "Could happen."

Could happen.

Once night fell and Kukowski tied up the boat, we had a working TV and way too many channels for it. The day had made us hungry, and taquitos were the obvious choice for that night's dinner for three. I ate mine in silence.

"Are you hanging out with Cat again tomorrow?" Troy asked me at the kitchen table.

"In the afternoon, yeah."

"Who's Cat?" Kukowski asked as he closed the door and came over to us.

"A friend of mine," I explained, rubbing at my sore head. The lake had baked me, and no bottle of water or aspirin seemed to ease the pain. "From elementary school."

"Oh, was she at your party?"

"Um, no." I looked down at the last taquito left on my paper plate. "She has this, uh, condition of sorts." I picked at the taquito, but it rolled off, and Troy snatched it.

"It's fair game when it's outside the plate," Troy said to me. "Anyway, can I borrow your copy of *Krijg de Tering*? I didn't think to bring mine, and I might as well get started on this poetry paper before we head back home."

"And when's that?" Kukowski asked.

"We'll figure it out," I told them both. To Troy: "Yeah, it's on the desk. At least you have time to actually read a book." To Kukowski: "Is it all right if I ask Cat if she wants to come here to the cabin with me?"

"Like a date?" He looked at me skeptically. "Do you think she'll say yes?"

"Yes," I answered, a bit annoyed. Troy laughed. "And why'd it take you till today to get here, anyway? You said you'd be back yesterday."

"Yeah, sorry about that," Kukowski said, scratching the back of his neck. "On Saturday, while you all were driving around, drinking, doing drugs, and ripping off houses, I was at the prison. I'd rather've been with you both, *believe me*. All right, maybe not drinking and driving. What a mess. Just talk to the oldest Kukowski kid—two years and ten grand."

"Bubby's in jail?!" I asked him. At Troy's vacant stare: "That's, uh, that's what I called Kukowski's son when we were younger."

"It's not pretty!" Kukowski went on. "You do *not* want one of those tickets. I didn't frame it and put it on the wall and go, 'Oh, yay, Bubby!' That's not one of those parenting moments you live for. 'Cause, see, your mom Heidi would go, 'Oh, no! I gotta go get Bubby out!' I'm not about that. I'm like, 'Nah, he's tough, and surely it would take more than three guys to rape him.' He's a big boy!"

"Father of the Year material," Troy said, rolling his eyes in noticeable disgust. He then got up from the table and left the room. Kukowski shrugged at me, but I knew Troy's stance on paternity. I understood.

It was late into the night when Troy fell asleep above me after finishing his nightly jackoff. I was still up, playing and replaying events in my mind, waiting patiently for stillness, eager to see what Cat would have in store for us the next day. I kept hearing noises, though—whispers and far-off insects outside the lake house. They would not let me rest so easily.

The air was cold. I grabbed my hoodie, put it over my pajama top, and then walked over to the front door. It stood wide open, and the moon projected a deep blue light across the porch. On the welcome mat: a dead cat with a severed head, its blood seeping ankle-deep into the fibers of my conscience.

Ian found Aiden Bradford's phone number after looking through various yearbooks and emails and a half dozen websites. He slouched back onto the couch and clicked up the volume on the phone—an action he hadn't performed in years. Four rings, five rings. He stared at the photo of Karina smiling up at him from the opened eighth-grade yearbook. Eight rings, nine rings.

"Good morn—oh! Just turned afternoon," said a friendly voice, laughing. "Mr. Bradford of Bradford Trucking and Company here. How can I be of assistance?"

"Wow," Ian said into the phone. "It's been… a long time."

"Gallagher? *Ian Gallagher?* Is that you?! How ya doing, man!"

"I'm…" Ian suddenly felt weak. With a cough, he pulled himself together. "Listen, what was the name—"

"Now, I thought you didn't use telephones! Weren't you, quote unquote, deathly afraid of 'em?"

"Yeah, and I still kind of—hey, what was the name of that pond the third bus was found next to in eighth grade?"

"The *bisexual* bus?" Aiden laughed again, but quickly caught himself. "Oh, right. Not funny. After what happened… I'm sorry, I just—"

"Do you remember the name?"

"Yeah, it was some Native American word. Something like… uhh… Nasa… Nasagarresett! *Lake* Nasagarresett! Yeah, that was it. I remember 'cause they found THC in the town's water supply." Aiden sounded pleased with himself.

"Right. Thanks. Anyway, I've got to go—"

"Hold up there! You're just goin' to leave me like that after all this time?" The laugh once more. "Naw, I'm just messin' with ya. So what's so important about that lake? You're not lookin' for Karina again, are ya, Mikey?" He paused, concerned. "It's been ten years."

Ian hesitated. He wanted to tell Aiden about the call from Karina, but he felt like no matter what he said, Aiden wouldn't believe him. Again.

"I'm not too far from the airport, y'know," Aiden continued. "I could drive—"

Ian hung up on him. There was no way he would understand.

"Lake Nasagarresett," he reminded himself.

Ian got up from the table and looked at the letter. He didn't want to leave Makenna behind without her knowing where he was heading.

"I'm going to visit some old friends in Oklahoma," it began. "I'll only be gone a couple of days..."

He liked Makenna a lot; they had been together for almost two years, and he wouldn't stray from her. But before he could think about looking forward, he had to cast out the demons from his past. He had to know what had happened to the nineteen missing kids on that third bus. What had happened to Karina.

And he hadn't forgotten. He also had to give the Woodpecker a good punch to the nose.

"Hey. Mom." Troy kicked at my side. "Hey. Wake the fuck up."

I groaned. I rolled over. I was on the floor beside our bed.

"Come on." He grabbed me by the armpits and pulled me up to my feet. "Jesus, you look bad. Let's go eat cereal and watch TV."

"Was I..." I rubbed my head. "Was I on the floor this whole time? There was a... cat's body on the porch..."

"This some kind of power-fantasy dream you had?" he asked. "Or are you saying Bryce killed a cat now instead of B-Love?" He yawned, and at the mention of Bryce's name, I thought of the rats Cat's classmates had left on her doorstep when she'd revealed she was Otherkin. "Next you're gonna say there's a clown in the sewers. You were here when I woke up at one to take a piss, and again right now. So come on. It's eleven, and I'm ready for some sunbathing on the dock."

He was wearing his rainbow swim trunks, so this made sense. I was tempted to remind him those multitude of colors were liable to get him shot on this lake, but he knew what he was getting himself into, so what the hell.

I followed him into the living room, where Kukowski sat with his feet up on the coffee table, watching the news with a bowl of generic cereal. I got some myself from the kitchen and joined him on the other couch. Troy sat beside me. A dead spider clutched to the fabric of my sock.

"—after the desk clerk identified the man as Charles Dodgson, shown on your screen now," the lady in the suit announced. "Dodgson had been staying at Norman's Motel in Madison at the time of the abduction and murder. Kelli Ziegler, a cashier at a Mr. Swanky's convenience store in Madison, was discovered by morning joggers earlier today. According to law enforcement, Ziegler was found naked, mutilated, and strangled with what appeared to be braided rope. As of now, Ziegler is the third confirmed victim in the Hellenbach series of murders, named after the first victim, Natalie Hellenbach, the granddaughter of Arkansas state legislator—"

"Michael," Troy said, eyes wide and focused on the killer onscreen. "We know that guy."

I didn't want to admit it, but Troy was right; the man with the wild eyes, unruly beard, and long, black, and greasy hair just so happened to be our Charlie the Hitchhiker from the Arkansas rest stop.

That's when it clicked.

"Oh my God." I put the cereal bowl down and pointed. "I saw him yesterday! At the Big-Box by the Protzig! He was..." I struggled to think straight. "He was in the checkout line in front of me, talking to the cashier there. He had a fresh haircut." I stood up and looked at Kukowski. "How many haircut places are there in Madison?!"

"Uh, just the one, I think."

"Shit. I have to call Northcott." I started fast-walking to the bedroom. *"He had a haircut!"*

"Who's Northcott?!" both Troy and Kukowski asked.

"THE PRIVATE INVESTIGATOR!" I shouted from the other room as I grabbed the business card and unplugged my phone and got rid of all the pointless notifications that cluttered the screen. "He's the one who showed up here Sunday morning!"

"You had a *detective* snooping around this place?!" Kukowski asked, and when I returned, he was standing up as well. "What for?!"

"Willow Dusett," I tried to explain, "was invited to the party because she went to elementary school with me. But she couldn't make it because she had to work that night. And on our way here—to Madison—Troy and I picked up a hitchhiker named Charlie who looked *exactly* like the man on the news. Except he doesn't anymore, because I saw him yesterday when we went to Big-Box, but I didn't recognize him because he'd shaved and gotten a haircut. *Willow is a hairstylist.* Northcott showed up because *Willow went missing Saturday night.*" I stared at them, perturbed and out of breath. "Get it now?!"

"Sort of?" Troy told me. "When did this happen? You haven't been making sense—"

Whatever else he said didn't matter, as I'd already started dialing the number. I walked outside over the stained welcome mat, got inside the Big Nasty, and then waited there.

He picked up on the second ring.

"This is Detective Michael Northcott speaking," he said. "Can I ask who's calling?"

"Michael. Michael *Jackson.* We talked Sunday, and I saw you yesterday—"

"What seems to be the problem, Michael? You don't sound too good."

"Have you been watching the news?" I asked. "Do you know the Charles Dodgson guy who's been going around and strangling teenage girls?"

"I know of him. Why?"

"I think he might've confronted Willow at some point." I took a deep breath. "It makes sense, but just listen: I'm from Dreary, Alabama, and I drove here to my uncle's lake house in Madison to have a sort of elementary school reunion with my fifth-grade class at Hayes Elementary School."

"Michael—"

"On the way, I picked up a hitchhiker named Charlie at some rest stop on I-49, and he was bloody and said someone had stolen his stuff—point is, Charlie looked exactly like the man they just showed on the news. We dropped him off in town Friday night—"

"We?"

"Me and my friend Troy," I explained. "Look, I saw Charlie again yesterday at twelve thirty or so at the Big-Box by the Protzig, but I didn't know it was him because he had shaved his beard and mustache completely, and he must've gotten a haircut at some point."

"And there's only one barbershop in Madison," Northcott finished for me. I heard some shuffling on his end. "This hitchhiker—what else did he tell you in the car? How did he act?"

"He acted calm, for a guy who'd just been mugged." I ran my free hand through my hair. "He mentioned his dad had killed his mom, though. Maybe it was the other way around. And he said he wouldn't hesitate to choke a woman if she got on his nerves."

Northcott was quiet, and only in his silence could I ascertain how fast my heart was beating with each ticking second.

"Detective Northcott?"

"Charles Dodgson is the primary suspect in the Hellenbach series of murders," he stated. "The first girl was Natalie Hellenbach, nineteen, and if it weren't for Natalie's granddaddy, then Jacqueline Wright—age seventeen—probably wouldn't have gotten the media's attention, either. Natalie was found last Tuesday in the woods near the restaurant where she worked, as was Jacqueline; both girls were waitresses, and both were stomped on, cut up, and strangled with a triple-braided rope. Jackie was discovered Thursday in a small town maybe two hours from where Nat was, but Jackie was farther west—toward Oklahoma. Kelli—a cashier—was found today in Madison, same circumstances. All these girls were servers in one form or the other." He sighed. "Willow fits that description. And if what you're saying is true, and your Charlie and Charles Dodgson are the same man—"

"Then Willow's probably out in the woods here in Madison!"

"—then Megan Hawley's in bigger trouble then the APD is making it seem," he finished. "She works at the Big-Box on Thirty-First Street by the Protzig, like you said. According to my friend in the Arminster Police Department, Meg never came home last night." He sighed again. "They think the Hellenbach guy—we'll assume it's Dodgson—is abducting the girls after they serve him and get off work. Then he takes them back to a motel or a secluded place. The top guys aren't sure what he's doing with the girls—they aren't raped, and they're only physically harmed right before they're killed in the woods… aside from wounds sustained while trying to escape, maybe."

"What's the lag time?"

"About thirty-six hours between the kidnapping and death."

"Charlie was bleeding when we picked him up," I told him. "There might be another girl."

"Christ. What route were you taking?"

"The quickest way from Dreary to Madison using QuickSearch Maps."

"Got it." There was the sound of a page being ripped. "I'll talk to my guys and warn them about Dodgson's makeover and Megan. I'll also make sure Madison's PO's got their eyes in the forests and not on the damn lake." I heard the crushing of the mint in his mouth. "I hate to say it, since I know her family, but it might be too late for Willow if Dodgson did get to her. And from all you said, this case is bigger than me now—and I'm talking FBI big. Who knows? Maybe I'll finally get to retire for good this time. And Michael?" He paused. "Thanks for calling. I'm sorry if I came across as a hard-ass before."

"Yeah," I said. "Yeah, no problem." My mouth was dry, and my throat felt raw. "I'm gonna go now."

"Call me back if you remember anything else."

With that, he hung up, leaving me to my thoughts in the SUV.

This was crazy. *This wasn't real.* Troy and I had helped a *hitchhiking murderer.* Franklin Chambers had been alive *at my party.* Bryce Skinner had *shot and killed three people* with his little finger. We'd fallen in the lake and drowned, but apparently, I'd imagined it all; I'd gotten wasted, according to Troy. But he had been with Gabby that night—and she'd denied that. *What the hell was happening?*

Catherine. I still had Cat, and I was going to see her at one o'clock. She was the anchor keeping my ship in place. But she was the captain, really, steering me along in the right direction. What mattered, despite the craziness, was that for once in seven years, I was home. At least, that's what I couldn't help associating her with. *Home. Familiarity. Childhood.*

I got out of the Big Nasty, walked up the porch steps, and then went back inside.

"If you want to get rid of a body, hydrofluoric acid isn't the way to go, despite whatever you may have seen on TV," Kukowski said while clipping his fingernails over the trash bin. Troy shuddered, but Kukowski nonetheless appeared unfazed. "In this case, bases are better for the fleshy, tender meat. So if you're planning on committing a homicide like Dodgson, what you *should* do is stock up on a corrosive drain-cleaning product—great for this kind of stuff."

My horrified expression must have been priceless.

"Michael," Troy started, seemingly overwhelmed by my uncle's answer to whatever question he had asked. "What did the detective say? About Charlie?"

"He's going to talk to the Arminster Police Department," I said. "He thinks it's too late for Willow—assuming Charlie's responsible for her disappearance—but the info about the haircut and shave should help them find him."

"To think you both harbored a fugitive." Kukowski shook his head. "And you bring him into *our town*, too!"

Troy sat on the sofa, his elbows on his knees, his hands running through his long hair in panic.

"We did this." He looked up at me. "We did. *We did this.* We brought that guy into Madison, and he killed your former classmate and the girl at Mr. Swanky's." He crossed his arms. "Mae, this is on us. This is so incredibly *fucked!*"

"Hey, now." Kukowski sat down with him. "This isn't your fault, 'kay? There's no way you could've known… probably." He sighed. "And what's done is done. You both did nothing wrong—at the very least, in the legal sense. Just…"

Kukowski took the remote and started flipping through the channels. He stopped on a recent episode of *Penthouse Pursuit* set in Costa Rica.

"Watch TV," he advised. "Try to figure out which luxury apartment the couple will choose. Read a novel, surf the web, play with my spirit board, do *something* to distract yourself. Anything to get your mind off the real world." Kukowski turned to me. "Don't you have a date in an hour and a half?"

"Oh, yeah, that's right." I pulled at the bottom of my pajama shirt. "I need to change and shower. Or, shower and then change. And—"

"Do what you gotta do," Kukowski told me. "I'll be here, waiting for an important phone call."

"OK," I said, then left for the bedroom. I grabbed a pair of jeans, a hoodie in case it got cold again, and my Sylvia Plath t-shirt that read, "*The Bell Jar* by Victoria Lucas," with the silhouette of a woman trapped in glass. Then I went into the bathroom and set the shower water's temperature to warm before getting in to cry, soft but hard.

When I got out, the mirror was foggy, so I wiped it with my forearm and took a good long look at myself. While I was starting to grow hair on my chin and stubble elsewhere, I knew who I was and where I'd come from—what I'd done. If Willow and

Charlie had crossed paths, her death was on me, and the same could be said of Kelli Ziegler from Mr. Swanky's. Maybe even Meg from Big-Box, too.

My head hurt. My head *physically* ached. Troy, Gabby, even Cat's comments made me think Bryce hadn't killed those people Saturday night, yet it had been so real to me. I had *felt* the terror. I couldn't think straight—couldn't think at all. My mind kept focusing on Cat, on Dodgson, on Bryce's massacre, and that damn bisexual bus.

Someone knocked on the door. I wrapped a towel around myself and opened it to see Troy with my phone, which vibrated in his hands and displayed a picture of my mother on its screen.

I thanked him, shut the door, and then answered the phone.

"Mom?"

"Good news and bad news!" she told me.

"Oh, all right. Bad news first."

"Um… OK." She adjusted her script. "The bad news is that the University of North Carolina in Windhaven isn't offering you much in scholarships, but at least we'd get some government assistance."

"Dang. So what's the good news?"

"THEY ACCEPTED YOU!" I moved the phone away from my ear. "—proud of you and all you've accomplished this year. This is your first acceptance letter! With many more to come!"

"Wait, you opened my mail?" I asked, then guessed it was no worse than having her brother write me as my dad. "Anyway, Dreary Community College already accepted me last month."

"Yeah, yeah, but I want you going out-of-state! Experiencing life away from… well, here! Dreary is…"

"Dreary?"

"… definitely not a misnomer." She laughed. "Aren't you so excited?!"

"Well, if they're not offering me jack, then I'm not going."

"Who's Jack? Is that a drug?"

"What? No. It's an expression. I don't want you having to provide for me financially more than you have to, and with student loans..." I shook my head. "No. I'm not going if they're not helping. They must not want me that bad."

There was a long silence. Finally, my mom said, "Um, all right then. I appreciate it, but you shouldn't base your college decisions on my income. If this is something you want, we'll make it happen."

"I'll be fine," I told her.

"OK. Their loss. Maybe you'll hear back from Hartsett and Arminster, too."

"Yeah, may—"

"Oh my God, I forgot to tell you!" I could hear the worry in her voice. "Troy's mom came over yesterday. She had a big fight with Mr. Souse about Troy going to Oklahoma with you. He took their jeep and hasn't returned her calls."

"Where'd he go?"

"She doesn't know! Maybe to see his family?" She sighed. "Anyway, I'll call you if I hear back about the universities. Check your email! They might've sent stuff that way!"

We said our good-byes and ended the call.

Too much was happening all at once, and none of it made sense. I felt stuck, I needed out, and I had to do it fast. Back in Dreary, I thought the lake house would hold all the answers, but it had only led to more questions and disorientation.

Cat was my beacon. I needed to be with her; that much was clear to me.

Ms. Varsha let me in that afternoon with a smile on her face, which I appreciated. Cat was in her room, she told me, so I thanked her and went down the stairs, two at a time.

There was no singing to accompany my descent; when I knocked on the cracked door, she was at her laptop on her desk. She wore the same outfit as before, but this time, she was messing with audio software. For a moment, though, I heard the song.

And now it's very strange—

"Hey, MJ," she said to me, standing up and flashing her teeth as I walked over to where she stood. "The cover's almost ready. My followers like how I do the older ones. You know. 'Daisy Bell,' 'Will the Circle Be Unbroken?' and—"

I hugged her. I wasn't sure what came over me, but I did, and she accepted it, though only briefly. Then she backed away.

"My bad," I told her. "It's just… I'm happy I've gotten to see you and talk to you these past couple of days. I didn't know if I would. And you're cool, and you're funny, and you're exactly how I remember you."

She laughed. I wasn't expecting that.

"Sorry," she said. "Just… total flashback. I thought you were about to ask me out for a second." She laughed again, but then her eyes widened. "Oh, shit. You *were* about to ask me out right then!"

"What?! No, I wasn't! Seriously!"

"Please." She went over to her multitude of blankets and held a pillow to her chest. "I don't think you know the kind of girl I am. Things were different when we were ten. You say I'm the same, but I'm everything but. I've changed. I'm not what you want. I'm eighteen, you're…"

"Turning eighteen this week."

"… turning eighteen this week." She curled her fingers. "Absence makes the heart grow fonder. I've read your book, and I've seen your stories on Uprorrr. You're a horny teenage boy—I get it, and that's totally fine! But I'm just not like that. I'm asexual."

"You're a sexual what?"

"I don't experience sexual attraction," she explained. "We needed to get that out of the way sooner—end the possibility of something… something *more* between us. For your sake, and mine. I don't want to toy with anyone's emotions. Sure, I enjoy cuddling, and I find some people aesthetically pleasing, yeah. And sometimes, I do get aroused. But arousal isn't necessarily attraction, and for a lot of people, that's a hard concept to grasp. You, on the other hand, clearly experience sexual attraction, and I don't give a fuck. Like, I don't. *I don't want to be intimate with you.* I don't mean to be so blunt about it, but yesterday, I tried to make it obvious… or maybe I didn't. I don't know… Jesus, that's what got me in this catastrophe in the first place."

I didn't know how to respond. I was confused and angry at what she was saying, even if it was true. Something had changed inside her, but my response drowned on my lips. So I said the first thing that came to mind.

"Willow's been murdered."

"Murdered?" Cat stared at me with disbelief, then looked down at my feet. She put her hands on her head, and for the third time, I noticed the circular scars on her palms. Her eyes met mine. She looked horrified. "Was it Bryce?"

"Huh? No, it was Charlie. Charles Dodgson. Haven't you been watching the news?" She wasn't listening anymore.

"Willow and I haven't talked in years," Cat said, mostly to herself. "She moved up to Madison because… the condoms had expired, she got pregnant—"

"Why did you want to know if Bryce did this?" I asked.

Cat looked up at me and jumped back as if she'd seen a monster. Once she realized it was me, she calmed herself and went over to the red curtains. She then grabbed the side handle and pulled them back, revealing a tiny window in the shape of a triangle. Light seeped into the room from it, creating a path that ended at her makeshift bedding.

"There's nothing hiding behind my curtains," she said, then pointed for emphasis. "Bryce has a lot behind his. Water drips down the walls and from the ceiling. I only saw a glimpse, though, in our time together. 'Too long a sacrifice / Can make a stone of the heart.' That's 'Easter, 1916' by Yeats."

"I'm not following. What do you mean he—"

"Bryce—" She held up her hands. "—did *this* to me." The scars were on both sides, and she turned them back and forth to illustrate her point. "I opened up to him in his pickup in this construction site we used to make out in, and you know what he does? He denies me. He *screams* at me. And then he tries to rape me. These scars?" She waved her hands, and her body trembled as well. "These are my constant reminder. The one guy I trusted the most—and he does *this!* I RAN FROM HIS TRUCK AND TRIPPED ON SOME BROKEN PIECE OF WOOD! THERE WERE *NAILS* IN MY HANDS, AND I HAD TO GET A *FUCKING TETANUS SHOT THANKS TO THAT DRUNK FOOL!"*

She had fallen to the floor, crying softly. I wanted to help her, to wipe away the years of sorrow and turmoil she'd written about online. She didn't deserve this—being locked away in this basement. She needed guidance back into the real world. I thought I could be that person for her.

"I'm so sorry, Cat," I told her. I reached out my hand. "I didn't know—"

"Don't!" she begged. "You think you can fix this? Fix me?! Be my *best friend* and make it *all go away* and feel better for making *me* feel better?!" She shoved me. *"How can you be so… fucking arrogant!"*

"Hey, Cat?" Ms. Varsha called from the stairs. "Your group is waiting for you in the living room!"

"Thank you!" she shouted back, wiping her face with the top of her t-shirt. Her red nose and watery eyes just about broke my heart. This wasn't what I'd intended. I didn't want any of this.

"You invited people over?" I asked, pulling out my phone to check the time. "But you—"

"I forgot," she told me, annoyed. "I have to go up there."

So she did. I grudgingly followed her up the stairs and to the left, where eleven kids ages anywhere from thirteen to eighteen sat in a lopsided oval in front of the TV. An armchair had been pushed in front of it; whoever sat there would be overseeing the guests. I figured it was for Cat, making me wonder the reasoning behind their meeting.

"Sorry, everyone," she told them. I stayed by the doorframe while she delicately stepped over them and to the chair. She sat before it, leaning against the leather. "This is my friend Michael. We went to elementary school together."

"*Hi, Michael,*" most of them said in unison, as if this were Alcoholics Anonymous and I needed to state my addiction. They were all of different races and genders, though I did notice most of them wore hoodies. A couple of adults were chatting quietly with Ms. Varsha in the kitchen. There were plates of cookies and cups of lemonade on the counter. Each kid had one.

"Hello," I said.

"So last week," Cat recapped to the group, "we talked about the times when we question our kintype. After all, it seems canines and felines are the most, um, *represented* among us." She briefly touched a brown book with a seven-pointed star on it, then looked up at me. "Actually, I'll be right back. One sec."

Cat stepped out of the circle, walked over to me, and then led me into the foyer and out the front door. Cool air brushed against my face as she looked around—first at the cars parked alongside the street, then at me.

"You ... must have a lot of questions," she said.

"Yeah, I do." I didn't mean to sound irritated, though that's how it came out. "What is this? Who are they? I thought we were doing our thing today!"

"I know, I know. But just like you want answers, so do they. I run this group for teens who identify as Otherkin. Most of them live in Arminster, but one of the boys is from Red Springs. They're nice kids, and it's the least I can do for the Otherkin community."

"So all those..." I moved my hand in the direction of the house. "People. They think they're cats, too?"

"They *believe* they were once *non-human*," she corrected me, "spiritually or otherwise. Two of the girls are cat therians—which is cool for me—but some of the others associate themselves with otterkin, dogkin, bird-of-paradisekin… swankin and rabbitkin… I feel like I'm forgetting someone." She snapped her fingers. "Wolfkin!"

"So… in your house… are all these Otherkin who identify as a bunch of animals—"

"No, sorry, but Jared is plantkin, though he's still searching to narrow it down. And that's completely OK! He can take all the time he needs."

"Did…" I stared at her. "You said 'plantkin,' didn't you?"

"Well, yeah, sure. There's plantkin, spacekin—who's to say planets don't have souls?—and a whole bunch of other Otherkin. It's not *just* animals. It can be anything—even otherworldly."

"Jared thinks he's a *plant*? Like a cactus or a grapevine or an alpine shrub?"

"*Spiritually*, Michael. That's the keyword here. We've been over this."

"Oh, no!" I told her. "Oh, no no no no no no no. You were talking about *animals* yesterday. No, scratch that, you were saying *you* believe you were a *cat* in a former life. And that's fine—I can accept that! But this is… well, a bunch of kids who think they were once a… *a bird of paradise!*" I laughed. "I mean, you like that jerky and milk drink, right? What does Birdy do? Pretend he can fly?"

"Look, you ass," she started. "You don't go around claiming someone's religion is false and wrong and stupid, do you? Same with someone's sexual and gender identities—you don't bash those, right? I fucking hope not. So what makes us any different? Where's our respect; where's *our* kindness, huh? Why stand there and make fun of all the hard work we're doing as Otherkin?"

"These kids are *impressionable!*" I reminded her. "They look up to you as their leader, and they'll believe anything you say! And you were… you were in the hospital when you discovered your Otherkinly-ness. You were doped up! *You weren't all there in the head!* And then you read this book, and you think you're a domestic cat—"

"You don't know what I think."

"I'm just having a hard time understanding how Jared can spiritually believe he… is a plant? Connected to a plant? Is this some Native American sort of—?"

"Michael, stop." Cat rubbed at her temples. "You're making me angry, and I have to go back in there. And if you're not going to be an ally, you might as well leave."

"Leave?" I echoed. "I went through hell and high water just to get here! What about me and you?! What about our date?!"

I recognized the Freudian slip as soon as I'd said it, as did Cat. This wasn't a date; it was anything but.

"Go," she told me. "There's nothing for you here."

"Fine." I turned around and grabbed the handle to the SUV. "Fine, I'll get out of your life. Is that what you want? You want me to leave again?"

"I want you to find whatever it is you're searching for." She shrugged. "I'm not that. I never will be. You're like those boys on Chipper who complain about being 'stuck in the friend zone.' You didn't break up with Olivia for this, did you? Tell me: did you hang out with me these past two days just to see if I'd date you?"

"No, of course not!"

"Did you?"

"I mean… maybe! I'm only human! I've thought about you a lot. The way you make me feel—"

"That's sick, Michael. That's pathetic—trying to be a girl's *amazing friend* in hopes she'll change her mind, decide you're the one, fall in love with you, and let you fuck her brains out some night after dinner. That's not OK. That's disingenuous. You can't 'win me over.' That's not fair; I'm not a goal. *My attraction to you isn't something you can earn.* Get it now? I'm more than a contact on your phone for when you're bored and lonely. So meow meow, motherfucker. That what you wanted to hear? Stop using me and go get your goddamn happiness somewhere else."

"Cat—" I tried. But she'd already gone inside, and I was alone once more.

I went back to the front door and pulled on the handle. She'd locked it. So I started knocking, then pounding against it furiously, whispering, "*Come on, open the door, open the fucking door...*"

Ms. Varsha answered.

"What are you doing?!" she demanded. "What's gotten into you?!"

"I just need to talk to Cat."

"I don't think that's such a good idea—"

"Just let me talk to her!"

"Michael, it's time for you to go home. Are you OK?"

"No, I'm not OK!" I shouted at her. "This doesn't make sense. Nothing's been making any sense. Everything's all wrong..." I looked past her. "Cat!"

Ms. Varsha slammed the door in my face. I knocked a few more times, then figured it was pointless. The *whole trip* had been pointless. The only ulterior motive was me trying to relive the past. Was that so wrong?

Someone shut the blinds on the left side of the house, followed by the right. I cursed under my breath and kicked at the grass. Then I went.

I took a different route to the cabin that afternoon, going north and feeling defeated. The weather was pleasant, though the temperature had dropped, and for the first time since entering Oklahoma, I turned up the heater. This was undoubtedly the state I remembered, where fireflies were called "lightning bugs" and "y'all" was a proper noun. Yet things were different. I wasn't sure I liked it.

The water of Lake Nasagarresett was a rich blue at three o'clock. The sun was high, a couple of confused osprey were touring the coast, and an army-green open-top jeep was tailgating me. I couldn't see all of the driver from my rearview mirror, though I could see from his rolled-up sleeves and beefy arms he was a man—an angry one, at that, by the way he gripped the wheel—and I struggled to recall if he'd started following me before or after I'd entered Madison County.

I purposely took a wrong turn. He swerved, nearly nicking some grandpa's red sports car. I got back on the correct road and pulled into 902 Honey Deer Drive. The jeep parked behind me.

What bothered me most was I had seen this jeep before, but when or where, I couldn't tell. Yet as Troy opened the front door to the lake house—happy to see me— and instantly scowled at the car behind the SUV, I knew then the driver must've been his stepfather.

Mr. Souse stood extra tall that day. He had slicked-back, immobile gray hair—the same color as his eyes, mustache, and perhaps his heart—and he wore not one, but two Julian Morrissey wristwatches. His eyes were bloodshot, and light stubble sprouted from his sagging cheeks. Mr. Souse was a mean man, and it was just Troy's awful luck they lived in a house divided.

"Troy!" Mr. Souse shouted up at him, pushing me to the side as I got out of the SUV. His voice was distinctly Southern in accent, though he slurred a little, and his stomp wasn't too steady. "Get your ass in the car right this instant!"

"Why are you here?!" Troy demanded.

"Because you've embarrassed your family—*your mother*—for the last time!" He went up to the second-to-last step on the porch, looking down at Troy. "You've disrespected her, your sisters, *and me!*"

"You're out of your mind," Troy whispered, his body shaking slightly. He took a step back toward the door. "Driving all the way here—"

"I'm out of my mind?! I'm the one having to check that Find My Family app and your debit card history to figure out where the hell you've ran off to!"

"You're not supposed to have access to that!"

"And why the hell not? It's my money—"

"It's Uncle Julian's money, dickweed!"

"Bite your tongue!"

"It's not Troy's fault!" I told him, walking to the left to look at them both. Mr. Souse turned to face me. "I invited Troy to go on a road trip—"

"Frankly, Michael, I don't give a crap what you do because you're not my son."

"Yeah," Troy said, "and neither am I." He stepped forward. "So back off, Cole."

"Who do you—?!"

"I don't need your approval!" Troy continued. "I'm way past that, motherfucker. All you do is emotionally abuse people and then refuse to acknowledge the shit you say is hurtful."

"You've never listened to a damn word I've said—it's always *Troy Rico* this, *Troy Rico* that." He laughed. "You aren't shit, Troy. You're a defensive child who thinks he's the goddamn king of the world."

"Fuck you!"

"And maybe that's what you want, but at least I know who I am: a hard-working father of two little girls and their *worthless* older sister." He spat to the side, and I watched in complete disgust as he surveyed Troy, who was crying from both eyes. Mr. Souse smirked. "What a joke."

The door opened, causing Troy to stumble to the right. Kukowski stood there in a blue Havana shirt and khaki shorts, his hands folded across his chest. He was shorter than Mr. Souse, but Kukowski had the expression of a chemistry teacher who'd taught for over a decade at an underfunded public school. Cole Souse had nothing on him.

"Get off my property," Kukowski told him with little to no emotion in his voice. "Do it now. And if you come back, I'll call the police, and don't you dare think I won't."

Mr. Souse's left eye twitched. I could tell he wasn't used to following someone else's orders, which was to be expected for a man who'd lived his whole life in the same town and ran his own trucking business.

"You can't tell me what to do," he said.

Kukowski pulled out the Leiden 21 handgun from behind his shirt.

"There are some things in this world that require very little activation energy."

"What the—?!"

"And some things need a ton of it." Kukowski admired the gun for a moment. "Do you know what nitrogen triiodide is?"

"I… do not, no."

"Basically, you take concentrated ammonia and concentrated iodine—which is very hard to get now 'cause you can make a contact explosive out of it. 'Kay? Put it together, and it makes this black kind of precipitate, and then you filter it. That black stuff, when it dries—and sometimes when you walk by it—it explodes. When it does, it makes a pretty big noise—and not a fire explosion, but of iodine gas, which is not the best thing to be breathing in. You're supposed to touch it with a feather because a thin amount on filter paper is enough to ring your bell. It is loud and it is painful."

"What're you—?"

"I actually have a bit of iodine left for horse injuries, and sometimes, I used to think about putting it on the seats in my classroom before school started." Kukowski waved the gun. "Do you see how government regulations have helped you now? People like me should *not* get involved in things like this. I don't like you, so it's possible when you go back to your jeep, you check out the seat, 'Huh, what's this black stuff?' Sit on it, it'll bust your rear. *And then you can snort the iodine gas and die!* I bet you're tempted to call the FBI the minute you pull out—'Got us a terrorist in Oklahoma!' But the only terrorist I see right now is you, terrorizing your stepson."

"Mind your business," Mr. Souse said. "I got enough crap to deal with."

"Sir, with all due respect, I will chew you up and spit you out." Kukowski walked up to him. "And don't get too smart with me, neither, 'cause I'll destroy you if you do."

Kukowski aimed the gun between Mr. Souse's legs. He crossed them instinctively.

"I think a 'Your Majesty' would be appropriate," Kukowski said. Mr. Souse cursed under his breath. "*Thank you!* Now I can go on." To Troy and me: "There was a bit of a curtsy there, too. Well, more like a jerking head motion along the lines of 'You're a real pain in the ass'—but I'll take it as a curtsy."

Mr. Souse was already on his way to his car. As he opened the door, he spat into the grass and then turned to us. He gripped the handle hard as he did so, his knuckles white and fingers red.

"I'll see you back at the house," he said to Troy, then scooted on into the vehicle. He stared Troy down for a few more seconds before starting the engine and going off down the road. Within seconds, he was gone, yet far too close for comfort.

I looked back at Troy, who was still shaking and sweating. I'd never seen him this nervous about anything, whether it be a statistics test or his sisters coming home early while he and Clyde were upstairs with the door closed. Troy was frightened—and not by a werewolf or zombie or anything. True fear can't be translated, only felt. Sometimes, it can be witnessed, as I experienced then, secondhand through the awful father/son dynamic that belonged to Cole Souse and Troy Valdez. It was awful. Troy had done some messed-up shit in the past, but *nobody* deserves an abusive parent, physically or emotionally. He was a good kid, deep down. We all were.

"Sometimes..." he started, weeping as he did. "God, sometimes I wish he would just *hit me*. At least then my mom would leave him. Blames his mood swings on his migraines, but that's no excuse." He took a deep, shaky breath. "Cole cares about her. A lot. But he doesn't care for me. And in my dreams... I get to yell back, you know? And he listens."

"I'm sorry," Kukowski said. He slowly put an arm around Troy, who came in for an embrace and started sobbing into Kukowski's shirt. "That's OK. That's OK. Let it all out."

"What an asshole," I said.

"Agreed." Kukowski started to cry as he looked to me. "I miss my daughter. She doesn't call much anymore. And Bubby—I should stop teasing him. I..." He gripped Troy tighter. "I'm just as bad of a father. And I know that's relative. But I don't mean to be. It's not easy. My own dad said I'd do fine, but ... *fuck*. Here I am, you know?"

I moved over to join them, and so we stayed like that on the porch for a while, comforting each other's losses. It'd been a strange couple of days, and no form of divine intervention could've prepared us for the week. The people had changed, yet I'd returned expecting more. It was a time-lapse video on loop.

Once inside the safety of our room, I shared with Troy my brief time spent with Cat and of our ending conversation. He smirked—not necessarily in that I-told-you-so way, but to point out the irony in me brushing off his breakup of sorts with Gabby. The tables had turned, but Troy would listen. So I vented.

"Life might've been so different for me here," I finished from the desk chair. He sat on the bottom bunk. "That much is clear to me now."

"Yeah, but forget about the years that've passed," he said. "Think about it. Recent days would've been altered or never been."

"Eva's still in Alabama, but she's the smartest of us. Her guidance could have helped me with Cat, or you with Gabby..."

"Sounds like you don't want Eva here for Eva."

"It's not that." I struggled to connect my thoughts with the right words, a recent habit of mine. "It's a quality I appreciate, is all. I like Eva."

"No, you like having someone to complain to—not with." He got up. "Jesus Christ,

Mom. Was there *anyone* in our friend group you actually liked?"

"I do like Eva!"

"Keegan? Leah? Clyde and Olivia?"

"I liked Olivia."

"You liked the fact she was around for you." He shook his head. "You think the same way about me, and look where I am because of it." He gestured with open hands toward the window. "How much longer do you need here, anyway? When are we going back? I'd like a good heads-up before I have to face step-dick again."

"Soon," I said. "I need some time to... sort out some things."

"So Thursday? Friday?"

"Definitely by Friday."

"Fine," he said, walking out of our room. "Whatever."

◆━━━◆━◆━━━◆

I ate cereal alone as the sun set over Lake Nasagarresett. I read the former forest that was *Krijg de Tering* while I waited for Troy and Kukowski to return to shore via the *Caldecota*, which I could see zipping along with life against the vast blue of the water from the open door leading to the shattered back deck. Little birds chased fireflies as I sat there with the empty bowl beside me, admiring van der Kolk's word choice and imagery of winter.

Thinking of Cat, I pulled out my phone, went to blackmissy.uprorrr.com, and then scrolled through the list of songs she'd uploaded. Her covers were calm and slow, but also seductive and haunting as they played into the chilling air. Finally, watching the last of the deep amber clouds making their way 'round the bittersweet sky, I turned up the volume to her version of Sarah Bethe Nelson's "Paying," repeated my restless regrets, and dreamt of all that could have been, all that should have been.

PART THREE: D.S.

"When I was younger I could remember anything, whether
it had happened or not; but my faculties are decaying now,
and soon I shall be so I cannot remember any but
the things that never happened."

—MARK TWAIN, 1924

T he flight to Arminster took longer than Ian had expected, much like the final miles of a marathon can seem to drag on and on. After he had left the note on the table for Makenna, he'd dashed for the airport, grabbing only his wallet and dark brown jacket; the wisps of snow that greeted him as he opened the front door kept him from forgetting it. He didn't even know how he was going to get to Lake Nasagarresett in Madison, Oklahoma. "I'll figure it out when I get there," he told himself aloud.

Ian walked away from Arminster International Airport and took a moment to take in his surroundings. It was dark, and the drizzle of snow in the air acted like tiny mirrors reflecting the light from passing cars. His eyes followed a single flake as it slowly drifted toward the road, melting upon contact.

Ian hugged his jacket closer and used his now-perfected two-finger whistle to try to get the attention of a cabbie who had parked a couple of terminals away.

There was a short, plump man by the front doors attempting to pass out flyers to people entering the nearest terminal. As he tried to get one couple's attention, a gust of wind came from behind, causing the man to lose his balance and drop his pile of papers. Instead of helping, several bystanders only snickered as the man jumped and slid on the slippery sidewalk while chasing down flyers, not unlike a walrus trying to gobble down flopping fish on an ice floe.

Ian caught a flyer and stepped on another. MISSING: TANNER THE TABBY was the heading. A close-up photo of the plump man holding his dear kitty took up most of the page.

"Three and a half weeks," the man said tearfully as Ian handed him the papers. "Three and a half weeks without my Tanner. God bless you, sir."

"I'm sorry," Ian said. "Real sorry." A taxi pulled up. "I know how it feels."

Ian got inside, sunk into the leather backseat, and then turned around as the driver pulled away. He was happy to see a few others were now gathering the flyers.

Ian redirected the vents. The warmth of the big cab's heater was comforting, and yet he was still aware he was shivering deep inside.

"Can you take me to Lake Nasagarresett?" Ian asked the driver.

The cabbie stopped the car and faced him. He had a dark, messy head of hair with a goatee to match. He looked to be in his early twenties. The name tag on the man's orange uniform shirt read: TAXI DRIVER 021, TONY.

"What on Earth makes you wanna go to there?" Tony asked, obviously startled.

"Look, I just need to get to Madison, all right?"

"Sir, do you know how many lives that damned lake has taken? How many *suicides* are committed there? Lost souls thinking that drownin' in unholy water's the only way... Do you know how many headlines have featured that godforsaken pond? And lemme tell ya, not one of those headlines has been good! Do ya, mister?"

Up to this point, Ian had assumed the disappearance of the kids was the only tragedy involving Lake Nasagarresett. Was there a greater mystery to those depths?

"I had no idea." Ian shook his head and stared out the window for a moment. He then pulled out his wallet and handed Tony a few twenties. "I once lost someone close to me there. I need to look around."

Tony glanced down at the cash and sighed. "So there's no way of talkin' you outta this? They say the Devil herself lives in those waters."

"That's not the only place she's been living," Ian muttered. "Please, can we just go?"

"Oui, oui, monsieur." Tony mockingly saluted Ian before putting the cab into drive. "Votre funéraire."

Ian sat in silence for the rest of the trip. Tony looked in the rearview mirror on occasion, probably wondering why he always got the crazies. And he wouldn't be too far off; Ian felt crazy, as the miles went by. He thought about his letter to Mekenzie, who was probably crying over it, and then cursed himself for being so vague in his writing. Plus, he'd left without telling work. *The boss is sure gonna love that.*

"There's Madison County's Grand Canyon!" Tony joked after hitting a particularly deep pothole. Ian wasn't used to these kinds of road conditions and felt like he might lose the meager dinner the airline had served him. He wondered if Karina's bus had taken these same awful backroads before disappearing. He put his hand on the handle to roll down the window, but taking a deep breath, he stopped himself. He didn't want to feel the freezing winter air against his neck just yet.

It's the perfect setting for a horror novel, Ian played out in his mind. *The search for a missing girl on a dark road, leading to a lake with an even darker history, surrounded by dead trees with bones for branches just waiting to …*

The clock on the old taxi's dashboard read 9:02. Despite all the potholes, exhaustion rolled over Ian. Closing his eyes, he drifted into a deep slumber.

He thought he smelled something funny. He thought he smelled rotting fish.

I didn't remember falling asleep; I didn't feel quite like myself anymore. It was as if I were a pentimento alteration with the traces of a better painting still there, cracked and exposed to the light. I was simultaneously Dr. Henry Jekyll and Mr. Edward Hyde while I held up my phone and caught my reflection in its screen. Ten in the morning on a Wednesday—the first day of spring—with dark chin hair and a faint mustache. But I was also the protagonist, and further beyond, the author himself.

Troy lay on the couch facing the TV in the living room, going through the channels one at a time. I hadn't seen anyone do this in years.

He stopped on the local news station, watched for a while, and then put the remote down.

"The news is so random," Troy told me as I sat down on the other couch. "Crime reports, virus outbreaks, international relations fucked up by some white-guy politician who shouldn't even be there, and then: 'Peach Growers Turn on Sprinklers at Three A.M.' Like, where did that come from?"

"It's supposed to be in the high twenties tonight," Kukowski explained from the entry to the kitchen. "That's why the weather people are saying there's goin' to be a freeze warning, so whoever has delicate plants, they'll turn on the sprinklers at about three in the morning."

"How come?" I asked.

"When liquid water turns into solid water, it gives off heat, and that's just enough to keep the peach bud alive for another hour. I'd explain the rest, but you don't care—

believe me, I know high schoolers. If I ask you to repeat it after, you'd be all, 'Dude, like, it sprinkles on it, and the ice, um, insulates it, man! That's how come Eskimos don't have to wear clothes, and they jump in the river and their swimming pools, and they get out and turn into icicles, and they're happy and warm! That's why they always have smiles on their faces and eat fish because fish taste good with ice on them!' And just keep going on like that and blurt out the stupidness. And your mom would go, 'I knew I shouldn't have drank when I had that child in me! I knew I should've stopped my whiskey every day!' Maybe that's what my mom did." He paused to think, then looked to me. "Probably why Heidi's such a weirdo."

"Hey!" I said, but Troy and I stilled laughed, anyway.

"What?" He laughed, too. "You guys are goin' to miss my humor, aren't you?"

"Are you going somewhere?" Troy asked him. He turned to me. "Or are we?"

"I'm breaking Bubby out," Kukowski told us. "Well, paying for it, anyway. You both have inspired me to be a better father to my kids, so I'm going to start by doing that. Just got to beat the blustery weather first."

"I thought it was only getting cold out tonight," I said.

"Never trust Arminster news when it comes to the weather. They figured it out with that weather guy Russ Carpenter 'bout four years back. He said there would only be a light frost one Christmas, *and boom!* Thirteen inches of snow, the idiot. And three people ended up dying." He looked out the window. "Nah, I'm guessing it'll start snowing tonight instead of by the weekend. I suggest you boys head out of Oklahoma sooner than later so you don't get caught in the middle."

"Oh, Gabby texted me back," Troy said to me as Kukowski left for his room. "We're hanging out today. Gonna talk things through. She should be here any minute now to pick me up."

"What for?"

"Her house." He cupped his right hand and sniffed his breath. "Could you get me after? Like, four or five-ish?"

"Sure," I said. Troy proceeded his flipping through the channels. "Um, did the police find out anything about Charlie Dodgson and Willow?"

"Yeah, they did." Troy kept his eyes on the screen. "She was found in the forest nearby, strangled with rope. They found another girl by that rest stop at the crossroads in Arkansas, and a sixth at a 'Mistletoe Park' by that Big-Box we went to Monday. That girl was alive, though—Megan Hawley—but barely. In a lot of shock. The cops still haven't caught Dodgson yet. They're so useless. *Fuck.*"

I felt awful as I ascertained the reality of the situation. I stumbled out of the living room and into the bathroom, where I fell to my knees and heaved several days' worth of junk food into the stained toilet. Their names flashed across my eyes in my head: Natalie Hellenbach, Jacqueline Wright, Willow Dusett, Kelli Ziegler, Megan Hawley, and another, unnamed girl. But they were more than names; in the case of Willow, she was a mother and a confidant to Cat. As for the others, they were at the very least daughters, friends, *people*. Dodgson had taken that away from them—and for what? What kind of twisted motive could he possibly have to justify his actions? Even Megan Hawley, the sole survivor, would be haunted by their encounter for years to come.

I'd driven the SUV.

I'd taken him across state lines.

I washed my hands and my face, then glanced up at the mirror. For a second in the reflection, I thought I didn't see anyone staring back. Yet there I was, with scraggly facial hair and sad, socketed eyes. I wasn't the hero to any story. I saw that. So who was I?

◆——◆—◆——◆

The TV was off when I left the bathroom. Troy was busy packing some things into a plastic Big-Box bag. I went over to my phone, put my thumb on the passcode reader, and then saw I'd received one new text from a 918 area code.

UNKNOWN NUMBER

Michael, this is Bryce. I would like to talk to you at my house in New Baines about what happened Saturday night. I have a lot on my mind. Can you come at six? It won't take long. I'll even provide dinner. You can bring your friend, too, if that makes you more comfortable. I shouldn't be too hard to find, since my stepdad is the mayor here, but if you need directions, please let me know.

It's been a long seven years. I hope you understand.

Talk soon.

"That's her," Troy announced regarding his own text. I looked out and saw Gabby's silver liftback parked in the driveway. I followed Troy through the door.

"Hey, Michael," she said. "Troy told me you're picking him up at five, right?"

"Uh, yeah," I said, still confused about Bryce and Gabby and Troy and Willow. "That should work. But, um, what exactly happened Saturday night? I need to know. I've heard... different stories. I want the truth, and don't take this the wrong way: did Bryce kill anyone?"

"Shit!" Troy exclaimed. "I need my phone—just one second."

He left us there in an awkward silence. Gabby drew a lazy Fibonacci spiral with her foot.

"I got a call the other day," she said when we were alone. "From a private investigator in Arminster."

"Detective Northcott."

"He started asking about Willow, but then we started talking about Bryce." She looked around, then back to me. "I think this could be our guy."

"Our what?"

"Think about it! We all have this messed-up crap hanging over our heads from fifth grade, but really, it wasn't our fault. *Bryce* talked us into it. If we make it look like someone from the outside is snooping around—*and he's on our side*—then we'll be off the hook, and Bryce will get what he deserves! We'll be put into, like, a witness protection sort of deal. For coming clean. Damn the consequences."

"What are you—?"

"I know you saw what happened Saturday," she told me. I nodded. "You know what he said to us. It was so… fucked up. Cat knows, too—more than she'll say."

"She mentioned his curtains," I recalled. "Or something that's behind them."

"We need proof. If there was some sort of way…"

Gabby trailed off. Because Troy was still inside, I took out my phone and showed her Bryce's text to me.

"Now *that* is an invitation to die for," she said. "This is good! This is exactly what we want. Bryce never invites people over, and Cat told me once that he wouldn't let her go near his closet while they were dating, under any circumstance. Nothing's scarier than a white boy with too much freedom. If you can get up to his room and figure out whatever it is he's hiding—whatever skeletons he's got up there—take pictures and send them to me. All right?"

"Look, I just don't understand—"

"No, you must not." She leaned against her car, and I could see her eyes starting to tear up. "Bryce is not a person. He's an idea—a bulletproof force completely consumed by his ideals. We dived too deep, and Bryce is a rabid dog. We have to put him down. He's certifiable! And if you haven't been affected by everything, then fine, whatever. But it's not just me, all right? It's Christian, it's Belle, Cat, Pete…" Sirens blared in the distance. She stared at me. "It's Zach, Morgan, and Bobby, too. Maybe even Blank Frank."

Troy returned then with his phone in hand; it'd been pushed between two couch seats, he said. Gabby turned away from me and got behind the wheel. She wasn't happy, but whether it was about Bryce, Troy, me, or the situation, I didn't know. There had been a lot of that as of late.

"I was gonna ask," Troy whispered to me before getting in with Gabby, "if you've seen my neon green boxer briefs. The Kleidüng ones. I wore them Saturday and put 'em with the rest of my things."

"I haven't," I said. "Sorry. I'll, uh, keep an eye out?"

"Yeah." He nodded his head. "OK, thanks. Gabby'll text you the address. Be there at five?"

"See you then," I said.

Gabby didn't look at me as she drove away—only behind her as she pulled out, straightened the car, and then sped off. I looked down at my feet, which had bits of gravel stuck underneath. I brushed them to the ground with the back of my hand as I returned to the cabin to rest before meeting with Bryce.

Kukowski had a backpack he was filling up with knickknacks from the shelves. After he admired the mallard statue, he put it inside, then zipped the backpack shut.

"Oh," he said as he noticed me. "I thought you already left." He sighed. "Well, I'm off. The key to the house is on the counter. You can put it under the welcome mat when you both leave—just be sure to lock up, clear out the fridge, and unplug any appliances. I don't know when I'll be back."

"But the TV you bought," I pointed out. "You're leaving? Is that why you're taking all that stuff?"

"Huh?" He looked down. "Oh, no. I didn't want to tell you. I saw the way you looked at this old place." He smiled faintly. "I got another job lined up. Guess my reputation precedes me. Who needs Hennigan, anyway? I'll be doing a zoology course in Arizona next year. It won't be a real intense class in terms of academics, but I do want to do a bone project with five or six people in a group to cut up a critter, scrape it down, and put the bones back together. The first skit I wanna do is three coyotes—which are *sort of* like dogs—with two of them playing pool and the other watching. I'll need a hat for at least one of those coyotes, and maybe even a shot glass and cigar for another." He laughed. "I'm goin' to really push the boundaries of this new school. What can I say? It's what I do."

I hugged Kukowski, just as I had five days before. This time, though, we were both fully clothed, save for my bare feet. He hugged me back.

"You still going to send me double the birthday cash?" I asked, smiling.

"That was your mother's doing," he explained as we let go of each other, "and she always paid me back. Besides, aren't you too old for birthday money?"

"That's up to you, isn't it?"

"You got me there," Kukowski said. His eyes drifted toward the backpack. "To think I thought I'd never see another teenager again unless I was flying over campus with a machine gun." He grinned at his own brutality. "Nah, my sophomores loved me. Other teachers, they'll say, 'Oh, have a great weekend.' Me? I tell 'em I hope they drive off a cliff. Except not really, 'cause there are no true cliffs in Oklahoma, and all you'd do is screw up your car. And since you're driving Heidi's Alpinist, maybe that's what you need, huh?"

"Maybe," I allowed.

"Anyway, it's time for me to get out of here, 'cause I'm about ready to divorce Oklahoma." He put the backpack on his shoulders. "Good luck, Mikey. Hope you found what you came for."

Kukowski walked down the hall and opened the front door, making sure to grab the black motorcycle helmet by the entryway before getting on his bike. Then he turned back, flashed me a sorry smile, nodded, and continued his ride out. I didn't expect to see him again for a long time. Arizona would be good for him, just as leaving Dreary had been helpful for my own journey of self-discovery, and meeting with Bryce would most likely mark the end of it.

According to the Internet, Bryce's stepfather was Samuel Hill, a war veteran who had served the past four years as mayor of New Baines. He, Bryce, and Bryce's mother lived in an $850,000 mansion near the Shaughnessy Country Club, which was about an hour-and-a-half drive from Madison, maybe less. The country club also wasn't too far from Shaughnessy Estates, the neighborhood where Bryce and I had grown up together, as well as Hayes Elementary. If Troy wanted to go after I picked him up from Gabby's place, I figured I'd take him there for a brief tour of my childhood. We'd come all this way; we might as well go full circle.

It was 10:25 in the morning. I decided to leave at 3:30 to get Troy at five, then potentially drive around New Baines before seeing Bryce at six. In the meantime, I read Ard van der Kolk's poetry. It was much different than prose, but I found myself appreciating the form with each stanza. English classes had led me to study haikus, cinquains, and limericks, but Ard was focused on raw emotion, relying less on flowery words and more on poignancy. He was a World War II poet describing the issues of his time. And what was I doing with my talents? Selling a half-baked YA horror story, that's what.

My mom called as I was about to leave for Gabby's. She was thrilled about something and speaking incoherently. After a full sixty seconds of me trying to calm her down, she revealed her big news to me: I'd gotten accepted to the University of Hartsett with a $25,000 scholarship toward tuition, not including federal aid, which I had yet to receive.

"We'd still have to come up with the other twenty thousand," Mom went on, "plus room and board—but still!" She laughed. "You did it!"

"I did it!" I said, laughing with her. "And the University of Arminster?"

"Same scenario: admittance and a little over half off. We should celebrate! When will you be back? I'll call Mrs. Souse, we'll get her, Troy, and the girls over for lunch, and I can invite your friends, and I'll buy some sparkling grape juice or something—"

"Mom," I said. She stopped. "It's fine. We don't need all that. We have to save up, and I'll start working day and night at Big-Box again. I'm serious. All right?"

"OK… but I'm still throwing you a mini-party."

"Fine."

"Good." I could hear her smile. "I looooove you."

"And I love you. I'll see you soon."

She ended the call. Then I smiled, too.

I wore jeans, high tops, a green plaid button-up, and my brown hoodie. In the Big Nasty, I found an old denim jacket with fleece on the inside, which I considered wearing if it got any colder. *Such Jubilee* seemed the only album appropriate enough to listen to on the near-hour-long drive to pick Troy up at the edge of Arminster, a city of illusions and its delusional taxpayers. I'd lived in this county long enough to know their mindset, to know they were too poor or too stupid to venture out beyond the view of the three skyscrapers, as if those enchanted objects alone constituted the peak of all experience. There was so much more past this place: the water on the Gulf Coast, the battleship in Windhaven, cities like Memphis, states like Arizona, universities like Hartsett in California. *California*, the end goal for so many of my generation. *California*, where the sun conjoins with the stars and anything is possible. Even a useful degree in creative writing. What a concept.

The sky was a cloudy gray of rain or snow. I didn't run into any bad weather on my way through Arminster County—only stillness and a light wind. The grass on either side of the four-lane road was pale in comparison to the previous days; the cars appeared rustier, the orange cones more apparent, the highway with additional cracks and debris. A wheelchair tumbled out of an ambulance, causing traffic to slow. The drive was eerie, though the town's welcome sign did provide some comfort, if not unease at its relevancy. *New Baines. Population 51,201. Make Yourself at Home.*

But first was the turnoff for Gabby's Arminster neighborhood of Greenland Hills, known for its affordable luxury and lookalike European-style homes. The entrance was designed to look like that of a castle, though any grand effect was diminished by the minivans in the driveways. I could see the appeal of the 4,000-square-foot living area of Gabby's home, but after studying it for a while, I realized it wasn't for me—too cookie-cutter for my taste, despite its bay windows, three-car garage, and the willow tree in the backyard.

I pulled up to the house and parked beside the still-yellow grass while sirens blared in the distance. There was somebody on the front porch, standing near the door. She looked familiar, and as I got closer, the big black girl turned out to be none other than Eva Green from Dreary, Alabama.

She waved at me and started walking over. I got out of the SUV, stood there, and then met her halfway.

"What are you doing here?" I asked, looking from her to the house to my phone. "Isn't this 7497 Sir Alexander Boulevard?"

"Uh-huh," she said, a quizzical expression on her heavily pierced face. Her lipstick matched her pink hair. "We ready to go?"

"Go where?"

"To Bryce's house?" She punched my shoulder. I winced. "You're not wasted, are you? At least, more than usual. You want me to drive?"

"What? No, I'm not 'wasted' or... whatever." I shook my head. "No. No, this is insane. You're supposed to be back at Troy's house in Alabama! We left you there! Remember?"

Eva frowned. "Stop joking around. This isn't funny, all right? So cut it out. You're being a bigger dick than Troy, you know." She laughed suddenly. Giggled. "You really are screwed up. Who do you think I am? Who were you expecting? You've always been the forgetful one. Birthdays, buying concert tickets, rides to Rochester... Remember that girl you kissed in the creek behind the school? You told us that never happened, but the footprints are there. All thirty-eight of them."

"What are you talking about?!"

"Are you on something, Michael? Seriously, are you on drugs right now? Did you smoke a little—" She mimed rolling a joint and taking a hit. "—before you drove here? Twist it eleven times to the right for a perfect one?" She eyed my keys. "Are you *dead certain* you don't want me to drive you to Shaughnessy Estates?"

"I'm fine," I declared. "Just... get in the Big Nasty. I don't..." I rubbed at my temples. "I think I'm seeing things. I don't know what's real anymore."

She put a hand on my shoulder. Then she flicked me on the head.

"What the hell?!"

"See?" she said. "I'm real. So stop being weird. Now what time do you have to be at Bryce's house?"

"Um, six."

"Then we still have time to stop by your old neighborhood." She went over to the passenger side and got in. "If you want, that is."

"I don't want to," I admitted as I joined her. "I *need* to."

"So go." She kicked her feet up. "No one's stopping you."

"Yeah. Yeah, you're right."

Eva took my phone and plugged the aux cord into it. If she played a song that afternoon, I sure didn't hear it. I was too focused on my own set of issues. Everything was so out of control that all I needed was something to remind me of myself.

The Shaughnessy Country Club was infamous for featuring a heavily contested fountain by its entrance depicting 1902 peace advocate Garvin D. Shaughnessy severing Native American Chief John Redman's head, where the water flowed out. Shaughnessy had been deemed a hero by Finbarr Hennigan, then-mayor of Arminster, for disallowing the chief and the rest of the nearby tribe from causing harm to early Arminster County, and thus, most of New Baines was named after Shaughnessy. Almost a century had passed when the truth of Shaughnessy's frequent embezzlement of government funds, bribery, and "illicit sexual relationship" with Chief Redman was discovered by a historian, according to QuickSearch. But by then, everyone was too apathetic, so his name remained.

The Country Club in New Baines was only a six-minute drive from where I needed to be, which was thirteen minutes from Greenland Hills via the turnpike. Eva and I paid the toll as our price of admission, and just like that, we'd gone back in time down roads I truly did remember. These all led me to Hayward Street, where the long-awaited movie theater had finally been built. Directly across from it was a neighborhood, with old picket fences and a chipped sign stating all I already knew: SHAUGHNESSY ESTATES.

My hands started sweating profusely onto the steering wheel, and I felt a trickle slide down from under my arm to the tip of my boxers. Gray was the color not just of the weather, but of my mind as well. Nothing made sense, but I felt—deep down in my heart—the clouds would soon clear so I could see past my waywardness.

"Don't be scared," Eva said teasingly.

All at once, "Just Let Go" by Sturgill Simpson was on the radio. The green grass was much taller as I drove past the entrance, and the trees were in full bloom. Sunlight touched the leaves and created a hard shadow on the asphalt. The air was warm, the sky was blue, and the signpost for South Shaughnessy Avenue was no longer crooked, but brand-new and proud. Outside chairs held cushions and pillows, station wagons sat patiently for their owners, and insects roared with the summer heat.

Most of the houses were one story and smaller than I'd remembered. The lawns were well-kept, though, and every other driveway seemed to sport a trailer for four-wheelers. I saw basketball nets, signs promoting the annual garage sale, yellow bags holding that day's edition of the New Baines *Ledger*, and pickup trucks—red, white, and blue. There were flowers, too; it seemed like years since I'd last seen flowers. I nearly cried at the sight of the redbud trees hidden between cul-de-sacs. The speed bumps and roundabouts had nothing on me.

Life was perfect here. The trees made way for the freshly painted telephone poles, and together, they coexisted. The street names weren't pretentious, but simple and named after a single man: South Shaughnessy Street, South Shaughnessy Road, and good ol' South Shaughnessy Court. A mail truck idled to my left, but no one stood beside it. Everyone had gone.

The sun disappeared then and fled behind the impending storm. The sky was white and covered by a deep, dark, and angry gray of gloom, smoke, and cloud. The grass returned to the ugly yellow, and the trees and hedges were bare once more. Police chatter replaced any music. This was the reality I had feared—my childhood homestead at 7401 South Shaughnessy Avenue.

It was a single-family residential built out of brick in 1978. A couple of shingles were missing from the right side of the roof, and piles of tree limbs lay before the two elms that made up the front yard. The blinds were drawn, but I could map the inside and all its seven rooms, two bathrooms, fireplace, and 2,182 square feet regardless of my sight. The left-side window peered into what had once been my bedroom, the main window to the left into what was to be a sibling's room, and the one on the right into the dining room—the site of so many neighborhood parties and birthday celebrations.

What was foreign to me was the single pair of running shoes propped against the front door. They didn't belong to me. I didn't know whose they were.

"Someone else lives there now," I realized, "with their own pickup in the garage and their own feet on the carpet, the hardwood floor, the tile..."

"There are four registered sex offenders within a mile of here," Eva said as she scrolled through her phone. "Thirteen foreclosures, three former drug labs, a total of six environmental hazards—"

"Stop," I told her.

"You need to hear it."

"I don't *need* anything." I gripped the wheel tighter, staring at the house. "I thought I did, but it's like I'm dreaming wide awake. I feel like a ghost."

"What else?" she pried. "Do you sense it? Something in the way?"

"I feel their frustrations with me," I continued. "I hear the air as it leaves their nostrils at a slightly faster rate. They bring the background to the foreground, and I want them to quit watching me—stop reading my thoughts."

"Do you need to walk up there and knock on the door?" she asked me. "Or scribble something down on a receipt and stuff it in their mailbox?"

I started to move forward, but Eva reached over my body and grabbed the wheel from me.

"What are you doing?!" I yelled at her, shoving her off my lap.

"I could ask you the same thing, considering you were about to go through this person's bills to find out their name!"

"And so what if I was?!"

"This isn't your house!" Her words echoed between the buildings. "You don't live here anymore! The neighborhood pool isn't yours, the neighborhood park isn't yours, and these neighbors—"

"Mr. Grantham," I whispered.

"Who?"

I pointed up ahead to the corner house, where campaign yard signs urged voters to reelect Sam Hill as New Baines mayor. Like 7401, the Grantham's was ranch-style, and it, too, had bundles of broken branches in front of it. My mind went back to a hot morning at the end of June when I'd woken up to find a dozen or so of those aluminum tuna cans—with jagged lids pried up, still partially attached—sprawled from Mr. Grantham's yard into ours. Nearly seven years later, Mr. Grantham was nowhere to be seen. My mother had heard he'd shot himself the fall after we'd moved. So he and I were both replaced.

Past the stop sign was what South Shaughnessy Avenue children called "the T," also known as West Florentine Street, which connected us with the rest of the neighborhood. Directly ahead was the swimming pool, where most of us kids spent our summer days when not in the air conditioning and watching cartoons. Beside it was a small park with a wooden fort, a yellow slide, and a roofed area for social events.

"Did you come here a lot?" Eva asked.

"Oh, yeah." I took a right so that the park was on my side. I kept going. "My dad would take me there all the time and buy me whatever candy I wanted from the snack shop before the pool area. He had this sort of talent—like, he could guess how much the total price for the candy would be before the guy rang it up. I think the highest was twenty-three dollars or something ridiculous. It's crazy my teeth didn't rot out. He definitely spoiled me because I was an only child, whereas he had three brothers and a sister. They don't live in Oklahoma, though."

"Wait." She leaned forward. "What in the world is that?"

Up ahead was one large dirt mound after the other in an otherwise flat area with cleared trees and little grass. We were about a mile away from Shaughnessy Estates, and an old sign advertised the area as CALVARY HILLS. It was a planned subdivision started while I was at Hayes Elementary, but even a decade later, it remained unfinished, abandoned. Most of the roads had been completed, but other than the concrete, a toppled-over port-a-potty, and a faded yet still legible JESUS LOVES YOU scrawled across a tall water tank in the forest, Calvary Hills consisted only of the dirt mounds where one might build a home.

Eva and I got out of the SUV and started to walk around that place—that cemetery of endless possibilities.

"My dad and I used to come here after he was off from work," I recalled. "It was supposed to be a subdivision with giant homes that all looked the same, kind of like Gabby's neighborhood. We would just walk here from the house and get back before it got too dark. I would bring my toy army men and… and I dunno. It was nice."

"Seems spooky," she noted.

"One time, he asked who my favorite was between him and my mom. I said he was. I don't remember if that was the truth or if I just told him that because it's what you do, but I know he was happy to hear it."

There was heavy history to be found in the dirt mounds of Calvary Hills: sunbleached cones, torn bags of cement, a can of cherry dipping tobacco, a broken flashlight, a pair of sunglasses with one lens, and a soda bottle advertising the 2005 Super Bowl. Eva kicked at something in the dirt. She bent down, brushed the brown off the metal plate, and then stood back up.

"Hickman Construction," she said. "Huh. Don't you know a Hickman?"

I was crying. I didn't mean to be; it simply happened, just like everything else. Coming back to this place brought back so many memories: Fourth of July fireworks, babysitters, spit cups in the middle console, diving board jumps, apple cider drinks, ice storms, Christmas songs, Christmas mornings, Mother's Day, Father's Day, *family*.

"Hey." Eva's hand was on my shoulder. I was on my knees in the dirt, shivering. "It's OK. You're doing fine."

"I don't mean to… don't mean to be so…"

"Don't tell me," she instructed. "Write it down."

"Huh?"

"In the notes app." Eva tapped her pocket. "On your phone."

"But I haven't written anything good in months."

"So do something different. You write stories on your laptop, right? Try some other form of self-expression."

I took out my phone and opened the notes app. Then I clicked "New," and after much thought, I sat myself in the dust and began a youth-inspired free verse poem—a love letter to the quiet magic of childhood summers.

After a few minutes of writing, revising, and tweaking, I titled the poem, "Soldiers on Death Mountain." I tried showing it to Eva, but she stepped back, not wanting to be anywhere near my words.

"Your business," she told me. "Share it if you want, but give it a while."

"What time is it?" I asked.

"Five twenty-nine."

It'd been seven years for Bryce and me. We'd waited long enough.

Eva and I returned to the SUV, and from there, we did a U-turn back to West Florentine Street. Through bare branches, I saw my tree fort had been taken down as we took a quick right onto South Shaughnessy Court. We passed first Pete's house, then Christian's, followed by another right onto Truman Street, which was one of the major roads in New Baines. This took us to the intersection of Truman and Packard, and at the corner to our left was the old gas station my dad would drive into to avoid the stoplight while taking me to school. So I did just the same.

As I drove past Bundy Brook Apartments, I didn't see the connected portable buildings that made up what I remembered of Rutherford B. Hayes Elementary School of 8800 South Horne Place. I thought I'd taken the wrong street, as there was only more construction equipment and a sign promoting the future Shaughnessy Soccer Complex. The playground, the bike racks, and the main buildings that weren't trailers were all missing. Yet the creek was still there, way off in the distance. Of all the landmarks, the creek had made it.

"Your elementary school," Eva acknowledged for me. "It's gone."

"It's gone," I agreed. No use denying it.

"This is all Hickman Construction, too," she went on. "They must specialize in this region of Oklahoma."

"Who cares?" The sky darkened as I peeled out of there. "I wish I had some shitty wine. They're taking everything away from me. Every... *fucking thing* I had left in this stupid-ass town."

"You sound like Troy."

"Huh." I looked at my hands shaking on the wheel. "I do, don't I?"

"And the city of Troy was destined to fall. You read that in the *Iliad*. How far until we're at Bryce's?"

"Ten more minutes," I said. "God. I spent so many years dreaming about coming back to this place. And here I am. Now what?"

"Finish what you started."

"What's that?" I asked.

She said nothing, so I kept driving.

◆————◆—◆—————◆

We next drove to the high school—so large, it had to be split into two separate campuses. New Baines High, with all its "Go Cougars!" and such, seemed too big for me after staring at its buildings and clock tower for a few passing seconds. Whereas Dreary County High was meant for five hundred students, NBH was built for a whopping 2,300 teens trying their hardest to get by. After four years, they would either apply to the workforce or find themselves attending nearby Northeastern Oklahoma State College the following September. Perhaps the situation had changed in the handful of years I'd been away, but if NBH was anything like DCH, everyone did the bare minimum, and that was all. Few made it out of the county, let alone the state.

Yet even the promise of Hartsett University—the school of my dreams—wasn't enough to stop me from wondering about four years spent at New Baines High School. I imagined myself turning into the NBH student parking lot with the Big Nasty, getting laughs at first, but having it soon become part of my character. I'd walk to class talking to Christian, see Gabby at my table in art class, chat quietly with Belle in the library, and maybe even go with Nate for a bite to eat at Happy Cow.

Cat would be waiting for me against my locker, her binders against her chest, her smile wide and inviting. We wouldn't date; I knew that now. But I would still have her as a friend, and she'd be a whole lot better than Troy, Keegan, Leah, Clyde, and Olivia ever were to me. Cat cared. I hadn't enough. It was so easy to imagine.

"You talk about all these things that could've been different," Eva said, "but I don't get why you don't ever think like this for Dreary County High. You spent four years there. There are a hundred seniors graduating this year. You could've befriended any of them if our little group was such a waste of time for you."

"It's not that," I told her as we carried on through empty streets. "I just had it so good here."

"Michael."

"You can't see how much happier I would've been?!"

"Your dad would still be dead, and Cat would still be homeschooled. And no matter if you intervened, Frank would still kill himself, Willow would get pregnant—"

"I get it."

"No, I don't think you do. You're no fun to be around because you're always so mopey. You need to practice what you preach."

"Well, it doesn't matter," I declared, driving faster than the speed limit. "It doesn't matter what I think might've happened or what did happen, here or in Dreary. Nothing really matters. Everything is pointless."

"Don't blame your nihilism and lack of ambitions on this fantasy of yours."

"Lack of—?!" I couldn't believe what I was hearing. "I have ambitions! I'm the only person at Dreary who has any idea what they want to do with their future! I want to write. So what did I do? I published a novella—and you, too, can buy the ebook for ninety-nine cents. So at least I did something. I will *not* waste my life at Dreary Community College with Troy. If it was Arminster, that'd be different, but there is *nothing* left in Dreary."

Eva didn't say anything to this, and how could she? I was right. I'd always been right, but without a way to properly express myself. Being back in New Baines, I understood perfectly. Everyone else was losing their minds, not me.

We toured Main Street in silence. I didn't comment once on the changes I saw.

Bryce's manor was on the outskirts of New Baines in the more rural part of town. It had been built on what had been ranchland, according to QuickSearch, and the vast forest behind the property also belonged to Bryce's stepfather. The gated Tuscan home was an immaculate two-story with balconies, arched windows, fountains, and a solid front door with knockers that resembled the heads of Egyptian dogs. It was intimidating. Definitely Bryce.

With the gate already open, I pulled up to a parking space to the side of the separate garage. I expected someone—a guard or security personnel—to be patrolling the perimeter, but there was only Eva, me, and the dog heads that evening.

"Pharaoh Hounds," Eva said, pointing to the door knockers. "Either that or Anubis, the Greek name for the god associated with mummification. He was the keeper of graves in ancient Egyptian religion."

"I knew I'd heard that somewhere before." It was seven past six. I turned to her. "Well, you ready?"

"Sorry, Jonah. Not my whale." She looked around. "I'll stay in the car. We can pick up some Taco Kick on the way back."

"All right." I opened my door. "Should I lock you in?"

"It's the mayor's house."

"Touché."

I left Eva alone there and pocketed the keys.

The wind swayed the trees. I tugged at my hoodie as I fast-walked to the door, noticing my breath as I did so. The knockers seemed too much, so I used my knuckles against the rosewood.

I waited. I tried again.

In my peripheral vision, the curtains to the right parted ways, then came back together. Soon after, the lock was undone, and the door opened slightly.

Bryce looked much older than he had Saturday night. His hair was unkempt, and on his face was a blond beard that must've taken months to grow out. He wore jeans and a white t-shirt, but his feet were barefoot. He looked drained. The years were scars to him.

"Michael," he said. "It's good to see you again."

"Yeah," I said. "Yeah, you, too."

"It's cold out," he noted with a shiver. "You, uh, want to come in?" He looked past me and gulped. "Is it just you?"

"Just me," I told him, stepping inside. He shut the door behind us.

We were in a brief foyer, but straight ahead was the real catch of the house: an enormous living room with a soaring ceiling and only a couple of couches in front of a large fireplace. Aside from that, it was all empty space and tall windows. I pictured it to be perfect for mayoral campaign parties and such, but what truly caught my eye was the ice-blue pool behind the house, where I was certain one could swim many freezing laps. The interior décor seemed to be mythology-based, with statues of leviathans, paintings of phoenixes, and several burial boxes up against the walls. The whole place was astonishing, though Bryce seemed impassive about it all, making me question his true motives for inviting me over.

"Want anything to drink?" Bryce asked over by the kitchen. "I know it's only March, but I like having apple cider on dreary days like this."

"That sounds good," I said.

"Do you want to pour it, or do you want me to?"

"I can do it," I told him, remembering my conversation with Cat.

I followed him to the kitchen island with the granite countertop. On it was a hot brewer with a touchscreen, so I took one of the mugs Bryce offered and put it underneath. I told it to dispense hot water, selected six ounces, confirmed, and then repeated. I then took a spoon from the silverware drawer and started the blending of water and apple cider mix. While this happened, I took note of the photos of Bryce and Belle on the magnetic sides of the refrigerator. He cradled her frequently, and she kissed him in return. They appeared genuinely happy together. He didn't look like a killer.

It was then that I saw the magnificent fish tank in the next room. It was a gigantic aquarium eight feet high and ten wide, filled with water as blue as the pool. I watched as a purple-and-yellow fish swam between the rocks around a sunken ship. Another floated by itself in the corner, watching the other creatures. Then it started watching me.

"They're my mom's," Bryce said while he worked on his drink. "She's got a Moorish

Idol, a Yellow Tang, a Royal Gramma, a Humbug Damselfish, a Pacific Cleaner Fish, and an Ochre sea star in there somewhere. Maybe a pufferfish, too, if it didn't die. I can't remember. Fish don't have feelings, anyway."

I tried to take a sip of my apple cider, but it burned my tongue. So I scooped some up with the spoon, held it over the mug, blew on the spoonful, and then took another sip.

"We can take these over to the sitting area," he informed me, walking over there himself with his Santa mug. "Watch the rug."

There were three couches surrounding an expensive-looking table in front of the fireplace on the left wall. I set my drink on a coaster and chose the couch facing the pool while he turned up the flames. After that, he settled on the couch facing the heat and sat there.

Above the fireplace was an enormous painting of a woman in white draped over a bed, as if in a deep sleep. On her chest sat an incubus, watching her face. A black horse had its head poking out of the curtains in the background, as if curious to the fate of the fair maiden.

"That's *The Nightmare* by Fuseli," Bryce informed me. "One of the most profound Gothic paintings, and it's just a goddamn pun. It's infuriating."

To the left of the fireplace was an entryway elsewhere. Bryce noticed me spying it.

"That leads to the bathroom," he said. "And upstairs."

"I see." I took another sip with my spoon. Not as scalding. "Your house looks great. It's simplistic. Minimalist. A lot of, oh, *negative space*." I paused at his look. "I'm in an art class. It was either that or world history."

Bryce shrugged. "It's to give my stepdad some character so he doesn't appear boring to the public."

"Is he?" I asked.

"Wouldn't know," he answered. He took a big swig and grimaced. "So what brought you back to Oklahoma?"

"I missed you all." I took a drink as well. When he didn't say anything, I elaborated: "I've always had this nagging feeling I'd forgotten something here. Like, a better life or another part of me."

Bryce laughed. "Really? That's funny. While we're all trying to leave this town with our test scores and whatnot, here you are, coming right back. I understand. People who get nostalgic about childhood must've never been children themselves." He drank some more. "I'm getting out. Even if Oregon doesn't accept me, I am, one way or the other."

"You don't like it here?"

"No, I can't say I do." He set the Santa mug down, then stood up to walk over to the windows. The blue light accentuated his gaunt features as he stared out into the rain. "I made myself great works. I built myself houses, I planted myself vineyards. I made myself gardens and parks, and I planted trees in them of all kinds of fruit. I made myself pools of water, to water from them the forest where trees were reared. Whatever my eyes desired, I didn't keep from them. Then I looked at all the works that my hands had worked, and at the labor that I had labored to do: all was vanity and a chasing after wind, and there was no profit under the sun."

He looked back at me, smiling faintly. Then he shook his head and returned to the couches.

"I'm sorry about what happened at your party when I showed up," he told me, running a hand over his drooping eyelids. "I know I said and did a lot of things back in elementary school that weren't too cool of me, but I didn't expect everyone to bring up the past like that, you know? Maybe some of them who moved farther away from New Baines, but not people like Gabby, Pete, and Christian."

"What about Zach, Morgan, and Bobby?"

"Them, too. I just..." He stared down, then looked at me. "I didn't expect them to be so hostile, you know? We all made mistakes. But that stuff was *seven years ago*. I didn't expect Gabby to scream at me and for Rachel to run off crying. Even Sammy was about to punch me. So I'm sorry I was the cause of all that—that choir of criticism. I should have left sooner. Probably shouldn't have come at all."

I laughed. It was so crazy, that was all I could do.

"You came in there ranting about gay marriage," I reminded him. "They weren't talking about things you'd done or whatever! You got everyone worked up about racial issues and transgender issues—I think religion was brought up at one point—and when you'd finally divided everyone, you *shot* Zach, Morgan, and Bobby!"

Bryce just looked at me, his mouth slightly open.

"You..." He shook his head once more. "You think I did what?"

"Think?! I know that's what you did! I was there! It doesn't matter what anyone else says about it—*you killed three of our former classmates!* You messed everything up for me and the party, with your 'Hell calls hell' and whatever else it was you went on about!"

"Hell calls hell," he echoed, as if he were trying out the phrase. "As in, one wrong deed is a gateway to another?" Then it was he who laughed. "Please, Michael. You know me. We were friends. We swam together. You, me, and... and Catherine." He sighed. "I said *awful* things to her." His right hand began to tremble, so he grasped it with his left. "I don't care what gay people do. I'm indifferent to all that. Ever since my dad died, I realized how stupid it is to care about politics and morals, what's right or wrong—that's what got me into Saturday night's mess in the first place, remember? I was way too uptight back then." He took a breath. "Probably got my dad killed, now that I think about it. Except I think about it *all the time.* That thing we did—what do they call it? 'Five Twenty-Nine'? My dad's heart attack was my punishment for getting us all involved in... that *fucked-up shit.*"

Bryce was crying. He looked down and put his head into his hands, and I could tell life weighed heavily on him. The sight startled me. Bryce wasn't supposed to cry.

His eyes widened as he looked at me, scared and apologetic. He then pushed himself off the couch and ran upstairs, leaving me to wonder what the actual fuck was going on in Oklahoma.

Bryce returned with a thumb-sized baggie in his hands. He stepped slowly toward me, set the baggie on the table, and then sat back down. Written on a piece of masking tape on the side: RAMMIOL.

"What is it?" I asked him, turning it over. I saw a small amount of white powder inside. I didn't dare sniff it.

"I suffer from… a lot of emotional distress," Bryce tried to explain. "So I take pills to combat it, like risperidone, diazepam…" He noticed my confused expression. "Nevermind. My stepdad is Mayor Hill. He's got money. But you know what? I don't like him all that much; he's never around for me. He tries to pass off my problems as nothing. God forbid my mental issues ruin his reputation and end up in the *Ledger*, as if anyone reads that garbage. I had to pay for my own therapy. That's crazy, right? Please tell me it's crazy."

"That's crazy," I said.

"And he tries to buy me off with his money—except for when I need it, like for the therapy and treatment. He covers his tracks, as do I. But I don't want his big bucks. And Nate… well, I don't know if you've heard this about Nate, but it's not a huge secret: he's a drug dealer, and I fund him. Big whoop. I know it's stupid, but I need something more than the doctors will give me. So I took some of my stepdad's money then, but only to start up Nate and his projects. Rammiol was one of those, and it helps. It's scary, at first, the way it alters your mind. I *hate* manipulation. I get enough of it here. But I can accept what that white magic does for me. And Nate and I—we think it could do a lot of kids out there some real good."

He stopped talking, so I took that as my cue to respond.

"Wow," I said. "That is… quite the story I was not expecting." I scratched my head. "What's, uh, what's this got to do with me?"

"I think he might've slipped you some," Bryce admitted. "Or it could have been Jimmy. We use his dad's cement mixer sometimes. Point is, if that's the case, you probably hallucinated a lot that night. That's how it works. I won't even begin to describe to you the monsters I saw my first time. It gets easier, though. And with this operation we have going on, I can pay tuition with my own money, assuming I don't get any scholarships." He sighed. "But if you were given that drug against your will, please believe me when I tell you I am so, so sorry. That wasn't cool, and I will take full responsibility. If there's anything I can do to make it up to you, I'll make it happen."

I didn't know what to say or do, if anything. I'd felt out of my element since crossing state lines, but *this*—this was something entirely different.

"The effects of—" I turned the baggie over. "—Rammiol. How long until they wear off?"

"Um, the first time?" He glanced around, and that was when I noticed the patch of silver hairs in his beard. "Maybe a couple of days? It's been a while. Sorry. But Nate has the time tables, if you want them. We're narrowing it down, but it fluctuates."

"It fluctuates," I repeated. "And what does it do again?"

"Well, it's supposed to aid you psychologically in confronting traumatic life events or scenarios. Like, if you want to put it in basic terms, it helps you face your fears. So, for example, you said you saw me—and correct me if I'm wrong—but you said you saw me shoot the Millburns and Bobby about…" He laughed. "Wouldn't we have heard by now if someone like B-Love had died? But anyway, what did you say we were arguing about? Gay marriage?"

"Something like that, yeah."

"Were they for or against?"

"For," I answered, a bit embarrassed. "You were opposed to the notion."

"And what about you?" he asked.

"I'm for it," I told him, but by his face, Bryce expected more. "I'm all for gay rights, but I don't necessarily *appreciate* people thinking I'm gay. Maybe it's the way I dress, or because I'm short and skinny, or…"

"Or what?" Bryce pressed.

"My best friend is gay." I thought about this. "Well, these last few days have been questionable. But back home, he's the proudest gay you'll find for hundreds of miles. You see, Troy is open about his sexuality, and because we hang out together a lot, people think I'm gay as well. And it's not about me being selfish, either, 'cause it reflects on my girlfriend, too. Uh, ex-girlfriend. Basically, I'm heterosexual. So it bothers me when people assume I'm something I'm not."

"And that's your biggest nightmare?" he asked.

"It's your drug," I countered.

"Then maybe it's identity you're most concerned with. Or your reputation. That's what my stepdad obsesses over." He popped his fingers. "I think it's interesting, though, that it's sexual orientation. You hear you're gay so often enough that you start to believe it. You start saying, 'Maybe I am.' I don't think you'll know for sure until you try it, though, and I'll bet those arguments you heard from us were your own thoughts on the subject all jumbled together. History shows we are often afraid of what we don't understand, and a lack of alternative explanations can lead anyone to become a believer in anything. In this mundanity, we find epiphany."

"Bryce—"

"But I trust in conditioning," he told me, "which is the process of getting someone to act a certain way when placed in a repeated situation. That's all Rammiol is! Conditioning and telepathy. A hypnosis of sorts. For example: right now, I want you to imagine some dirt and a red shovel. Go on. Think about it. Some dirt and a red shovel. Some dirt and a red shovel. That's what's in your head—some dirt and a red shovel. The color of the dirt and the height of the shovel might differ, but for all intents and purposes, we're both thinking the same thing. You can't reach or feel them, but I've passed them along. I got them in your brain, but I'm sitting over here, not even touching you. You experienced Rammiol. Now think of all the rest it could do."

"Stop," I said, standing up, my face burning. "I've been high before, but this? You're talking about drugs, science, telepathy, shovels, and… and gay people."

"None of which are bad."

"But it's a lot to process! These past few days, I thought I was losing my mind. I thought I saw Franklin at my party, warning me about a flood, and then you walk in and start shooting people, and we fell into the lake, and… and now you're saying I was drugged and my own subconscious was working against me? I mean, if anything, I'm even more confused than before I took your… Rammy-thing."

"Rammiol," he corrected me, then squinted his eyes as he studied my expression. "You really don't know, do you? But that makes sense. Your mind is desperately trying to put the pieces together—so much so that you constructed a version of me at your party based on your memories of what I was like when we were kids. You imagined the Bryce you remember. Who knows? Perhaps it was for this moment you felt compelled to return. Must be easy to sleep when you're ignorant."

"Why are you telling me this?" I asked, slowly easing my way back down.

"Because you deserve to know." He sat up straight, looking past me. "We identified the problem, right?"

"There wasn't a problem! Not one that requires hallucinogens, at least. What you've been through is your prerogative, but I'm nowhere near needing—"

There was a sharp rasp of the door knocker. Bryce checked himself quickly, then sped over to the curtains.

"Did you tell?" he whispered to me, a sharp accusation in his tone.

Bryce opened the door without giving me the chance to answer. From my position on the couch, I could see two older women talking to him. One of them held pamphlets, and the other a large book with a cross on its cover. I heard "God's kingdom" and "spiritual paradise" before tuning out, focusing instead on the entry to the other hall—and, allegedly, the way to Bryce's room.

The door then shut, and Bryce returned with an annoyed look in his eyes.

"So many interruptions," he said. "I'm surprised neither of us have gotten a text up to this point."

More knocking.

"Dammit," Bryce muttered. "Where's Chauncey when you need him? Just… stay here, all right?"

"I, uh, I think I'm gonna use the bathroom," I told him, getting up and taking the Rammiol baggie with me.

"Oh, no, I'll only be a second."

With Bryce occupied with the women again—I heard "Jehovah's Witness" this time—I went under the arch and into the bathroom, briefly checking on the man in the mirror. Then, realizing how much time I was wasting, I shut the door, pocketed the baggie, and then went up the ornate staircase. At the first landing was a window, where I noticed how late it was getting by the way the sky was a faded blue around the grass, and how the clouds were black above the pines. The pool was lit, though. Like a spotlight.

Something darted across the roof. It didn't sound like rain. Probably a squirrel.

After passing by a couple of more Anubis statues, I found myself above the living room, looking down. I held on to the intricate railing and admired the chandelier momentarily before trying the first door to my right, also made of rosewood. But before I opened it, I turned around to catch that the rug below was a homemade bird's-eye view of New Baines with all the places I'd been that day: Shaughnessy Estates, Calvary Hills, the Shaughnessy Soccer Complex, New Baines High, and Main Street. They weren't labeled, but I knew this map and its locations. They were special to me, which made its presence in Bryce's house all the creepier. I'd come too far to give in to fear, though. It was like reading a novel to its end—one page at a time. So I opened the door.

I thought maybe I'd been there before. The lights were off, and I couldn't find a switch. But from the hallway fixtures, I could see the walls of Bryce's room were covered with framed abstract designs, all black-and-white scribbles and distorted shapes. On the right wall was a muted sound system and a flat screen showing home videos on loop. To the left were the bed and closet, and in front of me, a recliner facing the TV. Over a hundred pictures of our childhood, taken with an instant camera, were spread across the hardwood floor—some grouped, others not. I was one of the few in my own pile, away from the rest of my fifth-grade class. My pictures were mangled, ripped in half, then taped down the middle, yet each had been smudged by the drippings of candle wax. The pictures covered a faint circle made of chalk, the remnants of a pentagram within.

I took out my phone, turned on the flashlight, and then took a picture with flash. I then cursed myself for being so slow and went over to the closet. As I opened it, a baseball signed by Michael Gillenwater fell from the top shelf and rolled underneath the bed. I bent down with my phone to grab it and put it back, but along with it, I found a pair of neon green Kleidüng boxer briefs. Written on the tag: TRV.

It was all so perverted and disorienting, I almost screamed. I wasn't sure what I was expecting, but finding Troy's missing underwear wasn't it. So I put the boxer briefs in my back pocket and continued examining the contents of the closet, confused as to what to be looking for.

"Come on, Cat," I said, pushing back suit jackets. "What am I—?"

Behind the coats was a door, small and square. I undid the deadbolt, opened the door slowly, saw the pull chain, and then reached for it, turning on the single bulb.

A massive cork bulletin board leaned against the support beams of the attic. On it were pictures and files and papers and emails of all sorts, each broken up into specific sections. It took me a while to figure out they were organized by initials: CB, BB, GC, FC, WD, PF, JH, MJ, SK, SL, MM, ZM, NO, EP, BR, RS, CT, MW, and IG. Two items stood out in the middle: the first, a map with red thumbtacks in Texas, North Carolina,

Alabama, California, and various regions of Oklahoma; the second, a torn-out page from our fifth-grade yearbook with red X's across the faces of Franklin Chambers, Willow Dusett, Morgan Millburn, Zach Millburn, Bobby Royals, and Christian Battenfield. Christian's X was scribbled over, as if a mistake.

There were notes, too, with red strings connecting our yearbook pictures to the items collected. Attached to Blank Frank were emails between him and a hateful "Dom Sheldon," as well as copies of the New Baines *Ledger* reports on Franklin's highway accident and suicide. Below Mekenzie's name were plane tickets to Windhaven, North Carolina, as well as candid shots of her on the boardwalk with the USS *Goodwin* clearly in the background. Willow's was mostly empty, save for that morning's *Ledger* website report on her death, a red question mark beside it.

There were pictures from Photofixer and statuses from Chipper for the others as well, and a whole list of Otherkin papers and that seven-pointed star again under Cat's initials. I saw a list of therian websites, interview transcripts, and an article from QuickSearch about a man named Takuya Nagaya who was killed by his father in 2013 for slithering around and being "possessed by a snake demon." There was the picture of Cat at the Arminster LGBT+ club from the *Ledger*, high-quality photographs of Mountain Vista's gate and security system, and even a list of possible aliases for her song covers: "Miss Black? Madame Blackie? The Black Cat?"

I noticed my Coffeefolder invite to Bryce under my initials, along with a printed-out copy of the *Beneath the Makeup* product description on Coffeefolder. But there were also scanned pages from the book itself, with every instance of "Cyiarra" and "Dr. Ivan Galloway" circled in red. And at the bottom: a picture Troy had posted on Chipper once of him, Eva, Clyde, Keegan, Leah, Olivia, and me. His head and mine were circled. A photo of the Big Nasty and its license plate was pinned beside it. Next to that: a picture from Friday night of Troy, handcuffed to the railing of the cabin's front porch. He had looked right at the camera, scared and helpless. I hadn't believed him.

I raised my phone carefully, steadied my shaking hands, and then took the picture.

"You found it," a voice said. I quickly turned around to see Bryce standing there by his bed, gripping pamphlets. "I've been keeping up with you all for seven years, and nobody's found it. Not even Catherine."

"What is this?!" I demanded, moving past him and into his room, then turning around to point. "That is invasive! *That's crazy!*"

"I'M NOT CRAZY!" he shouted at me, throwing the pamphlets aside. "I'M NOT... I'm... I'm not crazy. Come on. You're saying you never looked any of us up? Don't act holier than thou. It's all publicly accessible. I had to do some digging—"

"And some drives and plane rides!"

"—but it was the only way to be certain!"

"Of what?!"

"That you weren't breaking the rules!" he exclaimed. "The rules, Michael! Why can't you understand we made those for a reason?! And yet you decide after seven years that it's fine to go against everything we've worked so hard to keep by breaking the biggest one of all!"

"What are you talking about?!"

"DON'T JOKE LIKE THAT!" He ran up and pinned me against the wall like one of his photographs, knocking down a painting as he did so. In its corner, I recognized Bryce's own set of initials. "THAT ISN'T FUNNY! THIS ISN'T A FUCKING GAME!"

I pushed him off and watched as he fell onto the bed, reached under the pillow, and took out a railroad spike. He lunged it at my head, but I ran, nearly slipping on the marble hallway floor as I heard the spike break the glass of another abstract design.

"GET BACK HERE, WACKO JACKO!" he yelled from his room, but I was already running down the stairs. "WHERE'S YOUR WHITE FEDORA?! WHERE'S SPIKE THE RABBIT?!" The signed baseball hit me square on my lower back and rolled away as I reached the bottom. "YOU GONNA TURN INTO A SKELETON AND DANCE

FOR ME?!" I staggered—grabbing the bathroom door for support. "YOU KNOW DAMN WELL WHAT WE DID ON MAY TWENTY-NINTH!"

He jumped on top of me, reaching for my neck. I shoved him off and bolted for the front door, but he threw pillows in that direction, so I instinctively ran for the kitchen.

"BRYCE!" I screamed, hiding behind the island, trembling. "WHAT THE FUCK?!"

The Santa mug shattered against the refrigerator in front of me. I got up to run, but I ran into him, knocking him back momentarily. Then he put his arm down on the counter and scooped all the cups and dishes in my direction. I stepped back to avoid them, so he reached for a stainless-steel ladle while I grabbed a butter knife off the floor.

My phone buzzed in my pocket. He took the ladle and swung it like a baseball bat. I ducked just in time and kicked his left knee, knocking him to the ground. I then grabbed ahold of a sarcophagus and pushed it down onto him. But it was lighter than I thought, and soon, I'd found myself in front of the fish tank with nowhere to go.

"Bryce," I said, holding the butter knife in front of me as he pushed the coffin to the side and managed his way up. "I—"

He flung the ladle in my direction. I jumped to the side and dropped the knife in surprise as the glass broke and the water flooded the living room, knocking Bryce over onto his back with the flopping fish.

"OH, YOU BITCH!" Bryce wailed, echoing all throughout the house as I dashed around the spill and out the back door.

The air was freezing cold, but the adrenaline kept me warm as I fled, jumping over lawn decorations and the back gate as I did so. It was nighttime, and I had only scattered stars and a full moon to guide me across the field and into the woods to hide me from that monster.

"Somebody learn all your dirty little secrets?!" I heard him yell. "They figure out you've been lying to them?! Can you *live* with denial?! *I know you can see me!*"

The trees were spread apart and without a single leaf on their branches. I kept going farther and farther within, but I still felt hopeless and lost. I briefly touched my back pocket and cursed as I realized Troy's underwear had fallen out during the commotion.

"Goddammit!" I cried aloud. A coyote pack howled in the distance.

I leaned against a random pine with my back facing the manor, pulled out my phone, and then checked for notifications. Six missed calls, but I didn't have a signal to return them. So I turned on the flashlight again to see a pair of tattered blue socks nailed to the tree in front of me. I didn't know why, but that image alone frightened me more than Bryce's secret archive on our fifth-grade class. I was scared. I hadn't been so scared in my life.

I continued through the forest, and forty-five minutes later, after having been turned around on numerous occasions, I stumbled upon a country road. From there, I walked east until I found the mayor's mansion and the big blue rays emitting from the pool. Yet the inside lights were out, as if Bryce had somewhere else to be.

The gate was still open, so I got on my stomach and crawled my way to the Big Nasty in hopes of not setting off any alarms. Finally, when I was sure there was no visible danger, I opened the SUV's door, started the engine, dimmed the lights, and then backed out of Bryce's driveway and onto the street. I faced forward as I passed the country club, Main Street, New Baines High, the soccer complex, and the neighborhood. I'd paid my dues, and it was time to run.

I drove straight and fast to the other side of infinity. I focused only on the sound of the radio music and the deep sensation of needing to piss. The whole trip took an hour and thirty minutes in the dark, taking the turnpike for fifteen miles, then I-44 for fifty-eight. The snow fell as I signaled and turned left onto US-59 South. Blurs of trees passed the window. Time felt off. Suddenly, 902 Honey Deer Drive.

A light dusting of snow covered parts of the porch, but it was nothing, really. I parked the Big Nasty in its usual spot, took out the cabin key, and then opened the door. The inside was just as freezing, and in the air was a strange smell of wet clothes. I switched on the lights.

The keys were still in my hand.

The door had been unlocked.

I couldn't imagine Bryce driving up the whole way, but then again, he had the night I'd arrived. And for what? To scope out the place? And what car did Cat say he drove—a pickup? Had she mentioned the color?

"Now I'm the crazy one," I muttered to myself, looking again at the full moon before closing the door behind me. "Watch me turn into a werecat with yellow eye contacts." I laughed. "Uncle Herbert? Kukowski? ... Troy? Or Eva... Are you there?"

Kukowski's bedroom door was still locked, and ours across from it remained untouched. My laptop was still there, overlooked, as was the TV in the living room. We hadn't been robbed.

I kicked off my shoes and set them beside the bunk bed. Then I went to the TV and clicked it on for some noise—*any noise*—so I wouldn't feel so alone. But there was only static.

A floorboard creaked. I stood up and swerved my body around, searching for the source, listening for footsteps behind me. I then slowly moved over to the fireplace and reached above the mantel, not taking my eyes off the rest of the rooms. But my fingers didn't touch anything. The gun was gone.

"Bryce?" I asked to no response. "If you're there, this isn't funny. I could call the cops."

The wind shook the windows as the snow continued to spread outside. The weather ran west to east, but it sure felt like the storm from Dreary had followed me to Madison.

I looked around the fireplace, wondered why the hell Kukowski didn't own a poker or something I could use as a blunt weapon, and then settled for a worn Stephen King collection from the bookshelf. Would the taxidermy bear beside it protect me further? Probably not. So I continued my rounds, closing my eyes and opening them again, hoping it was all in my imagination.

The grandfather clock sounded. I pissed myself, but only a trickle down the leg. Embarrassed, paranoid, and afraid, I went to the hallway, raised *Four Past Midnight*—at least two inches thick—high in my right hand, and then slowly opened the bathroom door with my left.

I screamed at Bryce, hitting the top of his head with the book. But then I was hitting myself, then staring at myself, or rather, my reflection. I lowered the book slightly, but then I did see Bryce, and our eyes met in that mirror. He grabbed my hair from behind and slammed me into the polished metal, the paperback suppressing the blow but still cracking the mirror like a spider web. I then toppled backward, and Bryce shoved me hard against the wall and towel rack by the toilet, where I slumped to the floor with the shards.

He was straddling me—choking me hard with his icy grip. I was going in and out. Bryce was drowning me.

"YOU CAN'T JUST SAY SOMETHING LIKE THAT!" he screamed into my face. "YOU KNEW WE COULDN'T ALL MEET AGAIN! IT'S THE SECOND RULE!"

"Bry... Bryce..."

"YOU CAN'T GET THE POLICE INVOLVED BECAUSE YOU'D BE CHARGED, TOO!" He gripped me tighter. "I KEPT TABS ON YOU TO MAKE SURE YOU WOULDN'T FUCK UP—*AND YOU DID!*"

He let go. I clutched my upper chest and turned to the side, gasping for air, thinking each might be my last. Meanwhile, Bryce took out his phone, typed something into it, and then shoved it in front of my face. It took me a second in the darkness of the bathroom to see I was looking at the product page for *Beneath the Makeup*.

"Why are you showing me—?"

"Read the description!" he demanded. "READ IT!"

"'The Canopy Creek Sanatorium and Dr. Ivan Galloway—'"

"NO!" He slammed his phone against the tile, cracking the screen. He forced it again to me. "READ THE DESCRIPTION!"

"IT SAYS, 'THE CANOPY CREEK SANATORIUM AND DR. IAN GALLAGHER BOTH LOST PATIENT MADISON FITZGERALD IN LESS THAN A MONTH!'"

"THANK YOU!" He stood up then, and that's when I realized I was sobbing. "That was the first rule you broke—but I couldn't do anything while you were in Alabama! And then you think you can enter the state and call an assembly without any consequences?!" He spat on my face. "THIS IS WHY I'VE GOT QUICKSEARCH ALERTS ON ALL YOUR NAMES! IF SOMETHING POPS UP, I ADD IT TO THE BOARD! But then you—" He pointed. "You are *much more difficult*, since your name is the same as Michael Jackson the singer. So I have an alert set for Ian's name, too!"

"The kid from the bus?!"

"DAMN YOU!" Bryce yelled. He kicked me hard once between the legs, then landed several more blows to the groin. "HE'S NOT JUST A KID! HE'S THE REASON WE'RE IN THIS FUCKING MESS!" More kicks, more pain, coughing up crimson, capillaries bursting. "You're probably one of those writers who thinks there's really such a thing as good and evil, black and white. Tell me it's that simple, Michael. Go on! *I dare you.*"

I was sopping wet in a pool of my own piss, blood, and tears, but Bryce didn't seem to care. My whole body ached and burned with pain and exhaustion. It wasn't any comfort catching glimpses of Bryce's eyes and seeing he didn't enjoy any of the misery he brought me. To him, this was punishment for a crime I couldn't recall committing.

Bryce waited there, standing in the doorway so I could see only his silhouette. Then he leaned against the frame as he slid to the floor, his hands trembling.

"There's nothing we can do," Bryce said, eyes downcast. His voice shook as he spoke and turned to me. "And that's the worst part. It hangs over our heads. Every instance of pure silence when we're alone with our thoughts, it's all that comes to mind. It's human nature. And it's all my fault. But you… you will never know what it's been like. How hard it's been. *Never*."

Bryce cried with me. I was so confused and hurting and too scared to say anything to him. I moved onto my back and whelped at how quickly I'd been reduced to nothing more than ashes.

"It's the road to hell," he went on. "Good intentions. I tried to do what my dad would've wanted, but I messed up. It's what I thought was right. 'Cause that's what they teach you—what they taught us. The home is the first school; the parents, the first educators. But you never see how much it hurts others until you're too late. So the horrors remain. And my dad died because of it. Christian, Gabby… It'd be easier if they'd just kill me. My dad…" He broke down. *"Father, my God, I killed him. And there's nothing I can do!"*

We sat there in a gross placidity. Then he straightened.

"Wait a minute. Wait seven years!" Bryce laughed, frightening me further. "We were doing all the right things, just executed improperly. We have to try again." He looked to me. "We have to try again!"

Bryce jumped to his feet and ran off down the hall, slamming the front door on his way out. After a few more seconds of waiting in worry, I continued to sob once more.

◆━━━◆━◆━━━◆

It felt like years had passed when I finally managed to get off the floor just to have to hold onto the sink to stop myself from fainting. When I could walk, I slowly picked up the shards and started mopping up the fluids with some old rags I found in a drawer. I then put them and my clothes in a laundry bag to wash and set the shower temperature to warm, wincing as the water hit each aching part of my body. I scrubbed and scrubbed and I kept scrubbing until my hands were raw. Had they always been this red? I didn't know. I didn't know I didn't know.

Afterward, I carefully dried off and limped naked to the bedroom. Then I found some warm pajamas and eased my way into them.

I had heard once that every time we think of a memory, we begin to recall less and less of it, creating our own bias as the mind instinctively fills in the gaps. This, I hoped, would be the case with my assault that Wednesday night by Richard Bryce Skinner. I thought of my options, such as filing a police report, but for what? My bottom lip was swollen, and I had some nasty marks on my face, legs, neck, crotch, and lower back, but it wasn't serious enough for a trip to the hospital. I'd also inadvertently been the cause of so much destruction at Bryce's manor, self-defense or otherwise. And what was it he'd said about me going to the cops? With that bulletin board full of information, I wouldn't doubt he had some secrets of mine. Plus, his stepdad was the mayor of New Baines, and I'm sure the man had more than a little influence and connections, despite the attack occurring in Madison.

I heard the front door open, and this time, I did scream. It was only Troy, though, tracking in snow and staring at me with an irritated, resentful countenance on his stubbled face. If people could emit fumes, he was smoking from every orifice on his beanie-covered head.

"Where. The fuck. Were you?" he asked me, dropping his bag beside him. "You *said* you were going to pick me up from Gabby's at *five!*"

"I was there!" I told him, then swallowed, as it hurt to talk. "I showed up in the Big Nasty, but Eva—"

"What *about* Eva?! Did she call you with news that Olivia isn't a lesbian and wants to finally suck your dick?! Tell me: do you still wet the bed? Are you that much of an eccentric child? You're a ten-year-old trapped in a seventeen-year-old's body!"

"Go to hell!"

"Well, it's about time you said something you meant!"

"Do you not see my face?!" I demanded. "These cuts and bruises?! Can't you think about someone other than yourself for once?!"

"WHAT?!" he screamed. "I think of other people all the damn time! You're the one who's always making everything about you and your book and your poor relationships! And you know what? I'm sick of it! Gabby and I talked, and while she did say we had sex after your party, we're just going to be friends while she's dating Christian. I asked you for one favor—to pick me up at five—and where were you? Not answering my calls, not reading my texts… *nothing!*"

"Then it's a good fucking thing I got accepted to Hartsett so I can get the hell out of your life and stop causing so many of your goddamn problems!"

"You…!" He gulped. "You weren't accepted to Hartsett! How could you say that?!"

"My mom called me before I left!" I told him. "Maybe now you can find someone else to start blaming your shit on."

"You knew for almost *a week* and didn't tell me?!"

"She called before I left *today!*"

Troy didn't say anything in return. He only looked at me with complete disappointment in his muddy-brown eyes.

"Hartsett, huh?" He folded his arms across his jacket. "Makes sense. You were always so hopeful—always shaving your balls and wearing the nicest underwear you owned to every party in case you just so happened to get laid as a ninth grader. But life isn't like that for everyone. You can't go back and change your childhood. Some people aren't as optimistic as you—they don't have the brains you have, the abilities you have. Some of us throw fucking parties with total strangers because I don't have any real friends besides you." He kicked at the doorframe. "And now you're leaving. What an ingrate. Selfish fuck."

"It's not that simple," I explained. "I made mistakes. And whether it was my former friends or current friends, all I wanted was for everyone to be happy."

"No, Mom, you wanted *you* to be happy." Troy pushed past me—sending a sharp pain through my shoulder—and started grabbing handfuls of his things. "I'm not done with you, but boy, am I *done* with you. I'm putting wood in the fireplace and sleeping on the couch tonight. And if the weather's not too bad, we'll leave first thing tomorrow." He considered the moonlit view outside. "I hate this place. Can't imagine what you ever saw in it."

With that, he left me alone in our room. So I cracked the door, in case he had to come back for something, but he didn't. We slept separately that night.

I didn't need Troy. I didn't need him or Cat or Bryce or Oklahoma at all. I needed the end goal, which was Hartsett, and five more months wouldn't kill me. It was a waiting game, after all, and someone had to win.

I sent Gabby the pictures and then powered down my phone for the night, all the while thinking of the closet in my mind's teeming depths.

Ian Gallagher was underwater.

He was cold, but strangely relaxed. The cyan rocks formed a breathtaking landscape with blues and greens against an endless expanse that would have been any painter's dream.

There was only one obvious thing missing: the fish.

Ian's toes brushed against a cobblestone staircase. About fifty feet in diameter, it spiraled downward for what appeared to be miles. Ian understood he had to climb down these stairs, and then how silly the idea seemed. But gravity was different here, wherever this was. Ian didn't feel an urge to swim to the surface high above him to catch his breath, nor was he floating around. It was like walking normally, but with weights attached.

A medieval cosmonaut stood farther away, watching.

Ian peered over the edge and realized it would be easier to just drift down than to walk. Grasping the rusted railing, he put one leg over, then the other, and then let go. Ian closed his eyes and slowly descended into the abyss, never once considering how in the world he was to get out again.

There was a repetitive ringing in his ears, and Ian opened his eyes out of curiosity. The water was now a darker shade of blue, almost violet. The ringing seemed to come from an unseen telephone. Or was it two phones? He could clearly hear two tones, ringing in discord. Even more. Ian pressed his hands against his ears, trying to block out the sounds, which had gone too far past mere annoyance. Pain shot from one temple to the other, and it felt like a bowling ball rested on his chest—each breath more difficult than the last.

Someone, please, just answer the phone!

And there it was, out of nowhere—the butterfly's scream. Just as last time, the discomfort was unbearable. As Ian slowly drifted through the center of the spiraling staircase, he tried to grab onto the railing to stop what now felt like a descent into Hell, an icy prison. Yet the railing wasn't there; much to his horror, the staircase was falling apart in random places, creating gaping holes like jagged, ravenous mouths of monsters.

He heard it. The voice.

"The water's cold, E." Something was different. "We're waiting for *you*."

The image of Karina blurred in Ian's mind—contaminated by a deformed woodpecker with red, empty eye sockets. With a sinister grin, the Woodpecker looked up from the void below. Ian was terrified to fall any farther, but he had no choice; he had chosen this path. The *easy* way.

"Don't *bother*... looking for *me*," cried the Woodpecker, snapping its beak at him. The voice had shifted to a much deeper tone, as if being played back from a voice recorder slower than normal. "THERE'S... *NOTHING*... OUT... *HERE*."

If only he had listened.

Finally hitting bottom, Ian landed on his feet, lost his balance, and then dropped to his knees. It was pitch black. It took extra effort to stand.

In the distance, he saw a single light beaming down. The light illuminated a lone statue at the top of a mountain made up of thousands of broken sculptures, each knocked over and begging to be put back together.

He began to move toward the central stone figure, every step sending sharp jabs to his head. Walking over the dismembered busts, Ian noticed some of them displayed various outfits from eons ago, now slowly turning to dust.

Ian tripped over a centurion's bloated torso and fell into a pile of white rock bodies. Impossible to walk, he crawled his way to the top. His head throbbed. He had never imagined such agony.

Reaching the summit, Ian stared into the eyes of the last statue still intact. Karina's image was captured perfectly in the stone. Every detail was there. As he had dreamed of doing for years, he gently stroked her face. But his joy quickly morphed into horror as, beneath his outreached hand, her face began to seep dark blood—slowly, at first, in drops from her forehead, nose, and mouth, and then in waves of thick crimson.

Ian jerked back his hand. Inexplicably, his palm showed no blood, but the statue was covered in it and beginning to disintegrate right before his eyes.

The centurion's stomach collapsed then, revealing it to be hollow. Inside was a little boy named Childhood, his body curled, his face blotted out by years of nonexistence.

Ian heard the taunting laugh of the Woodpecker screeching within his skull.

I awoke in the morning covered in sweat. At first, I thought it might be other fluids from my body, but no, it was sweat. I couldn't recall my restless dream, though I did remember Bryce's obsession with Ian Gallagher. Why him?

The sky outside was white as the snow piled up against the sides of the lake house and across the trees. The cabin was warm, thankfully, and I suspected the fireplace had much to do with it. I left the bedroom to check on Troy, to be amicable with him. The multitude of blankets and quilts he'd slept with were still there, and though the fire continued to roar, Troy wasn't around to enjoy it.

I checked my phone on the nightstand. Several missed calls and texts from Troy the day before. One new text from him, received at nine o'clock that morning.

"Someone popped three of the tires on the BN," he wrote. "I called a mechanic to check on it. She'll be there around noon. $$$ is on the counter. I also took your clothes to the laundromat. They're in the kitchen. I'll be out today seeing what Madison has to offer (or whatever is still open). We'll drive home sometime tonight. Leave me alone."

I peered out the window. The Big Nasty had a fine layer of snow on its olive-green hood and roof rack, and I noticed it was sinking to the right. I hadn't run over anything on the way back to the cabin the previous night, so someone must have popped the tires, as Troy had suggested. He knew what he was talking about; being gay in Dreary meant having your wheels slashed on numerous occasions, whether it be at the school parking lot or your own driveway.

I went to the kitchen to examine the clothes, clutching onto my thigh as I did so, as my right leg hurt like hell. Sure enough, everything had been washed thoroughly. On the table was the business card for Detective Northcott. I put on the hoodie and denim jacket over my pajama shirt, slipped off my pants to wear my green boxer briefs under them, put on my shoes, pocketed the card once again, and then opened the door to a numbing nineteen degrees Fahrenheit. I couldn't see the ground in most places—only a quiet white.

The tires had indeed been popped. It looked like they'd been shanked with a shiv, which didn't concern me as much when compared to the chilling "PV=nRT" written on the rear windshield in lipstick. I'd originally thought the tires might've been Bryce's doing, but the tattoo story was Troy, myself, and Hennigan High School-specific. Was this a message for me, or Kukowski?

Whoever had done it cost Troy a thousand dollars, per the statement from the mechanic. She arrived thirty minutes later, bundled up more appropriately than me in my pajama pants. Limping back inside, I tried thinking of all the possibilities as to who had burst my tires. If it was a threat meant for me, it was most likely Bryce. But the "PV=nRT" pointed toward it being for Kukowski. So who would've done it? Maybe that woman he was with when I'd arrived at the cabin Friday night? One of his students? Colonel Mustard with the lead pipe in the conservatory?

"Not the lead pipe, the *knife*," I told myself, shaking my head in disdain.

In the bedroom, I opened the Chipper app on my phone and searched for all instances of Kukowski's name. I then started scrolling to find someone pissed off enough to where they'd slash my tires in case they were his. From the top statuses I read, it seemed his students either admired him or were offended by his rants to the point where they hated his guts. So there was @TheUnbiasedGamer saying, "My chemistry teacher is the sarcastic asshole I aspire to be. God bless Kukowski," while there was also @LilyliciousLilypop with, "Failed yet another chem test. :) Thanks, Kukowski," among others. My favorite was from @JoelHarrisonKnox: "kukowski sniffed my water bottle for vodka and then offered me some taco kick after school. we gonna bang or??"

The culprit, I suspected, was none other than @iKaylaLykkesboys with her Chipper status from two years before: "For the eighth time this year Kukowski claims I'm a stoner... #WTF." She didn't have much of a motive besides the seventy-eight-percent grade in the class, but she did know where he lived, and that was enough to raise my suspicions.

The phone vibrated in my hand. Someone was calling me, and though I hadn't found the chance to add him to my contacts, I sure recognized the number.

"Bryce?" I answered, my back aching as I spoke, my free hand clenching my leg.

"Michael," he said casually. "I hope you're feeling better meow. I know I am. I'm glad we hung out yesterday."

"What the fuck—"

"We're a lot alike, you and me, me and you," he continued. "We dislike people who don't play by our rules. Christian doesn't hear me, Troy doesn't hear you. It's all the same. Catherine, too. I'll admit, I wasn't completely honest with you last night. I'm sorry. I've tried putting out too many fires. I've actually been talking with Cath, and she and I both agree we want an end to the madness."

"You haven't talked to her," I told him. "Cat wants nothing to do with you."

"Well, that's interesting, considering I'm on a video call with her right now." There was some clicking on his end. "Say something to our famous author friend."

"Hey, Michael," said Cat's voice from someplace else.

"Cat?!" I asked, gripping the phone tighter. "I—I didn't think… I'm so confused. He tried to kill me, and I… Why… why are you with him?!"

"I'm not with anyone," she stated. She sounded removed, far off. "From what I've been hearing, your party shook up a lot of people. It's not fair what any of us have had to go through. We all need closure, and Bryce has done what he could, for the most part, to—"

"He has pictures of all of us!" I told her. "In his room, there were all these crazy… He had this… this, uh, candles and a chalk pentagram—and his closet! There's this bulletin board full of emails and photographs of Mekenzie walking around in North Carolina and stuff on the rest of us, and when I found out, he threw a *railroad spike* at me, and… and…" I swallowed. "And why are you with him now?! He tried to rape you! He… I mean, shit, this is just like fifth grade all over again!"

"No!" she commanded. "Don't you dare, Michael! This is not about you, and it's not about Bryce."

"You chose him over me."

"YOU LEFT!" she screamed. "I waited for a phone call, an email to my mom, anything! Bryce, didn't I wait?!"

"For too long," he agreed.

"Not once did you ever reach out! *Not once!* Until your girlfriend broke up with you, anyway. So why the fuck are you holding this against me now?! *I moved forward!* And now, we all have to!"

"But…" I started. "Cat—"

"All I am is a symbol to you," she stated. My heart dropped. "Don't patronize me, either. You had your chance. Bryce says he has a plan to make this right for everyone."

"What about Gabby?" I asked. "What does she think?"

"Funny you mention her. She told me you believe that me once being a cat is a kind of escapism—that we all have these *identity issues* because of what happened." Sirens blared in the distance. "By extension, I sure hope that's not what you think of all queer people."

"It isn't! And that's not—"

"Unless you're a necromancer, don't even bother," she told me. "I'm done, Bryce."

"No, wait, Cat—please, hold on a minute," I pleaded into the phone. To Bryce: "Put her back on! I'm not done!"

"Cat got your tongue?" he joked. "You're right. There's still much to do. That's why I'm having my own little lake house party tonight at eight for all our fifth-grade class to attend." Silence. "Well, what's left of our class, that is. Anyway, I already sent out the invites on Coffeefolder. We'll finish this then, once and for all. See you soon."

He ended the call. I was left staring at the phone.

"DAMMIT!" I screamed to the ceiling fan, then kicked at the bottom bunk. "FUCK, FUCK, FUCK, FUCK! GAAH!" I searched the room. "Where are you?! Where are the cameras?! What show is this?!" I flipped the mattress. "YOU GOT ME, GUYS! YOU GOT ME GOOD! EXCUSE MY POTTY MOUTH, 'CAUSE I'VE OFFICIALLY LOST MY FUCKING MIND!" I kicked over the wastebasket. "ARE YOU HAPPY NOW?! IS THIS WHAT YOU WANTED?!" I picked up my phone, saw I had notifications from Coffeefolder, grasped at my hair. "Make it stop… Please, God, make it stop…"

On Coffeefolder, I had two unread messages: one from Pete, the other from Bryce. Pete's was the latest, saying he wanted to have a get-together at his house on West Shaughnessy Lane at five that evening before we went to see Bryce, who Pete specified was not invited. Bryce's message was an invitation to his own party at 511 Quaint Lake View on Lake Nasagarresett. Both messages had also been forwarded to the rest of our former classmates at Hayes.

I thought of going to Cat's house in Mountain Vista—her own Neverland Ranch— but she didn't want anything to do with me, and the SUV was being fixed. Cat had been so upset the other day, and Ms. Varsha so authoritative as she'd told me to beat it. *Michael, are you OK? So, Michael, are you OK? Are you OK, Michael?* What a joke.

I scrolled through my contacts list and considered calling Olivia—"Ollie" in my phone—but guessed she wouldn't want to hear from me, either. I remembered saying "I love you" the night she'd dumped me. Had I truly loved her in that moment? Or would I have said anything to keep her with me? Was I that afraid of losing her?

I needed to talk to someone, anybody, about what had happened. All of it. I kept scrolling past names of people who either hated me, wouldn't understand, or both: Mr. Bradford, Clyde, Gabby, Eva, Keegan, Leah, my mother, my uncle, Troy, and his mother. Even Kelli Ziegler had made her way into my phone, and she had been murdered by the triple-braided rope of a serial killer. I felt dead, like her, in a wooden box buried by sudden snowfall. It wasn't cleansing; it was maddening. I thought I knew isolation from Dreary, but I'd been entirely wrong. Nothing could compare.

I cried. I wept into my hands and cursed the air around me. There was no one left for me. I had no friends, and I doubted I'd ever had any. Even Troy was gone, off exploring. Exhausted, half-delirious, and enraptured by his carefree attitude, I thought of the day he and I had first met. I hadn't understood Troy was hitting on me at the time, as our first conversation was about, of all things, Korean rapper Thorax Wang.

"He is *so* gay," Troy had said.

"What?" I had asked. "What makes you say that?"

"I dunno. He just *is*, you know?"

"No," I'd told him. "No, I don't know."

It was 12:47 in the afternoon. If I planned to leave at 3:30 for Pete's party in New Baines—to maybe confront Kayla about the tires—then I had a little less than three hours to kill. But Troy was my distraction; he'd always been. I needed a new one, but I wasn't ready for this much adjustment, this role reversal, this rapid transformation, so soon. I wanted to understand him better—to see how he could do it all. He made life seem so easy, yet I knew that wasn't true for him. The Troy in my head was different from the Troy in real life.

I imagined his laughter through the outside wind. It was comforting.

The email containing my EverbladeOnline.com username and password was nearly nine years old, but surprisingly, the login details worked. My character spawned randomly in the middle of a forest, trees in every direction. There was no universal chat, as the game stated I could only talk to players within a hundred steps from me. So the world was quiet as the mechanic towed away the Big Nasty.

The fall of Troy's town of Harmony was not well-known on the Internet. I only found one forum topic on the subject from a website dedicated to *Everblade Online* kingdoms. The conversation was between three members of a larger in-game city who I supposed were *Everblade* scholars of sorts trying to determine the history of the town for their records. Of the heroes they listed, Troixe was not among them.

I glanced at the top of the page and noticed it said that two users were reading this topic, both guests. When I refreshed, only one user remained.

I used a map and coordinates from the forum to locate Harmony. It took me several in-game days of trekking, each consisting of gathering berries to keep myself from starving, fighting off slashers during the night, and holing up in abandoned shacks on the hillside as I waited for dawn. I didn't see a single player during this time, though I did find the notes they'd left behind.

"Wendy, when you read this, please send me a message."

"I'll come back the first of every month at three Pacific."

"I tried to keep the fort, but it's been years. Forgive me, brethren."

It seemed almost silly to me, but really, who was I to talk? I'd driven nine hours to see my childhood classmates again after seven years; if these people wanted to check back periodically on their own friends, so be it. At least they were saving gas mileage.

On the seventh day, I found Harmony. It was a small city protected by a stone wall ten times the height of my player. The wall formed a square around the settlement, which was in a forested coastal area. The front gate—the only gate besides the one for boats in the water—was blown open. I sent my character through.

To the immediate right was Mayor Ghoul's mansion, the immaculate quartz structure Troy had mentioned during the road trip. The doors were locked, but one of the windows was missing, so I stepped inside. There were waterfall fountains on both sides of the staircase, which led to a master bedroom and its grand view of the city.

There looked to be something inside the fountain on the left, so I had my character walk into it. As expected, there was a door leading through to a large, hollowed-out oak tree against the outside city wall—the first of many secrets.

During the hour I spent there, I discovered more hidden passageways than a city named "Harmony" should have. Most of the houses had been ransacked by looters, though I did find some emeralds and preservatives stowed behind a shelf in a home belonging to a fellow named "Lotza." In the same house, I came across a door under the rug that once again led me underground and outside the gates. So much for peace and other synonyms.

To the left of the city was Maestro Manor, named after the hero of whom Troy had spoken highly. Maestro Manor was a simple wooden building, but beside it was a three-story country house with a sign that read: MAESTRO'S HOME FOR THE WEARY. Directly in front of it was part of the east-side city wall, which had faded graffiti and anti-Ghoul hype written across it. The right side of the Home for the Weary, which faced the sea, had been blown up or destroyed somehow. I suspected Mayor Ghoul's boats had something to do with it.

A diary I found under one of the beds revealed the truth to me. According to a person who went by "Griffinity," Mayor Ghoul and Maestro were the same player using trickery to keep the town together by creating the inevitable rebel to control the situation. The writer then went on about how it was symbolic of identity, "the given versus the chosen." Whether the plan worked, Griffinity didn't say, though the last entry did mention that the survivors—including Griffinity, Bunnicaro, Mountaines, and Swearyouloveme—were heading for the White Forest beyond the fifth lookout point. The diary was addressed to Troixe.

"Who are you?" asked a player named Antinous. I turned my guy around. Antinous wore armor that glowed green, and in his hands, he held an emerald sword. "Did you live in Harmony?"

"I'm just passing by," I typed out.

"Do you have any food?" he pressed, his sword still drawn.

"No," I answered.

Antinous killed me then, taking my berries, emeralds, preservatives, and Griffinity's diary with him.

I researched the members of Troy's group, including Swearyouloveme, for about ten minutes before the mechanic returned with the Big Nasty. I then signed some paperwork and took the SUV for a test drive around the lake. When I came back, I paid her the cash, she left, and then I put on my jeans, an undershirt, and a gray wool button-up underneath the hoodie and jacket.

I carried on via the interstate to "Cut Your Bangs" by Girlpool. The ladies sang of broken promises, a sad, monotonous song. The sky was a pure white, and for a moment, the snow had let up. Troy and I should've been heading back—our window of opportunity, so to speak—but he hadn't returned to Honey Deer Drive by the time I was ready to leave. It would've been so easy to drive off without him, but I wasn't a complete asshole. At least I'd texted him where I was going; whereas he hadn't been specific, I was the bigger person. I told Troy the truth: I was going to a party.

It was curiosity, mostly, driving me back to New Baines. There was no real reason to go to Pete's or Bryce's anymore. I'd seen my classmates. I'd talked to Cat. They were all crazy, and probably, so was I.

Yet I still wanted my answers. At least the roads were somewhat familiar.

Cars slowed as a white van spun out of control and slid to a stop. Everyone was going under thirty. The whole scene might've looked pathetic to anyone up north, but this was Oklahoma. Despite getting blizzards every four years or so, these were rough conditions, especially for new drivers. I was all right, though; I could handle my own.

Eva called my phone after I'd gotten off the turnpike. In some ways, the streets were more dangerous than the highways, as the neighborhoods weren't getting as much traffic, and thus, the snow got taller. Still, I answered.

"Eva?" I asked.

"Why haven't you been picking up?!" she demanded.

"Hold on. I'm in the Big Nasty. Let me pull over." I did. "OK, what's up?"

"What?! *Clyde and Keegan are in jail*, that's what's up!"

"Jail?!" I repeated. "Dreary police got them? For what?!"

"They're in Rochester. It was some party. Clyde was caught selling meth, and Keegan almost beat Leah to death. She's in the hospital there. This happened Saturday night. I would've told you sooner, but I just found out yesterday!"

We were quiet. I didn't know what to say.

"I'm sorry," I told her.

"You should be." I heard her sniffling. "If you and Troy had been here, maybe it wouldn't have gotten so out of control or…" She took a deep breath, then started to cry.

"Maybe," I said. "But, hey, Evangeline: when I get back, you and I are going to hang out, OK? We won't worry about what anyone else is doing. Just us."

"Why? What's the point?"

"Because I haven't been a good friend to you. I know that now. I need you in my life."

"And Troy? What about him?"

"I don't think he'll apologize, if that's what you're asking."

"No." She sighed. "I'm talking about… Your mom called my mom. We know about Hartsett. Congratulations, by the way. But… Troy was hoping you'd stay in

Dreary with us."

"You're going to that Alabama med school."

"I'll still be around."

"So what? You're saying I should throw away my future and dreams because Troy Rico wants me to stay in town?"

"Did you at least discuss this with him?"

"He doesn't want to talk about it."

"Then maybe you aren't trying hard enough."

"Look, I'm just going to focus on my personal projects when I get back—"

"Personal? What could be more personal than your best friend?!"

I sighed. "Me and Troy aren't on good terms. I'm not sure we will be by the time we get to Dreary tomorrow. But you and I… I want us to be good."

"Until graduation."

"Huh?"

"And then you're off," she explained. "You'll be checking out California and posting about it on your website. Whereas I want my friend group back together, you want someone to eat lunch with during school. I get that. But if you don't want to be friends, don't tell me that we are."

"Eva—"

"That's all I'm asking."

I was on Packard Street. I could see the sign for Truman.

"I'll make things better," I promised her. "How's Olivia?"

"Livi's fine. She's been with her junior friends."

"Do you know if she's dating anyone?"

"Um, yeah, she is."

"Do you know who?" I asked. "Is it Rikki?"

"Does it matter?" she countered. I contemplated this.

"OK." I scratched at the back of my neck. "I have things I need to do."

"Get back safe," Eva said, then hung up.

I put the gear in drive and got onto Packard. The stop sign had been run over, and it stuck out, disfigured, in the snow. I shook my head, signaled out of habit, and then turned left onto Truman. A minute later, I signaled left for South Shaughnessy Court.

The Fortescue residence appeared unaltered after seven years: same fence, same paint, same hedges, and the same grotesque lawn gnomes. Bryce's dad—his biological one— had asked the homeowner's association to request Mr. Fortescue's gnomes be removed because of them being an eyesore, causing a back-and-forth rivalry between the fathers. The feud had ended when Pastor Skinner died of his heart attack. So the elves and the fairies were there to welcome me back.

Of the vehicles in the driveway, I recognized Emily's blue hatchback, and in the garage, Pete's candy-apple red lowrider, with its dual headlights, rear wings, and all the rust from decades of ownership. I could distinctly remember Mr. Fortescue—who was miraculously alive, given everyone's unfortunate history with their fathers—driving Pete and me around in that convertible when we were younger, promising it would be Pete's when he turned sixteen. I was happy to see Mr. Fortescue had kept to his word, as I knew just how much Pete had been looking forward to the day.

The front door opened before I knocked.

"Well, if it isn't Lot's wife," Pete said, referencing Genesis. He shook my right hand, pulled me in for a quick hug with his left, and then put his hands in his pockets. He smiled as I closed the door. "Thanks for coming out. How've you been these past few days?"

"I'm not sure... how to answer that," I said, his eyes on my bruises. "It's a long story.

I've been better."

"You look like you've been through hell," he noted. "I bet it's weird being back, huh?"

I laughed. It felt good. "I would definitely say that, yes."

A smaller teenager walked behind him. Pete turned around and pulled the boy over by the shoulder.

"Michael, you remember my brother Tommy, right?" Pete asked, gesturing to the child, who did a half-wave, half-salute. "He's in seventh grade at Clarkson."

"Yeah, I remember." He looked like Pete when we were kids. To Tommy: "What I remember more is finding that wad of meat and cheese you hid in one of the kitchen drawers."

"That was you, Tommy?!" Pete exclaimed a little louder than I'd expected. "Momma blamed me for that, you little turd!"

"Whoa, there," Emily said with a drink in her scab-covered hand, joining us. "I haven't heard anyone say that in—"

"Seven years," finished the people on the couch in the living room. I spotted Jim, Sam, and Rachel, all watching TV. "We get it already!"

"Anyway," Pete said to me, "because you were so accommodating at your party, I've got some sodas, quesadillas, little sandwiches, fruit, Gletscher, and Red Harbinger in the kitchen." He then tilted his head at my expression. "If you don't drink, that's totally fine; it's only an option."

"No, that's great," I said. "It's just that I'd never offer produce at a party. I'm too cheap."

"Oh." He looked around. "Well, anyway, Rachel and Sam are playing *Annihilation!* in co-op mode, and Jim's watching."

"So no hide-and-seek and shooting at each other with fake guns?" I asked.

"Not anymore," he answered with a laugh, clearly not catching my hint of nostalgia. Probably for the better.

"Ha-ha!" Sam yelled, standing up and playing his air guitar in front of Rachel. "In the words of bionic badass Commander Ace Thunderbolt, you, Rachel Schoenhals-Zajac, just got… *annihilated!"*

"We're on the same team," she reminded him, sighing and placing the controller beside her. She then adjusted the reddish-pink beanie over her hair. "Anyone else?"

"I should've asked you to bring one of the board games from your uncle's bookshelf," Pete said to me. "But that's all right. Jim, didn't you have a game in mind?"

"Yeah, sure," Jim said. "Cards are on the counter. Everyone gets eight."

I got a call then, but I reached into my pocket and silenced it from there. This moment, after everything that had happened that week, wasn't about anyone else. Having fun with my elementary school friends was exactly what I'd needed that night—what I'd wanted since the beginning. To see them talking and laughing the same as years before was both comical and exciting for me. I didn't believe there was anything wrong with getting high or having orgies or drinking whatever shit was around, but that wasn't what we were doing. We were playing a fucking card game, and sober, at that. This was what I'd been missing out on. Decent, human interactions.

"So Saturday, I heard you telling Christian you might be going to Hartsett," Rachel said in my direction. One of her eyebrows had smeared. "My brother went there. He liked it a lot."

"That's good to know," I told her as I shuffled the deck for another round. "I got accepted there and the University of Arminster. Found out about both just yesterday, actually."

"We could room together, if you end up at AU," Pete told me. "I'm going for petroleum engineering."

"You and a third of all the other incoming freshmen," Sam pointed out.

"It has a nice English department!" Pete added.

"You'd really want me to be your roommate?" I asked him. Jim took a loud sip of his Gletscher.

"Of course," Pete said. "We're in this together, man. You're like a long-lost brother. We're all family here."

"Amen," Jim agreed. I raised my cup of water to that.

There was a knock at the door. Pete got up on his feet, counted heads, and then went to go open it.

I heard an exchange of greetings, followed by, "No, you're fine, honest." After a few more seconds, Christian shook the dust off his shoes as he walked into view, carrying his winter coat in one hand and a rotisserie chicken in the other.

"I was stocking up at Big-Box for the storm," he explained. "I still live down the street. Thought I should bring something by."

We laughed and invited him over, so he joined in, smiling just as we were. Pete wasn't.

"What's the matter?" Sam asked him.

"I guess I'm just confused as to why you came," Pete said to Christian. "It's almost seven. Shouldn't you be on your way to Bryce's?"

"Oh, crap," Jim said. He checked his watch and stood up, too. "I gotta get going before the weather gets worse."

"But you're my ride," Sam said, also standing.

I got up as well. Rachel frowned.

"You're leaving?" She gestured with her head. "To go there?"

"It's not like that," I told her, then to Pete, I said, "I… need to talk to Kayla."

"About what?" Sam asked too quickly for my liking.

"I think she popped my tires earlier," I said. He backed down.

"She must've thought it was your uncle's car," Emily noted, then shrugged. "I considered it, too. Kukowski can be sort of heartless sometimes."

"Bryce said Catherine might be there," Rachel told me. My heart began to race. She then lowered her voice. "Is it true? You saw her, right? Does she really think she's a cat?"

"What a joke," Jim said. "And of course he didn't see her—she's at St. Luke's."

"I heard she lived in a gated community," Emily added.

"I heard she was a German spy in the war," I teased. I didn't think they got it. "Cousin to the Kaiser? Anyway, she believes she once was a cat, yes. To my knowledge, she knows she's a human, but she likes to do cat-related things."

"Couldn't have been easy for Bryce, I guess," Rachel went on. "I heard she was wild at parties—like, in a sad way. She'd get blackout drunk and wake up on the concrete outside the next morning. And then she comes out as a cat? How would you have reacted?" She shook her head. I knew my answer. "So it's serious, then?"

"She's serious, yes," I told her, annoyed and beginning to understand Cat's frustration. "She believes she was reincarnated from a domestic cat into a human. It's called 'Otherkin.' It's super complicated. Gabby explains it better."

"Where is Gabby?" Emily said, mostly to Christian.

"I'm not sure," he said. "To be honest, she and I haven't been talking much these past couple of days."

"I thought you both were dating," Jim pointed out.

"We're… something." He scratched at his neck.

"Doesn't that make you gay?" Emily asked. "I mean, in a matter of speaking. And not that there's anything wrong with—"

"Being queer is biological," Pete stated, "and current science suggests that it has to do with the way certain genes interact. That said, there's no isolated 'gay gene' as of yet. I don't know about brain chemicals and stuff, but some studies show specific hormones play a role in a person's sexuality."

"So is he gay or not?" Jim asked.

"I'm not gay, all right!" Christian said defensively. To me: "And where's *your friend*, Michael?"

"Back in Madison," I answered. To Pete: "I don't want to leave, and please believe me when I say I've had a nice time tonight just being normal with you all, but it is getting late, and with the snow…"

"I get it," he told me. "It's fine. The offer still stands, by the way. How much did Arminster give you?"

"Same as Hartsett."

"Then I guess it depends on if you want the four seasons."

"Of *Sea Breeze Academy*?"

"What? No, like, winter, spring, summer." And as if to elaborate further: "Fall."

"Oh." I could feel the red on my cheeks. "Yeah, that."

"So who's all leaving?" Emily asked.

"I parked my car at my house and walked here," Christian said. "Can I ride with you, Michael?"

"I'll take you," Jim said.

"No, I think I'll ride with Mike," he declared. They looked to me. I shrugged. "So it's settled."

"Then come on, Sam," Jim continued. "Unless you're getting a ride to Red Springs elsewhere."

"I suppose I'm leaving, too," Emily said. "But I'm going home."

"Same," Rachel added. She stood to hug Pete. "Thanks for the party. It was fun. See you Monday in class?"

"Yep," he told her with a sigh, and after we shared our appreciation as well: "It was no problem at all." He walked us to the foyer. "Have fun, I guess. Drive safe out there."

I felt like a total dick as I stepped outside his home.

The sky was dark, but the ground was a thick layer of silver. With each step to our respective vehicles, there was a crisp crunch beneath our feet. I reached into my jacket pockets and found Northcott's business card and a pair of gray gloves. I put them on while the card stayed within; there was only so much a retired cop could do for me in this weather.

Christian got in the passenger seat, I got in the driver's. I started up the SUV and waited for the heater to kick in as the headlights created a tunnel of light. When we were ready, Christian and I followed Jim's minivan to South Shaughnessy Court, then onto Truman, then Packard, and then the turnpike.

"I'm sorry about all that," Christian told me after a few minutes of silence. "For throwing you under the bus, I mean." He sighed. "I like Gabby. A lot. It's weird having feelings for your best friend. Makes things messy. One minute, he's spending the night at my house. Then she can't because my parents won't let her. I'm happy for her. I really am. I like the time we spend together. And I know we're dating. I have nothing against gay people—or queer, or bisexual, or asexual, or all the other letters. I can't imagine how tough it is. But I'm not one of them. And that doesn't, like, make me better or anything! I'm just… not that."

"I understand," I said, wiping condensation off the windshield, "about being the straight guy people think is gay. It's hard—for me—because Troy is my best friend in Dreary, and he's the person who everyone there knows is gay and associates with being gay. So me being around him… they believe I'm gay, too, calling me 'burrito breath' or whatever because he's Hispanic. *But I'm not gay.* And my last girlfriend, she hated when people would joke around like that—again, not specifically because he's gay, but because I'm not, and they implied I was having sex with him and not her."

"Wow." Christian looked down. "They said that?"

"Said what?"

"You having sex with Troy instead of your girlfriend?"

"Oh, well, not exactly. We never did it. We never had sex, me and her."

"So then what? You were spending more time with Troy than ... ?"

"Olivia."

"Olivia."

"I don't know." I shook my head. "It was a normal amount, I thought. We were friends doing friend-things. Nothing weird."

"So maybe she was jealous?" he suggested. "Gabby's like that with Bryce. Well, not jealous, but worried. She says he isn't healthy—that he isn't a good influence. I don't blame her. You know what he's done. But I'm his best friend, so I try to be there for him. Wouldn't you do anything for Troy? I know, I know, it's a perverse loyalty. Bryce has me and Belle, but after Cat left New Baines, he lost it. Now all he wants is to get out of here—Oregon, for him. But he's caught up in drugs, and he's always suspicious about little things. I don't get him. It's been *years*."

"When I was at Bryce's house yesterday," I started, "because he invited me over, I, uh, I snuck away and saw this ... this cork bulletin board in this attic behind his closet. These bruises ... he tried to kill me after because I found it. There was a torn-out page from our fifth-grade yearbook—*our page*—and some faces had an X over them."

"Whose faces?"

"Franklin ... Willow ... You."

"Because I broke one of the rules?" He laughed, but it was quiet, and I sensed it was more out of anxiety than anything. "I can only think of two years ago. He and Cat had broken up, and he was mad and not eating, and we were arguing at his house ... I brought up Ian Gallagher in front of Gabby, Belle, and Nate. That quieted him. But I spent the night afterward, and it was cold out—not like this or anything, but cold enough in June to where I suggested we turn on the fireplace. You know how Oklahoma weather is."

I kept left and continued onto I-44 Eastbound.

"I'm a heavy sleeper," Christian continued, urgency in his voice, "and I didn't notice he'd never raised the flue. It's a gas fireplace, and if Bryce's mom hadn't woken me up in the middle of the night, I could've died in my sleep from carbon monoxide poisoning." He pounded once on the glove compartment. "It would've been the perfect murder. I can't believe he tried just because of a stupid name." Christian shook his head. "He called me a Judas."

"Please," I told him. The snow fell harder, the SUV's wipers barely able to keep up. "Don't brush me off or yell at me. I keep asking, but no one will tell me anything about Ian Gallagher and why they're all so afraid of him. What did he do?"

"What did Ian do?" Christian echoed. "Nothing. Really. We did it. You, me, Bryce, Cat, Gabby… the whole nineteen of us, minus Bobby, since he'd already left for Hollywood by that point. I guess if Ian did anything, it was wearing skirts to school. You remember him, don't you? The little fourth grader? He was your neighbor. How do you forget—?"

"My neighbor?" I asked. The radio blared static; I clicked it off. "The Granthams?"

"The *Gallaghers*, Michael. 'Grantham' was a codename. Like, 'grant them peace.' But it was Mr. Gallagher, his wife Cyiarra, and their son Ian. *They* were your neighbors."

Christian looked away momentarily. I thought I would hear those sirens again. I didn't.

"Ian…" Christian continued. "He'd been wearing skirts and other girl clothes to school. Bryce was afraid Ian would end up a transvestite or a drag queen—you remember how Bryce was, always forcing us into his dad's morals. But not even Pastor Skinner was that crazy. He was laid-back. I don't know where Bryce got it from. You *seriously* don't remember Ian Gallagher? I saw you both kissing during recess once."

"What?"

"Yeah, and then Blank Frank and Pete tried to do it, too, but they got all the shit. I kept quiet about you and Ian, though, and truth be told, it's mostly 'cause I was scared of how Bryce might react if he found out. You were my friend, and being gay was... different back then."

"But I'm not gay!" I told him. "I'm not even bi! M'i lcerfepyt olranm; roy'ue hte rcyza noe!"

"No one is saying you're gay," Christian said. "I'm just telling you what happened." He started to cry, growing hysterical. "You... you must've blocked it. *Repressed it.* Lucky you. We all responded in various ways, I know that. Lots of cognitive dissonance. Bryce drew this messed-up, abstract shit and got sent home from class because of it. Pete took up Brazilian jiu-jitsu, I turned to baseball, Belle prayed, Sam played his guitar... but he also starved himself. And Nate started selling drugs as a means of distraction, as if anything could be worse than what we did. I'm pretty sure Emily self-harms, and Rachel pulls out her hair. And while they all were doing that, Frank avoided us, Willow got into bad relationships, and Cat cried *every single day* for years. It was heartbreaking. And we weren't allowed to talk about it."

"Talk about what?!"

"*We killed Ian Gallagher, Mikey.*" He was crying, and so was I. "Don't you get it? Bryce convinced Ian he'd go to hell if we didn't convert him! So on May twenty-ninth, the rainiest day of the year, Ian stayed behind during recess while the rest of the fourth graders went inside, and it was our turn to play. We all had our different roles: Emily and Rachel were to act as normal, Nate and Jim were lookouts... Then we snuck through this hole in the fence and went to the creek. Ian *told us* he couldn't swim, and Bryce knew it! We held him down anyway—you and me both—while Bryce kept sermonizing over *forgiveness* and *strength* and *encouragement* and *sins* and *love* and *wickedness* and *being born again*, as if he had any idea what that all meant as a fucking ten-year-old!"

I knew this story, except it wasn't one at all. I had been there next to Christian, next to Bryce, above Ian, who wouldn't stop struggling. Yet we were too afraid to disobey. No matter what god Bryce thought he was serving then, it wasn't worth the life of that boy.

"Cat and Gabby had screamed we were holding him under for too long," I recalled, "but Bryce ignored them. And when he was done—"

"Ian wasn't breathing," Christian finished for me. *"But Bryce said it was OK because Ian was saved now—that it was a necessary death! And if any one of us came forward, we would all be punished for being accomplices!"*

The storm continued.

"So we left him in the creek," Christian stated. "Bryce told us to pretend it didn't happen. That's when he made the rules: never mention Ian's name, never call an assembly in case one of us cracks, and never stray from the flock like Ian did. And we agreed, because what else were we supposed to do? We didn't know what was happening. Then Ms. Albertine called us in from the rain. So we went."

I watched my deepest fears manifest into physical sickness as I rolled down the window and spewed several days' worth of junk food onto the side of the Big Nasty, adding to it all.

"Michael, the road!" Christian yelled out, grabbing the wheel and stopping us from hitting the white van in front of us. He wiped the tears from his eyes with his shirtsleeve. "Shit, that was close. Are you…?"

I put up a hand to signal I was fine. I felt a mixture of hatred, menace, and desolation, but I knew in my head and not in my heart the only awareness I could truly discern: that right then, in the middle of the interstate during the beginning of a blizzard, was not the time to grieve Ian Gallagher. I'd had my opportunity, if not as a kid, then as a near-adult seven years later as I'd driven through our neighborhood and passed our shared elementary school. His death was on me. I couldn't believe it, yet I fully did.

"I need to pull over," I said. "I need… I'm not feeling…"

"Hey, hey," Christian said, snapping in front of my face. "Don't trip out on me. Wait until we're someplace safe. Like…" He pointed. "Over there. Take that exit. I can figure out the rest of the way."

I did as he instructed; I'd proven to be good at this, for the most part. In an empty parking lot, Christian got out to switch seats. I moved over and placed my head against the cold window, my eyes unable to rest from shock.

I heard Christian weep as he whispered, "He would've been sixteen years old."

———

He awoke to the sound of the blaring taxi horn. His right leg hurt like hell, and the windshield was shattered, allowing the winter air to engulf his lungs. The dashboard's internal clock read 10:02 p.m., but he didn't know how accurate it was. Reaching in the side-door pocket, he found a flashlight and tucked it inside his jacket.

Ian limped outside and, looking back, saw Tony, unconscious, forehead bleeding and slumped against the wheel. He pulled on the driver's door, but it wouldn't budge. Lying in front of the cab, a wide-eyed deer was slowly dying.

He pulled his jacket tighter as the snow kept falling. It covered the road, and drifts had already blown up against the side of the cab. A strange sound caught his ear. He shined the flashlight down the road and found what looked to be a homemade sign, creaking and swinging from a tree branch. Carved into the weathered wood: NASAGARRESETT.

Ian was suddenly aware the honking had stopped. He turned. The deer and the cab, along with Tony, were gone—

"Mikey?"

—without a trace.

A tug on my shoulder.

"Hey, Michael, wake up. Don't fall asleep on me."

"I'm not," I said, stretching. The Big Nasty's heater was on full blast, which meant the stench of Clyde's vomit was all around the two of us. "Sorry. This guy threw up on the seats last summer, and it never went away."

"It's interesting," Christian noted, "the stories we choose to tell people and what details we leave out. I guess it happens over time." He rubbed his hands back and forth. I remembered our conversation—my revelation. "Anyway, here we are."

I looked out his window and saw in the dark what he was referring to: a giant lake house so large and obnoxious, it was sort of regal, in a way. It sat there isolated in the snow, far from the other neighbors and the thin, dormant trees encircling us. It was everything I could've asked for in a cabin on the lake. Yet that wasn't enough to make me want to go inside.

"Gabby sent us all the pictures you took," Christian told me. "She and I have… differing opinions on how this needs to be handled. She believes Bryce should be punished and the Gallaghers compensated, even if we're all locked up in the process."

"And you?" I asked, trying to understand how I'd forgotten all of this—how, as twisted as this was, it made perfect sense as the context I'd been missing.

"We can't let this get out," he explained. "I mean, you know how quickly these things spread. Like wildfire. I'd lose my scholarship if Northeastern knew. It's all I've got." He put his hands together. "We can't gamble that. Dance with the devil you know, you know? Besides, Mr. Gallagher is dead, and Mrs. Gallagher, who knows where."

"I think I'm gonna hold off a minute," I managed. "Still… collecting my thoughts. You don't have to wait up."

"I'll get a feel for it," he said. "But tell me first, before we head in there: if Bryce divides us further, and I need you, you gonna play ball?"

With no other choice, I nodded slowly. So he left me in the Big Nasty.

I watched as he trudged through the snow to get to the house. He passed a black SUV, a red pickup, and a white convertible with the roof up, all of which must have arrived not too long before, as they were just barely covered in snowfall. Once Christian reached the doors, they parted for him, and he went inside, causing me to wonder if I'd ever see him again.

Cat's concern with my memory, Gabby's plot against Bryce, and even Franklin's warning—real or imagined—at last made sense thanks to Christian's honesty. Yet the confusion still swam in circles around in my mind, and there was a sudden crater of fatigue for it to fill. *His name was Ian Gallagher.* I couldn't recall his face, but what had happened, I remembered. I felt disgusted with myself, resentful of Bryce, and enamored with the innocence I'd had the week before. Or, at least, the virtue I had perceived. It was a lie, though, and a damn good one at that. But a lie, nonetheless. *Suffocate such lullabies.*

Sam was leaning against the side of the house by the pines. I noticed from the porch light's illumination he held a cigarette in one hand and a lighter in the other. When he couldn't get it to work, he threw them both into the snow in anger and crossed his arms, shivering.

I turned off the Big Nasty and took the keys with me as I approached Sam. His cheeks and nose were a loud red, and the tops of his shoes were wet.

"Hey," he said. "Glad you made it. Jim and I saw you guys nearly wipe out."

"Yeah," I said. "Thanks. Uh, who are you again?"

"I'm Sam," he told me. "I live in Red Springs, the town over. I've been in love with Kayla since we were kids—when she went by Sam as well. You and I just saw each other at Pete's party. I'm possessive."

"Oh, that's right." I shivered with him. "Sorry. Is Christian in there?"

"Yep," Sam said, looking back. He pointed past me. "And that's Kayla's car. The fancy convertible. She bought it herself. You were looking for her, right?"

"Uh-huh."

"Well, no time like the present."

"I feel like there's something I'm supposed to ask you."

"Why I act the way I do?"

"OK."

"Sam—" He corrected himself. "Kayla and I promised we were going to wait for each other. But then we moved cities, and she starts fucking other guys." He spat to the side. "Well, you know what? I say, fuck her. Who needs her?"

"It sounds like you do, no offense."

"It's the same as you and Catherine," he went on, "so don't think I'm the strange one, all right? You both liked each other in elementary school, got separated, and then you saw her again this week. You obsessed over her for seven years, too, and look where it led us." He kicked at the snow. "Fucking Bryce and his charnel house."

"But I had a girlfriend," I said. "I thought about Cat a lot, but... are you saying you *never* dated anyone else?"

He shook his head. "Not once."

"Did you discuss this with her?" I asked him. He shook his head again. "Then you should. Cat and I at least talked some things through. It was weird for me—"

"What was weird? That she thinks she used to be a cat?" Sam laughed at this. "Man, fuck that. We drowned a little boy and went to outrageous lengths to cover it up. Bryce thinks he's a god, Willow got abducted by a serial killer, we're right next to a lake where the fish all suddenly died after those schoolkids disappeared... and you have a hard time with Catherine once being an animal?" He laughed again. "I'm conservative as hell, but after this week, I'll believe just about anything—and you'd be wrong not to do the same."

I thought about this. "Huh. I guess you're right."

"I'll talk with Kayla if you apologize to Catherine," Sam promised. "Or is it Cat now?"

"It's Cat," I answered, smiling. "She went from Catherine Anne Thomas to just plain ol' C-A-T."

"She's incredible," he said with a grin. "Anyway, it's time for you to go inside."

"Why?"

"Because that's what you're supposed to do."

"Oh, yeah," I said. "Yeah, you're right. Are you coming, too?"

"Sure," he told me. "Let's get this over with."

There was a murky quality to the pine-paneled cabin as Sam and I walked in. Thick crisscrossed beams hung overhead, threatening to fall and collapse upon us. The only light came from the moon out over the lake, setting a cold blue aura around the empty place. Kayla paced in circles, Christian and Jim waited against the wall, and Nate messed with his phone by the windows. Belle sat on the single sofa in the center, facing the outside world. She looked pale.

"Michael," Kayla said. She wasn't smiling, but she wasn't angry, either. "Sam. You both came."

"And you popped my tires," I said right back. "Olive-green Alpinist SUV parked in front of my uncle's cabin."

"Good to see you," Sam told her for both of us.

"Yeah," she said to him, then to me: "Michael, I'm so sorry—I honestly thought it was Kukowski's. I, uh, I got the news yesterday that I didn't make it into OSC's medical program because of my chem grades."

"So Bryce didn't put you up to it?" I asked. "Or rather, he didn't do it himself?"

"Of course not!" Belle said, turning around to face us. "He's not like that. He's a good guy under a lot of pressure."

"Yeah, and he did *this*." I pointed at the various bruises on my face and neck. "He kicked the shit out of me at my place, and he tried to kill me over at his."

"No," she told me, standing up and walking to us. "He wouldn't. He—"

"Belle," Christian said, joining us. He put an arm on her shoulder, but she pushed him off. "Bryce is my friend, and I have faith in him. But you remember what he said about there having to be 'consequences' for breaking his rules, or else—"

"Or else we all end up at Red Springs Penitentiary," Kayla finished for him.

I glanced around. "Where is he?"

"Looking for Gabby," Nate explained, "who's supposedly bringing Cath."

"I'm not sure what's going on anymore," Kayla added.

"Tell me about it," I said.

"He never tells us anything," she went on. "We don't see him for seven years, and then he shows up at Michael's party, he freaks the fuck out, and now he's telling us to come to his stupid cabin so we can put this all behind us. That's all anyone knows because he won't tell us shit, which is why we have to talk behind his back all the damn time."

"What do you even see in him?" Sam asked Belle. "He's a total dick!"

"Bryce wants to help," she told us. "He feels awful for what we did to that kid. But he has this thing—I don't really know much about it." She looked to Nate. "What's it called? Rammiol?"

I reached into my left pocket, and sure enough, the baggie was there. Kayla eyed it, so I tossed it to her as Nate sighed.

"It's a drug," he told Belle.

"But you promised!" she shouted, sitting down again. "You said you were going to get him to stop drinking and snorting and—" She was crying. "It made him manic! Forgetful! He… he kept calling me Catherine."

"It's salt," Kayla said, the white powder on the tip of her wet finger.

"I needed his money," Nate explained. "It's only a sinus cleanse. He kept going on about psychology and conditioning... but it works, the power of suggestion. He believes it's curing him. I just hope he's still taking his prescription meds." Nate laughed a little. "Bryce thought, once we got everything figured out, we could sell it to people with emotional trauma."

"But he doesn't know it's fake?" Christian asked.

"No, and he can't know."

"Wait," Kayla said. "You were going to try and sell us a *placebo* to cure our PTSD? What the fuck kind of scam is that?! Is that what this assembly's for?!" She threw the Rammiol to the ground in rage, scattering the salt crystals across the hardwood floor. "This is messed up, and we all know Cath isn't coming. Bryce can kiss my carnal ass. I'm leaving."

"Sam!" Sam called out to her as she went for the door. He followed her outside. "Kayla, wait up!"

"Nate," Jim said. "Can I talk to you for a minute?"

He nodded, so they went over to the other side of the barren living room—nearly as frigid as the outside. Christian said he'd be watching for the others by the front window, so I went over to Belle.

"How're you doing?" I asked her. "We haven't really gotten a chance to talk."

"Oh, I'm fine," she said, pulling her orange winter jacket tighter. I moved to the couch with her. "Life's been strange, but you know that much."

"I don't know who to trust here," I admitted. "Everyone has different angles. We're all biased, but there are so many lies. Too many secrets."

"Too big to keep," she reminded me, referencing Franklin's last words. "Nate could be protecting his drug business. Christian is Bryce's best friend. Catherine has psychosis." Belle covered her eyes with her hands. "I don't even trust myself!"

"Tell me what you do know," I said. "Help me understand."

"I know we killed that boy," she stated. "I know that after the pastor died the next Sunday, Bryce stayed inside for a month. In middle school, he started dating Catherine, and by the end of sophomore year, they'd broken up. Gabby told me once he tried to force Catherine into having sex with him, but that's not the Richard I know. He's caring, he's sweet, he sings me duets, and… he loves me. I know he does. He doesn't lie; he's extremely direct. He doesn't manipulate people. It was weird, though, when he wanted to go to Windhaven for spring break last year, because that's where Kenzie lives, and we'd kept in touch some. This year, we were planning a drive to Alabama. I'm guessing your town of Dreary."

"He has a bulletin board full of our information in his attic," I told her. She pulled out her phone and then stared at its blank screen, which reflected her image. "It's not right."

"Gabby sent us the pictures. I don't know why she trusted me with that. Bryce and I tell each other everything. It pains me not sharing with him that you all know."

"You knew?"

"I knew he was researching," she stated. "It's not my business."

"It's not his, either."

"Well, antagonize him all you want," Belle said, "but he's been through a lot. More than you'll know. The fact it was he who said we should cleanse that boy—"

"Ian Gallagher."

"—*that boy*… It messed with his head. I don't expect you to care for him, but Bryce has struggled, too. I think everyone forgets that. *He has a mental disorder.* I won't excuse his behavior, but it's not entirely his fault. Bryce is broken. He's damaged. He's not evil, but occasionally misguided, like all of us. There are many kinds of hallelujahs."

"Well, he did try to kill me last night," I said.

"Then I'm sorry you saw that side of him," Belle told me. "It's no fun." She then touched her left eyelid with her index and middle finger, and with her bottom nail, popped her eyeball out of its socket and into her palm. She looked at me directly, smiling. "I've learned to avoid it."

Bryce and Gabby stormed inside then. They were in a heated argument, and Rachel and Emily sheepishly followed in behind them. Jim, Nate, and Christian stepped forward.

"Where's Catherine?" Jim asked the two. Bryce shot him a hard glare.

"Michael," Gabby said, noticing me. Bryce turned in my direction as well, his beard white with snow. "You're here."

"You…" Bryce began. He looked to Christian. "… arrived."

"And you tried to kill me just like you killed Ian Gallagher," I said.

"That isn't what happened!" he screamed at me, then in the same tone, he said to Belle: "That isn't what happened!"

"We know," Jim assured him. "He's making it up, Bryce."

"Fuck you!" Gabby shouted, stomping over to punch him. Christian pulled her back by the shoulder. "Why are you defending him?! I sent you all the pictures! We know he's been watching us—he has stuff on everybody!" She turned to Bryce. "You didn't just kill Ian with his 'rebirth' or whatever. You drove Blank Frank crazy with your emails until he shot himself!"

"HE BROKE THE FIRST RULE!" Bryce screamed at her. "IF A HIGH SCHOOL COUNSELOR SUSPECTS A CRIME, THEY HAVE TO REPORT THEIR CONCERN!"

"AND WHAT ABOUT WILLOW?! DID YOU SEND THAT SERIAL KILLER AFTER HER—OR DID YOU DO IT YOURSELF?!"

"OF COURSE NOT!" he yelled, shaking the whole house. "I DIDN'T WANT ANYTHING TO DO WITH YOU ALL AFTER MAY TWENTY-NINTH!" He pointed at me. "But thanks to Cookie or Chop Sticks or whatever you are, this is where we're at! So we might as well fix this."

"There's nothing to fix," Belle said in a quiet voice. "What's done is done."

"We have Rammiol!" Bryce said, then to Nate: "If it helped me, then it can help them!"

"Dude, cut it out," Nate whispered back.

"What's he talking about?" Gabby asked the room. She looked to me.

"A recreational drug," Bryce announced, his mood suddenly changed, "made from a perennial plant with hallucinogenic seeds. It can be used to treat emotional trauma. And it works! I've been on it for nearly—"

"Rammiol's just pretend," Nate told him. "I made it up. It's salt. I'm sorry. But they knew about it—Jim, Michael, Christian, and Belle. I thought I should be the one to—"

"You told us five minutes ago, you lying piece of shit!" Jim shouted. "Don't try to get us all on his bad side just to save your own skin!"

I saw something sinister turn then in Bryce's eyes, staring past the uneven floorboards and sodden earth below. His right hand began to tremble, so he grasped it with his left.

"You hear that, Dick?" Gabby asked Bryce. "We do talk—behind your back, 'cause everyone's scared of you. You don't have any friends here. You force us to chat in private if we want to find out anything—like how you beat up Michael last night. Christian texted me that."

"Have a little faith!" Christian exclaimed to her. "Bryce might be extreme at times, but he's done a pretty good job of keeping this all under wraps. I don't deny what we did was wrong, but putting it all behind us is our best bet right now!"

Gabby ignored Christian and walked up to Bryce, no longer afraid.

"Is that why you got us all here?" she asked him. "To kill us off, too? Is that what you want to do to Cat?" She laughed. "You still love her, don't you?"

"Oh, man up," Bryce taunted her. Gabby's eye twitched. "You're a fool if you let a girl get in the way of your ambitions. Besides, I have Belle now. Catherine means nothing—do *not* put me in that category. We need her to move on with this." He faced the crowd. "Not to go on all-fours; *that is the Law.* Are we not Men? And let me remind you I was not the one who physically killed…" He stopped. "Ian Gallagher. That wasn't me. We all had our responsibilities that afternoon. Christian and Michael—they were the ones who held him down. They didn't have to listen to me. They *felt* him struggle."

"Don't put this on us!" Christian said. He was tearing up, and so were a few others. As I touched my face, I realized so was I. "That was all you, Bryce, and you know that! We helped, yes, but that wasn't my—"

"Funny how memories change like that," he said. "See, I made those rules for a reason. They were to keep you safe. But some people broke them along the way, and Michael, you saw what happened to the Millburns and Bobby B-Love."

"Wait, what happened Saturday?" I asked him. Bryce didn't answer. He just sneered at me. My eyes widened, so I turned to the crowd in desperation—to Christian, to Gabby, to Belle, Nate, Jim, Rachel, and Emily: "What happened the night of my party?!"

"They all followed along," Bryce told me. "Or maybe not. It doesn't make sense, and that's the point." He laughed. "Maybe we're all crazy here! Either way, you'd be surprised at the lengths some will go to when their future is on the line. That's why Emily and Rachel are here tonight, despite stating they wouldn't be. My stepfather will do whatever it takes to keep me out of trouble, which is why you should never question the inner machinations of a politician. But you all don't have that luxury, so every now and again, you worry how a certain crime from seven years ago might come back to haunt you—how it would affect your colleges, careers, *everything* should one of you slip and tell."

We were quiet, all of us. I then remembered clearly that was the way it had been when Bryce had first proposed we cleanse Ian in the creek. He'd herded us in like cattle or sheep, and so history would repeat.

"Michael, I'm actually glad you invited us to your lake house," he continued. "I'm glad we got to meet one last time to finish the job. I think you all know what I mean. I've thought long and hard about that day for so many years, and I've figured out what we did right—and what we did wrong. I didn't want it to come to this, but at least now we have a chance to correct ourselves. We've been seeing these shadows on the wall for far too long. We need to make amends, and actions speak louder than words."

Bryce looked around the room at the eight of us. He smiled.

"Jim, go to Hickman Construction and collect the equipment we talked about," he instructed. "Nate, take Gabby home. Christian, you're coming with me to the city. Now, Rachel and Emily, you both get a good night's sleep. And Michael, you get rid of your Troy. This is a 'No Moonwalking' zone, you know, and he's seen too much already. We can't have loose ends. Belle can go with you." He clasped his hands together. "All right. Let's move out."

"And what if we say no?" Gabby asked, arms crossed.

"I won't kill you, if that's what you're asking. You've seen how much trouble that is to bury. Not worth it. Thou shalt not murder." He sighed. "No, you'll kill yourself. I won't have anything to do with it, but that's what you'd like to think. The guilt will force you into silence, but I know what you'd rather hear me say." He turned to Emily. "I will get inside your head and *break you*." He faced Rachel. "I will make you go insane to the point where you think you were once an *animal*."

He smiled at me.

"What do you fear, Michael?" he asked. The rest waited for my response. "I'm talking honestly—strip away your ex-girlfriend, colleges, your mom, your dad, your book, and people thinking you're gay. What terrifies you? Is it death? I don't think so. That'd be too easy. You're afraid of change." He shrugged. "Me, too." He looked to our former classmates. "But I also have dreams. All you people want is a scapegoat to shift the blame, and I know how to play the part. You *let me* play the part. But I am done being that guy—that designated black sheep. After seven years, it wears you down, takes its toll. We subscribe to these social scripts. We have to put an end to this."

He laughed to himself.

"Oh, but that's not what you want me to tell you." He pointed out the back window.

"See that light, Michael? It's faint and green and looks like a fallen star, but if you're looking for it, you'll see it. That's your neighbor's dock. I know where you live. It's just a boat ride over, as you probably should've figured out by now. So come on—walk on the water with me… and I will show you something different. But in the end, it doesn't matter the number you roll. I own the game. So don't get in my way… *or I will put you in the ground.*"

Bryce left then, and the rest moved mindlessly like zombies to the door, one by one, to carry out his tasks. They didn't question it—that had stopped at some instant I couldn't pinpoint. I screamed at them, yelled at them, even tried to grab Gabby. She only shrugged me off, resigned to the absurdity.

"Come on," I said to Belle as I found us alone in the cabin. "I'll take you home."

"It stopped snowing," she noted, looking out the window. Yet we both knew in full honesty the worst was yet to come.

Belle and I drove away from the lake in an eerie silence. I asked if she wanted to listen to the radio. She said not really. I asked if she was cold, as I was. She said no. So we kept on.

"I don't know why he told you that in there," she said after some time. "Nothing happened to Morgan, Zach, or Bobby. They left soon after. He's not normally like that." Belle stared at her reflection in the side mirror. "When you came back to this state, after everything we'd been through, it must've been too much for you. You fell back on our familiar selves, but Michael, we've changed. You created a different Bryce that night, and now that character… he's left the page. He became real. My sister is a psychology major. Some people, after a traumatic event, will imagine an alternate universe of sorts to cope with the pain… but I think you went too far with this one. You poisoned the well, and we need to know: are you there, in that dream? Or are you here with us?"

"I'm here," I said. "You've got me."

"We didn't need you," she told me. "Didn't need *this*. Now I'm not so sure." We passed abandoned cars and empty homes. "Your phone?"

"Yeah. It's been a couple of years, but I'm due for a new one in September."

"No, it's vibrating."

I checked, and she was right. It was a 539 area code. I answered on speaker.

"Hello?"

"Is this a, uh, Michael Jackson?" a man asked. He sounded older. I heard country music in the background.

"That's me."

"This is Dwight Wagers at the Hickory Horned Devil bar on Cooper Street. Your friend Troy's been here a while, and I, uh, I don't think he's in a state to get home by himself. Said to call you—had your number memorized."

"OK," I said. "That in Madison? I'm about twenty away."

"He'll be here," Wagers told me, then hung up.

I looked over to Belle, who had her head down and hands together. "Is it all right if we—?"

"Just let me pray, goddammit!" she exclaimed, then immediately apologized. "Sorry, sorry. I, um, think… sure. Go ahead. Can't say no, anyway."

I made an illegal U-turn. I thought if I got pulled over for it, that wouldn't have been the first time a cop had stopped me because of Troy Rico. It was hard to believe my encounter with Bleakman had been two weeks ago to the day. So much time had passed. Too much, in fact.

The Hickory Horned Devil stalked a lonely road on the east side of Madison. A tall neon sign above it advertised BAR, BEER, and LIQUOR, while the Devil itself was a yellow building with a red awning across it. There were pines to the left and a parking lot to the right with a single truck occupying the EMPLOYEES ONLY section. A banner on the side mentioned two-dollar cocktails during happy hour, pretty girls only. The redneck feel was astounding, but at least it was genuine, unlike myself in recent years.

Belle and I had been quiet on the drive over, but I couldn't contain my annoyance any longer.

"I'm always having to keep track of him," I told her. "It's frustrating. Like, why do I have to be the designated driver from wherever he dragged me to? Most of the time, he doesn't even text me the address, so I have to figure it out on my own."

"Some phones come with a locator app for people on the same carrier plan," she said. "It's called Find My Family. Bryce would use it at his house to see where his mom and stepdad were so he'd know how much time we had alone. Maybe you could use it for Troy."

"I probably won't need it after this weekend." I admired the frost-covered building and all its brokenness. "You want to go in or wait here?"

"I'd feel safer with you."

I killed the engine and got out of the Big Nasty. We then passed the overflowing trash can and through the red door on the left. Belle stayed close behind.

Immediately in front of us was the bar, with the bartender on the left side and the stools for patrons on the right. The walls were wood, the floor was wood, and the furniture was wood, but the neon was alive and everywhere in the beer advertisements, arcade machines, and jukebox playing "I Am the Fool" by the Bros. Landreth. I spotted Troy by the pool table with a glass of something in his hand, his back to us. He wasn't so much as playing traditional pool, but rather, he grabbed the cue ball with his free hand and rolled it across the table to hit the others—very Troy Rico-esque.

"How old are you two?" the bartender asked me while peering over his aviators. He had long sideburns and fat cheeks. In his mouth, he held a toothpick. "Y'all don't look twenty-one."

"My name is Michael," I explained. "Michael Jackson. I spoke on the phone with Mr. Wagers about—"

"Yeah, that's me," he said, then pointed at Troy. "There's your friend."

"He's not my friend," I told him. He shrugged and went back to watching his program on the mounted TV.

I limped over to the pool table while Belle ordered a lemonade. I was still sore, yet I knew it was almost over—everything. Troy didn't care. He only ever worried about his fantasy back in Dreary, where he was always up on top. As distorted as the past week had been, it was reality, and I was glad Troy had gotten to experience it for once.

"T," I said. He didn't respond. "Time to go, so hurry it up."

"Oh, hey, Mom," he said to me, slurring his words and pointing to Belle. "Lookie there! You got *another*. She your new girlfriend?"

"That's Belle, jackass."

"All the same to you."

I took him by the coat sleeve and dragged him over to the bar.

"Hey, he still needs to pay for the drinks," Wagers told me. "The pool sticks, too."

"He's underage," I stated, ready to leave, but Troy waved his hand.

"No, no, it's fine," Troy said. He produced his wallet and threw out the silver plastic. Wagers picked it up, swiped it, and then handed it back to him. "God, I hate you, Michael."

"I know," I said. "Let's go."

"But we were having *such* a good time singing songs about *tobacco* and *cowboy boots* and *Jesus* and *whistling at girls*, weren't we, Dwight? Not as much fun as you, I'm sure, but…"

Wagers looked to me with pity. "Get him home, all right?"

"Nooooo," Troy went on as I led him to the door. Belle paid for her screw-off bottle of lemonade and then quickly rejoined us.

She and I went back out into the snow and helped Troy get settled in the middle row of the SUV. He was cursing, I was ignoring him, and Belle was as silent as ever. She sat next to me up front, keeping me company.

I pulled out of the parking lot, and soon, we were on US-69 South.

"I want a Happy Cow," Troy said, then farted. "Oh, Christ. If there wasn't a crack there before, there sure is now." He laughed. "And I don't want just a chocolate shake, but the *whole* Happy Cow, you feel me? You could work there, Keegan could work there, Clyde and Olivia could work there. Eva, too. We'd have sooooo much fun."

"Keegan and Clyde are at the iron hotel," I told him. "Leah's in the hospital."

"Let's go to the Irish pub," he went on. "I went there first. Good Ol' Days. Nice older woman there who listened to me vent."

"Because I've gotten sick of it?" I asked him.

"Because *you* were at that party," he explained, choking up, voice trembling. "And *you* thought you hung up on me. But I was listening! The whole time! And you're a real jerk, you know that? An awful friend. Why can't I be enough for you, huh? You hate me 'cause I'm gay."

"I don't hate you, Troy." I gripped the wheel tighter. He was crying. "Look, we're taking Belle home to New Baines. So stop talking. You're drunk, and you're an idiot."

"I wish I was straight," he finished.

I opened my mouth to respond, but he was snoring back there with a hand down his pants. I rolled my eyes. What a conversationalist.

We got off the turnpike and turned right onto Packard, then left onto Truman a block later, and then finally into the Shaughnessy Estates neighborhood to drop Belle off at her house. It was ten past eleven, and all the streetlights were lit. I noticed tiny paw prints in the snow, and of course, they belonged to a cat. I couldn't help laughing then, which woke Belle up beside me.

"Home, sweet home," I announced.

"Yep," she said, opening the car door and stepping out. "Thanks for the ride—"

"Wait!" I said. Belle stood there, shivering. "I'm curious. What is it like, living in the same house your entire life?"

"Repetitive," she answered, then shut her door.

It was a dangerous lie. Maybe it was dull for her, but so was Dreary. Perhaps that was how all small towns were: monotonous, tiring, lonesome. Maybe it wasn't so much about the person coming back than the ones who were left behind. I had gone to where I'd needed to be, yet I still hadn't been to the reasoning for my being there.

Troy was asleep, so I didn't ask what he wanted. It didn't matter, anyway. We had one more stop before Dreary. I turned around in Pete's cul-de-sac, drove to Truman Street, and for the first time since sitting where Troy was with my mom in the driver's seat, I took a left for the Shaughnessy Grove Cemetery a few miles away.

It was snowing again, as evidenced by the tiny fractals reflecting off the SUV's headlights and billowing behind me. The windshield was covered in snow except where the wipers had been, and the roads were smothered in uneven patches. Some fences and the tops of trees had toppled over from the weight. Too big to keep.

The sky was cloudy, but I could still see the dark when I wanted. I came across mostly empty land with a few trees looming here and there. To the right, I passed a two-door beater pickup and wondered why, in all seriousness, its driver was holding on to the past like that.

The voices in my mind came up for air.

"I need your help," Bryce had told us. "All of you. I can't do this on my own."

"I don't know who I like," Cat had said to me. "I like you and Bryce both. Can't we talk about this some other time?"

"Bryce, please, listen to yourself," Christian had pleaded with him. "You're being crazy. He doesn't know what he's signing himself up for."

"HE STOPPED MOVING!" Gabby had screamed. "CHRISTIAN, MICHAEL, STOP HOLDING IAN UNDER!"

"Baby, sweetie," my mom had gone on. "This is a fresh start for us. A new state, a new town… I know you're going to miss your friends, but you'll make new ones. This will be good for us. I promise."

The Shaughnessy Grove Cemetery was to the right. It had a long road leading to the church in the distance, but it also had tiny ones for walking between sections of graves. An iron fence with sharp spikes kept it looking official, but there was no gate or security guard, so anyone could come and go as they pleased. Even me.

I parked the Big Nasty facing west in the lot by the church. The inside lights were off, and a marquee to the right read: WELL, YOU DID ASK FOR A SIGN. The world was quiet here, and I was afraid of what I would find in the snowfog. I hadn't been to this place since Ian's death. Bryce hadn't attended the funeral, but Mr. Gallagher had, with his pale, angular face and combed-over hair. He hadn't spoken a word that day, so Pastor Skinner had, instead.

I pulled on the ends of my gloves so they were tighter against my fingers. I then looked back at Troy, sighed to myself, and shut the door against the chilling air.

The crunch of snow under my feet was familiar to me, as was my shadow. Using the flashlight on my phone, I saw crooked crosses, spears, and thorns ahead. I checked the first few headstones I saw: Carroll Cochran, Jaime Melendez, Danelle Duvall, Jennifer Reiter, Julie Staton, Guillermo Maduro. Too many people going home, but none were my guy. I did this for several minutes until I found a name I did recognize: HARPER PERMINDA ALBERTINE, fifty-nine when she had died. Later: FRANKLIN JOSEPH CHAMBERS, age fourteen. Nearby, a couple of Dusetts, which lead me to wonder if this was where Willow would be buried.

Finally, in the middle of all the other graves: GUY JACKSON, FATHER AND HUSBAND. He had been forty-eight during the prison riot. Etched into the corner of the stone: MURDERER.

The wind rose, turning my sweat cold. I examined the inscription closely, touched it, and then waited.

I didn't feel any different. I wasn't going to throw up like I thought I might. It was a slab of rock with a name, description, and a couple of dates. It tried to be personal, but it wasn't. That wasn't my dad under there. My dad hadn't been the man who chewed tobacco to the point where his teeth turned an ugly yellow. He hadn't been the scary alcoholic, the man who abused painkillers, the man who had drunkenly spilled his pills all over the carpet and then came at my mom with a kitchen knife, her locking the door to the master bedroom, her mother crying on the phone, him pounding on the other side and commanding that she not call 9-1-1, and him plowing into that family the very next day. My dad was at the end of West Florentine Street, among the toy soldiers and dirt piles that made up Calvary Hills. He was alive in my memories, as was the rest of the neighborhood and town. These things didn't change up there because of what was printed on a mere death certificate. That would have been nonsensical. I would have been nonsensical.

"There it is," Troy said behind me. I didn't turn around. "Started it all."

"I'm glad you figured it out," I admitted. "Back in Dreary. That he was dead."

"Even after everything we've been through this week?"

"Here," I said, taking his hand. "Let me show you something."

We walked down the row and up one. There were two headstones separated from the rest: one for Ian, the other for Mr. Gallagher. On our way, we'd passed the pastor's, as well as an empty grave, where weeds poked out of the snow. I sat there, in front of Ian, age nine, and Mr. Gallagher, age forty. Troy crouched beside me as I paid my respects, though I had a gut feeling he was still asleep in the Big Nasty. Nonetheless, I shared with him then all I had learned—the truth, the secret—about my fifth-grade class at Hayes Elementary.

"Reminds me of that one Ard van der Kolk poem," he said on our way to the SUV after I'd finished. "The one that goes, 'Men are merely animals / With their heads off of the ground.' But I don't know, Mom. I don't know if I can believe that. I'm not sure you believe *yourself*, drowning a kid for a hate crime. It's just so…" He shook his head. "Sorry. It's late. I need to, like, process everything, and those crosses all look like little dicks. What time is it? Midnight?"

"Where's your phone?" I asked, checking mine.

"Dropped it in the toilet at Good Ol' Days. Left it there."

"It's twelve fourteen."

"If we leave now, pack, and get a few hours of sleep, we can be back in Alabama before sunset tomorrow."

"I'm too tired," I said. "And sore. Dead on my feet, as they say in Oklahoma."

"No, mae, we need to get back." He shivered. "We've spent enough time in these towns, and besides, it's cold as balls out here. I know how these stories end, and trust me—not a fan."

"It's been a long day, and you don't know the way to the cabin."

"I have a physics project I haven't started."

"Let's—" I opened the driver's door and slowly got in; Troy did the same and spread out across the backseat. "—do it… tomorrow. All right? We'll… we'll stay here for the night."

"Stop yawning. This is important, and I have to take a shit."

"Pass me a blanket and pillow."

"I'm serious. You just don't know when to stop."

"Thank you."

"Michael?"

I closed my eyes and saw Cat, half dead and half alive in her living room. She shivered in front of the struggling fireplace as water dripped down the walls and from the ceiling. It pooled in the middle, submerging her in years of remorse as someone knocked, knocked, knocked at her front door, which had been bound by duct tape and twine. The tormenter was her father, clawed and mutilated, who was Bryce, who was me, and then, last, a little boy she did not know. Cat could neither swim nor break from them, and so her breath remained ever steady all the way through the prison house of childhood.

It took Ian thirty minutes to walk the path to the lake. He went over his strange, vivid dream multiple times in his head.

"This is crazy," he said aloud. "I'm crazy! This is wrong… but it'll all be over soon, one way or another. Karina's out here… somewhere."

When Ian reached Lake Nasagarresett, he was shocked at the beauty of this cold and lonely place. He imagined families and couples on their honeymoons boating and playing without a care. All that was missing was a marina to complete the picture.

An old blue pickup was stranded beside the lake. The truck's tires were missing, and its windows had been shattered. Vandals had covered it with graffiti, and the driver's-side door was wide open. Ian reached behind the sun visor and took out a photograph of a large group of people. They were standing on a deck with a view of the lake, the crowd all facing the camera. On the seat, Ian found two things: a crowbar as rusty as the truck, and a torn envelope with DAD written across the front. Curious, Ian slipped a small piece of paper out of the envelope and felt a sudden chill as he unfolded it. The note was signed by "Wendy" and addressed to her father. It said she intended to look for her friend out in the woods, where he had disappeared. It also indicated neither of them came back.

It's as cold as a grave here, but don't worry about me. It'll be okay because I'll be seeing Frankie again soon. I feel so numb right now. It's the pills. I hope you'll forgive me.

Ian walked farther down toward the lake. With the help of the flashlight, he could see a thick sheet of ice stretching from shore to shore. He bent down to feel it, but he quickly withdrew his hand. It was abusively cold, as if the ice had scorched him.

There was no way he could touch that ice, but there was something he *could* do. Ian went back to the pickup and grabbed the crowbar.

"I was blind before, Karina, but now I know what I must do to save you. It's simple, really. Why didn't I think of it before? All these years…"

The wind stirred. Ian walked out onto the frozen lake. He was exhausted and shivering and didn't care if the ice could support his weight. Gripping the crowbar tightly, he lifted it high above his head and stabbed the straight end into the ice. Again. And again. Seven times in total, forming a crude septagon. Then, using the hooked end of the crowbar, Ian slammed the center of that septagon with all his might. The impact created a small, jagged opening just big enough for a person to fit through.

"I can't do this, Karina. I can't live my life in fear any longer. These demons haunt me because I tried to ignore you—tried to let you go. But I won't. I'll fix this. For us."

Ian looked into the empty void beneath him, closed his eyes, and jumped. He sank into the black abyss, chilling him to the bone and dragging him deeper. He couldn't hold his breath much longer. Allowing his body to go limp, Ian fell into the endless depths and dreamt of Karina.

I awoke to the sun in my eyes.

I closed them, groaned, and reached for the recliner handle. I then straightened my seat, pushing my grandma's old quilt to my shoes. The SUV was freezing, and the snow had been pushed off its windshield. Something about Karina.

"You awake this time?" Troy asked behind me. "The things I do for you—made me crap in a Big-Box bag and throw it out in that trash can over there. Then I walked east for a couple of miles before I found a gas station. I think the Big Nasty's battery died."

"No, it's—" I yawned. "That's no problem. We can get a jump from Pete's dad, if it's not too early in the morning."

"Huh? Mom, it's six in the evening." He raised his watch, which was when I noticed the red in his eyes and dark beard on his cheeks. "You kept getting up and going back to sleep. So I let you. Anyone ever tell you you snore?"

"Olivia, once."

"Two years with the girl, and you've hardly mentioned her at all this week. I mean, I broke up with Clyde, but I still think about him. You didn't cry once over her."

"I've kept my..." I yawned again. "Kept my mind busy."

"Something like that."

I looked around. The wind blew wisps of snow at the SUV, and every other second, the sun would shine through the storm clouds. But it was setting, not rising.

"Where's my phone?" I croaked, throat dry. On the floor was Belle's yellow bottle of lemonade. I held it up to Troy. "Is this...?"

"You're good," he said. I twisted off the lid and drank it all. "I think your phone's between the seats. You kept playing that band you like on loop, but you'd fallen asleep, so I turned it down."

"You turned the volume down?!" I exclaimed. As expected, when I found it and checked, the phone's battery was at two percent. "Great. Today's Friday, you don't have a phone, I'm about to not have a phone—"

It vibrated repeatedly in my hands. The screen displayed an unknown number with the Arminster area code. I tapped the green button and held it up to my ear.

"Hello?"

"Michael?" someone asked. She sounded older. "This is Varsha. Cat's mom. Are you still in Oklahoma? Is Catherine with you?"

"No. Well, yes and no. Yes, and then no." My head felt stiff. "I'm in New Baines, but Cat isn't with me."

"She never leaves without asking first. *Never*, especially in a blizzard!"

I sat up. "Cat's missing?"

"I saw on the TV what happened to Willow Dusett," Ms. Varsha told me. I could hear the regret in her voice. "Our car is in the garage, but the front gate to Mountain Vista was busted open from the inside, and that Charles Dodgson man is still out there—"

"Whoa, whoa, slow down. She's missing, and you haven't seen her since when?"

"This morning."

"This morning." I thought of what Belle had said. "Ms. Varsha, does Cat have a cell phone?"

"No. She doesn't." I sensed the instinct in her tone. "She didn't want one."

"OK, let me rephrase: does she have a phone she takes with her to contact you? Like, if she goes to the store or for a drive somewhere, does she carry one on her?"

Ms. Varsha hesitated. "Yes. But she isn't answering my calls!"

"All right. I can work with that. See, there's this Find My Family app on your phone that lets you track people you're already connected with via your network. So touch the home button, see if you have the app, and if you do, use it to find her."

"Um." There was some tapping on her end. "I don't… uhh… oh. It says… she's in Shaughnessy Estates. She's at an empty lot on West Florentine Street—at the end of it."

"That's Calvary Hills," I said. My phone flashed red. "I'm at the cemetery right now, but my phone's about to die. I'll head over there and call you then, all right?"

"Michael—"

The screen turned black. I got out of the SUV, and Troy followed.

"Another mission?" he asked me as we trotted through the snow. "I'm surprised. Since when did you start helping others? Or is this because she's Cat's mom?"

"She's *missing*," I reminded him. "What part of that don't you get? Look, it can't be more than a thirty-minute walk—"

"Thirty minutes?!"

"And we'll stop by Christian's or Belle's or Pete's house on the way over!"

"Pete the gay guy?" he asked.

"He's bi."

"Oh, Mom. 'Gay' is an umbrella term for anyone in the LGBTQIA community."

"What about asexuals? Isn't that, like, misrepresentation?"

He snorted. "As if you know what that's like."

I rolled my eyes. "Look, one of them—Christian, Belle, or Pete—can help us jumpstart the Big Nasty. Then we'll check out Calvary Hills."

"Should've stuck to the reunion." He trekked beside me, the snow stinging our faces. "Always trying to be the hero, always wanna be starting something… This isn't fun anymore. Your friends are crazy. Man, I am *done* vacationing with white people. We were supposed to leave *two days ago*. I don't even know what 'Calvary Hills' is, anyway."

"It's a… *subdivision!*" I ran my hands through my greasy hair, then over my face and eyes. "God, you can be so inept sometimes!"

"And what the fuck is that supposed to mean?!"

"It means you can't do shit, Troy! It means you're so content with going to school in the same town and throwing parties for ninth and tenth graders that you don't have a clue as to what you want to do with the rest of your life. At least I've taken the initiative to write—"

"Again with your book?! Is this you needing attention?! Juepuña."

"Yeah, well, tell me about some of your accomplishments!"

"Well, for one, I'm supportive of my friends!"

"And that won't get you far when you're hanging out with Keegan and Clyde."

"Is that why you wanted to go on this trip?! Is that why I buy you Taco Kick and pay for new tires and make a playlist and pretty much fund an entire vacation for you to hang out with some people I don't even know?!"

"Do you even remember why we're in Oklahoma?! I would've made this drive with or without you. You tagged along because you're afraid of being so goddamn lonely!"

"So we're not going to this 'Calvary Hills' so you can find Cat and get her to suck your dick, right? Be honest: is she real? Tangible? A symbol, a metaphor? I sure haven't seen her, and from the looks of it, no one else has, either." He clapped his hands together. "Or! Wait a second! I bet Bryce killed her, too! She's only an entity in your subconscious space! Unless it's Bryce who's been dead all along. Some climax you got there. That's what they're thinking, you know!"

"I'm done listening to this crap."

"You think you've been through hell? Well, I've gone through my own here. Ever think about that? Of course not! Why would you?! It's always you and your problems! You, Michael Jackson, are a *terrible* friend."

"Oh, I'm sorry, would you rather me throw you out of a *moving vehicle?!*"

"You know what, fuck it! I don't think we made it to Madison! I think we died in a car crash on the way, and this is my eternal punishment for using the Lord's name in vain, 'cause nothing you've said since we got here has made any fucking sense!" He raised his hands above him. "Ah, Father, thy kingdom come! Praise and hallelujah! We fell asleep at a *cemetery*, for fuck's sake."

"No, this is definitely real life. I know because even now I'm still having to drive your ass places."

"Do you hear how selfish you sound?! You're the one with the car! But everything's always about you because you truly believe you're better than everyone else. *Especially me!* You're controlling, you're jealous, and you're competitive. You keep changing the reasons, but that's why Olivia broke up with you, you know—you never made time for her, you never showed you care for her, you would repeat the same I-love-you crap to try to make up for the times when she'd finally stand up to you and call you out on it—"

"Is that it? I'm too independent and think about myself from time to time?"

"No—"

"You're pathetic, Troy. You're irrational, you are careless, you're quick to criticize, you're sometimes *violent*, and you keep fucking me over."

He snorted. I shook my head.

"That isn't what I meant."

"Well, excuse the fuck out of me, 'cause for a straight guy, you sure talk about gay sex a lot—that's all I'm saying." He sighed. "Actually, you know what? That is all I'm saying! It's always me listening to your problems! When was the last time you heard me out about mine, huh?"

"When your stepdad showed up."

"That's different! You were forced to be there."

"All right. What about when you and Clyde were about to break up in February?"

"You only came to get away from Olivia."

"Forget it. We aren't even halfway there, so will you *please* shut up?"

"Not letting me talk about myself again, are you? Wanna talk about your book, instead? Or how you're going to California in the fall?"

"Maybe the University of Arminster—"

"What, so you can be with your new friends? With Cat?!"

"People actually give two shits about me in Oklahoma! And you want me to go back to Dreary?! Go fuck yourself!"

"Keegan—he tries to hide his homophobia, but he does a piss-poor job of it. You, on the other hand, are amongst the worst breed of homophobes because you disguise it and get away with it! Talk about sexual repression. If you're *so upset* about people thinking you're gay, then just calmly tell them you aren't without having such a goddamn fit. I mean, Christ, it's because of authors like you that gay people never get the happy endings we deserve."

"I don't have a problem with gay people!"

"Yeah, but they make you uncomfortable!"

"I have a problem with *you*, Troy!"

"This friendship is *toxic!* You know that, right?! I did my research. Cat could sense it between you and her, and that's why she called it off so early with you both! I just wished I'd seen it sooner." He was crying. "Because things were good, once. Not anymore. Now I bow to no one."

"You're insane."

"My anger is appropriate!" he yelled at me. "You don't accept me as I am, and you make it so we're not equals!" He took a deep breath. "Toxic people don't often know they're toxic. I put way too many of my eggs in your basket, thinking you actually care about me, thinking we were friends for life. But you have a victim mentality, and it's your insecurity that—"

"God, did you even want me to get accepted to Hartsett?!"

"OF COURSE I DID! I JUST THOUGHT WE'D TALK ABOUT IT!"

"TO THROW EVERYTHING ASIDE FOR YOU?!"

"FOR *US*, MICHAEL! FOR FUCKING *US!* THAT'S WHAT BEING A FRIEND IS—NOT THINKING ABOUT 'YOU' OR 'ME,' BUT *US!* I'M HERE FOR YOU, NOT ANYBODY ELSE! AND YEAH, WELL, I GOT SOME PROBLEMS WITH ME, TOO! SO GET IN LINE, PAL!"

"WE ARE *NOT* FRIENDS, TROY."

He pushed me hard into the snow, which cushioned my fall, but not his kick to my side. He then flipped me over and shoved my face into the cold, grabbing me by the hair as he moved my head around.

"I'M THE BESTEST FRIEND YOU'VE GOT, YOU SELFISH FUCK! YOU CAN'T TRADE ME OUT FOR SOMEONE YOU KNEW SEVEN YEARS AGO! THAT'S NOT HOW IT WORKS! THEY DON'T KNOW YOU LIKE I DO! THEY DON'T KNOW ABOUT THE WEED AND MOONSHINE AND ALL THE OTHER SHIT WE'VE DONE! LIKE THE TIME YOU ALMOST DIED AT THAT BAR IN SAN VALLA?! *WHEN YOU WERE CHOKING ON YOUR OWN VOMIT?!* DO YOU THINK THEY KNOW ABOUT HOW I SAVED YOUR ASS THEN?! I WAS THERE! WHERE WERE THEY?!"

He let me go. I rolled over on my back, gasping for air, each breath hurting more than the last. The snow was burying me, so I eased my way onto my knees before it could finish the job.

"Who was that one guy?" Troy asked me. I couldn't physically respond. "He offered to room with you—what's his name? Pete? I hope you treat Pete better than you've treated me." He started off. "Well, come on. Let's go see this motherfucker."

He walked faster through the snow then, dragging one leg at a time, as if he had any clue where he was heading.

I was glad I'd said it. I hated his apathy. Everything was always a joke to Troy Rico Valdez. He needed common sense—some measure of boundaries and self-control. He was stupid when it came to anything of importance, he was ignorant regarding basic manners, and he was horribly obnoxious without remorse. I knew how helpless he was going to be once I was gone. He needed to be thrown in the deep end, and despite how cold-blooded it might've seemed, I was happy for his suffering. He'd caused enough of mine, anyway.

Fair's fair, and hell calls hell.

Troy started banging on Pete's door before I could stop him. I'd pointed out the house, and he'd only trudged on, anger in his stomp and rage in his bleary eyes.

The door opened. It was Tommy in his pajamas.

"Are you Pete?!" Troy asked him.

"That's his brother, you idiot." I stepped around Troy. "Hi, Tommy. Is Pete home?"

"Michael," Pete said, entering the foyer from the other room. "Troy. What are you two doing here?"

"We need a jump for his SUV," Troy explained.

"We need to talk," I simplified. "Can I come in?"

"I'd rather you not," Pete answered. "Whatever Bryce is doing, I don't want to get involved."

"What are you talking about?"

"You didn't get the message? How he's 'trying again' or whatever?"

"Trying what?"

"Doesn't matter," Troy said, his teeth chattering like a Halloween novelty skull. "None of it. We need to get back to Dreary."

"Cat's missing," I told Pete, ignoring Troy. "Her mom tracked her phone to Calvary Hills."

"Shit. The subdivision off the T?"

"That's the one. And if Bryce is planning something—"

"Look, let's not and say we didn't," Pete went on. "I told you I don't want any part in this. I have a lot on my conscience from—" He looked back at Tommy, then leaned in. "From Ian and Franklin. If you want a drink of water, I can get you that, but whatever this is, I'm staying out of it."

"It could take us another half hour to walk there in this weather!" I told him. "You have to drive us. We need your car for the jumpstart, anyway."

"I'll help you with your SUV, but not with Calvary Hills, and not this minute, either. I'm watching Tommy while my parents are at Big-Box."

"So take him with us!"

"*I am not putting my little brother in danger, too!*" Pete yelled at me. He took a deep breath. "That's out of the question. I'm sorry."

"But Franklin would want you to put an end to this!"

"Excuse us," Troy said, closing the door in Pete's face.

I stared at him in total fury.

"The hell are you—?!"

"This is bullshit, Michael," Troy told me. "You are asking *way* too much out of everybody. You have nothing to prove, nothing to see to the end… It's over. It ended seven years ago. *Close the book and go home.* You're messing with people's lives here. This is *not* your call to make."

"I don't need any more of your input."

"You're out here with your *conspiracy theories* and your *antagonists* and all these *excuses* you keep making. Stop it. All right? Stop avoiding your responsibilities. What you need is to get the cops involved if you're so worried about this."

"Bryce's stepdad owns the police," I pointed out. Then I remembered something.

The door opened again. It was Pete, wearing a hoodie and winter jacket over his thermal shirt and pajama pants.

"After what happened to Franklin," Pete said, "I transferred schools to South Intermediate. I needed to get away from the past, from the memories, the monsters, but Frankie… he followed me. I kept seeing him in places, like, physically, out of the corner of my eye or as a face in the crowd." He shifted his weight. "Do you truly believe this thing of yours'll end it? Like, we'll finally be able to put everything behind us?"

"I think we can get pretty damn close," I allowed. I held the business card between two gloved fingers. "Can I use your phone?"

"Sure," he said, handing it to me. "Here, you both can come inside."

"Thank you," Troy said for us. Meanwhile, I dialed the number.

He picked up on the second ring, mint-gnawing and all.

"This is Detective Michael Northcott speaking," he said. "Can I ask who's calling?"

"Hey, this is Michael Jackson," I told him, stepping into the bathroom and locking the door. "I heard the news on Willow."

"I'm so sorry—"

"I need your help. It's about Bryce Skinner."

"Stepson to Mayor Hill. What's the matter?"

I started sweating, but I had to go on.

"You asked me when we first met if Bryce might have killed Willow for Five Twenty-Nine," I recalled. "He didn't, but now I know he would have, if necessary. *He's dangerous.* I understand that now. And he might be responsible for a lot of other stuff."

"There's no need for histrionics," he said, "so don't worry about that bit. I've already done some digging, and I spoke with Miss Gabriella Cabello." I heard the jangling of keys on his end. "From the pictures you sent her, which she forwarded to me, as well as the evidence recovered from law enforcement, there's a definite link between Richard Bryce Skinner and the suicide of Franklin Chambers. Bryce posed as a man named Dom Sheldon and sent death threats to Franklin via email. I think it's safe to say Bryce indirectly killed him—"

"Oh my God."

"—as well as Ian Gallagher. In fact, there's evidence linking you, Bryce, and sixteen other individuals to Ian's death, and all on that one bulletin board. The police never suspected foul play, you see. The creek was high, the boy couldn't swim, and the rain washed a lot away."

"So you know what we did."

"I have a good idea what happened on May twenty-ninth, yes."

"Well, it just might be happening again."

"Tell me what you need."

"Come to Calvary Hills," I said. "It's a subdivision that was never finished. It's by the Shaughnessy Estates neighborhood in New Baines."

"On my way now."

"Maybe bring a weapon and officers you trust, but not the FBI. I can't get the others in trouble."

"I can't promise they won't."

"Well, this isn't Charles Dodgson. It's Bryce. The mayor will cover it up, right? Bryce says he's extremely concerned with his image."

"Every politician is. But corruption has its limits."

"We need an end to this."

"Your uncle—the teacher. What's his name again?"

"Herbert Kukowski."

"I'll be there soon."

I hung up, and welling inside me, I felt instant regret at calling him. But for once, Troy was right in that this was beyond me. We had been so obsessive over our reputation that we didn't want an outsider's aid. Yet this was much, much bigger than we could've ever pictured it to be. Gabby had known that long before the rest.

"I'm sorry, guys," I whispered to myself—to the nineteen of them. "I hope you'll forgive me."

I swallowed my pride and opened the bathroom door.

After he finished telling Tommy to lock us out and stay away from the windows, Pete kissed his brother's forehead and took us to his lowrider in the garage. Somehow, despite all the wear and the pool of oil beneath the engine block, it started nicely enough. Pete told us he'd gotten the studded snow tires only at his dad's insistence. I, nonetheless, was thankful.

"I can't believe you talked me into this," Pete said as we pulled out of the driveway— he, Troy, and I. "Oh, God. What were we thinking?"

"There might not even be a problem," Troy noted. "Cat might've—"

Pete shook his head. "Bryce said in his message for us to meet him at Calvary Hills at sunset. If Cat went there, it must be serious."

"Certainly didn't go on a nature hike," Troy went on, staring out the window. "Not in this snowstorm."

"Bryce could have kidnapped her," I pointed out, "meaning it's even more serious."

"How much farther, then?" Troy asked as Pete signaled and turned left onto West Florentine Street. I didn't dare look for my house.

"A couple of miles," Pete told him. "Maybe. I don't know. Something feels wrong. God, my heart's racing."

I wanted to say something supportive, but it just would've added to the multitude of lies. Pete was right. Gabby had been, too. Christian had tried to please both Bryce and Gabby by serving as the mediator. I couldn't imagine how hard it must've been for him, being so close to Bryce and living with the guilt I had buried so deep into the recesses of my mind.

The sky was covered with snow and getting darker by the minute. The houses, park, and forest were devoid of life, the ground a sea of whitecaps. It should've been beautiful, and it shouldn't have been Ian. It should have been Bryce under Christian's hands and mine. There was time enough at last.

Gray. That's all there was around us, except for streaks of deep orange light in the sky, which made the falling flakes look more akin to ashes. Everything blended in together so perfectly that we could hardly see the trees or tall mounds of snow-covered dirt, and Pete definitely couldn't see the road. So he stopped the car.

"She's struggling," Pete told us. "Even with the tires, it doesn't matter, 'cause there's too much snow."

"So we'll walk," I said. "We've come too far, and this has to stop, one way or the other."

"You could die out there in the cold," Troy stated, "and you won't be a martyr."

"This isn't about me," I told him. "This is it. Now pass me those Big-Box bags."

"I feel like we're being watched," Pete said, looking around.

I took off my shoes, put my feet inside the plastic bags, wrapped them up, tied the bags tight, and then put my shoes back on. Troy grudgingly did the same, as did Pete after a moment of prayer, hands together and everything. I then got out of the car and into the deep snow, and we began our glacial walk into Calvary Hills.

"I can't…" Pete started after a couple of seconds. "I can't see anything."

"There's something there," Troy said, pointing ahead with one hand and shielding his eyes with the other.

I saw it, too. "It's blue."

"It's Emily!" Pete said, then started running. "Emily!" he shouted, then louder, over the howling winds: "KAYLA!"

They turned around and ran to meet us. Beside Emily's blue hatchback was Kayla's convertible, half-buried in the snow, both cars parked in front of one of the mounds. The girls were crying, and their tears hung from their faces like icicles. They, too, had needed closure.

"He's got them!" Emily told us. "Bryce, Belle, Nate, Rachel, Jim, and Sam. They're all there!"

"Where?!" Troy asked. "What's—?!" The wind picked up. "WHAT'S GOING ON?!"

"OVER THE HILLS," Kayla explained, pointing the way from one of the mounds.

I tried to join her, but Emily pushed me back, her hands on my chest.

"WHAT ARE YOU DOING?!" I asked her.

"JUST GO!" Emily said. "THIS ISN'T WORTH IT! I THOUGHT IT MIGHT BE, BUT IT'S NOT! WE HAVE TO GET OUT OF HERE!"

I pushed her aside and kept walking, legs pumping, the air of dust and wildfire. Emily tried again to stop me—taking my left glove—but again I kept on. She bawled in the background, but soon, it was but white noise to me. Kayla stood on top of one of the several mounds around us, and when I managed my way beside her, all at once, I saw the cross-beamed wooden posts in the near distance.

Tied to the one on the left was Christian, suspended at least a yard from the top of the snow, his arms stretched out across the horizontal post. Each hand was bound by rope, as were his feet, which were exposed and coated in a cracked casing of blood. His head twitched, side to side, either by his own doing or from the polar gusts of suffering. Nate was positioned close by, a metal baseball bat in his gloved hands.

On the right swayed Gabby, who was luckier than Christian, as she appeared to be unconscious. Her dark hair covered her face, and her body hung limp. Jim stood below her. He held a hatchet to his chest.

Between the couple was Catherine Anne Thomas, higher than both. She was wrapped in a black tarp but spread out just the same. She screamed to the sky, yet whatever she said was drowned out by the blizzard. In front of her stood Bryce, wearing a hooded jacket and aiming my uncle's Leiden 21 handgun at Belle, Rachel, and Sam, each with their own jerry can next to them.

I ran. The air made it harder to breathe, but after a while, I wasn't able to feel my lungs or body. I was numb, which made it easier, as I couldn't allow myself to imagine my singular pain when Christian, Cat, and Gabby were experiencing an entirely different agony beyond words and feelings.

"MICHAEL!" Bryce shouted, smiling happily. "I'M GLAD YOU DECIDED TO JOIN US!"

"WHAT THE HELL, BRYCE?!" I asked him as Kayla, Pete, and Troy arrived. I moved toward Nate. "GET THEM DOWN FROM—"

Bryce fired the gun, and Emily collapsed beside me. Kayla and Troy quickly got on their knees to help her.

In shock, I looked again to Bryce, who smiled still, despite his shaking hands. Way off to the right, I saw the same black SUV and red pickup—the latter's front bumper now dented and askew—from the night before, along with some spades, buckets, and additional posts.

"I'M NOT PLAYING AROUND," he told me, then gestured to the condemned. "THEY DID! OTHERS, TOO!"

"SAM!" Kayla shouted as Troy lifted Emily over his shoulder and carried her away from our mess. "GET OVER HERE AND HELP US, GODDAMMIT!"

"YOU MADE ME A PROMISE!" he screamed back at her.

"IN THE FIFTH GRADE!" She sobbed as she walked up next to me, facing Sam's direction. "PEOPLE CHANGE! I CHANGED! PLEASE DON'T GIVE INTO THIS CRAZINESS JUST TO SPITE ME! YOU WON'T EVEN BE IN THIS COUNTRY NEXT YEAR! WHAT DO YOU WANT ME TO SAY—THAT I'M SORRY?! I'M SORRY MY PLANS DIDN'T MATCH UP WITH YOURS! OK?! NOW WILL YOU CUT IT OUT?!"

"PLEASE, BRYCE!" Rachel begged of him. "I DON'T WANT TO DO THIS ANYMORE! I THOUGHT WE WERE HELPING CATHERINE, NOT KILLING HER! SAME WITH IAN!"

Bryce aimed the gun at Rachel. Sam immediately stood in Bryce's way. When I looked back, Kayla was running off to help Troy with Emily.

Bryce laughed above the wind. I thought of the time he had wanted Ms. Albertine's attention in class one day, but everyone else was talking, so she couldn't hear him. Upset, he'd stood on his chair and yelled, "Silence! I am the Lord!"

"TWO WOODPECKERS WITH ONE STONE, HUH?" he said, aiming at Sam and Rachel, his smile tainted with catastrophe. "I CAN WORK WITH THAT!"

"RICHARD!" Belle commanded. "THIS HAS GONE TOO FAR! CHRISTIAN IS YOUR FRIEND!"

"IF YOU CAN'T FOLLOW THE RULES, THEN YOU'RE NO FRIEND OF MINE," he told her. "WORK WITH ME, BELLE. I DON'T WANT YOU UP THERE NEXT!"

"WHAT ARE YOU TRYING TO ACCOMPLISH?!" I asked the executioner, my eyes wide in the truest fear I'd ever known. "WHAT IS THIS?! I KNOW THE MESSAGE, BUT WHAT'S THE PURPOSE?!"

"WE CAN'T KEEP LIVING LIKE THIS!" he shouted. "YOU THINK I'M A MONSTER, BUT WE'RE NO DIFFERENT, MICHAEL! YOU AND I ARE ONE IN THE SAME, AND YOU KNOW MORE THAN ANYONE WHAT WE'VE LOST! OUR FATHERS WERE TAKEN AWAY FROM US AFTER WE TRIED TO SAVE IAN GALLAGHER! BUT WE DIDN'T DO IT CORRECTLY BECAUSE IAN DIED BEFORE HE WAS CLEANSED! BUT HERE..." He gestured around with the gun. "THE PRISONER HERE MAY BREAK HIS CHAINS; THE WEARY REST FROM ALL HIS PAINS; THE CAPTIVE—"

"He's quoting a hymn," Pete whispered in my ear. "He's completely—"

"—FEEL HIS BONDAGE CEASE; THE MOURNER FIND THE WAY OF PEACE!" The wind died down as the sun's light disappeared. "Don't you all see? That maybe, just maybe..." He turned to Jim. "Offer Catherine some water."

"I DON'T WANT YOUR HOLY WATER!" Cat screamed at him. The earth quaked and the mounds split. "THIS WON'T CHANGE ANYTHING! WE'VE SUFFERED, ALL RIGHT?! WE KNOW WHAT IT'S LIKE TO HAVE REGRETS! *YOU ARE SCARING PEOPLE!* THERE ISN'T ANY NEED FOR THIS!"

In an abortion of all rationality, Bryce's temper broke away, leading him to unscrew one of the jerry cans with the gun still on us, balance the can on his right knee, and then topple it over onto the bottom half of Cat's post. With the gasoline spilled, he took out an old utility lighter from within his jacket and waved the flame around in front of us, a deranged smile showing once more.

We held our breath.

"Oh, Catherine," he said with his back to her. "Won't you accept me as your savior? Here faith reveals to mortal eyes a brighter world beyond the skies. Here shines the light which guides our way from earth to—"

"SHUT THE FUCK UP!"

He bent down and blindly placed the long tip of the lighter against the base of the post, causing the gasoline to instantaneously ignite and the lighter to explode in his right hand. Bryce dropped it immediately, cursing at whatever god he was serving— perhaps himself—and then stared at his hand in complete surprise. I saw him cry out in pain as he held it with the other hand—still gripping the gun—and ascertained that he was missing three fingers.

Sam and Rachel threw up at the sight, and I nearly did from the smell of his burning flesh. The smile was no more, and I knew his visage in that moment would haunt me beyond my death. Some sights, I figured, follow us into the afterlife; this would be one of those.

The flash fire didn't remain for long on Cat's post, but seeing then how far Bryce was willing to go for this fight of his—even years after lamenting the first killing—was enough for Jim and Nate to stop following his orders. They dropped their weapons and rushed to his side, and it appeared they wanted to give him their honest aid. Yet

Bryce wouldn't budge, and he aimed the gun at them, too, from the ground, backing up against the middle post, weeping in dismay.

Belle walked up to him, slowly at first, as the gun was then raised in her direction. But she went along normally, got up close, and then held him dear in her embrace.

I made eye contact with Jim, who was behind Bryce, and then looked to Gabby's post. He nodded, as did Nate, and soundlessly, they began to free Christian and lower Gabby into the snow.

"The fourth rule of sacrifice," Bryce said to Belle. I envisioned their relationship, his abuse, her love, his relentless anger—all in her smile at his words. Then he shot her.

She fell on top of him, and he cast her aside as Rachel screamed as loud as she could. Bryce then darted his melted hand into the snow as he crouched beside it and waved the gun around in all directions, not knowing whom to trust and whom to open fire on. He looked less like a man and more like a scared animal with his head barely off the ground, snot all over his face, blood on his clothes, and visible scars over his psyche.

"STAY AWAY!" he yelled at Jim, who then backed up slowly. "ALL OF YOU! I KNOW WHAT I'M DOING!"

"IT'S FINISHED!" Cat cried out to him. He kept shaking his head—kept beating the side of it with the butt of the gun as if there was creek water stuck in his ear. "Please! Let us go home!"

It was pointless, all of it. This wasn't the way to atone for our sins, and deep down in the frozen abyss that was his heart, I could see Bryce knew it, too. He was desperate, and for a while, so was I. But enough was enough.

"Bryce," Pete said, crying through our pain and looking behind Bryce at Christian, who gripped the metal baseball bat without fear. "Put an end to this madness."

"THERE'S NOTHING I CAN DO!" Bryce shouted at us, pointing the gun first to Pete, then to me, then past us. He was wide-eyed and trembling. Nothing could save him. "I'M SO SOR—"

The bat struck his head. His mouth was still open, but not another sound came out of it as he dropped the gun so he could pull back his hood, losing his balance in the process. So Bryce fell forward into the snow with Christian standing above, demanding an answer to the one question we all were asking—the one Christian kept repeating over and over as the police sirens wailed behind us: *"Why?!"*

Sam and Rachel sat on their knees while Jim and Nate helped Gabby and Belle, respectively. Christian remained motionless, clutching the bat with his blue hands and white knuckles. Pete tugged at my arm, but I didn't respond. I was still afraid.

Christian tapped Bryce with his swollen foot. He was the only one of us not crying.

"Damn you!" Christian told him, then spat on his body. *"Damn you to hell!"*

The police and two ambulances made their way around the mounds and over to us. They circled us in, and then men in uniform swarmed out, armed and bundled up. They ran to each of us, barking in our faces, but I didn't hear the guy in front of me. I was too focused on the emergency responders loading Belle and Gabby into the ambulances, the officers lowering Cat to the ground, and then Northcott getting out of his black sedan with Kukowski.

I was so wrong. I had coped through ignorance and dreams of a lost man, all while there had been hallucinations of Frank and Eva, the triggers of rain and water, shattered memories, drowning, and sirens blaring out the truth. Each moment of my time in Oklahoma that week was despicable. It finally, *truly* occurred to me what I had done to Ian Gallagher—one of my friends—those seven years ago at the command of Bryce, Childkiller, who was also my friend. I had naïvely assumed my childhood to be so much simpler than reality, and I had been wrong. And I was exhausted. And I thought I might be sick, too, in the head. Everyone was, but me and Bryce especially.

I'd kissed Ian because we had wanted to see what it felt like.

Wasn't that how all kisses were?

I broke down under the pressure of it all—a sacrilegious sacrifice misinterpreted by a madman and the people he manipulated. Kukowski ran over and held me in his arms. He told the officers to get away. He said he loved me. He cried like he had as he'd talked about his children. I thought of my mother.

Troy stood there, amid all the chaos, watching. Then he looked at me, and we made eye contact. Then he glanced the other way. So the silence returned, as had I.

"We all have normal schedules we rely on, Michael," the psychiatrist had said after the move to Alabama. "When something abnormal occurs that we weren't expecting, several aspects of life may change without warning. Suddenly, with little room for flexibility, the anxiety builds up, and your mind doesn't know what to do or think. This is the irregularity, and what often follows is a living nightmare."

Early Sunday afternoon, two days after the police interviews and aftermath, the snow began to melt outside the cabin. Where it vanished, soppy mud and yellowed grass replaced it. I sat at the edge of the landing over the half-frozen lake, and by the neighboring dock, a white man and woman played with their daughter, who I guessed was no more than two. Her parents were young as well—maybe in their late twenties. The girl ran around in her pink hat and boots and tossed a snowball at her mother. They laughed together.

"I'll be back, Elena," the man then said, running a hand through his short blond hair before taking the stairs to their own lake house.

"We'll be here," the woman said sweetly. She caught my stare, so I looked away. When I looked back, she was playing with her daughter again. In their eyes, I saw hopeful possibilities. I saw life and the good it can bring—the good that always, always outweighs the bad in the end.

"She has great aim," I said. The woman—Elena—smiled. "What's her name?"

"Saphnie," Elena answered. I smiled with her.

"Michael!" Troy called from the top of the steps. "I'm packed and ready."

"See you," I said to them, then got up and headed for the stairs. Saphnie waved at me as I did so, and with the dark water lapping in the distance, I made sure to wave back.

We were quiet up until we reached the Alabama border. I wanted to say something to him. I realized there was nothing wrong with people thinking I was gay because there's nothing wrong with being gay. I was wrong to have been offended. I had perspective, but I didn't know how to apologize. So I waited.

"See that?" Troy asked, tapping the glass. I was behind the wheel, and he was admiring the view out the passenger-side window. "That's what my old man used to call 'sky-blue pink.'"

"My birthday was Friday," I said.

"Too many will kill you," he noted.

"My favorite part about my birthday was getting an email from Santa and the elves at the North Pole." I sighed. "This year, I didn't."

"Guess you grew up."

"Her name is Sandra Goldsmith," I shared with him, then clarified: "Your online friend. Swearyouloveme. I did some research on her while you were out Thursday. She lives an hour away from Dreary with her dad and sister. She's twenty. A college girl."

"Enough," he said.

"I thought you might want to know."

"We moved on. If anything, this trip has taught me some things are better left unsaid. Would've saved us both a lot of trouble."

"I haven't been a good friend to you."

"Stop."

"I'm going to do my best to make things right between us."

"Please stop."

"I'm going to Dreary Community College with you—"

"STOP THE FUCKING SUV!"

"What?!"

He reached for the wheel. I turned right for the immediate exit. A mile later, when it was safe, I signaled and pulled the Big Nasty over on the side of a forested two-lane road. We were the only ones there.

Troy unbuckled his seat belt.

"What are you doing?" I asked him.

"I think I'm gonna walk from here," he said simply.

"Huh? That's ridiculous. We're not that far from—"

"I need to clear my head." He opened the door. "I'm sorry we—"

I pulled him closer by the shirt. We both stared into each other's eyes, him more out of concern than anything.

I kissed him.

He pulled back and shook his head.

"You would've done anything just then." He emptied most of his wallet into the cup holder, got out, and then shut the door. I rolled down the window, and he glanced in my direction. "Good-bye, Michael. It's been… quite the ride."

With that, he started walking forward. I drove at his pace for a while, but I soon came to the realization that one did not control Troy Rico Valdez; he wasn't a dog with a leash you could grab. So I drove on without him, looking back to see he was smiling to himself, Kaleo's "All the Pretty Girls" playing from my phone to ease our gentle way.

EPILOGUE

All of that happened what feels like a long time ago. That's probably how it should be. I'm typing this from my dorm at Hartsett University. I've lived here for a couple of months now, and if I'm being honest—as I have been to the best of my knowledge—I'm loving California. There's always just enough sunlight, and when there isn't, you can find some. It's exactly how I imagined it.

Glad I got something right. To learn is to suffer.

Unsurprisingly, the mayor of New Baines bought the silence of our parents, who agreed at our insistence. We kids didn't need muzzling; we were used to it. This way, our futures would be free of that May 29th, as we had always dreamed. With Bryce in a deep coma—and with minimal brain functionality, at that—it seemed as if things were starting to go our way for once. We were clear. We could move past this. No more rules.

That doesn't mean we kept in touch, though. If anything, the ordeal drove us further apart instead of bringing us together. But I did make a list of people to check up on and include here what had happened to them. I've mostly talked to Gabby since, as she called me after she got out of the hospital, so I have her and the Internet to bring this up to speed. That and intuition. Group texts only reveal so much, and once they stop, the faces blur fast.

Christian lost his scholarship to Northeastern Oklahoma State College because of his feet, which had required extensive repair and physical therapy. Belle survived the gunshot to her shoulder, though the blade will pop out of place when she moves in certain ways—her constant reminder, as if we needed any keepsakes. Pete sent me a Wish You Were Here postcard featuring the Arminster city skyline, and on the back, he'd added: "… but I understand why not." Emily hadn't been hit by a bullet; she'd collapsed from shock. She's apparently doing a lot better now, and she and Rachel occasionally go to counseling together. They invited Gabby, but she declined. "Too soon." Too real.

I'm not sure exactly what happened to Nate, Jim, and Kayla, but they've since updated their schooling information, and their families posted high school graduation photos, so they must be OK. I'm assuming Sam made it into the Israeli Defense Force, but I've been hesitant since that spring break to draw such conclusions. So I'll just say that I hope he's doing well. All of them.

Ms. Varsha called my number over the summer, then gave the phone to Cat. We talked for five or so minutes—very brief. I told her I was happy she'd started uploading her songs again. She asked if I was writing a new story. I told her no. Fiction doesn't feel right to me anymore. As of now, I'll major in English, but I don't want to teach. I told her I was sorry.

"I still taste the smoke," she said. Then she wished me the best, as I did her. I don't fully understand her beliefs, but that's why they're individual and personal. Me being around her wasn't healthy, I figured. So I didn't bring it up, which was no doubt the adult thing to do.

I haven't seen Troy since he left the SUV, but according to Eva, he did make it back to Dreary. I got an unsigned card for Mother's Day addressed to me, and I like to believe it was Troy who sent it—but he never answered my texts, calls, or messages to confirm. Sometimes, I think I hear his voice. I hope it was him. I truly do.

The reason I went to Oklahoma that March was nostalgia, and yet that isn't why I'm writing this confession. It's not the nightmares, either, where an adult Ian Gallagher searches endlessly. I've heard the best way to overcome your fears is to confront them, but what a joke that is. If this were the case, we'd all be cured. It's never as simple as we make it out to be.

Northcott showed up on campus the first cold day of October. He was waiting for me in the student parking lot, as I guessed he'd recognized the Big Nasty. I thought about running, but he said I wasn't in trouble. He only wanted to talk.

We went over to one of the benches by the palm trees, overlooking the Pacific.

"How are you?" he asked me, a peppermint in his mouth.

"I'm fine," I said. "What are you doing here? How did you find me?"

"Your mother let me know," he said. "What? Don't look at me like that. I got you all out of years of courtrooms and endless paperwork. You're saying I can't visit every now and again?"

"Preferably not."

He leaned back, grabbed his left wrist, and then stretched his arms forward to pop it. I hated that sound.

"Well, I don't know about you," he continued, "but I haven't been sleeping too good since this all started, and I was a cop for twenty years. I served as sheriff's deputy for a small town in Maine called Cinder Heights. Do you remember the shooting at Lincoln High School?"

"Nope."

"Probably too young. Anyway, my point is I've seen a lot of messed-up shit in my time, but *nothing* beats what your friend Bryce organized in New Baines. It was so…" He shook his head. "Jesus Christ."

"Why are you here?" I asked him, tired of whatever it was we were doing.

He told me. I wish he hadn't.

But I'll write it here, if only for the misery to end, as that's what triggered Bryce. Then I'll head to the university library and print off a copy to place in my desk. Manuscripts might not burn, but in time, I believe the words can change. If I distract myself for a few decades, maybe the details will alter, and we won't have done what we did. Maybe Troy and I will have brought Eva along after all, or perhaps Willow will have made it to the party that night. What if it was God's plan for Jesus to die on the cross, but not for Him to be raised from the dead three days later? Jesus feared death, and so God comforted His Son, and maybe Jesus has been walking the earth with His disciples ever since. Present day, He goes by Cat and has noticeable scars on her hands.

Maybe Jesus took seven years off to travel. Maybe Satan was working overtime.

Hell calls hell, I hear him say. But it's my expression just as much as it is his.

Hell calls hell.

Hell calls hell!

Richard Bryce Skinner awoke from his coma in a dark place. The assisting nurse noticed and rushed to his side.

To her, he tested five simple words.

"Take me to the cat."

REPRISE

t *was a cold morning,* and Mekenzie was confused. She had every right to be; her boyfriend had abandoned her with merely a letter before committing suicide six states away. Now she was in a putrid taxi with a driver to match, heading to the lake where Ian had killed himself.

As the taxi pulled up beside Lake Nasagarresett, Mekenzie could already see the police examining the hole in the ice an officer had described to her over the phone. She had cried hard when she'd discovered Ian's letter, and the later call from Oklahoma law enforcement did not ease the pain. "We found your name in the victim's wallet, ma'am. Do you know Mr. Gallagher, Miss Willis?"

Mekenzie paid the young driver and walked carefully down the steep hill. She counted five heads: two police officers, a television news reporter, her cameraman, and another figure—a wrinkled man with a sad smile and a crew-cut hairstyle.

After the police questioned her, Mekenzie asked to see Ian's body.

"Ma'am, we haven't actually found Mr. Gallagher," one of the officers informed her.

"What?! Why not?!" She sounded exasperated. "It's obvious he's under the ice—you'll probably find him floating off a couple of yards away!"

"I don't know about that," said the wrinkled man.

"And who are you?" she asked him.

"My name's Aiden Bradford—an old friend of Ian's," he answered solemnly. "I gave him the name of this here lake just a few days ago. I knew I shouldn't have." Seeing her raised eyebrow, he added: "I was with him when one of our eighth-grade buses was found here. All the children were missing."

"Hey, I remember that!" the reporter chimed in, and then to her cameraman: "Didn't you work on that piece? Over a decade ago?" He shrugged as his response.

"Mr. Bradford, do you know where Mr. Gallagher is?" an officer asked.

"Well, I have a hunch," he answered.

"So where is he?!" Mekenzie demanded, starting to cry. "Where is my boyfriend?!"

Aiden looked out across the lake and toward the horizon. "He's out there… swimming with the ghosts and demons that have haunted him for so long."

"Stop it!" she shouted. "Why are you playing games with me?! There's no such thing as ghosts and… *whatever!*"

He frowned at her. "Do you honestly believe that?"

Mekenzie rubbed her sore eyes. This guy didn't make any sense. But strangely, she believed him. The Internet did say Lake Nasagarresett had a history of unexplained deaths and disappearances.

"But why him? Why Ian?"

Aiden shrugged. "He was seeking closure."

Heavy tears rolled down Mekenzie's cheeks. "I don't understand."

"I don't think Ian understood it, either. He just knew… that this is where he belonged."

"Will we ever know for sure what happened?" asked the reporter.

At this, even the cops turned to listen to what Aiden Bradford had to say. He sighed deeply and looked away from Mekenzie—toward the dark storm clouds in the distance.

"Not today, not tomorrow. His pain died with him."

A glimmer of white caught Mekenzie's eye. Trapped between the ice and muddy shore, a dead fish, mouth gaping open, stared up at her... No, not at her, *through* her. For a terrifying moment, she couldn't move. She realized she wasn't even breathing. With a shiver she felt through her entire body, she forced herself to look away.

She never returned to Lake Nasagarresett.

Except in her nightmares.

ACKNOWLEDGMENTS

This novel was made possible with help from the following people: Tara Waugh, Sarah Walker, Essence Collins, Makenzie Ellis, Cora Hasegawa, Brooklyn Groves, Bryna Frohock, Wes Florentine, Eliza Dee, and my mother Grettel. Thank you, all, for your invaluable support.